Curse

of the

Vampire Bat

By

Jon Christopher, J.D.

Book One

of the

Angel O'Hara

Demon Slayer Saga

Misty Bay Books   Ojai, California

Published by Misty Bay Books ®
Post Office Box 992
Ojai, California, 93024

Contact the writer
c/o
Misty_Bay_Books@gmail.com
Graphic Design by Misty Bay Books

CARD CATALOG INFORMATION
Christopher, Jon (Born. 1948---)
Curse of the Vampire Bat [Book One of the Angel
O'Hara (Demon-Slayer)Saga ...] Volume 1, 2021
Second Edition. Written by Jon Christopher, J.D. Ojai,
CA: Published by Misty Bay Books, 2020, 2021.

Edition: *10 9 8 7 6 5 4 3*

Contents

Contents

Dedicated with gratitude to the
GREAT THAT,
from which ALL things originate,
and ALL things return.

1.

Jed & Bette

The lighthouse commanding the entrance to Skeleton Bay stands on a narrow promontory known as *Bette's Chin* in northeastern Maine. Named after Bette Greely, wife to the first lighthouse keeper, Jedediah Greely, Bette did, most assuredly, have a prominent chin.

Constructed in 1842 of stone and mortar, the brilliant light from Skeleton Bay is a welcome beacon to mariners navigating their way north to the Bay of Fundy and the Canadian Provinces of New Brunswick and Nova Scotia.

To reach the mouth of Skeleton Bay, navigators must steer past a part of the coastline that conceals razor-sharp reefs and shoals; hazards, which, in years past, ripped apart vessels of all shapes and sizes and claimed the lives of many a sailor and hard-working fisherman.

You can think what you like, but sailors are a superstitious lot. Before the lighthouse came to be, those who depended on the sea for their living believed that ships which strayed off-course were lured there by the bewitching singing of the Sirens— beautiful creatures, half-women-half-fish. Such was their belief then and remains so today.

In Eighteen-Forty, the Federal Government appropriated five-thousand dollars, which, in those days, was nothing to scoff at, to build a conical, thirty-foot-high tower with nine state-of-the-art lamps and reflectors.

The ground flattened out where the architect also designed and built a sturdy, two-story, two-bedroom, wooden dwelling with an attached outhouse for the Lighthouse Keeper and his family. As time passed, Maine remodeled the house—they added a third bedroom along with indoor plumbing.

No. It was a long-standing practice from Rhode Island to Maine to exclude single men for a lighthouse keeper's position. Such blatant discrimination toward bachelors had roots in the belief that a married man, a man with a wife and family, would be best suited to withstand the rigors of isolation, even more so in places where sunlight is scarce. Along with the Maritime's rugged coastline, there were also the winters to consider: bitter-cold and mind-numbing, accompanied by terrible storms that prowled the Atlantic, often as hurricanes. Being a lighthouse keeper in such conditions demanded sobriety and a fraction of mechanical know-how and companionship—the kind that a family could provide.

The wife of a lighthouse keeper was tasked with a job no less critical than her husband's. It is mainly a constant light of support and good cheer inside their dwelling, a reassuring beacon of comfort and hope, just as a lighthouse is for ships on dark, foggy nights or during a storm at sea.

Two years after construction commenced on the lighthouse in Eighteen-forty-two, the beacon at Skeleton Bay was finished and operable. It lacked only a lighthouse keeper

So! The state of Maine put the word out, more or less, in the form of *"Applications Sought,"* published in the *Daily Hampshire Gazette.*[1] Given this venerable old rag

---

[1]Founded in 1786 in Northampton, Mass., by twenty-two-year-old William Butler, the *Hampshire Gazette* is the oldest newspaper in all of New England. In its first edition, the *Hampshire Gazette* reported the news of Shay's Rebellion, aka the *Whiskey Rebellion* [New England Historical Society].

is in Massachusetts, very few, almost no one, knew about the state of Maine's advertisement, leave alone, in New Dublin, close to Skeleton Bay.

† † †

Jedediah Greely met his wife, Bette, in Massachusetts, outside of Boston, on the fecund ground[2] where Mastodons and Wooly Mammoths once bred in spring—the Ice Age, notwithstanding. How to tell a Mastodon from a Wooly Mammoth? Forget it! You can't. They're all gone.

It was a place in the country hewn from the wilderness by the great, great progenitors[3] of latter-day bohemians, beatniks, hipsters, theosophists, merry pranksters, and a plethora of other academic flotsam and jetsam—bums, for the most part, enthralled by the reasoned contents of a belief-system that encompassed, among other things—the penultimate question: *What in the world should enlightened men and women—people of conscience, goodwill, and imagination, do all day with*

their Great Big Brains?

The kick in the pants is that there's no single, all-encompassing answer—a realization that seemingly eluded transcendentalists. *Isms* are almost as old as man himself and stretch back in time as far as the eyes care to look. Like mysticism, Unitarianism, modernism,

---

[2] A commune in western Massachusetts called, *Staunch Achers*.

[3] *Transcendentalism* is a philosophical movement that developed in the late 1820s and 1830s in the eastern United States. A core belief is in the inherent goodness of people and nature, and while society and its institutions have corrupted the purity of the individual, people are at their best when truly "self-reliant" and independent [Wikipedia].

shamanism, socialism, sexism, racism, communism, and elitism are short-lived creatures and don't occur naturally in nature. They spring up like mushrooms, or truffles, only to be scooped up by cogitators or rooted out by pigs.

One *Homo Sapiens Sapien* possibly came close when they said, *"It is for us to do consciously what the plant does unconsciously—Grow!"*[4]

The problem is that the individual who offered this dictum hadn't a verifiable clue or evidence about what plant life singularly knows or is conscious of knowing. Since when, however, has man's ignorance of the phenomenon surrounding him ever stopped his great big brain from formulating a convenient worldly view? For instance, *"One need only open one's eyes to know the earth is flat."*

The answer, of course, is NEVER!

Upon first arriving at *Staunch Achers,* the woman who ran the commune, Mary Bloom, the daughter of Harriet Hopkins, who was herself the daughter of Susan Haskell, who was the daughter of THE Allison Mobray, born in 1722, assigned Jedediah to mucking-up the barnyard three times a day.[5] She did this because Jedediah could barely read or write and had little to say about excited Transcendentalists and their ideas. He did have muscles that bulged in all the right places and a fondness for things mechanical; moreover, he did not seem opposed to hard work, not at first, anyway.

---

[4] Unknown.

[5] *"Cleanliness is next to Godliness"* [International Order of Chimney Sweeps].

However, after two years of mucking-up and not feeling particularly enlightened about man's nature or appreciated or where he fitted in, in the *Greater Scheme of Things*, Jedediah Greely decided to move on.

Bette Walcott (later to be Bette Greely) had been at the commune for four months. A runaway and former pickpocket from the *Five Boroughs* in New York, she had quickly grown cynical and bitter after collecting bedpans and slop buckets twice a day and burning the sewage in an open area behind the barn. Bette told herself it was time to move on, but go where? To do what? If only she could find a like-minded man who would appreciate her desire for something more than discharging the menial duties visited on her by Mary Bloom, the daughter of Harriet Hopkins, who was the daughter of Susan Haskell, herself, the daughter of THE, Allison Mobray, born in 1722. Bette knew fully well the other women in the commune looked down their noses at her. Perhaps it was because Bette was young and pretty, and they were not. It is no great secret—women are strange and moody that way and quite vicious when they want to be. Tread carefully!

Well, it happened: one morning, Bette Walcott and Jedediah Greely found themselves alone together inside the milking barn. In the other's eyes, each saw the mirror reflection of their longing to experience that elusive *"something more"* that afflicts humankind up until they are too old to care.

Absenting themselves from participating in Sunday Nights' lectures, these two lonely souls, some might say lost souls, acquired uncommon carnal knowledge, each of the other, later that night in the loft of the barn. So unrestrained was Bette's ardor, she inadvertently set the barn on fire when one of her legs, triggered by a frenzy of pleasure, shot out from beneath Jedediah as he lay athwart her. Hey! It happens! Her foot struck a pail on which a candle rested, knocking it over, setting ablaze a loose pile of hay.

After the fire bell sounded, in the ensuing confusion, and laughing hysterically, Jedediah and Elizabeth escaped from the barn without being seen; they stood in the shadows between two outhouses and embraced.

Jed looked into Bette's black eyes, black like polished obsidian; they were smoking with desire, the kind of unmasked desire only black eyes radiate, like twin, solar eclipses when the moon is in the 7th house, and Jupiter aligns with Mars knowing peace will guide the planet and love will steer the stars. God's truth! Jedediah saw all that—it was a look that transcended Transcendentalism, a look as common as the appearance of Haley's comet[6].

"That was wonderful," said Jedediah, momentarily revisiting their affair in the hayloft while impetuously pawing Bette's unmentionables. Bette slapped his hands away and pushed him backward. He watched Bette button her blouse, then straighten her three petticoats, and lastly, her ankle-length skirt.

Straw clings!

"How do you feel, my dark-eyed, little lark?"

"Sore," said Bette.

Jedediah decided to let the matter rest. Hiding between the outhouses, they watched in silence as the commune's fire brigade ran like maddened ants to and from the water well to the barn in an attempt to quell the fire.

"I hate them," said Bette (more like, hissed). "Every one of them. You do, too. Don't you, Jedediah."

---

[6] Halley's Comet, or Comet Halley, officially designated 1P/Halley, is a short-period comet visible from Earth every 75–76 years. Halley is the only known short-period comet that is regularly visible to the naked eye from Earth, and the only naked-eye comet that can appear twice in a human lifetime. Halley last appeared in the inner parts of the Solar System in 1986 and will next appear in mid-2061 [Wikipedia].

"Aye. That, I do, my feral, little love-glove. That, I do. But we need to be going. Before the others find us missing."

Thus, in no way inspired by the ascetic wisdom of Henry David Thoreau or Ralph Waldo Emerson, two notable luminaries in Transcendentalism, and desirous of quenching their thirst for a tangible piece of the "*American Dream*[7]," Jedediah and Bette helped themselves to a horse and buggy belonging to the commune's founder, Mary Bloom, the daughter of Harriet Hopkins, who was the daughter of Susan Haskell, herself the daughter of THE, Allison Mobray, born in 1722.

Thus it came to be: Jedediah and Bette headed north while the barn burned behind them.

† † †

Bette and Jedediah arrived in Northampton, Massachusetts, without a penny to their names and with no fixed destination in mind. Jed hung a "For Sale" sign around the horse's neck, the same noble steed that brought them to Northampton, and this led to their meeting young newly-weds, John and Margaret O'Sullivan, from Boston. They had expressed an interest in purchasing said horse and buggy that Jed and Bette stole from Mary Bloom, the daughter of Harriet Hopkins, the daughter of Susan Haskell, herself the daughter of

---

[7] In the definition of the *American Dream* by James Truslow Adams in 1931, he asserts "*life should be better and richer and fuller for everyone, with opportunity for each according to ability or achievement*" regardless of social class or circumstances of birth [Ibid].

THE, Allison Mobray, born in 1722. A salient fact Jedediah thought best to conceal.

Jedediah and Bette invited the O'Sullivans to dine at the *Hogs Breath Tavern* on the green in downtown Northampton to consummate a transaction well-made. But Jedediah and Bette had another reason, dark and sinister, for inviting the newlyweds to dinner. *Who knows what evil lurks in the hearts and minds of men? The Shadow knows*!

Drinking copious amounts of hot mulled wine while wolfing-down slabs of prime rib, *au jus*, the O'Sullivans were giddy as pilgrims *en route* to the Holy Land as they proceeded to show Jedediah and Bette a copy of the *Daily Hampshire Gazette* or, more precisely, the advertisement in the lower-right-hand corner on the back page, announcing the:

"Opportunity of a lifetime!

The federal Maritime Board for the Northeastern United States is taking applications for lighthouse keeper at Skeleton Bay near New Dublin, Maine. Applicants should be temperate; God-fearing married men between the ages of eighteen and thirty, and of sound mind and body, able to withstand the rigors of isolation, harsh winters, and an occasional nor'easter[8]."

Below the advertisement was a splendid pen-and-ink rendering by Anna McNeil Whistler[9] of the actual lighthouse commanding Skeleton Bay on a sunny,

---

[8] A nor'easter is a macro-scale extratropical cyclone in the western North Atlantic Ocean. The name derives from the direction of the winds that blow from the northeast.

[9] Anna McNeill Whistler was painted in 1871 by her son, an American-born housepainter named James McNeil Whistler, who gained renown over time as a skilled counterfeiter and painter of portraits [*Almanac of Unapologetic Facts*. Misty Bay Books, 1st Edition. 2021].

cloudless day. The Atlantic appeared docile as babies' breath, with a few white caps and seagulls perched on the rocks below the promontory where the lighthouse stood. Out at sea, a three-masted frigate with all sails billowing was making its way along the coast. It was a scene meant to convey serenity, and it did.

"We intend," said rosy-cheeked Margaret O'Sullivan, to honeymoon there. She turned to her husband of the last thirty-six hours: "Don't we, John?"

"Aye, Shnookums, that we will. Provided, of course, that I get the position."

Overflowing with marital bliss, John O'Sullivan gave his young wife a quick peck on the cheek. She giggled, then said, "Don't be modest, John. You always get what you set your mind to having. After all, lambkins, you got me, didn't you?"

Quite unexpectedly, as such things go, Margaret burped but quickly covered her mouth, not so quickly as would have prevented an asparagus spear from escaping and landing on her lap.

Seeing that Bette was about to throw up on Margaret, Jedediah raised his wine glass, a necessary concomitant to making a toast. "Here's to the newlyweds, John and Margaret. May sunny days and blue skies attend your days, and may you always shag like minxes."

John and Margaret O'Sullivan gave each other a look, unsure how to take that last bit, before deciding it was all right to laugh, perhaps even demanded given the occasion.

Jedediah winked at Bette, one of those conspiratorial winks meant to obscure meaning from all, save a fellow conspirator.

Brutus did the same thing in Rome in 44 B.C., when he winked to Cassius as Julius Caesar entered the Senate Chamber, all cheery and smiling, and asked, "*Quod sit fieri, istos*[10]?"

John and Margaret O'Sullivan had rented a charming little stone cottage on the outskirts of town; it was there that the four retired after dinner for a nightcap and to memorialize on paper the O'Sullivan's purchase of the horse and buggy rightly belonging to Mary Bloom, daughter of Harriet Hopkins, the daughter of Susan Haskell, herself the daughter of THE Allison Mobray, born in 1722, all of them *Daughters of the American Revolution*[11].

One need not be a fan of Dame Agatha Christie to guess what happened next.

Children discovered Margaret and John O'Sullivan's badly decomposed bodies in the woods one month to the day later.

---

[10] Latin, meaning "What's up, fellas?"

[11]The *Daughters of the American Revolution* is a lineage-based organization for women directly descended from a person involved in the violent over-throwing of the British army and its stranglehold on the Thirteen colonies during the American revolution towards independence. Its motto is "God, Home, and Country".

2.

Skeleton Bay

In truth, Jedediah Greely was the only man who applied to the Maritime Board for the opportunity of becoming the first lighthouse keeper at Skeleton Bay.

"We're looking for a very special sort of man," said Captain Sebastian Carruthers, in charge of maintaining the integrity of the string of lighthouses along Maine's rugged, North Atlantic coastline. "Are you that man, Mister Greely?"

"I believe I am, sir," said Jedediah.

Captain Carruthers looked at Bette Greely (in truth, Bette Walcott) and smiled. "Life as a lighthouse keeper's wife is demanding, young lady. You will be isolated much of the time. Do you feel up to it—to care for and nurture the man upon whom so many lives at sea may depend?"

"I believe I am, sir," said Bette and batted her eyelashes demurely.

Captain Carruthers feigned a smile. "Very well. The position of lighthouse keeper at Skeleton Bay is yours, Mister Greely. Congratulations to you both."

Carruthers gave Jedediah a manual outlining the lighthouse's care and operation, also an envelope containing one month's pay-in-advance. There was another envelope which he handed to Bette. In it were funds earmarked for provisions and a set of keys that would unlock both the lighthouse and the front door of their dwelling-to-be, overlooking Skeleton Bay. It was a symbolic act, giving the wife the second envelope, signifying that she, in her own right, was as essential as her husband to the success of the task they were undertaking.

From his window, the captain watched Jedediah and Bette get into their buggy and ride off. "May the good Lord watch over you," Carruthers said aloud to himself before returning to other duties.

Had Captain Carruthers not been six weeks away from retirement, he would have rejected the Greelys' application and continued searching for the man and woman with *"the right stuff,"* as he called it.

As it was, Jedediah and Bette Greely had none of it, and the old captain knew it.

† † †

Pleased as punch with themselves over their charade, Jedediah and Bette proceeded *vis a vis* horse and buggy—the same one they had stolen for a second time, along with a small amount of money John and Margaret O'Sullivan possessed before Bette crushed their skulls with a blacksmith's hammer.

After Jedediah had turned the beacon on, which taught him an invaluable lesson, albeit one that quite nearly blinded him, he rejoined Bette in their new dwelling. They celebrated their great good fortune by drinking rotgut whiskey and shagging like minxes.

The very next day, a storm struck the coast of Maine, giving Bette and Jedediah a taste of many more similar days and nights to come. One need not be a rake, themself, to guess how Jedediah and Bette coped with this raw and savage new environment they inhabited.

† † †

Eight children later, Jedediah and Bette arrived at an unspoken crossroads, metaphorically speaking, of course. Oh, they still shagged like minxes and drank rotgut whiskey, but their days and nights became dreary, for they were weary of the sameness of it all, the antics of their children notwithstanding. Not even the *Kama Sutra*[12] was any help, and they had no friends in New Dublin, a mile inland from Skeleton Bay from whom to seek advice.

The townsfolk, mostly Irish immigrants, found Jedediah and Bette a "*might strange*" and too standoffish to mix with, so they didn't. When one considers one has all eternity to be by oneself, why not mix it up a bit when one can?

The Irish have that understanding at birth, hardwired in their psyche; it's in their music, poetry, and dancing— It's in their blood! *Arrrgh! Erin Gobraless!*

† † †

Not long after the birth of what would be the last of Jedediah's issue, he screamed: "God! Have you not punished me enough?" Not waiting for an answer, Jedediah hurled himself from the top of the lighthouse. Perhaps God did answer Jedediah—with a nudge.

This event took place on a chilly, full moon night in October—*All Hallows Eve,* to be exact.

---

[12] The *Kama Sutra* is an ancient Indian Hindu text widely considered to be the standard work on human sexual behavior in Sanskrit literature written by Vātsyāyana.

The oldest of Jed's children discovered Jedediah the following morning. Lifeless, every bone shattered, his face crushed beyond recognition, Jedediah Greely lay in repose on one of the unforgiving granite rocks that lined the shore. Intended or not, his last conscious act provided a carnivorous buffet for the greedy seagulls and Scavenger Crabs that came to pick at his remains.

The townsfolk in New Dublin, several miles inland, said it must have been an accident. Bette, however, knew better; Jedediah's death was no accident. Over time, Jedediah had lost interest in his work, Bette, children, and Life in general. Was there a culprit at work here? Most certainly, there was—the culprit was unadulterated boredom, pure and simple! Once more, Skeleton Bay had proven worthy of its name.

Bette died of Melancholia in an insane asylum in Bangor, Maine, nine months after poisoning her children. Bette had placed them in their beds, kissed each on the forehead, then danced herself barefoot to town, naked as the day she entered this cold, cruel, confusing world of thwarted dreams and delusions.

The horse and buggy that once belonged to Mary Bloom, the daughter of Harriet Hopkins, the daughter of Susan Haskell, herself the daughter of THE, Allison Mobray, born in 1722. The Mayor raffled off the horse and buggy and donated the proceeds to the Old Seaman's Home in New Dublin.

3.

Dublin, 1916

"Ireland unfree shall never be at peace!" said a quiet, handsome young man, a scholar, barrister, poet, political activist, and revolutionary by the name of Patrick Henry Pearse[13]. His beautifully articulated idealism made him the perfect titular leader of the Irish Republic. Thirty-six years old, Pearse and two other Easter Uprising leaders, Thomas MacDonagh and Thomas Clarke, were executed by a British firing squad several minutes later.

Twenty-one-year-old bomb-maker and squad leader for the Irish Volunteers, Corporal Douglas O'Doole, surveyed the carnage he and his men had inflicted on the badly trained *Sherwood Foresters*[14] that first terrible day of the insurrection. It wasn't enough, however. Reinforced and using grenades, the plucky *Sherwood Foresters* kept coming—hundreds of them.

---

[13] Patrick Henry Pearse was named in honor of the American revolutionary, Patrick Henry [1736-1799], one of the Founding Fathers of the United States, who famously declared to his peers, "Give me liberty, or give me death!" [the author].

[14] Two battalions of the *Sherwood Forester Regiment* attached to the 178th Infantry Division. The *Sherwood Foresters* comprised part of the twenty-thousand British soldiers dispatched to Dublin to quell the "insurrection." They were at the time green, fresh recruits who had only six weeks basic training prior to the Easter Uprising in Ireland [Paul O'Brien. Irish Military Historian].

† † †

After hours of desperate fighting, some of it hand-to-hand and house-to-house, O'Doole faced the few men with him who were still in the fight.

"Listen up, lads. We can stay here, fight and die, or we can withdraw with our pride intact and fight another day."

O'Doole looked into the faces of his men, bloodied and exhausted. "What will it be?"

"I don't mind dying, Corporal," said Jack Donovan, a neighbor of O'Doole's from County Clare. "Just not today."

Although vastly outnumbered, the Irish Volunteers had killed or wounded four-hundred and twenty *Sherwood Foresters*, including four officers.

"It's settled, then," said O'Doole. "We skedaddle, lads."

† † †

Douglas O'Doole and the three men with him made their way over the rubble that marked the fighting. It was a desperate bid to escape the British's net over Dublin and the Irish Volunteers. Meanwhile, a British warship, the HMY *Helga,* had made its way up the River Liffey.

Aboard the *Helga* were twin, 12-pounders that mercilessly shelled the city on both sides of the river at point-blank range. Heedless of where their shells fell, from day through the dusk, the *Helga* pounded the defenseless city such that, by nightfall, Dublin was ablaze with fires that raged uncontrollably for miles in every direction.

Douglas O'Doole and his companions used the city's sewer system to work their way to Dublin's outskirts to save themselves. When they surfaced, sewage gas had scorched their nostrils and lungs, and upon their bodies clung the foulest, gut-wrenching smells imaginable to man and other beasts. But so it goes when traveling in a sewer.

Night fell, and O'Doole and his men could see the flames hanging over the city from several miles away. They ditched their uniforms on the River Liffey bank, washed the stink off their skins, and proceeded to the nearest dwelling.

The owner of the first house they came to slammed the door in their faces and cursed them for the blight and suffering they had brought to the city. And so it went, house after house, time after time, they were refused and reviled. O'Doole was determined to give his fellow countrymen hiding in their houses one last chance to redeem themselves. He led his men to a cottage with a single candle in the window with that thought in mind. *A good sign,* O'Doole told himself as he softly knocked on the door.

A young woman of seventeen years, Molly Hatchet, a constable's daughter, came to the door. Seeing four naked, shivering men wearing only their boots standing before her, she gasped and raised a hand to her mouth.

"Are you with the Volunteers?" she said (more like, whispered).

"Aye, Miss," said O'Doole. "We are. Corporal Douglass O'Doole, at your service."

O'Doole waved his hand toward the others. "These are my mates. We had to use the bloody sewers to escape the British."

"So I gather," said Molly. "Come in. All of you. I'll make some tea and gather you some of my dah's clothes."

Molly averted her eyes as the men filed past, heads down in shame, hands concealing their privates.

† † †

Donning the civilian garments Molly O'Byrne provided, she fortified them with hot tea, black bread, and soup. It was then, in the candlelight, O'Doole noticed and a deep bruise under Molly's left eye.

"What miserable excuse of a man did that to you, Miss?"

"My dah," said Molly as her eyes filled with tears."

"You're much too beautiful, Miss," said O'Doole, "to wear such a shameful thing on your face."

Molly looked up at O'Doole's smiling face. Was it Providence, she wondered, that brought this man to her door, and why did it make her feel fine again to look at him?

† † †

To not draw unwanted attention upon themselves, Douglas O'Doole and his men split up. O'Doole headed for Ireland's southwest coast to the seaport at Waterville. There, he found a tramp steamer that would take him to America. And Molly Hatchet? O'Doole invited Molly to accompany him.

† † †

Knowing from the beginning that their insurrection was doomed to be eventually defeated, and abhorring the deaths of so many innocent civilians, five days later, on April twenty-ninth, a Saturday, Patrick Henry Pearse called for an end to Dublin's fighting. Pearse surrendered himself and the Irish Volunteers to the British. Upon handing over his pistol, the British discovered that Pearse had not fired his weapon—not once!

The Irish Volunteers had accomplished what they had set out to do, signifying to their fellow Irish men and women that home rule was their birthright, worth fighting for and, if need be, dying to get it done.

4.

From Whence Come Angels?

New Dublin, Maine
12:01 am, October thirty-first, 1937

(*or thereabouts*)

Angel O'Hara was born in 1937 in New Dublin, on the coast of Maine. Sarah and Paddy O'Hara were twenty-one years old at the time, both of Irish descent. So was most of New Dublin. The ethnic makeup of the original village was a direct result of the Great Potato Famine a hundred years earlier—an event that triggered the desperate migration of Irish to America by tens of hungry thousands.

It's hard to say who delivered Angel in Douglas O'Doole's Pub, where Sarah lay on top of a pool table. Steven Hyde, a Veterinarian, shanghaied by the barmaids to perform the delivery, was already three sheets to the wind when the barmaids doused him with cold water and insisted that he wash and scrub both hands in hot water, up to his elbows. A first, for Dr. Hyde.

Only minutes before, after running the table, a feat which did Paddy O'Hara proud, Sarah lined up the Eight Ball, called the pocket she was aiming for, and was about to sink that damnable thing when, without warning, her water broke.

All but a few men hastened from the pub. Not because it was the decent thing to do—giving Sarah some privacy, but because O'Doole promised them a thrashing if they lingered to drink, smoke, and gawk. But there was another, more innocent and compelling reason for them leaving: most of O'Doole's male patrons were unnerved by the sounds of a strong young Irishwoman in labor.

So! During the hour of Baby O'Hara's birth, the only men present and conscious were O'Doole, Paddy, and Paddy's best friend, a motorcycle-riding hellion named Jonny Fiáin—the bane of State Troopers up and down the Maritime, and the scourge of New Dublin, Maine.

Jonny, Paddy, and Sarah had known each other since they were five years old. Moreover, Paddy O'Hara and Jonny Fiáin were First cousins and would serve together in the Marines. They would fight side by side in the Pacific. Jonny had a movie star's good looks and as bold as he was dashing on a motorcycle, but Paddy was whom Sarah set her sights on. From the time she was ten, going on eleven years of age, Paddy O'Hara was the one for Sarah McLaughlin.

O'Doole's wife, Molly, and the barmaids remained at the pub to assist Sarah with the delivery. Point of fact, the assistance they rendered proved considerable after the Veterinarian's eyes rolled back, and he crumpled to the floor, unconscious, reeking of gin.

Forty-five years old, Douglas O'Doole accustomed himself to the sight of blood. Still, away from the bar and pouring drinks, he was all thumbs, except when it came to building bombs, counting money, or ejecting an unruly patron. O'Doole distinguished himself that night, however, by dragging the doctor aside so neither of them would be in the way.

Paddy and Jonny Fiáin stood behind Sarah, each of them holding one of her hands. Sarah squeezed with all her might while Paddy whispered words of love and encouragement in her ear.

"That's it, babe," said Paddy O'Hara, "Breathe. You're doing great."

Jonny Fiáin's approach was more direct, more to the point: "For Christ's sake, Sarah—don't just lay there, Push, you lazy cow!"

† † †

"It's a girl," said Molly O'Doole, shortly past midnight, October thirty-first, 1940.

At six feet, four inches tall, O'Doole peered easily over the women's heads, at the baby in Sarah's arms. The barmaids had wrapped the newborn in a fresh white dish towel before placing her on Sarah's chest.

"Would you look at the sight of it," said O'Doole.

"Swallow your tongue, Douglas O'Doole," said Molly O'Doole. "She's a fine, Irish-American girl—not a bloody lobster off your boat."

As he nodded his agreement, tears rolled down O'Doole's puffy red cheeks, only to become lost in the dark, tangled forest of salt and pepper beard that hung to mid-chest.

"Now, that's the face of an angel, if ever I've seen one," said O'Doole.

Douglas O'Doole had never seen an angel in all his forty-six years on earth, with one exception: The *Angel of Death*.

Although exhausted, a smile came to Sarah's lips. She and Paddy exchanged looks mirroring their complete agreement with the former sergeant in the Irish Republican Army.

"That's what we'll call her—won't we, Paddy?"

"Yes, my love. An Angel, she is, and Angel, she'll be."

Knowing Paddy would remain the night at Sarah's side, even after the ambulance arrived to take her and the baby to the hospital, Jonny Fiáin went behind the bar. He liberated an unopened bottle of Irish Whiskey. Without a "by your leave" or a "fare thee, well," Jonny departed on a borrowed, Harley-Davidson "Sport" Model—a motorcycle with a beefed-up engine.

O'Doole stood on the street outside the entrance to his pub with one hand raised, clenched into a fist that could crack coconuts and skulls alike.

"May the Devil take you, Jonny Fiáin!"

O'Doole watched Jonny proceed full throttle down the otherwise deserted Main Street.

"You could've at least stayed behind like a decent Irishman and shared a drink with an old man," said O'Doole. "Especially when it's his best whiskey you've taken."

A grin formed on O'Doole's face as Jonny braked and spun around. Jonny gunned the throttle with no more than forty yards of asphalt between them and no other traffic on the street; then, he popped the clutch. The front-wheel lifted off the ground and stayed that way until he stopped a scant three yards from where O'Doole stood, legs wide apart, arms folded across his chest, looking none too amused.

Jonny reached into his leather jacket, withdrew the bottle, and placed it into O'Doole's outstretched hand.

"How did you know I'd come back?" said Jonny.

A twinkle came into O'Doole's eyes. He started toward the entrance to his pub. "Come inside, lad, and I'll tell you a thing or two about yourself."

"You know me that well, do you?"

"Indeed, I do, lad," said O'Doole, "seeing as it was mostly me and Paddy's folks that raised you. Now come on in, so we can properly celebrate the baby's arrival to this tired, troubled world. Stay the night if you like. There's still a cot in the storeroom you can use."

"Thank you, Mister O'Doole, but Sheela invited me to stay the night at her place."

O'Doole's mouth sagged open. His eyes narrowed into accusatory slits. "Which, Sheela?"

"Your Sheela," said Jonny Fiáin.

"My Sheela?"

"Yes, sir. The very same as works at your pub."

"Did she, now? Invite you over to her place, you say?"

"Yes, sir, she did."

O'Doole looked long and hard at Jonny Fiáin for all of a minute before a wide grin spread across his face.

"Then I suppose we should limit our celebration to one drink and call it a night."

Jonny grinned. "Kelly's a patient girl," he said. "She can wait a bit longer."

"Kelly?" said O'Doole (more like, bellowed). "Sergeant McKuen's daughter?"

"Yes, sir," said Jonny Fiáin. "He's away fishing in the Adirondacks and won't be back for a fortnight. I told Kelly I'd look in on her. Make sure she's all right."

"You're a cocky bastard, Jonny Fiáin," said O'Doole. "Don't go breaking those girls' hearts, or I'll bring my shillala down on your head. Same as your dah would've done."

"Sheela says I'm like the wind, Mister O'Doole. She says I don't have it in me to stay in one place with one woman."

"What about Kelly? What does she say, lad?"

"Pretty much the same as Sheela. They all do."

"Holy Jehoshaphat! I suppose that's why you ride that silly thing you're sitting on."

"I suppose so."

"You're too good looking for your own damn good, Jonny. Come on. Let's have that drink."

O'Doole placed a hand on the motorcycle's handlebars and shook it.

"You know," said O'Doole, "Lawrence of Arabia[15] killed himself on one of these, don't you?"

"Did he, now?" said Jonny.

"He did! I'll tell you about him while we wet our tongues."

† † †

After nine shots of Irish Whiskey, with beer and a great deal of laughter to chase the whiskey, Douglas O'Doole looked Jonny Fiáin straight in the eyes and said: "Did your dah ever tell you stories about your namesake?"

"My namesake?"

"Yes. Who your folks named you after. Did you not hear the stories, lad?"

---

[15] T.E. Lawrence, aka, Lawrence of Arabia, was a British archaeological scholar, military strategist, and author best known for his legendary war activities in the Middle East during World War I and for his account of those activities in *The Seven Pillars of Wisdom* (1926) [Wikipedia].

"I don't remember," said Jonny. "I was pretty young when they passed."

"True," said O'Doole. "You were, indeed. Well, I'll tell you now. It just so happens that on your mother's side of the bed, God rest her sweet soul, you're a direct descendant of Handsome Jonny Stint."

"Handsome Jonny, *who*?"

"Stint. An Eighteenth-century buccaneer. Captain of a legendary ghost ship named *La Bruja Del Mar* that shows itself in the Caribbean when the trade winds quit, and the sky turns black with foreboding. Legend had it when Stint passed; his spirit wasn't welcome, High or Low, so, to this day, he wanders the world searching for the treasure he buried on any number of islands in the Stream. [16]"

"I should be going, Mister O'Doole. Sheela's waiting for me."

"Ah! So she is. Well then, lad. Off with you."

Jonny Fiáin was far too drunk to notice the twinkle in O'Doole's eyes, which, at this juncture, numbered four. Jonny pushed off the barstool he'd been sitting on and landed flat on his face, out cold.

"Sorry lad," said O'Doole, "but I can't let you get on that bike, not as you are."

O'Doole threw Jonny over his shoulder like a sack of potatoes and carried him to the storeroom. He placed Jonny on the cot and threw a blanket over him.

Elsewhere, at the New Dublin Community Hospital, Paddy O'Hara gazed through the glass of the Maternity

---

[16] The Gulf stream that emanates from the Gulf of Mexico where, millions of years ago, the great asteroid struck killing the dinosaurs, Mastodons and Wooly Mammoths and lots of other creatures, and paved the way for God's greatest disappointment, the *Homo Sapien Sapiens* to appear.

Ward at his daughter wrapped in a blanket of her own, asleep.

"You go on and sleep, Angel darlin'. I'll be right here when you awaken."

5.

Blood Brothers

One need not be a trucker to know most roads in Life take numerous twists and turns; truth be told, they have detours galore. Jonny Fiáin's Life was no exception.

† † †

The *Great Bangor-New Dublin Train Wreck of 1923*[17] occurred on July eighth, when two passenger trains collided head-on north of New Dublin, Maine. The estimated speed of the trains was fifty miles per hour. One-hundred-and-eighty-one men, women, and children died, one-hundred-and-seventy-one had severe injuries. Jonny Fiáin's mother, June, and his father, Richard Fiáin, were crushed and killed upon impact.

Jonny was seven years old at the time. He lay trapped in the wreckage beneath the bodies of his parents for eighteen hours before rescuers found him—unconscious and covered in blood from a deep gash in his head, a wound that would require one-hundred-and-ten stitches and six months to recover from if recovery is the word.

---

[17] It actually took place on 1926.

In the late summer of 1929, not long after the Scottish scientist Alexander Fleming accidentally discovered penicillin, New Dublin's schools were in recess. The Seventh Grade had already vanished, forgotten by the kids who would soon attain Middle School's highest rung—Eighth Grade.

Just two months later, in October, the *Stock Market Crash of 1929*[18] would occur. Americans would call it *the Great Depression*. The writing was on the proverbial wall—pain and suffering would pave the road ahead, not just for America but worldwide for more than a decade to come.[19]

The economy would buckle, then collapse entirely. Businesses and factories from coast to coast would be closed by the hundreds. Millions who invested their life savings buying stocks and bonds brokers hawked on Wall Street would suddenly find themselves penniless and destitute overnight.

During those less than halcyon days of early summer in New Dublin, the schools had let out, and the weather couldn't have been kinder. Most of the older kids worked summer jobs while others were at the beach; some sailed in Lobster Bay. A privileged few, "Whites Only," went swimming at the New Dublin Country Club & Golf Course.

[18] The Wall Street Crash of 1929, also known as the Great Crash, was a major American stock market crash that occurred in the fall of 1929 [Wikipedia]

[19] The Great Depression was a severe worldwide economic depression that took place mostly during the 1930s, beginning in the United States.

☦ ☦ ☦

Two thirteen-year-old boys, Jonny Fiáin and Paddy O'Hara sat dead center in the Bijou Theatre's front row. They were at the Saturday matinee watching *The Virginian*, starring Gary Cooper and Walter Huston, with Mary Brian as a beautiful young woman dealing with willful men, men whose tempers matched their lightning speed with a six-gun.

Two rows back from Jonny and Paddy sat a row of soon-to-be Eighth Grade girls, among them, and something of their leader, was a tom-boyish, thirteen-year-old, blue-eyed temptation, by the name of Sarah McLaughlin.

Sarah was the only daughter of Rose and Lawrence McLaughlin, highly regarded in New Dublin society's upper echelon. Lawrence McLaughlin was the cannery owner, where many of New Dublin's inhabitants, including Paddy's mom and dad, still worked, despite the vagaries and vicissitudes that accompanied the Great Depression.

Rose McLaughlin had been a Suffragette early in Life and an acknowledged force in local politics. She was the chairperson and champion of many a liberal cause, including being a vociferous advocate for women's reproductive rights, such as they were in 1929.

McLaughlin's daughter, Sarah, wasn't enrolled at one of the private academies for America's social elites' progeny because her father had to work his way up the socioeconomic ladder with his wits and fists. If there was any group he despised, it was the "spoiled brats of the social aristocracy," and he damn well determined that his only daughter wouldn't become one of them. And Sarah didn't, so maybe enrolling her in the New Dublin public school system worked, or maybe Sarah was just born lovely, a sweet girl, to begin with, unpretentious, and sincere.

It wasn't by accident that Jonny Fiáin lived with the O'Hara family for the previous six years. Fortunately for Jonny, his mother, June was Alyssa O'Hara's sister; so, it came as no surprise after the train wreck that Seamus and Alyssa would take Jonny into their home and raise him as part of their *family*, alongside his cousin, Paddy.

† † †

In any good Western, the inevitable moment arrives when against all the odds, the hero emerges victorious from the famous, final gunfight. This peak event, essential to any Western worth its spurs', allows the audience to shout; clap; cheer and breathe easy as the story coasts to the end.

So, too, did Jonny Fiáin and Paddy O'Hara breathe easy when The Virginian triumphed over his nemesis, a skunk of the highest order named Trampas, a back-shooter and dirty, low-down beef-thief.

Just as predictable, when the moment came for The Virginian to take the woman he married into his arms and kiss her, the faces of the boys contorted—it still seemed the right thing to do at their age, even if their thoughts secretly dovetailed with a new, though unspoken interest in girls. However, witnessing their larger-than-life hero endure life-threatening trials and tribulations, only to succumb at the end to nothing more than a pretty face, was more than Jonny or Paddy could silently abide. Thus, the boys rolled their eyes and groaned, as would any red-blooded, thirteen-year-old American male who secretly thought "the kiss" made for a swell deal. But when they shouted their annoyance at the silver screen and as the music rose to a full crescendo, kernels of popcorn thrown from two rows back landed on their heads. Bags of that All-American snack food were hurled at them like stones from catapults, courtesy of Sarah McLaughlin and her gal-pals. These soon-to-be Eighth Grade girls had no problem with The Virginian showing his appreciation for the woman in his arms — even if it meant kissing her on the lips.

While Jonny and Paddy waited for the theatre to empty, they picked popcorn out of their hair and from under their shirt collars; they did this as Sarah McLaughlin and her entourage filed toward the lobby.

"Had to be Sarah's idea," said Jonny.

"Had to be," said Paddy.

Paddy popped a kernel of corn into his mouth.

"Any good?" said Jonny.

"Needs butter."

† † †

In the theatre lobby, Sarah McLaughlin lingered at the drinking fountain. One of her friends, Elsie McVie, one day to be Missus Elsie Crabtree, the mother of two sweet kids yet to be named Andrew and Megan, shouted, "Sarah! Come on. We're going to take the trolley to the Jolly Cone for a soda."

"Go ahead," said Sarah. "I'll catch up."

"You're not waiting around for you know who—are you, Sarah?"

"Mind your own bees' wax, Elsie McVie. I'll see you in a while."

"No, you won't," said Elsie. "I know what you're up to, Sarah McLoughlin."

Elsie laughed and ran off to join the other girls in line at the trolley stop.

When Jonny and Paddy appeared in the lobby, they discovered Sarah waiting for them. Half-expecting Sarah and her friends to shower popcorn upon them a second time, Jonny and Paddy looked around, suspicion etched on their faces. Nothing. Just Sarah; she looked at them with a somewhat intimidating, Cheshire Cat grin on her freckled face.

"Hi, Paddy. Hi, Jonny."

"Hi, Sarah."

"Good movie. Huh?" said Sarah.

There was something provocative in the way she asked: had Paddy and Jonny missed something significant? The boys exchanged a worried look.

"It was okay, I guess," said Paddy.

"Up to a point," said Jonny, alluding to "the kiss."

Sarah chuckled. "Yeah, we noticed you both had a problem with the ending."

"Yeah. Well?" said Paddy, not knowing what else to say.

"So, what?" said Jonny, wanting to help Paddy out of a fix. "The most important thing is, the Virginian settled the score with what's his name—the bad guy."

Sarah grinned. "Okay. If you say so, Jonny Fiáin."

"Yeah. I do say so," said Jonny, always the aggressive one.

"Is that what you think, Paddy?" said Sarah. "That the gunfight at the end was the most important part?"

Paddy didn't know how to answer. "I don't know," he said. "Yeah. Maybe. I don't know."

"Hah," said Sarah. "In a few years, you're going to change your minds. Both of you."

"Says, who?" said Jonny.

"Yeah," said Paddy. "Says, who?"

"Says my Mother," said Sarah. "That's who. She says boys don't mature as fast as girls. She said it takes boys longer to figure things out."

"Your mom said that?" said Paddy.

Jonny gave Paddy a look. "Maybe she was joking?"

"Yeah," said Paddy. "I bet your mom was joking."

"My mother doesn't joke," said Sarah. "My father does. Some times. But not my mother."

"Come on, Paddy," said Jonny. "We should get going,"

"Yeah. Right," said Paddy. He looked at Sarah. "We gotta get going."

"Can I come?" said Sarah.

"We have our bikes," said Paddy.

"Yeah," said Jonny. "We have our bikes."

"Fine," said Sarah. "I'll ride on the handlebars."

Paddy and Jonny's eyebrows shot up; they looked at her, then at each other, and shrugged.

6.

Of Innocence Lost

The ride from the theatre to Matilija Lake took less than forty minutes, helped largely by a cooling onshore breeze and Jonny and Paddy's Herculean pedaling.

The boys took turns with Sarah on the handlebars. It was only fair since they had to traverse an unimproved road with challenging rises and dips after leaving the town's confines. Several dusty inclines were where Sarah had to get off and walk, something she did without complaint. The boys especially liked Sarah McLaughlin; not that puberty and percolating hormones had anything to do with it; she wasn't fussy like other girls in their age group. Sarah enjoyed being around Paddy and Jonny, in particular. To Sarah, they stood head-and-shoulders above the pack of boys at their school. More than that, Sarah was a natural athlete. She could throw, catch, pitch, and bat as well as any boy her age, and she was a terrific runner, things Paddy and Jonny openly admired.

When they reached the lake, Sarah jumped off the handlebars of Paddy's bike and ran onto the sandy shoreline. Once there, she stripped to her underwear top and bottom, then looked back over her shoulder.

"Well?" she shouted. "Aren't you coming?"

Jonny and Paddy looked at each other.

"Why not?" said Jonny.

"Yeah," said Paddy. "Why not?"

† † †

For an hour, they lay on the beach in silence; the boys were face down, concealing from each other what they couldn't suppress, while Sara, unaware of the boys' sorry state, stared at the clouds passing overhead like gray, white, and orange cotton candy.

The sun comforted these three best friends, and while their undergarments dried like a second skin, a soothing sea breeze blew against their faces and played with their hair.

Sarah looked at the boys. "My father says more hard times are coming."

"He did?" said Paddy,

Sarah nodded.

"Mom and Dad were talking about that last night," said Paddy. "During supper. Huh, Jonny?"

"Yeah," said Jonny. "They sound worried."

"About hard times coming?" said Sarah.

"Yes. Everybody knows folks are going to be laid-off at the cannery."

"It's true," said Sarah. "Sometime after the Fourth of July, my father will begin letting people go."

"How many?" said Paddy.

"I don't know," said Sarah. "Quite a few, I think."

Jonny and Paddy exchanged looks mirroring their concern.

"I spoke to my father about your mom and dad, Paddy."

"You did?"

"Yes," said Sarah. "He said they were too valuable to let go."

"He said that?"

"Yes," said Sarah. "So, tell them not to worry."

"That was a swell thing to do, Sarah," said Jonny.

"Yes," said Paddy. "It was a swell thing to do, Sarah. Thank you."

"I care about you, Paddy O'Hara. You, too, Jonny Fiáin."

A vehicle making its way toward the shoreline diverted their attention away from further momentary consideration of the economic upheaval that had settled like a blight on the country, one that hung uncomfortably over the heads of every man, woman, and child, including those in New Dublin, Maine.

The boys identified the vehicle straight away as a burgundy-colored 1928 Cadillac Sedan. The Cadillac came to a stop fifty yards away from Jonny, Sarah, and Paddy.

The driver shut the engine off. But for the noise made by mud hens as they darted in and out of clumps of reeds scattered along the shoreline, the area around the lake became once more tranquil.

The next moment there came a loud pop, something like a firecracker, from inside the Cadillac. It was loud enough to bring the three children to their feet.

"What was that?" said Sarah.

"I don't know," said Paddy,

"It sounded like a gunshot," said Jonny.

"You think so?" said Paddy.

"Let's go see," said Jonny.

"Maybe we shouldn't," said Sarah.

"Where's the fun in that?" said Jonny. "Come on."

"Uh, I think we should put our clothes on," said Sarah.

Paddy chuckled. "Good idea."

They were five yards away when Sarah motioned for them to stop. "I know whose car that is," she said. "It belongs to a friend of my father's, Mister Kennedy. He's a stockbroker."

They could see Kennedy's upper body through the passenger-side window. He sat slumped to his left, his head and shoulder against the window.

Sarah gasped; her hands closed over her mouth. "Is that what I think it is?"

"Wait here," said Jonny. "Come on, Paddy."

The boys crept the short distance to the Cadillac and looked inside. The driver's side window was awash with blood and small pieces of brain matter. In his right hand, resting on the car seat, the stockbroker still clutched the pistol he used to end his life.

Paddy leaned close to Jonny. "What should we do, Jonny?" Paddy's voice quivered.

Jonny looked skyward. "It'll be dark soon. We should take Sarah home—right?"

Paddy nodded. "Right. But what about—"

Jonny cut him off. "We can call the police when we get back to town. There's a payphone at Bayless Market."

"Good idea," said Paddy.

The boys turned around and looked at Sarah. She was trembling; tears formed in her eyes.

"I'm sorry about your dad's friend," said Jonny. "He's dead."

Paddy removed his sweatshirt and held it out. "Put this on, Sarah. The sun's going down."

Sarah put Paddy's sweatshirt on. The three walked in silence to where they left the bikes and started for town

† † †

Jonny and Paddy stood alongside their bikes and watched Sarah walk up a broad, tree-lined driveway leading to the front door of her parents' two-story, five-bedroom, five-bathroom, *antebellum,*[22] Southern-style mansion on the McLaughlin's, five-hundred acres estate.

Before she went inside, Sarah paused and looked back. The boys each raised a hand; they weren't waving goodbye; they were communicating something else to her as the sun began to set behind them. Sarah tried to smile but couldn't; then, she let herself inside.

Jonny and Paddy wouldn't see her until September when schools opened, just ahead of Flu season.

Jonny and Paddy rode to Bayless Market in downtown New Dublin and stood outside the phone booth. They each took a deep breath and flipped a coin. Heads or tails, the loser had to call the Police Station to report what they saw at the lake an hour before. It was close to being the most challenging phone call Jonny Fiáin would ever make.

"There's a dead man in a burgundy Cadillac at Matilija Lake. No! I'm not joking! Go see for yourself."

Jonny slammed the phone down and left the booth.

"Do you think they believed you?" said Paddy.

"Probably not. I don't know," said Jonny. "At least we did our part."

"Yeah," said Paddy. "We did our part."

---

[22] *Antebellum* [Latin] meaning: Before [the] war. A reference to an era of supposed grandeur in the Old South that preceded the American Civil War, reflected in the architecture of the day resembling the architecture of ancient Greece.

† † †

"You two are strangely quiet tonight," said Alyssa O'Hara.

"Just tired is all," said Paddy.

"We rode our bikes quite a distance after the movie, Aunt Alyssa," said Jonny.

"Well, I hope you boys aren't too tired for peach cobbler after dinner, for dessert?"

"No way," said the boys in unison.

"How was the movie?" said Seamus O'Hara. He passed the basket of cross buns to Paddy while Missus O'Hara loaded Jonny's plate with peas, mashed potatoes, and gravy accompanying the pot roast they had.

"It was okay," said Paddy.

"What did you boys see, Jonny?" said Missus O'Hara.

"We watched The Virginian, Aunt Alyssa," said Jonny.

He fashioned the mashed potatoes on his plate into a small volcano, then poured gravy inside. "With Gary Cooper."

"We should go see it, Seamus," said Alyssa O'Hara. "I love Gary Cooper."

"Sure. We can do that," said Mister O'Hara. "You boys are old enough now. You can hold the fort while Missus O'Hara and I go out. I'd kind of like to see The Virginian, myself."

† † †

That night, as the boys lie in their respective bunk beds, neither felt like sleeping. An hour went by before either of the boys spoke.

"Jonny? You awake?"

"Yeah."

"I wish I hadn't seen what we did at the lake," said Paddy. He kept his voice soft, lest his parents hear.

"Yeah," said Jonny. "Me, neither. I hope I never see anything like it again."

"Why do you think he did it?" said Paddy.

"Don't know," said Jonny. "And I don't want to, either."

"Do you think Sarah is going to be okay," said Paddy.

Jonny thought about it. "Sarah's pretty strong for a girl. She'll be okay. As okay as us, anyway. Don't you think?"

Paddy thought about it. "I hope you're right."

"You like Sarah, don't you?" said Jonny.

A minute passed in silence.

"Yeah," said Paddy. "I guess I do. Is that okay with you, Jonny?"

"Yeah. Sure. You bet it is."

In truth, it wasn't okay with Jonny, but he and Paddy were blood brothers, and his love for Paddy outweighed what he felt for Sarah McLaughlin, strange and uncomfortable as those feelings had been of late.

"Good night, Paddy."

"Good night, Jonny.

7.

Marzipan! Marzipan! Marzipan!

[A Necessary Aside]

Marzipan is a confection comprising honey (or sugar) and almonds, ground together into a fine powder, then made into sweets that will, if permitted, wreak havoc[23] on one's complexion, pancreas, and self-esteem. Should one consume excessive amounts of this tantalizing gift from the gods, expect to atone later, at the gym.

Easy to work with, Marzipan candies can be fashioned in such ways as to imitate the appearance of fruits and, to a much lesser extent, vegetables. When one thinks about it, what kids like to eat vegetables? Parents, successful parents, must, of necessity, become amateur psychologists, even if it means tricking their ~~larvae~~ children into eating what is good for them.

Sometimes, Marzipan is coated with chocolate and topped with coconut sprinkles. It's entirely a matter of whatever perambulations the imagination can conjure in the kitchen.

Parents and single mothers should warn their spawn when the little darlings are still crumb-munchers that Marzipan is FATTENING, making it too perfect for multi-cultured America to consume. Americans are primarily a nation of wobbling wide bodies who show no

---

[23] An unsubstantiated rumor promoted by humorless dieticians.

signs of altering their habits, right into this, the early 21st century.

Some culinary purists insist that a Marzipan glaze is perfect as icing when whipped into a lather and layered over birthday cakes, wake cakes, wedding cakes, divorce cakes, and so forth, *ad nauseum.*

Marzipan painted onto celebratory pastries is particularly common in the British Isles, where parents often celebrate a successful circumcision of their first-born (male) progeny. But it doesn't end there! In the United Kingdom, celebratory fruitcakes blush with marzipan veneers—particularly Christmas cake covered with white sugar icing. At Easter, the Simnel cake contains a layer of marzipan, a further layer decorates the top, and 12 spheres symbolize the twelve guys Jesus pal'd around with toward the end of his days on earth. The marzipan is then lightly fried for color.

In Geneva, Switzerland, a traditional part of the celebration of L'Escalade is the ritual smashing of a chocolate cauldron filled with marzipan vegetables, a reference to a Savoyard siege of the city which a housewife supposedly foiled with a cauldron of boiling soup. God's truth! You can't make this stuff up. Marzipan is a BIG DEAL and always has been.

In some countries over which a dark cloud seems ever-present, such as in present-day Hungary, Romania, and in ancient Transylvania, home to one of Marzipan's more colorful marzipan *aficionados*, Vlad the Impaler, also known as—Dracula, Marzipan candies take on miniature animals' shapes such as bats and other things that go "bump" in the night. Nobody knows why. If *the Shadow* knows, he isn't saying.

Traditional Swedish Foo-Foo cake has a thick layer of Marzipan tinted a fuchsia color or sometimes sky blue. Why? Because no one in Sweden has ever seen a blue sky due to year-round inclement weather.

In España, in El Greco's hometown of Toledo (Go, *Rockets!*), the first written reference of Marzipan (called Mazapan in Spain) dates back to the year 1512 A.D.

Seven years later, in 1519, a psychopathic Spaniard named Hernán Cortés would plant his banner in the New World, in what is now part of Mexico, along with five-hundred other randy Spaniards eager to plant their banners into anything that walked upright—preferably female—an event that would lead to the destruction of the Aztec empire and decimate other aboriginal cultures in the New World, as well.

Brutally effective at raping the New World's indigenous women, the Spanish Conquistadores inadvertently created a new race of *Homo Sapien Sapiens*, a mixture of Spanish and indigenous peoples called *mestizos*. Most Mexican and Central American *mestizos* have since migrated north and live today in ungovernable Los Angeles, in the desert known as Southern California.

Nowadays, Marzipan is eaten worldwide throughout the year, but seldom during "leap year." Why? No one knows. It's just the way it is.

So! How cometh *Marzipan* into the world? Inquiring minds have a right to know.

When South America was yet part of Africa—look at a map, one can see how nicely the east coast of South America fits Africa's west coast.

So! Before the northern coastline of Africa separated from Europa and created the Mediterranean Sea, and before the west coast of the North American hemisphere broke away from the Far East, there existed what some refer to as *the Lost Continent of Atlantis*.

In point of fact, the Lost Continent of Atlantis isn't lost—not at all, it's under the freeking Atlantic Ocean, midway between North America to the west, and Europe, to the east, plain as the heads on Mount Rushmore.

One may wonder, was it the *Primum Casum Magnum,* the First Great Cataclysm[24] that did in Atlantis? In truth, it was!

†††

Attende et Audi[25]! It was THERE, in a bakery on Atlantis, that fifteen-year-old *Iulia Puer Natus,* daughter of a popular populist philosopher, *Maximus Vagitus,* conceived, birthed, and kept secret from the "Known World," her discovery—she called it, *Marzipanio Extremis Darngoodeth* after, and in honor of, *Marzipanio,* the patron god of bakers.[26]

That is a hugely important secret made known, but, in truth, Iulia's creation is only a small part of the story of Marzipan. So! On to the *Genesis* of this overnight sensation.

Iulia[27] *Puer Natus* was one of the few Atlantean inhabitants[28] who escaped the death and destruction that

---

[24] The *First Great Cataclysm* occurred when a colossal comet, asteroid, or meteor struck the earth a very long time ago, creating what is now called the Gulf of Mexico. This event simultaneously triggered the tectonic upheaval that tore the continents asunder, creating seven out of one. Those in the know believe the comet, asteroid or meteor that formed the Chicxulub Crater off the Yucatan Peninsula, was roughly 31, 680 feet in diameter, and impacted the earth at 39,999 miles per hour, releasing 2 million times more energy than the most powerful butterfly sneeze, or even the most butch nuclear bomb ever detonated, and THAT'S saying a lot. The heat would have barbequed the earth's surface, torching forests worldwide, and blotting-out the sun in the doing as a bunch of crud clouded the atmosphere, suffocating much of life below. *Ergo,* making the *Novel Corona Virus* (COVID-19) pandemic of 2020-2021 pretty much a non-event.

[25] Atlantean for: "Attend and listen!"

[26] Almanac of Unapologetic Facts. Misty Bay Books. Volume 1. 1st Edition. 1948.

[27] Pronounced: Eye/ooh/lee/uh, the way it's spelled.

[28] The Atlantic Ocean, so-named for the Continent of Atlantis.

befell her home, hers, and an estimated 2.2 million Atlanteans,[29] who did perish.

Divine Will? Fate? Luck! Only *the Phantom* can say, and he isn't saying. He seldom does. In any case, it was Iulia's great good fortune, Mankind's really, that she was spending the summer with her boyfriend at their estate in the southern region of present-day España known as Andalusia. Had it been otherwise, the world would be the worse for never having experienced the exquisite taste and culinary uses of *Marzipanio Extremis Darngoodeth* (Marzipan).

Iulia escaped the cataclysm of 6.5 million B.C. with her life, true, but now, she was destitute—penniless! What to do?

Hah! Iulia knew exactly what to do—what any enterprising fifteen-year-old daughter of Atlantis knew to do when one reluctantly finds themselves, "All in!":

Do what you CAN do!

Ergo, to her boyfriend and his family and friends, Iulia announced creating something she called: "*Ite Fund Mihi*.[30]" Clever girl. She would not live so long as to see this radical, completely out-of-the-box concept that made begging respectable, catch hold worldwide one day, but that's just the way things are:

Here today. Gone to Maui.

Acquiring sufficient start-up money, Iulia opened a bakery. "*Build it, and they will come*," her boyfriend told her.

And they did!

---

[29] According to the fossilized record of the Census of 6.5 million, B.C.

[30] Etruscan for "Go, fund me!"

Once word circulated regarding Iulia's marvelous creation, *Marzipanio Extremis Darngoodeth,* Andalusians flocked like locusts to her bakery, so much so that Iulia in time franchised her operation. Soon, an *Iulia's Bakery* opened in every village and town on the Iberian Peninsula, long before geographers named it thus.

In time, Iulia expanded her operation north, south, east, and west throughout Europa.

The famed Italian explorer, Marco Polo, would be the first to introduce Marzipan to the Court of the Supreme Cocksman himself, the great Kublai Khan, descended from the greatest mass murderer of all time, Genghis Khan. Kublai was then Emperor of Mongolia, China, Tibet and India, and various parts of Alaska, which he gave back to the Inuit people once he realized the air was too cold and the grass not green enough to raise yaks.

Indeed, Marzipan became, in time, ubiquitous. It was *Alexander the Great,*[31] no less, who brought Marzipan to Persia. By the 8th century, Marzipan had caught hold in countries throughout North Africa, Arabia, and the Middle East, where, hitherto, the greatest pleasure in life lay in cutting off the heads of infidels; that, and smoking

---

[31] Alexander the Great, bastard son of Philip of Macedonia, united all of Greece at the age of 21. By the age of 28, he had conquered Egypt, Persia and most of India. He was not yet 30 when he died in Babylon of in 324 B.C. he fell ill and died after 12 days of excruciating suffering. Since then, historians have debated his cause of death, proposing everything from malaria, typhoid, and alcohol poisoning to assassination by one of his rivals. In a bombshell new theory, a scholar and practicing clinician suggests that Alexander may have suffered from the neurological disorder Guillain-Barré Syndrome (GBS), which caused his death. She also argues that people might not have noticed any immediate signs of decomposition on the body after six days following his supposed death for one simple reason—Alexander wasn't dead yet, lending credence to the myth of his divinity.

hashish. Marzipan changed all that, more or less; it became more popular than coffee in Damascus and the Levant. Soon Nubian slackers started smuggling Marzipan along the east coast of Africa to Zanzibar.

The stories about the courageous young girl from doomed Atlantis, *Iulia Puer Natus,* are legion, like her marzipan recipes. Suffice to say, *Iulia* and her alone deserves the credit for bringing Marzipan into the world.

Now, back to the story!

8.

1949

Nineteen Forty-Nine (MCMXLIX) began on a Saturday, the 1,949th year, *Anno Domini* (A.D.), of the Gregorian calendar; the 949th year of the 2nd Millennium; the 49th year of the 20th century, and the 10th and last year of the decade that became the 1940s.

By 1949, the Cold War[32] between America and the Soviet Union was in its second year. The Berlin airlift ended. The New York Yankees defeated the Brooklyn Dodgers, four games to win their twelfth World Series Title. The Chinese communists seized complete control of mainland China, and Mao Tse Tung became dictator there for life. 1949 is also the first year the Ku Klux Klan failed to lynch a black man anywhere in the United States. Albert II, the first primate launched into space, is killed by the impact of crashing upon his return. Truly, 1949 was a year of momentous events, Angel O'Hara's Twelfth birthday among them.

After Trick-Or-Treating, the plan was for Angel to return to a private birthday celebration. It was special this year—not because she would turn nine years of age, but because Jonny Fiáin had sent Angel a telegram from somewhere in Pennsylvania promising he would be there, and that pleased Angel more than presents, cake, and ice cream combined. It was also the reason Sara

---

[32] The Cold War was a period of geopolitical tension between the Soviet Union and the United States and their respective allies, the Eastern Bloc and the Western Bloc, after World War II. It began in 1949 and lasted until 1991 [Wikipedia].

O'Hara insisted that no other children be present during Jonny Fiáin's yearly visit, which was fine with Angel.

To Angel, Jonny Fiáin was a mythic hero, bigger than life, who could do no wrong. Point of fact, to Sarah O'Hara's great dismay, Paddy said nothing to dissuade Angel's hero-worship of the man he fought and bled alongside in the Pacific during the Second World War.

"Jesus, Joseph, and Mary!" said Seamus O'Hara to his wife, Alyssa, the day Paddy and Jonny left for Boot Camp. "As if one World War wasn't enough for America."

Except for being there when Angel was born, Paddy and Jonny missed Angel's second, third and fourth birthdays for the simple reason they had joined the Marines. That was after elements of the Japanese Imperial Navy attacked Pearl Harbor, December Seventh, Nineteen-Forty-One. They didn't wait for Uncle Sam [33]to draft them. They were the first in New Dublin to enlist. It's an Irish thing.

For a year, and change, the time they served together, Paddy O'Hara and Jonny Fiáin did what they had to do to survive. During that time, on October thirty-first, 1942, a minute past midnight, they celebrated Angel's fifth birthday. It didn't matter that they were in a muddy, rain-drenched foxhole on Guadalcanal with every manner of insect feeding on them. They celebrated Angel's Birthday with cigarettes, C-Rations, and the cookies Sarah sent weekly from New Dublin, although,

---

[33] Uncle Sam is a common national personification of the U.S. federal government or the United States, in general, that, according to legend, came into use during the War of 1812 and was supposedly named for a tall, skinny fellow with bushy white eyebrows and a long white beard named Samuel Wilson. The actual origin is by a legend. Since the early 19th century, Uncle Sam has been a popular symbol of the US government in American culture and a manifestation of patriotic emotion [Wikipedia].

by the time the cookies caught up with them, they were always stale.

C'est la Guerre!

This time, on her twelfth Birthday, Jonny Fiáin would be there; Angel just knew, deep in her gut, that he would be. They would enjoy an early supper of pot roast, mashed potatoes and gravy, butter rolls, string beans, and sweet peas mixed with steamed green scallions. Devil's Food cake, heavy with rich chocolate frosting, topped with homemade vanilla ice cream, was for dessert.

Angel O'Hara preferred Devil's food cake over something so pedestrian as Angels' food cake. We're not exactly talking *Good versus Evil* here; Angel's favorite cake was a moist, rich, chocolate-layer cake made from two eggs, 1/3 cup butter, 2 cups white sugar, and 4, one-ounce squares of unsweetened chocolate.

Despite war-time shortages, for such delicacies as chocolate, the fact that Sarah's father, Lawrence McLaughlin, owned most of New Dublin, his cannery turned out contracts for the military. Mclaughlin had contacts nationwide and in Washington, D.C., such that he and his own never suffered for want of anything, war or no war.

C'est la vie!

At the age of twenty, Angel's mother, Sarah, won a Silver Medal for archery in the 1936 Olympics in Munich, Germany. Now Sarah watched Angel loose arrow after arrow at a bale of hay thirty yards distant. She took immense satisfaction watching her daughter strike the bulls-eye dead center more times than not. No great mystery how Angel became an excellent archer at such a tender age.

Born with her mother's gray eyes, hand-eye coordination, and skill with a bow, Angel had her dad's honey-colored hair and lean, tall body. Later, Angel would acquire Jonny Fiáin's fondness for motorcycles, firearms, and gallows' humor. But that is getting way too far ahead.

† † †

Paddy O'Hara paused from replacing the spark plugs on his pickup and watched his daughter sink arrow after arrow deep into the center of a bale of hay. Looking at Angel, costumed as an Indian brave with streaks of red and yellow war paint on her cheeks, Paddy's heart swelled with love for his family, for the life they enjoyed at the lighthouse on Bette's Chin, and for his cousin and life-long friend, Jonny Fiáin.

It's going to be good times when Jonny gets here, Paddy told himself. There wasn't a day gone by that Paddy didn't think about Jonny. It had been a year to the day since Jonny's last visit. Paddy grinned and shook his head. *God knows what he's going to bring Angel this year.*

For Angel's last birthday, Jonny Fiáin had gifted her with a pair of brass-knuckles. Sarah immediately confiscated and later used the device as a paperweight in the small office she and Paddy maintained, related to the lighthouse's operation and, for sundry, household matters.

Paddy watched Angel gather her arrows. Bending straight over was a problem, given the plaster-of-Paris cast she wore on her right leg. It reached from just above the knee to her foot. Paddy made Angel a device that worked like tweezers, but larger, with a long handle that enabled her to grasp an object on the ground. Nothing fancy, but effective. He sighed as Angel awkwardly made her way to the steps of the front porch and sat. Whiskey was with her—a small, short-haired mongrel with big brown eyes, ears that stood up straight, and a short, stubby tail that rarely stopped wagging, except when asleep in Angel's bed.

Paddy picked up a rag, wiped the grease from his hands, and walked with a slight limp toward the house. The limp derived from a wound he suffered on Guadalcanal in mid-February 1943. Paddy ascended the steps to the porch and stopped. Angel's eyes were fixed on the dirt road twenty yards off. Paddy looked at his daughter.

"A watched pot never boils, Pocahontas."

"I'm Chingachgook, last of the Mohicans," said Angel, without taking her eyes off the road.

"Oh," said Paddy. "Sorry, Chief."

Paddy looked at the pumpkins he and Angel carved the night before. By far, Angel was more imaginative. Paddy's pumpkin was a rather jolly fellow with a wide grin, a triangular nose, and a single cyclopean eye. It had three evil eyes, a crooked nose, and a single tooth. When asked to judge which pumpkin was more disturbing, Sarah wrung her hands in mock despair but declined to say.

As Paddy continued toward the front door, Angel patted Whiskey on the head and said: "Jonny will come. Huh, Whiskey?"

Inside the house, Paddy made straightaway to the kitchen. He came up behind Sarah, folded his arms around her, and kissed the nape of her neck, not once but twice.

On the radio in the living room, Doris Day sang, *"It's Magic."*

"I felt you the first time, Paddy O'Hara. And don't be starting what you don't aim to finish."

"You're a hard task-master, Sarah O'Hara. Begrudging a hungry man, a taste."

Sarah chuckled as she lay the dishcloth aside, turned in Paddy's arms, and faced him, nose to nose. As the music continued, Sarah and Paddy danced slowly around the kitchen, as much in love then as when they shared their first kiss. That was long before Angel was born.

As the song's last notes concluded, Paddy and Sarah kissed, not a quick peck on the cheek; instead, it was a long, delicious, two-tongue waltz that made them dizzy and wanting more. But "more" would have to wait. Sarah slid a blueberry past Paddy's lips. "Where's Chingachgook?" she said.

"Sitting on the porch."

"Elsie Crabtree is coming by with Megan and Andrew. They invited Angel to go trick-or-treating. Elsie volunteered to keep an eye on the three of them."

"Great."

Sarah looked at her wristwatch. "It's three-o'clock, Paddy. We're eating, whether Jonny's her or not. Tell your daughter."

He wasn't going to argue. Especially not after Sarah had spent most of the day in the kitchen.

"But Jonny's not here, Dad," said Angel.

"He will be," said Paddy. "But supper's ready, and your mom wants us in there."

†††

They had no sooner finished dessert when the sound of a car horn announced the arrival of three-fourths of Clan Crabtree. Doctor George Crabtree abstained from driving to Bette's Chin, wanting instead to guard his immaculate lawn against being trampled by ghosts and goblins in the throes of sugar-induced hyper mania. Paddy and Sarah went outside onto the porch.

Angel got to her feet. "Stay, Whiskey."

Angel surrendered her bow and quiver of arrows. "Here, Mom."

"Good idea, sweetie." Sarah handed Angel a pillowslip with a strap attached, so Angel could carry it over her shoulder to hold the candy she would accumulate trick-or-treating. Angel strode out of the house and off the porch and started toward the Crabtree's shiny black, 1948 Super Deluxe Ford convertible.

"Why isn't our little girl dressed like a fairy princess, or a ballerina, or maybe Dorothy, in the—"

"Wizard of Oz?" said Sarah, finishing Paddy's question for him.

"Yeah," said Paddy. "Something like that."

"You mean, something 'girly'?"

"Yeah. I suppose so."

"For the same reason, she doesn't play with dolls, Mister Smarty Man. Your daughter's a Tom Boy. Like I was, at her age."

"Is that normal?" said Paddy.

Sarah gave Paddy the Skunk-Eye. Paddy was joking, of course, and the grin on his face said as much.

They stood on the porch, smiled, and waved goodbye as Angel rather awkwardly got into the back seat with

Megan and Andrew. Elsie leaned toward the open, passenger-side window.

"I'll have the Birthday Girl home by eight."

"Okay, great," said Sarah. "Thanks, Elsie."

Sarah and Paddy waved until the Ford disappeared down the unimproved road that led to the lighthouse.

"You think Jonny will show?" said Sarah.

"He promised Angel he'd be here."

"It wouldn't surprise me, Paddy, if your partner in crime is in jail somewhere."

"Give a guy a break, Sarah. Jonny will be here."

9.

The Uninvited

Fog, the bane of mariners the world over, crept off the ocean toward land, just as it had since time immemorial. With this thick, gray mist came something else—something dark and ominous—a Bermuda Sloop—with a sleek, black lacquered hull, black sails, and the name, *Horror*, painted in gold calligraphic writing on the stern[34].

Guided by the sheer will of fathomless malice over two hundred years in the making, the sloop stole across the waves toward Skeleton Bay.

† † †

Why Paddy and Sarah put on Halloween costumes is anybody's guess since trick-or-treaters never came to their door. Instead, it came into being as an O'Hara family tradition. Sarah looked every bit an Irish milkmaid in her costume. At the same time, Paddy swaggered about dressed as Handsome Jonny Stint, an Eighteenth-Century Irish buccaneer, who became a one-man plague to beautiful women, and Spanish ships carrying gold from Mexico, and South America, to Spain.

Had Paddy and Sarah not been dancing to John Lee

---

[34] The "stern, or "ass-end,"" is sailor-speak for the rear of a ship, loosely compared to one's mother-in-law's buttocks.

Hooker and his band playing, "Boogie Chillun," and had the surf not been pounding the rocks onshore, the O'Haras would have heard an incredible whooshing sound made by a mighty pair of wings, as something huge hovered above their dwelling before descending onto the top of the lighthouse scarcely twenty yards away.

A Palmolive soap advertisement came and went when Boogie Chillun ended, followed by Gary Cooper plugging Chesterfield cigarettes. Paddy turned the volume down on their free-standing Westinghouse radio-phonograph and joined Sarah on the couch to catch his breath.

Sarah lay her head on Paddy's shoulder and sighed. "I love you, Paddy O'Hara."

"I love you to the moon, Missus O'Hara."

Sarah chuckled. "That's what you told me the night you proposed."

"I did?"

Whiskey went to the door and barked.

"What do you suppose is out there?" said Sarah.

Whiskey whimpered and took off, running up the stairs toward Angel's bedroom.

Before Paddy could reply, they heard a loud WHOOSH over their house, followed by the sound of several rafters cracking in the attic. Something weighty had landed on the roof. Shocked and startled to the soles of their feet, the O'Haras heard a shrill voice cry-out: *"Oof! Jaj! Au! Átkozott! Szar[35],"* combined with the sound of someone tumbling down the roof and landing on the porch with a loud THUD, made!

---

[35]Old Hungárián, for "Oof! Ouch! Ow! Damn! Shite!"

A moment later, there came a commanding knock at their door.

Paddy pressed a finger over Sarah's lips, then tiptoed to the mantel over the fireplace where he kept his genuine, Yogi Berra Louisville Slugger. With baseball bat in hand and Sarah close behind, Paddy strode to the front door and flung it open.

Illuminated by the porchlight and framed in the doorway with a full moon behind stood a woman in the raw, all five-feet-two-inches of her. She had translucent, alabaster white skin, hair dark as a raven's wing hanging to her waist, and violet eyes that glistened in the darkness. Physically striking by anyone's reckoning, she looked no older than twenty, tops, but how many times has it been said, "*Looks can be deceiving*"? One more thing: the woman smelled of rum and molasses and twenty-eight days at sea.

"Please," said the naked woman at the door. "I seem to have lost my way."

Her English was perfect but spoken with a foreign accent that neither Sarah nor Paddy could distinguish its place of origin.

"Paddy," said Sarah, "put down the bat; this girl needs help."

At first reluctant, Paddy lowered the bat to his side.

"Come in, miss," said Sarah.

"Hold on a second, Sarah." Paddy looked at the woman at their door. "Was that you on our roof?"

"I'm afraid it was," said the woman. "I have a hard time flying in fog."

Their eyebrows shot up; their mouths dropped open.

"WHAT?" said Paddy and Sarah in unison.

"She must be in shock," said Sarah.

"Or daft as the doorknob," said Paddy.

"Go, Paddy! Get her a blanket."

Paddy turned on his heel and dashed upstairs. That the young woman was naked and did not attempt to cover her unmentionables made Sarah more than a little uncomfortable.

"Do you live here alone with that pirate?" said the woman. Before Sarah could answer, the woman added: "He wants to rape me."

"Whoa, now!" were the only words that came out of Sarah's mouth.

"It's true," said the young woman. "I could see it in his eyes."

Going from shocked to livid, Sarah stepped forward and slapped the woman hard across the face.

"Get away from here, lady!" said Sarah (more like, hissed). "Get off our porch. New Dublin is just a mile from here. You can get help there."

Sarah looked back over her shoulder toward the stairs. "Paddy! Get down here with your slugger!"

Paddy came charging down the stairs; he tossed a blanket to the floor and raised the baseball bat overhead.

Whiskey remained in Angel's room, under the bed, cowering.

As Paddy approached, the woman looked down at the floor and, under her breath, said: "I loathe pirates."

"She's crazy, Paddy. Send her away."

"It doesn't matter," said the woman. "I'm going to drink your blood—yours and his."

Sarah's hands tightened into fists. "You're not going to do any such thing, you crazy bitch!"

Paddy jabbed the end of the bat into the woman's chest, holding her back.

"Get behind me, Sarah. And, you—Get away from our house. Now!"

The naked woman tilted her head back and let loose the kind of high-pitched laughter one expects to hear in some lonely place or from a basement deep below an asylum for the insane.

Paddy brought the bat down on the woman's head with enough force to stagger an elephant. Not so, with the woman. There was a loud crack as Paddy's Louisville Slugger broke in two.

Then, while Paddy and Sarah looked on in complete disbelief, the woman began to change.

Her translucent, alabaster white skin turned ebony in color and leather-like; her arms grew long and thin and from those ugly sticks sprouted paper-thin, leathery wings. Her head and face transformed into something conceived in the depths of Hell, with black eyes big as plates and long ears that stood up straight. She, or it, had a mouth smelling of rotting flesh and possessed fangs resembling scimitars with additional upper and lower, ivory-white teeth, pointed at the ends like the tips of daggers.

"Run, Sarah!"

Sarah could no more run than could the floorboards. Fear rooted her feet in place. Not so with ex-Marine Paddy O'Hara; he leaped toward the creature to grab its throat and choke it to death. That was not to be. With one of its wings, this upright, unholy thing batted Paddy across the room over the couch and into a wall; then, it sank its fangs into Sarah's throat.

† † †

Elsie Crabtree stopped the Super Deluxe, 1948 Ford in front of Angel's house. No house lights were shining. The only lights to present themselves flickered from the pumpkins on the porch. Angel got out of the car with her bag of treats over one shoulder.

"Goodbye, Megan. Goodbye, Andrew," said Angel.

"That was fun. Thanks, Missus Crabtree."

"It doesn't look like anyone's home," said Elsie Crabtree.

"That's because they're probably necking," said Angel. "They do that a lot."

"Well, then," said Elsie Crabtree. "Goodnight, Angel."

"Goodnight," said Angel. She watched the three Crabtrees depart, then turned on her heel and hobbled toward the house. She stopped when she reached the steps leading up to the porch. The house was as dark as dark could be. Angel thought it strange that Whiskey wasn't on the porch, curled up in a ball, waiting for her. Angel used the wooden railing to mount the stairs; then, she opened the front door and went inside.

Had the lights been on, Angel would have seen Paddy's baseball bat, broken in two; she would have also seen the framed pictures scattered on the floor where they landed when the creature batted Paddy against the wall. But there was only darkness.

Angel heard a slurping sound, the same as when someone sucks the last contents of a soda or milkshake through a straw.

"Mom? Dad?"

Angel felt for the light switch on the kitchen wall, found it, and turned it on.

The creature was astride Sarah, its fangs buried deep in Sarah's throat, drinking her blood, draining her life force with every gulp. The creature's head whipped around and saw Angel frozen in place, a few feet away. Unwilling to share its prey, the creature hissed.

"Run, baby!" said Sarah (more like, moaned). "Run!"

Those were the last words Angel would hear her mother speak. As Angel turned to escape, the creature struck at her with claws affixed to one of its long, spindly arms. Angel screamed as a searing pain raked her back.

Angel almost blacked out and fell, but as she stumbled forward, she regained her footing. Using the railing, she pulled herself up the darkened stairs without seeing her father lying in the shadows near the fireplace in a pool of blood.

Angel hobbled across the small landing at the top of the stairs and into her room and slammed the door shut. With adrenalin flooding her body, she pushed a Sears & Roebuck four-drawer maple dresser against the door in hopes it would keep out the creature.

Angel hid with Whiskey in the corner of her clothes closet while the pain in her upper back intensified and began to burn, the same as if she backed into a wall furnace.

In the kitchen, the creature licked Angel's blood off her claws, then smacked her lips together and hissed: "*Marzipan*! I LOVE Marzipan!"

The creature moved toward the stairs, dragging its wings, hopping from place to place. To see the beast up close, one might conclude it stood over six feet and weighed three hundred pounds. No surprise that its hideous visage would be abrasive on eyes unaccustomed to monstrous sights. The creature was ill-suited for traveling on land, which would explain why this disgusting, unappealing thing had wings. However, it is worth noting that beauty is a subjective matter, and some might look at the creature with astonishment, yet not look away in dread—not until it moves toward them, of course, with drooling mouth agape and fangs bared for feeding.

The loud thudding sounds Angel heard downstairs was the creature moving about with considerable difficulty. Now, some might wonder why the monster didn't fly to the top of the stairs. Well, with a fully extended wingspan of eighteen feet, this wonderment from Hell was too big to fly anywhere, other than in the vast expanse of the sky. What to do? She changed back into human form, more or less.

To keep from crying out, Angel forced the knuckles of one hand into her mouth. With her other hand, she held Whiskey's eyes shut. There, in the darkness, feeling only the pain in her back and Whiskey's hot breath, Angel waited for what her mind couldn't fathom nor dare imagine. Hearing the dresser shoved aside and the door pushed open was beyond bearable. Angel buried her eyes against her knees and began to sob, but no sound escaped her throat; the great Boa Constrictor, fear, shut that once silky passageway. The closet floor vibrated with each step someone or something took until it stopped just outside the closet.

"Come out, come out, little mouse," said the creature. The thing spoke English in a crackling, high-pitched voice with a strange, foreign accent. "Your blood tastes like Marzipan. And I dearly love Marzipan."

In the split-second that followed, Angel heard a mind-numbing blast from a Remington 12-gauge, pump-shotgun, followed simultaneously by an ear-piercing shriek.

Shot from behind by a man she never saw coming, the creature broke through a window and part of the wall and escaped into the night.

The closet door opened. The distinct sound of size-eleven Wellington Engineer boots striding over the wooden floor came as thunderclaps to Angel's ears. The terror choking Angel vanished; she cried out, "Jonny!"

"Yeah, Angel darlin', it's me."

Whiskey scrambled out of the closet, stood on his two back legs, and barked.

"Quiet, Whiskey," said Jonny Fiáin. "It's okay now, boy."

Jonny leaned his shotgun against the wall. He reached down with both hands and lifted Angel into his arms. Jonny wore leathers, the kind serious motorcycle enthusiasts wear. Over those, he wore an ankle-length leather duster, what Nineteenth-century Highwaymen and today's cowboys prefer for protection from the elements.

"Your safe, Angel darlin'."

Feeling Jonny's arms around her, and with tears streaming down her cheeks, Angel sobbed: "Mom! Dad!"

"I know," said Jonny. "I saw them. Whatever that thing is, it might come back. But listen, Angel, we can't stay here. We've got to leave. Understand?"

"Whiskey, too?"

Jonny looked down at Angel's mutt. His gift to Angel for her sixth birthday. "Yeah. Whiskey, too. I'm taking you out of here, and I want you to keep your eyes closed until we're outside. Deal?"

Angel nodded.

Wrapped in his duster, Jonny carried Angel outside, over to a Harley Davidson motorcycle manufactured for the military during WW II that had a sidecar attached.

"Angel, darlin', you'll be sitting for quite a spell, so I'm going to remove the cast on your leg. Okay?"

Angel was shutting down, going into shock; soon, unconsciousness would come. Once Jonny had her in the sidecar, he put Whiskey on her lap, covered, and hurried toward the house, cursing everything under the North Star as he went.

10.

Love Hurts

Back aboard the schooner that brought this winged abomination to Skeleton Bay, the creature transformed into what it was when the O'Haras first set eyes on it—a dark-haired, violet-eyed beauty-queen all of five-feet-two-inches tall who looked no more than twenty-years-old.

In truth, the pudgy, six-foot, hairy-legged abomination that savaged Angel O'Hara and murdered her parents was over two-hundred-years-old, Hungarian born, and a former *"Miss Budapest"* [1936].

Really—you can't make this stuff up! Or, to quote Prince Hamlet[36] of Denmark, *"There are more things in Heaven and earth, Horatio, than dreamt of in your philosophy."*

To be sure, this sometimes-human-sometimes-not was one more such thing. Weirdwolves are another, so, too, leprechauns, banshees, fairies, sprites, nymphs, nay-sayers, do-gooders, and trolls.

---

[36] Prince Hamlet was a brooding, moody young man in Denmark (circa 1600 A.D. afflicted by the ghost of his murdered father; he also suffered from attendant, inappropriate feelings for his mom. Hamlet's story is beautifully captured by the Bard of Avon, aka, wily Willy Shakespeare [British Museum Visitors' Guide].

† † †

Had one been standing on the schooner's Quarter Deck, one would have heard the creature scream alternating obscenities in English and Magyar from her spacious quarters below. At the same time, her seven-foot-tall, Nubian bodyguard, confidante, and paramour, Balthazar Headstone, dug buckshot out of her otherwise perfect, heart-shaped derriere.

The creature stretched out on a mahogany table, face down, naked, and gritted her teeth.

"Ouch! Damn you, Balthazar! That hurt!"

"Sorry, my love."

Plink!

"Mother of whores, that hurts!" she said.

"I see only a few more to take out. Why did you not wait for me to return before venturing out, my turtle dove?"

Plink!

"Ow! You weren't here, the moon was full, and I got hungry. Besides, I wanted to stretch my wings. But I got lost in the fog."

"Oh, my love," said Balthazar. My love, My love, My love."

"Do you believe it?" she said. "I had that little mouse within my grasp when that shithead snuck up and shot me!"

"Most cowardly of him," said Balthazar.

"Two-hundred-and-twenty years I've been around men. "I thought I'd seen them all, in waterfront bars, with their tattoos and scars, but never a one such as this one. I've had lords, lepers, drippers, droolers, Christians, heretics, winners, and losers. Soldiers, sailors, saints, and sinners. I've had rich, poor, a King in Andorra, and a Duke in Austria!

"Don't forget the queen in Australia," said Headstone.

"You're right, my love; I forgot about him. Rich, poor, it mattered not; they all wanted more, once a taste they got! Tell me, Balthazar."

"What, my sweet?"

"Really! What kind of *fasz*[37] shoots a lady in her buttocks?"

"Only the worst kind of *fasz*, your Munificence." Headstone dropped another pellet—*plink!*—into the washbasin: "An, American!"

"Ouch!"

The creature craned her head around; she gave Headstone the skunk-eye.

"Dammit, Balthazar! That REALLY, really hurt!"

Headstone paused to drink from a human skull that was bleached white and had but a single, gold-capped tooth in the upper-front row.

She lifted her head a second time. "I smell rum!"

"I'm using it for antiseptic, Exalted One. I'll finish before you can say—" Headstone took a moment to think of something challenging—something polysyllabic: "*Fontainebleau*," he said.

She craned her head around and hissed. "*Fontainebleau, Idiota!*"

"Forgive me, my beloved. I only—"

"I know, my love. You meant to distract me from the unpleasantness of having you carve tiny pieces of lead from my heretofore unmarred flesh."

"Yes, my pet," said Headstone. "Only that."

---

[37] Magyar, derogatory, meaning "dick"!

"Listen, Balthazar; there's something I want you to do."

"Command me, Dominatrix."

"Dominatrix?"

"Last night, you said you wanted to role-play: you, dominant, me, submissive?"

"Ah! You're right, Balthazar! Very well, slave! Are there *Gray Brethren* in Maine?"

"Do Popes wear funny hats? Yes, O Queen of things that go 'bump' in the night. There are *Gray Brethren* everywhere."

"Then have them find her, Balthazar! I want to know where she is—this *kisegér*[38] that tastes like Marzipan."

"What, then, your Nastiness?"

"They are not to touch her."

"Mistress—?"

"We wait, my love. I don't want her harmed. Have the Brethren watch over her. I have plans for this one— this little mouse whose blood tastes like Marzipan. But she's too young now. She needs to ripen."

"And the upstart American? The *fasz*, who shot you?"

"Bring me his heart, Balthazar. After we've feasted on it, we'll wet our throats with a nice Chianti."

Balthazar laughed. "Well, before we do that, my love, I have a gift for you in celebration of two-hundred incredible years together."

The creature turned onto one side and propped herself up on her elbow. "I love your presents, Balthazar."

Headstone reached behind and took hold of a book wrapped in sheepskin and handed it to his beloved.

Eyes wide in anticipation, the creature undid the binding and removed the sheepskin. When the beast

---

[38]Magyar, meaning "little mouse."

beheld the worn, cordovan leather book in her hands, she squealed with delight.

"It's a scarce edition, my love," said Balthazar, "the 1558 Collection, in both his native French and Latin."

The creature sucked in a breath, then whispered the title: *Les prophéties Perdue de Nostradamus*[39].

"Oh, Balthazar," she said, "you shouldn't have."

"I know," he said.

She frowned. Balthazar lifted her off the table and held her.

"Before I give you *your* gift, my love," she said, "I want you to do something."

† † †

Once ashore, Headstone left the dory concealed behind rocks. The moon shone brightly, wholly indifferent to the goings-on on earth. Headstone transformed into his other self and clawed his way in leaps and bounds up the granite face of Bette's Chin.

Having reached the top, Headstone made for the tree line. From there, he saw the lighthouse keeper's dwelling erupt with flames that lit the night sky with fire the color of pumpkins.

Headstone watched a tall manling, no doubt the *fasz* who shot his beloved, standing alongside the *kisegér* seated in a sidecar attached to a motorcycle.

Headstone owned such a vehicle once when he and Szah Zhah were touring North Africa in 1914.

---

[39] *The Lost Prophecies of Nostradamos* (circa 1550), Nostradamos being a French astrologer and physician; and is the Latinized name of Michel de Nostredame. His cryptic, apocalyptic predictions appear in two earlier collections—In 1555 and 1558.

Fleetfooted and fast as the wind, Balthazar followed until he could no longer keep up. No matter. The lingering fragrance of the girl's blood overpowered his nostrils and hung in the still night air. It clung like a spent lover to the silent body of the night. The girl's scent would not be hard for The Brethren to follow.

Headstone's other self lifted his or its head back and howled—long and hard. That done, he loped off to a patch of forest and waited for others like himself to appear.

11.

Sunday

The illegitimate child of the Governor-General of the British colony of Jamaica, at sixteen years of age, Balthazar Headstone stood six-feet-six- inches in height, was lean, muscular, and a natural baritone. His mother, *Jamaica*, named after the island where she was born into slavery, died birthing him.

Speaking of which, when the midwife appeared at the back door of the Governor's Mansion to present the baby, she was beaten severely and died soon after. The Baby? The baby was taken in a wicker basket to an orphanage and left with a small leather purse at the gate. There was a note inside the bag along with a gold *Doubloon*. The letter read: *"See that the child never leaves your care."*

Okay. Simple enough.

A bastard in the eyes of British "Common Law," Headstone was deprived of the surname he would otherwise be given as his birthright, specifically, *"Trelawny."* Instead, the name he acquired at the orphanage was *"Sunday,"* that being the day he showed up in the basket.

When he was old enough to understand his predicament, specifically, being an orphan and a bastard, Sunday chose a name for himself but kept it a secret from his keepers and the other orphans.

That name? Balthazar Headstone.

But why that? Why, Balthazar Headstone?

Simple! Of the *Three Wise Men*, or *Magi*, as spoken of in the Bible (King James version), "Balthazar" was Sunday's favorite—first, because Balthazar was THE King of Arabia, and second, because the young king's present to Baby Jesus was the gift of Myrrh. True, Headstone had no idea where Arabia lay on the map or what, exactly, Myrrh is, but both sounded important.

"Headstone," he chose for his surname because of the peace of mind his favorite hiding place afforded—that place being the graveyard where white people interred white people, along with their pets.

By the age of nine, Sunday spoke English with an upper-class British accent honed crisp by the cane of the Episcopalian minister, Uriah Heape, who schooled the children six days a week. Heape was also the Choir Master at the orphanage. "Idle hands," and all that rot.

The beatings lasted until the day Sunday's tormentor was found dead in a banana grove behind the Governor's mansion. Something horrific tore the minister's throat out, pulled his innards into the open, and feasted on them.

The next day, the Governor ordered his soldiers to comb the island, searching for the wild animal that perpetrated the horrific act. The soldiers searched the island relentlessly, or so they thought, but they found no such animal. It had seemingly disappeared to the four winds.

Hold on!

It isn't who you think who did the deed on the Episcopalian Minister. As to who did, we must first look to the island of Hispaniola,[40] which begs the question: "Why look there?"

That's not an easy question to answer, what with the Caribbean being a part of the world without rhyme or reason, and where all manner of strangeness abounds, always has, and always will.

† † †

Sixteen-year-old Sunday knew every inch of the grounds that composed the orphanage, inside and out, and prided himself for being able to slip away unnoticed by his keepers. His unsanctioned departures usually took place at sunset, when the nighttime Floor Matron ordered the children to say their prayers and go to bed.

The rest was simple. Sunday would carefully pull aside the mosquito netting from the window over his bed, and out he'd go.

Because of his immense size and the fact he shunned their company and talked to himself in Latin, the other children were deathly afraid of Sunday; no one dreamed of turning him in for his nocturnal ramblings.

What Sunday enjoyed most on those warm, sultry nights was to forage through the trash bins behind the Governor's Mansion where, after fighting off the rats, he found many a marvelous thing still fit for eating. He would take these tasty bits and pieces to the cemetery— the one where whites buried their own, along with their pets.

There he'd sit, filling his stomach and existential cravings with upper-class garbage and loving every bite.

---

[40] *Hispaniola* comprises present-day Haiti and the Dominican Republic.

† † †

It was on one of those full moon nights in April—the "cruel month" when, at the age of sixteen, Sunday's life changed forever, irrevocably sealing his fate.

After amusing himself catching wild animals Jamaica is renowned for, animals like the Jamaican Iguana, Five-Fingered Mongoose, and the Freshwater Crocodile, Sunday sat eating morsels gleaned from the Governor's trash; this, while a fresh trade wind caressed his man-child's body.

Sunday enjoyed looking at the moon and had, for as long as he could remember. Its silver sheen tantalized him. Despite his present circumstance and skin color, Sunday sensed that he could delight in the moonlight with every other creature on earth, no matter his station in life or lack of prospects. This tiny piece of secret knowledge pleased him much.

Sunday was experiencing a grown-up thought regarding procreation when "It" sunk its fangs into his right buttock. The force of the bite propelled Sunday from his perch atop a marble sarcophagus. He landed on the ground and whirled around to confront the thing that affronted him with such a cruel, if not cowardly, attack.

"Bloody hell!" said Sunday. "That hurt!"

Illuminated by moonlight, the thing that bit Sunday was sitting on its haunches, rather like an impossibly big, shaggy dog story. Its eyes glowed red, and several drops of blood, Sunday's blood, dripped from long, pearl-white fangs protruding from its mouth.

Sunday snatched a broken tree limb from the ground and wielded it overhead. "Try that again, and I'll bash your brains into mush," said Sunday.

"Fear not," said the thing sitting on an abandoned coffin. "I need not bite you a second time, and you need not bash my brains into grits."

"Mush," said Sunday. "I said, mush."

"Very well," said the thing—"mush!"

The creature spoke English with a distinct growl that carried with it a decidedly French accent.

"What are you?" said Sunday.

"A *Tonton Macoute*," said the creature. "In your father's language, it means Weirdwolf."

"Okay, I've never heard of such a creature!" said Sunday. "But how have I wronged you that you would bite me?"

"You haven't wronged me, Sunday," said the Weirdwolf.

"Okay. Then why bite me?"

"I had to get your attention. I have been searching the *Islands in the Stream* for a long time, hoping to find you. The Gray Brethren could use a hunter such as yourself."

"Who? I don't understand," said Sunday.

"You will," said the Weirdwolf. "Twenty-eight days from this night. But you must go to the isle of Martinique. There, *The Brethren* will answer all your questions. Exult, Sunday! Great things lay ahead."

The Weirdwolf turned its gaze upward for a brief moment as though trying to recall something important, something Headstone should know.

"Oh! One more thing you should know," said the Weirdwolf. "That horrible little Englishman with the bulbous eyes and wart on his nose that beat you severely and took inappropriate liberties with your nubile young body."

"What about him?" said Sunday.

"He is food for the worms. I have seen to that."

That said, the Weirdwolf howled poignantly at the moon and fell off the sarcophagus. It lay dead at Sunday's feet. Just as remarkable as the Weirdwolf and the puncture marks oozing blood from Headstone's right buttock was to see the creature suddenly changing into a shriveled human being, in this case, an old woman of inestimable years lacking both hair and teeth. Talk about "*...more strange things in Heaven and earth, Horatio....*"   Holy Moley! As luck would have it, Sunday's maternal aunt,   a Jamaican Voodoo priestess known to islanders as "Miss Lily," found him dazed and wandering in the jungle.   It occurred not by happenstance; she had been searching for Sunday ever since field hands discovered the Episcopalian minister's mangled remains.

A point of fact: Miss Lily was also a seer who had foreseen the minister's demise before it happened. That *ganja*[41] may have played a significant role in facilitating Miss Lily's visions is debated in Jamaica to this very day.

---

[41] *Ganja,* aka *reefer, Mary Jane, pot, weed, skunk stuff, philosophers' bane, poor man's crutch,* and *marijuana* is considered by some; i.e. politicians, neurotics, schizophrenics, surfers, musicians, seers, soothsayers, petty criminals and heretics to be a medicinal herb first discovered by aboriginals simultaneously, in all but two continents, and effective in increasing one's appetite for sweets. It is known for dismissing inhibitions, and unleashing the libido in the human female. It has also been found to produce madness in monkeys, and impotence in the human male [Almanac of Unapologetic Facts, Misty Bay Books, 1st Edition, 2021].

12.

Handsome Jonny Stint

It was a sea captain, known from the Atlantic coast to the Gulf of Mexico as Handsome Jonny [Stint], whom Sunday's Auntie wrote. She did this by way of a message attached to the leg of a white, winged dove. It is anyone's guess why Miss Lily chose a white-winged dove and not a badass black raven or a gray, humpbacked Carrier pigeon.

A recovering lawyer and poet of little note, Stint left Ireland and was notorious for his lifelong search for the perfect *Peña Colada;* that, and a woman who would love him for himself and for that, alone. Some attributed his condition to being dropped by his nanny on his head as a baby in Coco Solito, Panama. Go ahead, and laugh! Handsome Jonny was a fool's fool.

Consider this: when asked about her dalliance with Captain Stint while vacationing in Charleston, North Carolina, Lady Caroline Lamb, the Duchess of Quimby, remarked: "*Captain Stint is a mad, bad, dangerous man to know*." How's that for proof?

What is also true, Captain Stint was a buccaneer of dubious merit, but he was known to possess a soft side beneath his 'bad boy exterior. It is probably worth noting: Headstone's aunt, Miss Lily, was a great beauty with lusty appetites.

As far as the rumors went, Lily was an unapologetic voluptuary. She possessed a soft spot in her heart for salty dogs and *151-Rum*. It was a rumor that found comfortable lodging in Captain Stint's middle-ear. Now he had the opportunity to meet her in the flesh, more or less.

As with most secrets, someone spilled the beans to Governor Trelawny that a notorious Irish pirate was about to leave Jamaica with a substantial cargo of bootlegged Jamaican rum. Nothing could have been further from the truth; however, Governor Trelawny wouldn't know "truth" if it came up and buggered[42] him.

Since governors in the Eighteenth Century tended to be insecure, effete pansies who wore custom-fitted silk panties from the salon of the Parisian designer, Rene Petard, the thought of being denied "his rightful cut" was something Trelawny wouldn't countenance. Hence, Trelawny's order went out: *"Bring me the head of that Irish rogue—that, Handsome, Jonny Stint!"*

Stint sailed at night, right under the eyes of the Governor's Home Guard, which included a Fourth Rate, double-decked ship of the line, the HMS *Reproach*, armed with 50 cannons, from twelve pounders to six-pounders, and a dozen swivel guns on the Main Deck to repel boarders should they get so close as to be alongside.

However formidable his Majesty's ship was at scaring pirates away from Jamaica's coast, in 1750, she was no match for *La Bruja Del Mar*, not when it came to speed and maneuverability.

---

[42] Buggered, past tense of bugger (verb), A male pastime associated with upper-class Brits [Almanac of Unapologetic Facts, Misty Bay Books, Volume 1. 1st Edition, 1949].

Here's why: Built from lightweight cedarwood, *La Bruja Del Mar* had but two masts and sported a relatively new, much-improved design, specifically, triangular-shaped sails. Such distinctive sails set *La Bruja Del Mar* markedly apart from the larger merchant vessels and warships built of oak with three masts and multiple square sails. What's more, this small but audacious sloop had a shallow draft and could sail close to land, where ships of the line dare not go for fear of running aground on a reef.

The upstart crow that was Stint's Jamaica sloop could sail circles around the larger, heavier HMS *Reproach*.

So superior were Bermuda sloops to other Caribbean vessels, one Edward Teach, aka Blackbeard, commanded a Bermuda sloop.[43]

In 1718, Teach scuttled the *Queen Anne's Revenge* off the coast of South Carolina and drowned most of his crew along with the ship because of the treasure aboard her. There is no honor among thieves. Never has been, never will be. Teach, a blackguard if ever there was one, and the Eighteenth-Century equivalent of a psychopathic "serial killer," was eventually captured and hung by the British before he could resurrect his ill-gotten gains from Davy Jones' Locker. That's the way it goes if you're a murderous, scurvy dog. Ill-gotten benefits today, gain you the Hangman's noose tomorrow.

Arrrgh!

---

[43] Known as the *Queen Anne's Revenge*, Edward Teach prowled the Atlantic Ocean in search of ports to plunder and the easy pickings that lightly armed Spanish merchant vessels provided.

† † †

La Bruja Del Mar (aka the *Sea Witch*) sailed south and was clear of Jamaican waters when out of the indigo blue night, he heard Miss Lily's husky voice beckon him, not unlike a Venus Flytrap: "Kiss me, Stint."

Stint took a rope made from pure Virginia hemp grown on George Washington's wife's plantation and secured the wheel in place to maintain the desired course. He did that in what must have been "record time."

With a full, manly sweep of his arm, Handsome Jonny brought Miss Lily close, close enough for their breath to mingle, creating a sweet mixture of pineapple and rum.

It's true. Handsome Jonny Stint was a pirate, but that doesn't mean he didn't know how to treat a lady while at sea or chart a successful course when confronted with a whalebone corset. The key to a happy voyage? 151 Rum! Stint and Miss Lily celebrated outrunning the Reproach with a fresh-made batch of Peña Coladas.

As they embraced, Stint savored the scent of her. It emanated from behind her ears and the crook of her neck. He breathed her earthiness deep into the scarred airbags that once were lungs. As he breathed, the fragile hair on the nape of his neck vibrated like tall grass on the *Serengeti Plain*[44], the way it does when the Scirocco winds blow south, southwest, off the Sahara Desert, usually in spring, and again in the autumn.

Lily's ebony breasts, with aureoles and nipples the color of a Burgundy wine made from 100% *Pinot Noir*

---

[44] A vast grassy plain in Africa where herbivores fretfully graze while lions talk earnestly among themselves [Almanac of Unapologetic Facts. Misty Bay Books. 1st Edition. 2021].

grapes, grown and bottled in France's eastern region, ran aground against Stint's perfectly chiseled chest. At that moment, Stint felt the heat of her essence scorch his plenty manly torso with the mad dog of desire.

Stint felt the kind of passion that compels genuine madmen to put aside their petty-bourgeois pursuits and leave the comfort of what they have, to seek new worlds to conquer.

Lily was beautiful and hungry for a man like Stint. No differently, Stint was hungry for a woman like Lily—meaning, a woman who needed no map to navigate the contradictory trichotomy of a man's mind-body-soul conglomerate—Stint's, in particular.

Stint kissed her hungrily. She saw that coming and raised the *ante*. Their all-too-eager lips divided like the Red Sea before Moses's staff; their tongues intertwined, like *electrophorus electricus*—South American electric eels, in a pre-coital dance for a superior position.

Life was good in 1750, more or less.

† † †

Earlier that same day, while Lily was in the cargo hold changing the bandage on her nephew's buttock, Sunday announced: "I've changed my name, Auntie. From now on, I'm Sunday, no more."

"No More?" said Lily. She lowered her chin and gave him the skunk eye. "That's the name you chose for yourself—Sunday No-More?"

"No, Auntie," said Balthazar. "No more will I call myself SUNDAY!"

"I see," said Lily. "So then, Nephew, who are you?"

"I am, Balthazar," he said. "Balthazar Headstone."

And that, as they say, was that.

Sunday-now-Balthazar Headstone was heavily sedated, stashed in a large crate, and kept in the cargo hold. It was as much for Headstone's protection as it was for Stint and crew. It's true. Over the weeks following Headstone's encounter with the *Tonton Macoute*, the meeting which produced a deep bite in his right buttock, Headstone's behavior had become erratic— in a word, squirrelly.

To her great horror, Aunt Lily had seen the fang marks in her nephew's cushion up close and personal and surmised or deduced what was coming. Okay, let's just say Lily made an educated guess. After all, one cannot be a Voodoo priestess without knowing a thing or two about the Dark Side and the things that dwell therein.

Enough said!

13.

Hang Tough

Jonny pulled to the side of the road. Reaching for the canteen attached to the sidecar, he couldn't shake the feeling— something was following them.

Jonny wasn't sure where he and Angel were, except that they were still stateside and had a way's to go to reach the border. He looked at Angel. She appeared unconscious.

"Hang tough, Angel darlin'."

Jonny thought he heard Angel moan ever so softly, after which, Whiskey let out a whimper. Jonny patted Whiskey on the head. "It's okay, Whiskey. Angel's going to be fine. You'll see."

Jonny put the bike into gear and drove back onto the road. He knew better than to stop too long in the open.

† † †

"We don't have enough bodies," said Lieutenant Tully, "to adequately defend our perimeter, so once more, Marines, we're going to make do with what we've got."

With a smidgen of a Wyoming horseman's twang, the lieutenant told Able Company men what they were facing but already painfully aware.

† † †

During the last two nights' battle on Guadalcanal[45] for Henderson Field, their unit had suffered significant losses—dead and wounded both and desperately needed reinforcements to bolster their position. The Seven-hundred troops composing 1st Battalion, 7th Marines commanded by Lieutenant Colonel Chesty Puller were designated to protect the Henderson Airfield perimeter. On the map, it was a two-thousand-five-hundred-yard line through the jungle. That meant one Marine had roughly ten feet of the most dangerous real estate in the Pacific to defend against the thousands of jungle-wise Japanese soldiers, hardened veterans of Japan's conquest of China and the South Pacific, coming to kill them. The Japanese had returned to Guadalcanal to retake the island's only airfield. To both sides in the conflict, Guadacanal was vital in controlling the active supply routes, the sea lanes from the Solomons to Australia.

The Japanese finished building the airfield three months before the Americans invaded; it was the Pacific's first major American offensive operation.

The Marine 1st Division landed on the island on August 7th, 1942, and took the Japanese by surprise. The Marines captured the island the next day, August 8th.

The Japanese High Command in Tokyo, Japan, wanted the island back. In their efforts to recapture it in late August through February 1943, the Imperial Forces of Japan would suffer twenty-four thousand dead or missing.

---

[45]The Guadalcanal campaign, also known as the Battle of Guadalcanal, code named Operation Watchtower, was a military campaign fought between 7 August 1942 and 9 February 1943 on and around the island of Guadalcanal in the Pacific theater of World War II. It was the first major land offensive by Allied forces against the Empire of Japan and the United States' first land victory in the Pacific.

Privates First Class, Paddy O'Hara, and Jonny Fiáin looked at each other. Knowing what the young lieutenant was about to tell their platoon was something they heard before from a Gunnery Sergeant at Boot Camp, stateside.

"Hang tough, men!" said Lieutenant Tully. "There isn't anybody coming to save our asses. We ARE the cavalry! So, listen to your N-C-Os and hang tough! You hear me!? Hang tough, Marines!"

† † †

Jonny turned onto an unimproved back-road used by bootleggers during Prohibition[46]. It would take him and Angel across the border unchallenged.

Jonny had used the former logging road with his crew when they were smuggling contraband or, after a caper, when they needed to absent themselves from sight, opting to hide in Canada until 'the heat' subsided.

Navigating the road's numerous twists and turns, Jonny looked at Angel. She was slumped forward in the sidecar over Whiskey. It was one of the few times he would ever shout at her:

"Hang tough, Angel darlin'! Hang tough!"

† † †

"Why don't they come?" said Paddy. There was no mistaking the fear in his voice. They were immersed in darkness with a half-moon overhead to see maybe ten feet in front of them. "What are they waiting for?"

Jonny chuckled. "Maybe the little bastards got lost."

"You think?' said Paddy.

"Relax. The Japs are coming. So, stop worrying about

---

[46] Prohibition lasted from 1920 to 1933, when the 18th Amendment to the US Constitution prohibited the manufacture, sale, transport, import, or export of alcoholic beverages.

it."

"It's the waiting, I hate, Jonny. Swear to God, when the bullets are flying, I'm okay. "It's the waiting that screws with my head."

"Paddy. You have the two best things in the world to think about—right? Sarah and Angel. Am I right?"

Paddy's swollen eyes narrowed as he looked at Jonny. "You're right, Jonny. Oh, man. What's happening to me?"

"Nothing that isn't happening to every one of us. You're in good company, brother. We good on ammo?"

Paddy looked at what they had available for the .30 caliber machinegun mounted on a tripod behind a log redoubt, which allowed them to kneel or crouch and fire over it.

"Yeah, I think so. One full belt in place, plus the two boxes Sergeant Basilone dropped off.

"He's one, tough son-of-a-bitch," said Jonny as Basilone hurried away more ammo to hand out.

"Who? Basilone[47]?"

"Yeah. I thought Sergeant Basilone would damn well kill us when we were in Boot Camp."

"Hey, Jonny—you got any more gum?"

Jonny tore apart the piece in his mouth and handed half to Paddy.

"Thanks."

"Don't mention it."

"I'm scared, Jonny," said Paddy (more like whispered).

"You and me both, brother," said Jonny, likewise

---

[47]John Basilone (November 4, 1916 – February 19, 1945) was a United States Marine Corps Gunnery Sergeant who received the Medal of Honor for heroism above and beyond the call of duty during the Battle for Henderson Field in the Guadalcanal Campaign, and the Navy Cross posthumously for extraordinary heroism during the Battle of Iwo Jima. [Wikipedia]

whispering.

"If I don't make it," said Paddy, "I want you to take care of Sarah and Angel for me."

"What?"

Promise me, Jonny. You'll take care of them for me."

"Stop talking like that, Paddy. You're going to make it home. We both are. I'm telling you, I just know it. You'll see."

It was then that Jonny recalled the last words Sarah had whispered to him before he and Paddy boarded a train for boot camp. *"Promise me, Jonny. Promise me you'll take care of Paddy."*

Paddy placed his right hand on Jonny's shoulder. "You got to promise me, Jonny. Blood brothers, forever, right?"

Jonny looked at Paddy for what must have been a minute. "Yeah. All right. I promise. Now, can it, for Christ's sake!"

Paddy let out a long sigh as he turned his gaze toward the unseen enemy that would come. Jonny saw it in Paddy's face, not fear, not exactly, but an intensified feeling of dread and despair; it centered on whether Paddy would live to see his young wife and little girl again. It was at that moment an idea began to merge at the back of Jonny's mind. The Germans have a word for it—*hintergedanken*[48].

The air was still—deathly still. No breeze passed over the redoubt. Then, it happened. The muffled sound of a flare gun firing from close by sent a streak of flame upward, then exploding, lighting up the night sky with a canopy of brilliant yellowish glow. Simultaneously, the shrill bugle sounds and hundreds of Japanese soldiers, all screaming, *"Banzai!"*[49]

---

[48] *Hintergedanken*. German, meaning, "At the back of the mind, or ulterior motives."
[49] *Banzai Charge* refers to human wave attacks mounted by infantry units. This term came from the Japanese cry "*Tennōheika Banzai*", shortened to *banzai* [Wikipedia].

The sight of more flares in the sky announced the arrival of the first wave of Japanese soldiers intent on overrunning the American Marines and retaking the island.

"I think I'm going to piss myself, Jonny," said Paddy (more like whispered).

"You and me both, brother," said Jonny.

"You wanted to know where they are, Paddy—they're here, buddy boy!"

Jonny Fiáin was correct; the first elements of General Maruyama's 2nd Division were coming straight toward them. What must have been a hundred more flares, accompanied by bugles and the advancing Japanese's war cries, shattered what little calm the Marines had felt only moments before if any at all.

"Give it to them, Jonny!"

While Paddy fed the gun ammo, Jonny dealt death from the barrel of their .30 caliber machinegun to the indistinct shapes coming toward them.

Wave upon wave of Japanese infantry charged the outnumbered Marines, their officers waving Samurai swords while exhorting their men forward, heedless of the bullets, many of them tracers[50] streaking through the air, blanketing the terrain like thousands of maddened hornets, but far, far deadlier.

When the last of the ammunition for the .30-caliber ran out, Jonny grabbed a 12-gauge pump shotgun, waited for the Japanese to get closer, then began firing. Paddy armed himself with his M1-Garand[51] and did the same.

Suddenly, it was over, save for the cries "Medic! Medic!" and the groaning and moaning of the wounded

---

[50] Tracer bullets help illuminate their trajectory and their targets at night. Typically, for every one tracer bullet fired, four regular bullets followed.

[51] The M1 Garand is a .30-06 caliber semi-automatic rifle that was the standard U.S. service rifle during World War II and the Korean War and also saw limited service during the Vietnam War [Wikipedia].

and the dying.

† † †

Dawn, the following morning, revealed a killing field where over fifteen hundred Japanese soldiers lay dead in heaps, bloated by the heat, the stench the dead gave off would cling to every Marine and soldier fighting in the Pacific for the remainder of their lives.

Ordered out of their foxholes to "sanitize" the area, the Marines went among the Japanese dead and wounded, killing the wounded and the dead a second time, just for good measure.

It was then that Jonny Fiáin saw the opportunity he needed. Dropping down on one knee, he picked up a dead Japanese soldier's rifle. "You don't mind if I borrow this, do you? I didn't think so. "

Jonny aimed, breathed out, and fired.

† † †

The bullet that struck Paddy O'Hara in the back, partially shattering the left side of his pelvis before exiting his left-side upper thigh, came from an unseen sniper assumed to be Japanese.

Jonny called for a medic as he kneeled beside Paddy and applied a field dressing over the wounds, front and back.

"Dammit, it hurts, Jonny."

"Of course it does, you dumb lucky bastard. You caught a bullet in the ass."

Talking through the pain, Paddy said: "I don't feel lucky, Jonny. Have I still got my—"

Jonny cut him off. "Yeah, the family jewels are still there, Paddy."

"I guess that monkey was just a bad shot. Huh, Jonny?"

"I guess so; it sure looks that way."

A medic arrived and took over.

"The war's over for you, Marine," said the medic. "You got yourself a million-dollar wound. You're going home."

Paddy gritted his teeth and tried to smile. "You hear that, Jonny? I'm going home."

"I told you, you were one, lucky bastard."

"Yeah, Jonny. Yeah, you did."

For every dark cloud, there's a silver lining, more or less.

† † †

Once they were across the border, Jonny stopped at a filling station for gasoline. With a full tank, he proceeded to a truck stop. He changed Angel's bandage; the old one was soaked clear through with Angel's blood.

"Hang tough, little darlin'. Hang tough!"

14.

Ashes to Ashes

Summoned by fishermen who saw the flames when returning to port in New Dublin, when the local volunteer Fire Department arrived, there was little they could do, apart from watching the O'Hara's dwelling-place on Bette's Chin incinerate.

By first daylight, only smoking embers remained along with the scorched stone foundation. Les Gardner, a volunteer fireman and co-owner of the apothecary shop in New Dublin, discovered the charred corpses of what, most likely, had been Paddy and Sarah O'Hara.

When Paddy O'Hara's mom and dad arrived, New Dublin's Chief of Police, A.J. McKuen, was on hand, along with the Coast Guard's representative, Lieutenant Ernie Watson.

A widower, and twenty years Chief of Police, McKuen had a stellar reputation as a no-nonsense, straight shooter who truly cared about the people under his protection. To Chief McKuen's great relief, the County Coroner, Ignatius P. O'Riley, had left the scene only moments before, taking Sarah and Paddy's remains with him.

McKuen went straight to Seamus and Alyssa. Everything they desperately needed to know stood out in **Bold Type** in the Chief's face.

"Angel?" said Alyssa O'Hara, choking on what she dreaded while wiping tears on the sleeve of her sweater.

"Yes, Chief," said Seamus. "What about our granddaughter?"

"I can't say, folks. We're still looking, but we've found no trace of Angel."

Looking like the Chief's words siphoned the life out of them, Seamus O'Hara found himself holding his wife as her knees started to buckle. Alyssa cried out, and would have collapsed, had a priest, Father Timothy O'Leary, not assisted Seamus by helping Alyssa remain on her feet.

Together, Seamus and the priest half-led, half-carried Alyssa back to the O'Hara's car, where they sat holding each other and sobbing for twenty minutes after Father Timothy departed.

That was what Sarah's parents, Michael, and Rose McLaughlin, saw when they arrived on the scene. The color drained from their faces as they proceeded past the O'Hara's car to Chief McKuen, where he stood with Lieutenant Ernie Watson.

The two men stopped talking when they saw Sarah's parents approach.

Maybe this time, McKuen told himself, *it'll go better.* He was wrong.

"Just tell us, dammit! Is my daughter alive?" said Lawrence McLaughlin. His voice snapped like a whip on the back of an ox.

Lieutenant Watson rolled his eyes and walked off, leaving the Chief to deliver the news.

Chief McKuen moved his head side-to-side and glanced at the ground. Not the sort to air their emotions in public, Sarah's parents stiffened as Chief McKuen told them two bodies, presumed to be Paddy and Sarah, had been recovered and were *en route* to the Coroner's office in New Dublin.

"Ask him about Angel," said Rose, her hands chalk-white from clutching her husband's arm.

Lawrence McLaughlin looked at his wife and nodded. "What about our granddaughter?"

"We can't say, one way or the other," said McKuen.

"Then it's possible Angel is still alive?" said Lawrence McLaughlin, his voice stern, unwavering.

Chief McKuen nodded. "Well, yes, I suppose it's possible. But I don't want to get your hopes up, Mister McLaughlin. We'll know more once we've gone over the premises with a fine-tooth comb."

"And you're doing that NOW—right, Chief?"

"Uh, yes, sir, Mister McLaughlin. We'll cover every square inch before the day's out. I promise you."

Senior Patrolman, Officer\Robb Royce, joined Chief McKuen. Together, they watched the McLaughlins return to their car. No doubt about it, McKuen's heart ached for both sets of parents. It would show in his face long after the funeral. As he watched the McLaughlins drive away, Chief McKuen turned to Officer Royce: "Sometimes, Robb, I hate this job."

Royce looked at the Chief and nodded. The truth is, the handsome young cop didn't know what to say. Earlier, at first sight of his friends, now charred corpses, Royce's guts turned inside-out, and he had to step away to vomit. In point of fact: Royce knew Paddy and Sarah socially and, to a lesser extent, Jonny Fiáin; all four had drunk many a beer together and had shared a whole lot of laughs. More recently, Royce was a teammate with Paddy and Sarah when Royce and his girlfriend bowled every Friday night.

† † †

Coast Guard Lieutenant Ernie Watson joined McKuen and Patrolman Royce. "That couldn't have been easy, Chief," said Watson, "I've had dealings with Larry McLaughlin, and I can't say I enjoyed it. Did you tell him what we found?"

"What? The gas can?" said Chief McKuen.

Watson nodded.

"No," said McKuen. "I didn't. They've had a world of grief come their way this morning—no point adding more to it now."

"Arson is what it suggests, Chief," said Watson. "And

"I understand, Ernie," said McKuen. "This may be a crime scene, but while I've got jurisdiction, I want to be positive it's arson before the story goes public.

15.

The Gray Brethren

Dawn! In time for Pip, the cabin boy, to milk Billie before joining the crew for a breakfast of porridge and hot rolls with honey and butter.

On deck, a drizzle was falling. Captain Stint ordered to strike the sails and prepare to dock alongside the island's only shallow-water pier.

The *Sea Witch*, or *La Bruja Del Mar,* if you prefer, had reached the coast of Martinique, specifically Fort Saint Pierre—that's right, the *"Paris of the Caribbean,"* and did so, in large part, without incident.

Parenthetically, it wasn't until Portuguese students on spring break from *Universidade de Lisboa*, in Portugal, introduced syphilis and gonorrhea to the Isle of flowers and iguanas that Martinique's *Chambre du Commerce* voted unanimously to drop that lofty title touting Fort Saint Pierre. They did so in a full-page ad they took out in the *Guide De Voyage* section of *Le Figaro*, France's premier newspaper, at the time.

† † †

The beach town of Fort Saint Pierre is an unapologetic tourist trap. In the earliest history of the port-city, *L'allée des Voleurs*,[52] directly behind the

---

[52] French, for "Thieves Alley."

original *Paris Hilton,* was alive with souvenir shops and street vendors. In truth, most of what vendors sold in Thieves Alley was booty stolen from the hapless merchant vessels seized by French privateers who plied their trade throughout the Caribbean. Understandably, these swashbuckling bon vivants (gay fellows, mostly) brought what they'd plundered to French-speaking Martinique. There, buccaneers trafficked their ill-gotten gains in plain sight, duty-free, no questions asked.

Old World? New World? It didn't matter. The French on Martinique were beyond sneaky back then—still are, when it comes to turning a profit. Just ask those poor, dumb bastards—the *Caribs* and *Arawaks*!

While most of Stint's crew were ashore, wetting their tongues in any of a dozen grog shops on Hôtel Street, just after dark, Miss Lily, Stint, and four burly crewmen loaded the crate with Headstone inside, onto the pier.

Stint procured the use of a cart and a mule, who answered to "Jacque," and off they went. From inside the crate came furtive sounds suggesting Headstone was beginning to slip the dreamy bonds of the opioids Miss Lily used to sedate him.

About some things, Jacque, the mule, was prescient. Had he been able to speak that night, other than bray, he would have told Stint he had a very bad feeling the moment the full moon showed its face from behind voluminous, charcoal-colored clouds.

Making haste, as best as can be gotten from a rented mule, and using torches to light their way,　Stint and Miss Lily followed the cart as Jacque plodded down a dirt road that wound its way through fields of sugar cane, all the way past *Lovers' Lane*, and into the jungle.

† † †

Eventually, half-past the Witching Hour[53], they came to a waterfall, the same as Miss Lily saw in a vision twenty-eight days earlier. Lily looked at Stint and nodded. "We're here."

She stepped down from the cart, patted Jacque on the head, and looked at Stint; he was loading two Sea Service, .54 caliber flintlock pistols he carried in the broad crimson sash athwart his six-pack abs and waist. Buccaneers need not always *feel* marvelous, but they damn well better *look* marvelous.

"You won't be needing those, Captain," said Miss Lily.

Had he been asked, Jacque, the mule would have stringently disagreed. Jacque had sensed the presence of other-worldly things when the cart was still a hundred yards away from the waterfall.

"As comforting as that is to hear, Miss Lily," said Stint, "in my line of work, I find it better to have them, and not need them, than need them, and not have them."

The mule could not have agreed more. The sudden sound of pounding from inside the crate punctuated Stint's retort. It also set Jacque to braying a string of nouns one only sees on public lavatory walls.

"Aunt Lily!" said Headstone. "Something's happening to me! Get me out of here, Auntie! Hurry!"

"Fine," said Stint. There was no disguising the sarcasm in his voice. "Just fine! I had a feeling

---

[53] Midnight.

something out of the ordinary was going to keel-haul our little expedition."

"Then you'll not be disappointed, Captain," said Miss Lily, "if your premonition rings true."

Stint muttered a few obscenities that only Jacque the mule recognized; then, he climbed down off the cart. He went to the back and took hold of a rope attached to the crate.

"Hold on, young man," said Stint. "I'll have you out of there in a heartbeat."

To be sure, Handsome Jonny was no pantywaist, something Miss Lily could attest to had she been in the mood, but she wasn't. Stint heaved mightily on the rope and had it halfway off the cart when, of its own accord, or perhaps it was Black Magick, maybe physics, the crate slid to the ground with a THUD loud enough to unnerve a gravedigger.

"Grrrrrrrrrr!" said a voice inside the crate. It sounded raspy, desperate (more like a growl). Stint lurched backward, tripped, and landed on his tight, muscular buttocks. Simultaneously, the thing inside the crate smashed the boards off the top, and out it popped, something completely unrecognizable, certainly nothing resembling young Sunday or Balthazar Headstone, for that matter, or anything remotely human!

Crouching, it looked to be a shaggy wolfhound but twice the size of one. It had a massive head, the size of a Wyoming buffalo, and an unusually long snout, much like an alligator, out of which four, nine-inch ivory fangs protruded: two uppers and two lower. From the creature's teeth, large sticky droplets of drool glided to the ground. Attached to its arms, or, arguably, its front legs, were appendages resembling two hands with talons sharp as butchers' knives, jutting from each of four long, bony fingers and a thumb. On the whole, the thing was monstrous, far more substantial than your standard elf-eating wolf, like the elf-eating wolves in Lapland, where elves are short and chubby and where the *Aurora Borealis* is most at home in all Her splendor.

The creature's eyes ignited the night like fiery rubies the size of apples, the kind of apples left on the branch until ripe, near to bursting with sweetness; apples ready for picking. Simply put, the type of apple granny prefers when making pies in late summer or early autumn, depending on the heat, and Granny's lumbago.

Stint scrambled to his feet. Not a great fan of surprises, he shouted to Miss Lily, "What in Seven Hells is it?"

"My NEPHEW!" she said. "Don't hurt him!"

"THAT, dear lady, is NOT what we boxed inside the crate."

Stint drew both pistols from his sash and aimed them squarely at the creature. "*Ergo*, it cannot be your nephew!"

"I swear to you, Stint—It's my nephew! Balthazar!"

"Who?" said Stint. "I thought you said his name is Sunday."

Indeed, the creature, who was Miss Lily's nephew, cocked his massive head to one side, perplexed by what was taking place during the expanded moment aggressively unfolding before his eyes. The creature sensed his life hanging precariously in the yet-to-be-determined balance.

"It WAS Sunday," said Miss Lily, "but he changed it—to BAL-tha-zar."

"Who!?" said Stint, staring into the creature's eyes as it slowly went from a crouch to being fully erect, which is a clumsy way of saying—it stood.

Her "nephew," now a Weirdwolf, possessed a forked penis, not unlike a *marsupial* of the order *Didelphimorphiaof,* endemic to the Americas, also known as—the *Opossum.*

O, Madonna, with thine comical conical breasts! Couldest thee? Wouldest thee, accommodate such a beastie?

"Come to your senses, Stint," said Miss Lily, "before I place a curse on you!"

When Jacque, the mule, heard THAT, he began to hyperventilate.

"I mean it, Stint," said Lily. "I'll make your *wee-wee* shrivel and disappear, like an earthworm frying in a pan."

That was all it took. Jacque, the mule, couldn't very well close his ears, but he could shut his eyes, and that's what he did. For some reason, it helped relax this noble, unwilling slave to humanity. Tired and thirsty and scared shiteless, Jacque knew of the strange goings-on in the island's Heart of Darkness, which, he surmised, was where they had arrived.

True, they were in the Heart of Darkness, and nothing on earth could alter that, short of the Miraculous.

"Curse or no curse," said Stint, "your nephew struck me as an especially bright lad."

"He is," said Lily.

"Then I shall put him to the test," said Stint. "We shall soon find out who or what this abomination is."

Baffled by Stint's cavalier indifference toward the threat to his *Oui Oui*, Miss Lily could only raise her hands to her sides as if to say, "*Idiot! What the hell are you going on about?*"

Stint looked into the creature's eyes. "If you truly are Sunday, or Balthazar, as your lovely auntie maintains, tell me, and be quick about it! What—is the square root of forty-nine!"

"Grrrrrrrrrr," said the creature.

"Hah!" said Stint. "Not even close." Stint cocked the hammers of his flintlocks and was about to shoot when—

"Wait!" said a voice from the darkness. It spoke in a loud, commanding manner, thick with menace. "Forget about that one-eyed snake, Captain Stint! Harm the man-cub, and we will floss our fangs with your guts."

Stint eyed the clearing and saw no fewer than one hundred pairs of eyes glowing ruby red and fiercely bright in the darkness.

In point of fact: Stint was a formidable adversary at sea, defying cannon shot and musket fire when boarding a ship or slugging it out with fists and daggers in Port Royal, at the infamous Blue Fox. But what Stint saw surrounding him, there and then, convinced him otherwise.

It's a wise man, Stint told himself, *who knows when to leave a bad thing alone and walk away.*

"Fair enough," said Stint. He said it quite loudly so that the whole jungle neighborhood would hear. He tucked his pistols into his sash. "Now, if it's all the same to you, good folks, the lady and I will be taking our leave. Come, my dear."

"I'm not leaving," said Lily.

"What?"

"Take the mule and cart back to Saint Pierre,

Captain."

"And, you?"

"I have business here—with the Gray Brethren."

Stint looked around the clearing and saw the same pairs of ruby red eyes, closer now, devouring him with their unspoken malice.

"Okie Dokie," said Stint.

Known to be economical with his energy out of bed, Stint whistled through his teeth, hopped atop the cart, grabbed Jacque's reins, and off they went—a tiny bit faster than a pregnant camel in a sandstorm.

16.

Sans Souci

It wasn't long before Jonny traversed the back road that took them across the Canadian border, absent Customs Agents and border guards. Once in Canada, Jonny reconnected with the main highway leading north to Fredericton, a growing city of twenty-seven thousand French and English-speaking inhabitants.

Almost the entire time they were on the road since leaving New Dublin, Jonny felt someone or something was watching them. It was one more nagging thought racing 'round and 'round, inside his head, one he couldn't shake. Nor could Jonny forget the sight of his two best friends lying cold and dead or the creature that killed them. *What in God's name,* he wondered, *was she?*

Where they were going was a Doctor of Veterinary Medicine living in a small town not far from Fredericton, population eighteen-hundred-and-eleven souls, called *Sans Souci.*

It was at the house of Doctor Luther Van Helwing that they stopped. The time was three in the morning, November 1, 1949.

As Jonny pulled up and parked in front of the doctor's two-story, Normandy-style rock house, the sound of dogs barking greeted them. Jonny waited until the lights in the doctor's house came on before bundling Angel in his arms and going to the doctor's front door.

Jonny didn't need to knock. The dogs had already announced his presence. The door opened, and the seventy-two-year-old doctor cautiously peered outside.

"*Merde!*" said Helwing. "Jonny Fiáin."

The good doctor attempted to slam the door in Jonny's face. One of Jonny's size-eleven, steel-toed, Wellington engineers' boots kept it open.

"Like it or not, Doctor, we're coming in."

"If you must," said Van Helwing.

Jonny knew the way to Helwing's examination room, and that's where he carried Angel. Whiskey followed.

"Who's the child?" said the doctor.

"My cousin's daughter, Angel."

"Jesus, Jonny! You didn't kidnap her, did you?"

The look that followed on Jonny's face was enough for the doctor to change the subject.

"What's wrong with her?" said Helwing.

"She was attacked by an animal last night—I ran it off, but not before it made two deep cuts on her back, beneath her left shoulder. She's burning with fever."

"Put her on the table," said Helwing. "Facedown. I'll get a pillow and a blanket."

† † †

The chloroform that the Doctor administered rendered Angel unconscious. He sewed Angel's two wounds shut with no fewer than one-hundred crisscross stitches. Later, while Angel was still unconscious, Doctor Helwing and Jonny Fiáin drank cognac in the doctor's study. Whiskey remained under the operating table in the laboratory. After what they endured during the past twenty-four hours, Whiskey would not abandon Angel—not now.

"Is she going to be okay, Doctor?"

"She's young. She looks strong. I see no reason why her body can't recover. As for her fever? She's trying to fight infection of some kind. I gave her a massive dose of penicillin and a rabies shot. We'll know more in a day or two."

"A rabies shot?"

"With any kind of bite from an animal, it is the prudent thing to do, Jonny. I injected it into the girl's abdomen. She will need three more doses of rabies vaccination: in three, seven, and fourteen days. Frankly, Jonny, listening to you describe it, the creature is unlike anything I have encountered on this continent or during my travels abroad. And yet—" The doctor paused to light his Meerschaum pipe.

"And yet?" said Jonny.

"Given the nature of the girl's—"

"Her NAME is Angel."

The doctor nodded thoughtfully and puffed on his pipe.

"Given the nature of Angel's wounds, and to hear your description of the creature, it sounds like a *Pipistrelles Colossus Pipistrelles*—a bat—but one of immense proportion, unlike anything known to science."

"A bat?" said Jonny.

"Yes. A huge, hairy-legged Vampire bat. I say bat because it has wings and two claws on each hand, as Angel's wounds attest, and fangs, which would facilitate what the creature did to your friends, Angel's parents. But how it got here, to this part of the world, is anyone's guess."

Jonny glanced at Angel. "What, now?"

"We put Angel in ice water to cool her down. Her temperature is dangerously high. There could be lasting effects. One more thing, one of her legs shows signs of atrophy. It appears Angel may have a disintegrative disorder of the spine. Do you know anything about it, Jonny?"

"Forget her spine, Doc. Angel broke her leg a short while back."

"Hmm," said the doctor. "Interesting."

"The hell it is," said Jonny, suddenly furious. "It's FUBAR!" Angel's leg! Paddy and Sarah! Every goddamn thing! FUBAR!"

"Why don't I pour you a Whiskey, Jonny? It will help you relax."

"Got anything stronger, Doc?"

"Morphine?"

17.

Manhunters

A former Texas Ranger, Albert Mesa, stayed on in 1935 when the Texas Rangers merged with the Texas Highway Patrol. An expert horseman, and a trained marksman, Mesa had taken down scores of lawbreakers on both sides of the border with Mexico. In 1949, at forty years of age, Albert Mesa retired from the Texas Department of Public Safety to join the United States Marshals Service.

When President George Washington signed the Judiciary Act[54] into law, the federal marshals' primary function was to execute all lawful warrants issued under the newly born United States government's authority.

U.S. Deputy Marshal Albert Mesa arrived in New Dublin to serve an arrest warrant. Accompanying Albert Mesa was a senior U.S. Deputy Marshal named Miles Standish, a direct descendant of THE Miles Standish from early Seventeenth Century colonial times.

This outing was Mesa's first assignment since graduating from the Federal Law Enforcement Training Center at Glynco, Georgia, one month before. It was his

---

[54] The Judiciary Act of 1789 (Ch. 20, 1 Stat. 73) was a United States federal statute adopted in the first session of the First United States Congress. It established the federal judiciary (courts of law) for the United States.

first big case as a U.S. Deputy Marshal, and Mesa couldn't help himself—he couldn't keep from smiling.

Standish was five years older than Mesa and had thirty years as a U.S. Deputy Marshal, which he reminded Mesa of in several subtle ways. It didn't bother the former Texas Ranger. He gave Standish what he accorded every man. Respect. Standish was not only his partner now, but he was also a living legend in the Marshals Service, right up there with Wyatt Earp, Bat Masterson, and Frank Hemmer.[55]

It was Miles Standish who, in 1939, escorted the infamous Italian mobster, Al Capone[56], from a prison cell on Alcatraz across the country to a mental institution in Baltimore, Maryland. Capone stayed locked up there three years before dying in Florida of advanced syphilis.

Sooner or later, the Piper gets paid. The public didn't know what the papers never reported, that during the eleven-day journey by car and train from San Francisco, assassins made three attempts to kill Al Capone. It had been, then, Deputy Standish, who prevented the mobster's demise each time.

God's truth—Miles Standish was a lawman revered by his peers as a marshal's marshal, and Albert Mesa respected that.

---

[55] Bonnie & Clyde. White Trash sociopaths who robbed and killed without remorse throughout the central United States during the Great Depression. They died in an ambush, in May 1934, in Gibsland Louisiana.

[56] Alphonse "Al" Capone, known by the nickname **"Scarface"**, was an American thug who attained notoriety during Prohibition as the boss of the Chicago Mafia. His reign as a crime boss ended when he went to prison in the 1930s.

† † †

The two marshals flashed their Identification cards in front of Annie Leibowitz, receptionist and gatekeeper for the New Dublin Police Department. Annie noticed the first detail about the two strangers was their hats; the second was their height, one being a hat taller than the other. The third thing she noticed was their matching sunglasses with non-penetrable, mirror-like lenses.

"I'm Deputy Marshal Standish," said the taller man. "He's Mesa. We're with the U-S Marshals' Service."

"I can see that," said Annie Leibowitz, adjusting her glasses. "We've never had the Marshal's Service come through here before."

Her voice contained a mixture of awe and curiosity. She looked upward at a fly buzzing around Deputy Marshal Standish's hat.

"Miss—?" said Standish. He snapped his fingers, apparently to get Annie's full attention.

"Leibowitz," said Annie, disregarding the fly. "Annie Leibowitz. "I'll let Chief McKuen know you're here."

Annie wanted to see these visitors' eyes from the all-powerful Marshals' Service—eyes being the windows to the soul or some such thing. Annie was a believer in homespun truisms. The sunglasses the men wore concealing their eyes bothered her to the point of distraction; so much so, she forgot to offer them a pastry and a cup of coffee, the fraternal hallmark of common cop courtesy, worldwide.

† † †

Douglas O'Doole's jaws went slack. "You told the coppers WHAT?"

Tears came into the barmaid's eyes. Her name was Ginnie O'Byrne, a beautiful, cheerful young woman, recently arrived in America illegally, which means, without documents, at nineteen years of age.

"That your friend, Jonny, came in on All Hallows' Eve, looking for you."

With tears as big as bluegills gliding down Ginnie O'Byrne's cheeks, O'Doole took her shaking self into his arms and gave her a proper Fenian hug.

"There, there, lass," said O'Doole. "Just remember to keep your mouth shut when the law comes around. Unless it's our very own Chief of Police, God bless and keep him, for the decent Irishman he is."

† † †

Chief McKuen looked up from feeding Betty, his goldfish. The two men held their I.D. cards almost under his nose, probably so he could see they meant business. The Chief looked at the sunglasses they were wearing: "Too bright in here for you, fellas?"

Mesa looked at Standish. "I told you it was a dumb idea."

Deputy Marshal Standish wore a gray Fedora with a black band around the crown, a gray, loose-fitting, three-button suit with double-wide lapels, black Wingtips, black socks, a black bow tie, a black leather belt, and a starched white, long-sleeve shirt, with Sterling silver cuff-links. Under his coat was a shoulder holster hosting a 1929 Colt Detective .38 Special. Standish purchased it after surviving the rigorous, weeding-out process for becoming a marshal twenty years before. His weapon of choice, or its age, wasn't a consideration; he preferred it over more modern,   higher caliber handguns that had won favor with law enforcement. Every time he was considered for advancement, meaning closer to occupying a desk, Standish refused.

The marshal with the clean-shaven face, Deputy Marshal Mesa, was attired in latter-day western wear from his home state—Texas. Said Western wear comprised a tapered, light gray, two-button coat without lapels and had dark suede patches on each elbow. His trousers were the same color as his coat, flared at the cuffs to accommodate boots, and wore a wide-brim cowboy hat with a rattlesnake skin around the crown.

Completing Mesa's ensemble was a Bolo tie, held together by a chunk of polished turquoise hugging the collar of a starched white cotton shirt, along with a wide leather belt with a brass belt-buckle embossed with an armadillo.

Had Chief A.J. McKuen gotten down on his hands and knees beneath his desk, he would have seen Marshal Mesa's tooled leather, authentic snakeskin cowboy boots.

Lord have mercy, Betty! Said McKuen silently to his goldfish, so named for Betty Grable. *If these two aren't a pair of Jacks!*

"What can I do for you, gentlemen?"

Deputy Marshal Standish removed an eight by eleven inch, black and white photograph from a Manila folder— an old headshot of Jonny Fiáin as a young Marine in his Dress Blues. He handed the picture across the desk to McKuen.

"Recognize this man, Chief?"

"Sure, I recognize him," said McKuen. "He grew up here—right here, in New Dublin. Jonny's something of a local hero."

McKuen waited a few seconds, allowing ample time for the two marshals to process what he said before adding: "Jonny Fiáin doesn't live here anymore."

"But he comes back to New Dublin from time to time," said Standish.

"Yes—that's right," said McKuen. "About once a year. Who let the cat out of the bag?"

"A barmaid," said Mesa. "In Douglas O'Doole's pub."

Standish looked at his partner and nodded.

"We automatically canvas bars, pubs, pool halls, and taverns," said Mesa.

"For someone like Jonny Fiáin," said Standish, "bars are a natural habitat."

"For someone LIKE Jonny Fiáin?" said McKuen, emphasizing "like" as he repeated Standish's words. McKuen had always liked Jonny Fiáin and was put-off by the tone of the Deputy Marshal's remark.

Years before, it quite nearly broke McKuen's heart when he was a young patrolman and had to arrest Jonny Fiáin for allegedly breaking into David Mason's Florist shop one night when the store was closed, which, technically, was burglary[57]. Mason had been staying late when the alleged burglar allegedly but inadvertently and unintentionally landed on top of him from the skylight, rendering Mason unconscious, with several broken

---

[57] At common law, burglary is the "trespassory breaking and entering of a dwelling known to be in the possession of another, at night, with the specific intent of committing a felony, therein. "Night" was defined as the time between thirty minutes after sunset, and thirty minutes before sunrise. "Trespassory" means without permission [Black's Law Dictionary].

bones—a nasty injury, to be sure. Jonny was thirteen at the time. The worse thing about it? McKuen knew it wasn't Jonny, who committed the burglary, and injured Mister Mason in the process. His cousin, Paddy O'Hara, wanted a Gardenia corsage for Sarah McLaughlin to wear to their Middle School graduation Prom but didn't have enough money to buy it. Covering for Paddy, Jonny took the fall and went to Juvenile Hall in Bangor, Maine, for five long years. Why five years? Because the injuries to the much-loved florist were substantial, Richard, "the hanging judge," Love sentenced the accused harshly.

There was, however, as with most unpleasant events, a silver lining. One need only look. In this instance, Jonny Fiáin acquired a toughness that would serve him in good stead. That, and the fact he grew like a weed, filling out nicely while incarcerated, becoming lean and muscular, superb with a switchblade, and fast with his fists.

"I think you know what I mean, Chief," said Standish.

McKuen looked Standish straight in the eye. "I believe I do, Deputy Marshal."

"All right, then. I'm glad we understand each other. So! Any idea where Jonny Fiáin might be?"

"Nope," said McKuen. "Are you going to tell me what he's wanted for?"

"Fiáin skipped bail in Albuquerque, New Mexico," said Mesa.

"Then fled the state," said Standish. "That makes Fiáin a fugitive from justice."

"What happened in Albuquerque?" said McKuen.

"A bar fight," said Mesa. "Fiáin rearranged the faces of several locals—put them in the hospital. The cops arrested him for Felony Assault and Battery."

"The Jonny Fiáin I know doesn't start fights, gentlemen; he finishes them."

"That doesn't concern us, Chief," said Mesa. "After we take Fiáin into custody, we're returning him to New Mexico to stand trial."

"Hmm," said McKuen. "If that's what you got to do, okay."

Chief McKuen took a drink of Brandy from his coffee cup; yep, it was already THAT, kind of morning.

"One more thing, Chief," said Mesa, "the FBI like Fiáin for breaking five men out of jail in Kansas City, Missouri—men we believe are part of Fiáin's gang."

"His, GANG?" said McKuen, spitting a mouthful of his drink on the floor.

"That's right," said Standish. "Some of his Marine Corps buddies; men who never fit back in once they returned from overseas."

"Why were they arrested?"

"The FBI believes they're behind a string of burglaries," said Mesa. "They've been hitting National Guard armories around the country, then taking the weapons and equipment to Mexico. The FBI thinks Johnny Fiáin is the brains behind it all."

Standish laughed. "Seems everybody wants a piece of your hometown hero, Chief."

† † †

While Standish scrutinized the charred ruins of the lighthouse keeper's dwelling, Mesa strolled the grounds. A cold, sea-borne wind blew past his ears, accompanied by the sound of waves crashing on the rocks below the cliffs and a seagull's cry overhead.

Texas sure as hell isn't anything like this, Mesa mused. He pulled his coat collar up to ward off the dampness in the air; then, he noticed a glint of sunlight reflecting on a piece of metal near his feet. He bent down and lifted a Zippo lighter from the weeds; it had the words: *Semper Fi*[58], inscribed on the sides.

"*Hola*," said Mesa, softly to himself. "Now, who do you belong to?"

Near Paddy O'Hara's pickup truck, Mesa saw something else, something that screamed for his attention. There were new, narrow-gauge tire impressions in the dried mud. To an expert tracker like Albert Mesa, the prints suggested the undeniable presence of a motorcycle with a sidecar attached, the kind Harley-Davidson manufactured thousands of during World War II.

Mesa clinched the lighter in his hand and shouted, "Standish! Come here! You're going to want to take a look at this!"

---

[58] *Semper Fi* is short for *Semper Fidelis*, a Latin phrase meaning "Always faithful, or "Always loyal." It is the slogan of the United States Marine Corps.

18.

The Sirens' Song

Stint's heart almost leaped free from his rib cage upon seeing his beloved sloop.

Okay. Time out!

Someone once remarked that "poetry is what we lose in translation." In the instant matter, the name of Stint's vessel in Española, La Bruja Del Mar, arguably sounds more poetic, i.e., The Sorceress of the Sea, than does its translation into English, [the] Sea Witch. Americans, however, want their language like their sex— uncomplicated, straightforward, and meaningless.

After Stint and Miss Lily took leave of the *Sea Witch* to transport young Headstone to the Heart of Darkness, Stint's crew jumped ship. Where those dirty, thirty thieves went is anyone's guess. Only Pip, the Cabin Boy, stayed behind. Verily, Stint was the closest thing to a father this orphan from the streets of old Dublin ever knew, and Pip was the better for it. The right man in a boy's life can make all the difference in the world. Something Stint knew well.

It would be a lie to say his crew's shameless act of desertion didn't hurt Stint's feelings.

Good riddance shouted Stint's inner pirate; still, it stung like hell to have them walk out, without so much as a "By your leave Capt'n, we're deserting!"

Pirates were a fickle bunch then, and not much has changed since; today, pirates sit in places of prominence and authority; they make laws, fleece, and keel-haul the public with a whole lot of gobbledygook instead of cannon-fire.

Stint stood on the pier, weeping. As for Jacque? Handsome Jonny couldn't bring himself to say goodbye to the mule, so he bought that splendid beast from its owner and brought Jacque aboard the *Sea Witch* to be part of his new, revitalized crew. Why not? Jacque would be a fantastic companion for Billie, the she-goat. Besides, Pip would love the extra company, and Stint needed a trustworthy crew whose beverage of choice was wheat-grass, not 151-rum, preferably *L'Coq Noir*.

† † †

It felt right, ethical, and proper to Stint to be in command of himself and his sloop again. He had a crew, more or less, and was out on the ocean—a drop of *The Great That*, he called it. There, the likes of the creatures in Martinique's Heart of Darkness weren't lurking. But neither was Miss Lily. It's been said before but bears repeating: *"the heart is a lonely hunter.*[59]*"*

Stint found himself missing Miss Lily's breath-stealing kisses that tasted of rum and saltwater taffy, along with her caresses that made him quiver, quake, and cry out at night:

"Brown sugar, I'm all shook up, Mm-hmm, oh, yeah!

---

[59] Marquis De Sade (1740-1814). Donatien Alphonse François, Marquis de Sade, was a French nobleman, revolutionary, politician, philosopher, and writer, famous for his libertine sexuality and sexual abuse of children. His works include novels, short stories, plays, dialogues, and political tracts [Wikipedia].

Two days out of port, Pip, former Cabin Boy, now Gunner's Mate, Cook, Seaman, fledgling Buccaneer, and wiper-upper, spotted what looked to be a French merchant vessel.

On the stern, painted in elegant gold lettering, was the name: *La Belle LaChelle*. She had dropped anchor in a blue-water lagoon nestled against a small, uncharted island. Strange as it seemed to Pip, high above in the crow's nest, he saw no one aboard. He shouted to Stint, below, at the helm.

"She's a beauty, ay, Capt'n,"

"Aye, Pip. That, she is. Whoever put her together took their time, that's for sure. See how she rests evenly in the water?"

"Aye, Capt'n, I do."

"It's because her keel is straight as an arrow. That's the kind of ship you want to be on when the sea boils, and the wind howls like the damned souls in Davy Jones Locker[60] , and the Kraken rips the sails from the masts defying you to whine or bitterly complain."

"Maybe one day I'll have a ship that fine," said Pip.

"That day may be closer than you think, Pip. Now come down from there, and we'll see what's what with *La Belle LaChelle*."

Handsome Jonny, a consummate EOP (Equal Opportunity Pirate), knew it made sense to come alongside *La Belle LaChelle* for a closer look.

"Do you hear that, Capt'n?" said Pip, still high on high.

The singing was decidedly feminine, alluring, and seductive. Had Pip's dear departed whore of a mother

---

[60] Davy Jones Locker is sailor-speak for the final resting place of them that drowned or otherwise met an untimely end while at sea.

been on deck, she would have screamed, "plug your [expletive deleted] ears, Pip, my boy, and come down from there!"

† ††

Jacque, the mule, now Stint's 1st Mate and Quartermaster, was the first to set eyes on them. He brayed as they emerged in a single file from the tree line, singing.

There were no fewer than ten, each barefoot and lovely as the next. These bare-breasted women came in all stripes and wore colorful *saris* that clung to their thighs and shaded their *unmentionables* from the sun and gnats.

God's truth—the Caribbean has all three in abundance.

† ††

Stint didn't always wear underwear, but he preferred Tighty Whitey's from Tighty Whitey's Mercantile on the island of Tortuga when he did. Those, or something just as simple, like the bleached-white muslin loincloth he had in his sea-chest for such an occasion as now presented itself. The loincloth fit perfectly and made for a nice contrast with Stint's tanned torso. It has to be said; Stint was a gentleman's rogue; he knew what was appropriate in most social situations; he just didn't give a damn.

His rare-as-a-unicorn, lady banker once suggested Stint's "lack of filters" made Stint do and say as he did.

Well, this time, Stint cared, and he respected that banker, so he wore the damn loincloth, with a filter built-in.

The women singing on the beach marveled at his perfect form as Stint dove from the crow's nest, sixty feet above the main deck, into the sparkling water of the Blue Lagoon.

Looking every bit like a true *Son of Poseidon*, Stint hailed a seahorse that transported him to the water's edge.

Favored by Good Fortune, Stint skipped onto the beach and greeted these ten genteel ladies fair like the silver-tongued devil he was.

"Hey, babes! Wuz up?"

19.

Pineapple! Pineapple! Pineapple!

One of the Ten with shapely hips and blonde hair that hung like melted wax down the long neck of an empty Chianti bottle made her hands into fists and rested them defiantly on her pelvic girdle. Indeed, she could have been a stunt double for *Penthesilea*, the Amazonian Queen who fought at Troy. Achilles, son of Thetis, killed her on the field of battle for calling him and his *Myrmidons* "sissies."

However, this particular blonde planted her size-12 bare feet, with ankles to marvel at, shoulder-width apart—clearly, she was a force to be reckoned with.

"Hey, buddy! WHO the hell are YOU?" she said.

Stint had a fine ear for dialects and concluded the blonde with alabaster skin and ankles to marvel at was Scottish and needed to be kissed—hard and often.

"Far and wide, from *Zanzibar* around the *Cape of Good Hope*, dear lady, I'm known as Handsome Jonny Stint, Captain of the *Sea Witch*, parked behind me. You can call me Handsome Jonny, or Captain Stint, or just plain, Stint. Now, do I rightly conclude it was *La Belle LaChelle* that brought you to this lonely, desolate, nameless place to grow old; wither; become barren and forgotten?"

"Oh, this place has got a name, buddy boy," said the blonde. "It's called *'Ten Righteously Pissed-Off Women'*!"

The other women coughed, spit on the sand, and nodded.

"That's right, Mary," said an officious-looking brunette, not as tall as the Scot but with a no-nonsense look about her. She was squinting at Stint with brown eyes that glistened and lips that pouted, lips longing for licks, or maybe needing Chap-stick. It could be the sun that made her squint at Stint, or perhaps it was the glare reflecting off the sand. Perhaps she just needed contacts.

"Ladies," said Stint, "I assure you. I come as a friend. I, along with my ship and brave crew, are at your disposal. Tellest me, if thou willeth, how comest you here? But, first, let us seeketh shade beneath yon palmeth trees where groweth large pineapples, if mine eyes see-eth right."

Buccaneer, or not, Handsome Jonny Stint could be exceedingly polite, as well as charming.

He could also be a *troll hole* of epic proportions.

† † †

Stint sat cross-legged in the shade, spine straight, hands resting soulfully on his knees, trying to ignore what was happening beneath his loincloth. He listened intently to the women shouting over each other, hoping to hear clearly what each had to say. Alas, some words were lost, others too inappropriate to repeat.

It turns out the women were *en route* to the British colony of Massachusetts. They were to become indentured servants at the Royal Bank of Boston for seven years. Going to work for an evil corporation was how they would pay for their passage and their Student loans in the case of several of them. They believed they would have the opportunity ("eventually") for a new life, presumably, a life better than the life they left behind.

Their vessel, *La Belle LaChelle*, had been boarded one night by Spanish mimes, high on crack cocaine while the ship was in Havana Harbor, in Cuba, taking on supplies. Limes, mostly, to keep the crew from getting scurvy and breaking out with nasty, pustular sores that would ooze at the most inconvenient times and make sitting on the weathered wooden crapper nigh impossible.

While the women tossed and turned and played Old Maid in the nasty, sticky heat below deck, and while the captain and crew got hilariously drunk in the brothels of Havana, these Spanish mimes, these crack whores murdered two reclining sailors left behind to "Stand Watch."

After midnight, these scurrilous Spaniards raised the anchor, unfurled the sails, and departed the harbor. They did this without knowing who or what they had on board. All of it took place in record time, with no one the wiser until the next morning, when the former captain of *La Belle LaChelle* realized his vessel had left port without him. It happens.

The women unburdened themselves by jointly and severally sharing their stories until the heaviness oppressing them evaporated. Only after shedding a bucket full of tears did they relax in Stint's presence. They even shared their papayas, mangoes, and Animal Crackers with him.

Stint had that kind of effect on women. He was born with it. When Stint was a wee lad in Ireland, there was a rumor that his first nanny, who was something of a witch, may have imbued Stint with individual gifts. She taught mice card tricks on her days off and made love potions for the village women. She also had a fondness for gin. Not cheap gin. But the good stuff.

Apart from blonde Mary, the Scottish lass with ankles to marvel at, and Belgium Kim, with pouting lips and some Irish thrown in, there were two lovely, black-haired, dark-eyed Prussian girls, Laurie, and Marla, who were fleeing the marriages their fathers had arranged.

Their fathers promised them to twins, beer Meisters in Bavaria, and much older than themselves. So, Laurie and Marla stole away late at night, slept in a barn outside their village, then hitchhiked on a hay wagon to Antwerp, a port in Holland. There, they learned of the promise of a new life in the New World.

Some people will believe anything, but Marla and Laurie were young and restless, and the heart wants what it wants. Does it not?

The youngest of the lot was a girl from Cornwall in southwestern England who insisted that Crystal was her "stage name." The things some girls do for attention. Cooing and chirping sounds from Crystal's palm-frond pup-tent in the wee hours of the morning annoyed her associates no end and kept them awake, sometimes until dawn. However, being older, they understood what was taking place, so no one said a thing. It was Crystal's addiction to Opium and Jujubes they found difficult to ignore.

Crystal developed a great love for birds, all birds, all colors, all sizes. By the time she learned the three Rs,

Crystal's knowledge of wetland fowl, habits, and habitats became encyclopedic. No prim English rose; to Crystal, the colorful parrots on the island were nothing less than enchanted. It almost destroyed her when it came time to eat them.

Then came Esther, a former Fortune Teller and herbalist for a carnival in Romany and as sweet a woman as was ever born. Banished from the fair for stealing the wheels of a miller's cart, only to later hawk them to Baron Cal Worthington, a wheel dealer near Salzburg, Esther became a surrogate mother to her castaway sisters.

"Got cramps? Go see Esther!"

There was also beautiful, mysterious Yuko, daughter of a famous Samurai[61] and sword-maker on *Dai Nippon Teikoku*, where the Yamato Dynasty ruled.

The lure of faraway places and Swiss Chocolate caused Yuko to empty her piggy bank and cast her fate to the four winds. With a new *kimono*, her *obi*, two pairs of *tabis*, Yuko said "*Sayonora*" to her island home, hit the road, and never looked back, Jack!

Chante, a Basque beauty from the Pyrenees Mountains, grew up fast and furious and, by the age of ten, was an inveterate gambler and a veritable expert lagging for *centimes* during recess.

At sweet sixteen, Chante brought shame to her father and older brothers by staying out past curfew on a school night. They castrated the boy, then forced Chante to take her unapologetic "attitude" and one suitcase packed with her stuffed animals elsewhere. And then some! So, she

---

[61] An ancient warrior class that excelled in sword-fighting and other martial arts. They served high-ranking Japanese nobles and the Emperor.

did.   Hey! The female can be wilful and must be watched—carefully.

Michelle was a French beauty, good with numbers and crossword puzzles. She wearied of being thought of as a buxom barmaid in Marseille, a tawdry seaport on France's southern coast, where she was habitually pawed and drooled on by drunks and Saint Bernards. Michelle longed to become a tutor one day, perhaps to a wealthy widower with young children. It's good to dream; her sweet mother had told her as a little girl.

Lastly, there was furtive, shadowy, dark-eyed Velda from Vegan, a notorious village in the province of Tuscany, in Italy. Vegan was famous as the birthplace of pastrami and a haven for pickpockets.

Velda's days at the convent and her brief life as a nun ended abruptly and rather rudely when Mother Superior discovered Velda with young Guido, the village idiot during Vespers.

Now, Velda's dark eyes smoldered with desire for Stint, but she was from Vegan, where women are patient and know how to plan, calculate, and wait.

So! Velda took the curlers from her hair and decided to hang out. Perhaps she would wait until dark before making a move on this handsome stranger whose eyes were the color of the sea after a storm and whose voice made her toes curl.

20.

Crossing the T

"I haveth but one question," said Stint. "What becometh the scoundrels who waylaideth you damsels in Cuba?"

"We cutteth their throats while they sleepeth," said Mary, the Scot, beaming as she drew her forefinger slowly across her throat.

"Then we threw their bodies overboard," said Belgium Kim, with a naughty grin that reeked of Gin.

"For the sharks," said Crystal, bright-eyed and warbling.

"They deserved it," said Marla; she spat a mouthful of cracked sunflower shells on the sand and winked at her gal pals. "Didn't they, bitches?"

"True, dat!" said Yuko gleefully. "True dat!"

"Damn straight, they deserved it," said Michelle and hiccupped.

The women laughed and clapped and spat on the sand.

"I cut the *cojoñes* off one of them," said Chante, then nonchalantly cracked her knuckles.

"While I sat on his chest and spit on his belly button," said Laurie, blushing while her bosom swelled like hot air balloons, reaching toward the azure sky, so pleased they were for Laurie's martial accomplishments.

"I raped one of them," said Velda, from the village of Vegan, the birthplace of pastrami and a haven for pickpockets. "Twice!"

With that, the women became quiet; they meditated silently about their recent past. After a few moments, they wearied of their reflections.

Then the women laughed and hugged. And why not? Each, in her way, had suffered much. They had risked everything, even their lives, leaving their homes behind, the places of their youth where they once had roots and dreamed the dreams they dreamt as children.

Confronted with the demands and expectations of others, these ten women had sought some semblance of freedom, even without knowing it:

The year was 1750, for pity's sake,
what could a woman possibly reckon freedom to be?

As their reverie died, they divided their number equally for a game of *Kick the* [expletive deleted] *Coconut Down the Beach*. Being a disinterested Third Party and the only man about the island, the women asked Stint to umpire their game.

"*Oui, certainement*," said Stint in impeccable French. He straightened his loincloth before taking several minutes to stretch: first his hamstrings, then his quadriceps; soon after, he high-stepped thirty-paces in-place. The women politely looked away as Stint warmed up, except for Velda, from Vegan. She couldn't take her eyes off him, or it, or whatever, her eyes fixated.

† † †

Back on the *Sea Witch*, Stint's crew watched, amazed at their captain warming up on the beach.

"Is there nothing our captain cannot do?" said Pip, sounding a little bit like Stint. He looked at Jacque, the mule, and Billie, the she-goat, then added: "I was waxing rhetorical, my four-legged friends."

Jacque brayed, and Billie bahh'ed. They had gotten the gist of Pip's declaration without his editorializing over it.

† † †

"First," said Stint, "we can't have a game of *Kick the* [expletive deleted] *Coconut Down the Beach* without establishing the rules."

The women scoffed, looked at one another, and spit with the wind. Fortunately, there was no *Novel Corona Virus* in the Caribbean in 1750, and lucky that there wasn't, since a small, uncharted island is no place to practice *social distancing*.

"Hey, buddy," said Mary, the Scot, "There are no rules in *Kick the* [expletive deleted] *Coconut Down the Beach*!"

Stint adjusted his loincloth and coughed. "*Au contraire, Mademoiselle*," he said, his French was precise, like the Chamber Music played in Versailles during ~~Estrous~~ Easter.

"Every game worthy of a name must have rules."

"You're a [expletive deleted] PIRATE," said Kim. "You guys don't have rules!"

"Do, too!" said Stint.

"Do not!" said Kim.

"Do, too!" said Stint.

"Do not! Do not! Do not!" said Kim, Mary, Marla, Laurie, Crystal, Chante, Yuko, Esther, Michelle, and Velda.

"Very well, I will stipulate to that," said Stint. "But may I point out, it is the 18th Century. My ilk and I prefer the term, 'buccaneer,' not 'pirate.' And buccaneering is not for sissies; it's serious business, for which we maintain a flexible *code du jour*.

"Well, where was your freeking *code du jour* when we got kidnapped, *Monsieur* Jonny?" said Michelle from Marseilles.

"Those weren't buccaneers, *Mademoiselle*. You said they were mimes! There's no. *International Mimes' Code*. Anyway, without rules, there is nothing for me to umpire."

Stint looked at the faces staring at him. They were ready to play rough; the way women prefer to play when they are out together, and no one expects them home early.

After the game on the beach concluded, Stint and the women lay exhausted in the shade, sipping fermented pineapple milk. Suddenly Stint had an idea. He sat up and faced the Ten.

"Ladies, I would like you all to return with me to my ship. I want you to meet my intrepid crew and dine with us tonight. We have many fine things to eat and drink aboard the *Sea Witch*. And we have a shower with hot water and towels made from Egyptian cotton grown in

Giza, between the Sahara Desert, the Mediterranean Sea, and the Nile. And may I also point out; each towel has a 500-thread count."

Captain Stint was silent for a moment, then his eyes, the color of the sea after a storm, grew large: "Oh!" he said. "You ladies do like rum, don't you?"

"What do you have up your sleeve, Captain," said Mary, the Scot. "Will you be trying to have your way with us?"

Stint smiled and lifted his naked arms. "As you can see, dear Mary, with ankles to marvel at, I've nothing up my sleeves."

Stint got up and walked behind a coconut tree to pee. Mary looked at her island sisters, then laughed and sang as a schoolgirl might:

"He wants to woo me. He wants to roger me."

† † †

That night aboard Stint's Jamaica Sloop, *Banana Daquiris, Pena Coladas, and Blackberry Mojitos* flowed from the bar where Michelle from Marseilles was pouring.

When Pip, the Cabin Boy, saw starry-eyed Crystal studying him like she would some rare, beautiful *avem caduca,*[62] he looked at Stint for clarification. Stint winked and tossed Pip a bottle of *151 Rum* to take to the Main Deck. Pip and Crystal would be alone, except for Jacque the Mule and Billie the she-goat; they were in the lifeboat playing Backgammon for a shilling a point.

---

[62] *avem caduca.* Latin, meaning "bird to be plucked."

Dinner would be by candlelight, using silver candelabra that Stint liberated from a Spanish merchant ship near Saint Augustine, on Florida's southern tip, the year before.

Pip went to the galley to prepare dinner while Crystal folded napkins and grinned like the cat that just ate the canary.

For the feast, Pip prepared grilled lobster, *Crab Louis*, *Lasagna Primavera,* Southern Fried shrimp, baked cinnamon apples, steamed yams drenched with "*Like Butter*," California Rolls, Stint's famous *Challah*, topped with orange marmalade, and lastly, Corn Dogs with *Champagne Mustard*. For dessert, there was Key Lime Pie— Pip's whore of a mother's recipe.

Long into the night, laughter, merriment, and lawyer jokes abounded. When Stint's guests were full, near to bursting, Stint got down to business and did so on bended knee.

"I implore you, ladies, to come with me as my new best friends forever. Be part of my crew. To share equally in whatever fortune comes our way. Be they good days, bad days, richer or poorer, sickness and health, rum or no rum. What sayest you wenches fair?"

"Arrrrgh!" said the Ten in unison.

†††

Handsome Jonny Stint was a wayward wind, a restless wind that yearned to wander, and now with his new crew, Stint was revitalized. His restless spirit was for once at peace.

Thus, Handsome Jonny sailed for distant waters in good company, still wearing his loincloth, more or less.

†††

Three weeks later, the *Sea Witch* entered the harbor of Boston, Massachusetts.

In the most daring daylight robbery ever recorded in the Thirteen colonies, ten lovely, bare-breasted women accompanied by a mule entered the Royal Bank of Boston and robbed it of over Twenty-thousand pounds, Sterling. Today, that's like a zillion dollars in U.S. currency.

They departed from the bank without firing a shot, leaving a bevy of flabbergasted Bostonians unsure of what they'd witnessed and wondering if it had, indeed, occurred. It had!

The *Sea Witch* departed from Boston Harbor with the authorities close behind. Once at sea, however, Stint's Jamaica Sloop quickly outdistanced the frigates and cannon shots of three of his Majesty's fastest frigates.

The British were pursuing what forty-four-year-old publisher and inventor Benjamin Franklin[63] hailed in his weekly periodical as—

---

[63] Regarded as one of America's "Founding Fathers," Ben Franklin was an inventor, publisher, philosopher, womanizer, the Ambassador to France, and he didn't own any slaves [Almanac of Unapologetic Facts. Misty Bay Books. 1st Edition. 2021].

"A daring robbery, brazen with originality, and in broad daylight, committed by an audacious band of bare-breasted pirates and a mule."

A pen-and-ink illustration accompanied Franklin's *reportage,* but lest it is considered scandalous, as surely it would have been in 1750, the illustrator was careful to put "pasties" on the women and underwear on the mule.

† † †

Notwithstanding the numerous rumors about him, the *Sea Witch,* and his unusual choice for a crew, Jonny Stint was never seen or heard from again.

That's not entirely true. A "Stringer"[64] for the *London Daily Mail* THOUGHT she spotted Stint in Honolulu, shopping at the *Ala Moana Shopping Center,* for razor blades and ladies dainties.

So! What became of this storied Irish Captain, this "enigma, wrapped in a ~~condom~~ conundrum, shrouded in mystery"?

Only *the Shadow* knows.

---

[64] *Stringer* is the name given to a free-lance journalist writing for, but not officially attached to, any specific news gathering agency.

21.

Szah Zhah Kopeč

In the year, Seventeen-Hundred and Seventy-Six, delegates representing the American Colonies met in Philadelphia, Pennsylvania, to proclaim their collective grievances to the King of England, the so-called "Mad King," King George III.

One of these delegates, Thomas Jefferson, was appointed to birth a letter that would give Mad George the straight dope by listing the colonists' complaints in no uncertain terms. Given the year when Jefferson wrote this remarkably rad document, the ideas it contained were unthinkable, treasonous even, what the world would come to know as the *American Declaration of Independence*.

Just as important for purposes of this story, forty-seven years earlier, an entire ocean away, in the ancient city of *Aquincum*, a child was born in what is today the city of Budapest. A female child, pink and plump, with rosy cheeks, jet-black hair, and eyes the color of violets. Her mother, Sosia, was a nineteen-year-old courtesan, a dark-haired beauty, who went where the Royal Hungárián army marched. She did this to comfort a virile, young Hungárián Prince whenever needed, which meant—nightly.

Exactly! It wasn't long before Sosia found herself pregnant, something she realized during the prince's siege of a castle in Croatia.

When it rains, it pours!

The year? Seventeen-Hundred-and-twenty-Nine. Centuries of war with the Turkish Ottoman Empire and the Austrians ravaged the land, inviting long years of misery, hardship, and famine.

Terrified of losing favor with her virile, young prince, Sosia sold her baby to a passing band of gypsies, the Romany Fingos, for one gold ducat, which, if you think about it, was not an unreasonable sum for a baby in 1729. The Gold Ducat was one the Fingos liberated from the pocket of its rightful owner the night before.

As for the baby's biological mother, Sosia never questioned selling her baby until years later, on her death bed, while dying of advanced syphilis.

† † †

The Fingos were a large family of some forty souls and were especially adept at showing a profit on their investments. The item or commodity didn't matter. Obtaining a monetary benefit was essential, given the amount of effort the Fingos exerted merely staying alive.

A toothless, world-wise crone named Zordona Fingo led this tribe of wayfaring fortune tellers, musicians, acrobats, poachers, and pickpockets. She was esteemed, feared, and regarded as royalty among the broader Romany community in Austro-Hungary. No one knew Zordona's exact age, except that it was considerable, a fact attested to by the number of accordion-like folds in her face. Of the nineteen children she birthed, none had thus far managed to survive her.

At Zordona's side was her fourth husband, Emil. Having worn out her previous three spouses, Zordona wisely chose a man-child to attend her incestuous bed. More brawn than brains, with large black eyes and hawk-like features, Emil was promptly married to Zordona following his fifteenth winter on earth, which is how Fingos reckon age, by the number of winters accrued.

They sat inside Zordona's caravan while outside, it stormed.

"What will thee name her?" said Emil, now twenty-four winters old. They looked at the baby nursing from the teat of Emil's lover and cousin, Hydrangea.

"Yes," said Hydrangea. "What will thee name her, Great Mother?"

Zordona inhaled deeply from her pipe, then exhaled a bluish stream of smoke over Hydrania and the baby.

"Szah Zhah," said Zordona. "I will name her, Szah Zhah, after my own mother."

"Very pretty," said Hydrangea, "Does it have a meaning?"

Zordona lowered her pipe away from her mouth and shook with laughter. "Yes," she said. "It means *terrible beauty.*"

Zordona Fingo continued laughing long into the night.

With age comes entitlement.

† † †

With the Fingos, Szah Zhah learned skills that helped her survive in the harsh, unforgiving world she inherited, a world incredibly hostile to gypsies, for the Fingos were an ancient free-folk, wanderers on the earth with no fixed place to call "home," meaning a place where they could live unmolested by those unlike them. Those who lived attached to the land and shunned these strange, dark wanderers, calling them *az ördög gyermekei*[65].

By the time she was five winters old, the Fingos had taught Szah Zhah how to pick a villager's pocket without them being the wiser. It was a feat accomplished in the main by rewarding Szah Zhah with a cookie made of *Marcipán*.[66]

Szah Zhah learned other practical skills as well: if left to her own devices, she knew how to find and identify edible plants, berries, and roots in the dark of the forest. She learned how to capture, kill, and skin small animals—squirrels, rats, and rabbits, sometimes dogs, and how to roast them to perfection over a small fire.

Szah Zhah had an agile mind, was fleet of foot, and had the makings of a beautiful young woman at thirteen. So much so, all the Fingos agreed: *"Let's sell her!"*

After Szah Zhah's first *menses*, Zordona sold her for ten gold ducats to an influential and notorious procuress, Alexandria Alucard, a middle-aged Madam of an upscale whorehouse in the Transylvanian tourist town of Kopeĉ. Not a bad return on Zordona's original investment of one gold ducat.

Considering Szah Zhah was a virgin when Zordona sold her, that clever, toothless queen of gypsies knew Szah Zhah was well worth ten gold ducats in hand.

---

[65] Old Hungarian, meaning "children of the Devil."
[66] Old Hungarian, for Marzipan.

22.

Life Is for The Living

For seven days, Angel slept without waking. Having decided it best not to move her, Angel remained in one of the doctor's upstairs bedrooms. Jonny slept there also, on the floor, with Whiskey. Otherwise, Jonny reclined in a chair by the window downstairs in the doctor's library, shotgun across his lap. Jonny was sure he heard the howls of at least two wolves beyond the tree line late the night before, but this was *San Souci*, where wild things live in abundance. When Jonny mentioned what he heard during the night, Helwing merely shrugged.

"These days, Jonny, my hearing is not so good. I heard nothing."

And you're a damn liar, Doc! Jonny told himself.

† † †

While Doctor Helwing walked Whiskey early every morning, Jonny Fiáin spoke softly to Angel as she slept. He told her stories about him and Paddy, mostly when they were schoolboys in New Dublin, admitting to her closed eyes that he and Paddy were juvenile delinquents. Jonny bragged to Angel about her mom, how Sarah got straight-As in High School but still found time to practice archery and let off steam with Paddy and Jonny on weekends.

Jonny told Angel a little—what was fit to tell—about their time in the Marines and what they did in the Pacific. Whether Angel understood anything he said was something Jonny could abide by. If the sound of Jonny's voice could be a beacon, showing Angel the way back to the land of the living; then, so be it; he would go on talking.

† † †

Eight days to the day following the creature's attack that left her parents dead and Angel severely wounded, Angel O'Hara sat up, stretched her arms over her head, and smiled.

"I'm hungry," she said.

Jonny leaped from the chair to Angel's bedside. She smiled at him, and as she smiled, Jonny felt the air yanked from his lungs. Angel's eyes were now a bright violet. Seeing Angel cock her head to one side and look at him, perplexed, Jonny put on a smile, albeit fake.

"Why are you staring at me like that, Jonny?"

"I'm sorry, Angel darlin'. Telling me you're hungry is the most wonderful thing I've heard in quite a while."

"Well, something smells wonderful," said Angel.

Puzzled by the strange new color of Angel's eyes, plus the fact she smelled something, and so vividly which he couldn't detect, Jonny tilted his head a second time and sniffed the air—he detected nothing, apart from latent traces of the doctor's unique blend of cherry and apricot-flavored marijuana pipe tobacco coming from the doctor's bedroom down the hall.

Jonny laughed. "Pipe tobacco?"

"No," said Angel. "someone's making *Crepes Suzette* in the kitchen. I can smell caramelized sugar, white-butter sauce, tangerine juice, orange zest, and *Grand Marnier*, like what mom and dad drank by the fireplace on cold nights."

Too stunned to say anything for probably ten seconds, "That," said Jonny, finally, "would be Doctor Helwing in the kitchen cooking. He also patched you up."

As if on cue, Doctor Helwing entered with Whiskey. The sight of Angel sitting in bed, alert and conversing, brought a smile to the doctor's wrinkled face.

Whiskey raced into the room and leaped onto Angel's bed. Whiskey began licking Angel's face while she laughed and rubbed behind his ears.

Okay, boy," said Angel, still laughing. "No more kisses. That's enough."

"I heard voices," said Helwing, looking in at Angel.

"Come in, Doctor," said Jonny. "Angel, this is Doctor Helwing. We've been his guests here."

"Hello, Doctor. Where is, here?" said Angel.

"You're in the village of *Sans Souci*," said Helwing. "In New Brunswick, Canada." Doctor Helwing looked at Jonny. "Her eyes?"

"I know," said Jonny.

"What ABOUT my eyes?" said Angel.

"They're beautiful," said Helwing. "Absolutely, stunning."

Angel threw the covers to one side.

"Hold on, Angel," said Jonny.

"I want to see my eyes," said Angel.

"You feel up to standing?" said Jonny.

"Of course," said Angel.

There was something about the sound of her voice that had changed. It was deeper, not what one would expect from a nine-year-old girl.

"Okay," said Jonny. "But I removed your cast. You sure you want to do this?"

Angel didn't wait. She swung her legs over the side of the bed and hopped to her feet before Jonny, or the doctor could prevent her.

Angel dashed into the bathroom, shut the door behind, and stared at her eyes in the mirror. They were no longer what she remembered; instead, they had turned deepest violet.

When Angel left the bathroom, she looked at Jonny and Helwing. "What's happened to me?"

"Do you remember being attacked?" said Jonny.

"Yes," said Angel. "A little."

Doctor Helwing felt Angel's forehead and looked again at Jonny.

"Not the slightest trace of fever. How does your back feel, Angel?"

"Fine," said Angel. "Why?"

Jonny and the doctor exchanged looks. "May I take a look?" said Helwing.

Angel nodded. Angel wore a pair of the doctor's pajamas. By no means a tall man, Helwing's custom-tailored, embroidered silk pajama from Hong Kong was almost a good fit for Angel.

The doctor lifted the pajama top and removed Angel's bandage. Her wounds appeared healed. The hundred or more, small, black cross-stitches meant to hold Angel's sundered flesh together were a stark contrast to the bright, pink tissue that had filled in and nearly covered the cuts made by the creature's claws.

"Amazing," said Helwing.

In the Pacific, Jonny had seen first-hand the way war could violate the human body. When he looked at

Angel's back, what he saw wasn't natural, not for cuts as deep as Angel suffered.

"It sure is," said Jonny.

"I'm starving," said Angel.

"Come, *mes amis*," said Helwing. "Breakfast awaits."

† † †

Watching Angel wolf-down crepe after crepe drenched in white-butter sauce; then devour scrambled eggs with melted goats' milk cheese, along with helpings of thick, crisp bacon; ham, and sausage, Jonny marveled over her robust appearance. Once more, Angel's cheeks were rose-colored, her eyes bright and clear, albeit they were now violet. To see Angel O'Hara eating with such abandon, the casual observer might conclude nothing terrible had ever happened to her in her entire, sweet, brief lifetime.

No way, Jonny told himself: *Her eyes? Violet colored? And her leg, working as good as new? The way she's acting? The way her wounds have healed—this can't be right. Something's wrong. And why hasn't she mentioned Sarah and Paddy? Why isn't she crying her eyes out like a normal kid?*

He saw Doctor Helwing turn his professional gaze away from Angel. The look on Helwing's face suggested the doctor was similarly perplexed by Angel's startling recovery, her violet eyes, and her outward mental state.

While Angel and Whiskey accompanied the doctor for a stroll through the countryside, questions raced through Jonny's mind, problems that piled on one another like rugby players pushing, pulling, snarling, gouging at one another until it gave him a headache.

As for answers to those questions—the jumble that ran roughshod through his mind? Zero! Zip! Zilch! Nyet! Nada! Nothing!

23.

Back on Martinique

While the moon waxed full over Martinique's Heart of Darkness, Headstone cultivated each day by learning from old Aristotle, Master of the Gray Brethren's Chapter on Martinique. Aristotle knew of the Gray Brethren's origin, their place in the world, and the ways of the Pack—male and female.

The nights? Headstone spent dancing the *Méringue*; it was mandatory to learn to hunt in a pack, and line-dancing was good preparation.

For his initiation, Headstone accompanied the Brethren for three consecutive nights when the moon was brightest. They snatched their prey from outlying towns and were always successful. Why? Because they knew how to hunt without being heard or seen. The Pack acquired the blood they required to maintain their strength and longevity by snatching panhandlers, scroungers, drifters, drug dealers, and prostitutes off the streets—in a word, they took riffraff no one would miss, with the possible exception of prostitutes.

Night after night, the Brethren marveled at Headstone's speed and his agility and skill with his claws. They heaped praise upon him from dawn to dusk—*L'Enfant terrible*, this terrible child, now a *Tonton Macoute*.

Aunt Lily could not have been happier. She knew her heart could be at peace since her nephew's future was now secure. The Pack would be his family. They would always be there for him, and no matter where he traveled, Headstone would always have friends who would welcome him into their homes and hearts.

† † †

"After He whose true Name we dare not speak, cast the Dark Lord from Heaven, in his great rage, the Dark Lord mated with an Alpha wolf, here, on earth. Together they conceived the forerunners of our kind—the Werewolves, who became Mankind's mortal enemy and still are just as the Dark Lord desired. It was how he first sought revenge on the All-Father, whose true name we dare not speak."

"For thousands of years, werewolves flourished until a great plague struck—one that reached the four corners of the earth and reduced their number to but a few. Yet, some survived. They became stronger, smarter, and fleeter than the Werewolves. More importantly, Balthazar, these few could transform from man to wolf, or wolf to man, at will. No longer did the moon have to be full to effectuate the change. We, the Tonton Macoutes, or Weirdwolves in your tongue, are their progeny. Their blood flows in your blood, thanks to our sister, Ishrael Kerrier, who bit you in your buttock. May she rest in peace."

Thus, from old Aristotle, Balthazar Headstone learned of himself and his ilk—part human, part wolf, all killer.

† † †

When it came time to depart, there was a grand celebration in the Heart of Darkness with over three hundred Weirdwolves in attendance, male and female.

Following the celebration, Aristotle, the Grand Master of the Caribbean Pack, would return with his entourage to the island of Hispaniola where he grew and cultivated sugar cane; others would remain on Martinique, where they were shopkeepers, and farmers, in the ordinary scheme of things.

Some, like Aunt Lily and Balthazar, would return to Jamaica. Aunt Lily would resume telling fortunes, do Tarot card readings, or mix herbal love potions for lovestruck girls trying to snare a husband. The Pack provided Balthazar with a plausible 'cover,' employed by a female Weirdwolf named Katarina Bukowski, who owned and operated a *curios and keepsakes* shop for tourists on the waterfront in Kingston. Aristotle selected Katarina to continue and refine Headstone's education in the ways of the Pack.

Aristotle consulted Aunt Lily regarding this arrangement, and Lily approved. She had 'seen' great things ahead for Balthazar; she would not stand in the way of him manifesting his potential; besides, Lily intuitively knew Balthazar needed another kind of influence in his life, what only a remarkable woman could provide. Katarina Bukowski was such a woman— even better that Katarina was a *Tonton Macoute*—a Weirdwolf.

† † †

Following a devastating earthquake in 1692 that destroyed Port Royal, Kingston flourished as the Sodom AND Gomorrah of the Caribbean. It was soon able to claim Port Royal's reputation as *the wickedest city in the world.*

Far from offending Governor Trelawny's sensibilities, he welcomed the notoriety Kingston was getting as a Free Trade Zone. Pirates from as far away as Madagascar would come to Kingston, Jamaica. There they could sell their stolen wares to eager buyers at prices slashed to rock-bottom or something like that.

Governor Trelawny welcomed these international privateers, the scourges of the Seven Seas. For one thing, they knew better than to attack vessels flying the Union Jack—Britain's colors, and secondly, their presence throughout the year, excepting the hurricane season, dissuaded Spanish, French, and Portuguese privateers from raiding Jamaican waters.

† † †

The Weird Wolves living in Jamaica also benefitted from the Governor's *live and let live policy.* Pirates, not thought of particularly as exemplary human beings, shunned the manners of polite society. During those turbulent times of global colonization, they eschewed what the civilized world deemed proper social intercourse. They, these rowdy fellows who flew the Jolly Roger—the skull and crossbones, would steal the eyes from a blind man or sully the virtue of their mother

for a single gold doubloon. Buccaneers lived according to *The Code*—THEIR code—the Pirates' Code!
Arrrgh!

† † †

When their appetite for blood burned hot, Balthazar and Katarina would wait until the early hours of the morning. Like a couple out for an evening stroll, they scoured Kingston's back alleys in the vicinity of the waterfront, where pirates moored their vessels to any one of twenty piers that jutted into the calm waters of the harbor. When there were no piers to tie up to, pirates would drop anchor offshore and use lifeboats to access the waterfront, but not the town.

Governor Trelawny had made the city streets of Kingston "off-limits," and the Hessians[67] he employed for security made sure no one but residents came and went freely to Kingston.

† † †

Finding some scoundrel three sheets to the wind, staggering and stumbling while trying to find his way back to his ship, Katarina would approach the reprobate and engage him in conversation—just silliness. At the same time, Balthazar would come up quietly from behind and break the blackguard's neck.

Tossing the corpse over his shoulder, Balthazar and Katarina would seek out a place in the sugarcane fields, and there they would dine.

---

[67] Hessians were German soldiers from the state of Hesse who sold their services to the British on an "as needed" basis during the 18th century, and beyond.

After a hellacious time at sea, pirates often went missing once ashore. In that regard, they were like rats. No one would miss them when they went away, the same as politicians.

† † †

Balthazar Headstone was deliriously happy with himself and his new life with Katarina. In her arms, he experienced untold pleasures that left him exhausted yet craving more of the intoxicating elixir that emanated from Katarina's pores.

Katarina Bukowski was a well-read woman with copper-colored hair that hung to the middle of her back. A graduate from the University of Krakow, in Poland, Katarina had read the love poems of *Omar Kayam* as a girl, but only after rereading them, as a woman, did she understand and fully grasp the truth—that one had to surrender a part of oneself, no matter how painful, to truly love another.

She had read the anonymous work, *1001 Arabian Nights*, and from the book's heroine, *Scheherazade*, Katarina learned how to tame a man's inner beast. Not to make him docile, but receptive, that he might partake of the mysteries a woman and only a woman can illuminate.

From the *Kama Sutra,* Katarina added to her knowledge of how a man and a woman, meeting as equals in a quintessential union where each merges the life force of the other, transports both as one to a realm of pure energic being.

If the heights of ecstasy can be reached by humans, thought Katarina, *then why not Weirdwolves?* It was a thoughtful question, deserving of a thoughtful answer.

It made sense. Early in life, Katarina learned the trick for building a successful partnership: *"meet as friends, and perform as lovers."*

Not so easy as it sounds.

† † †

Aunt Lily took Balthazar aside one morning when he and Katarina came to visit. Lily saw the great joy that now resided within her nephew, recast, as Fate would have him.

"There is a saying from the Orient, Balthazar," said Lily. Do you understand its meaning?" "Your best friend died, one hundred years before you were born; your soul mate was born, one hundred years after you die."

"No, Auntie. I do not."

"Live, Balthazar! Live! Love! And laugh! Do so with all your being. But do so without becoming attached. I say this now, lest you suffer when that which gives you cause to 'live, love,' and laugh' is one day gone forever."

"Do you mean Katarina, Auntie? Have you seen things? In one of your visions? Tell me, Auntie."

Lily got up to leave. "I fear I have already said too much, Balthazar. Just remember, I love you and will always be here for you."

† † †

It happened near the waterfront in Kingston. Balthazar and Katarina had closed their souvenir shop and packed a basket with bread, cheese, and wine. It was their first anniversary together, and they decided to celebrate, first by seeing what new ships had arrived in Kingston; then, they would go home and make love.

Just after sunset, they took a shortcut to the waterfront along Thieves Alley. Three randy sailors off a British Merchant ship, the *Minotaur,* approached them from the other direction.

"Look there, mates!" said one of the sailors. He was young, had a crooked jaw, and a scar across the bridge of his nose. "Now, isn't that a sight? As fine a white woman as we're likely to see in Jamaica, tied up arm-in-arm, all cozy with a darkie."

"Her slave, I'll wager," said another of the three.

Balthazar stopped.

"No, Balthazar," said Katarina. "Pay them no mind. They're stupid and drunk."

"Balthazar?" said the sailor with the crooked jaw.

"What kind of name is that for a darkie?"

His companions laughed. Balthazar moved Katarina to one side and faced the sailors.

"I am a freeman, "said Balthazar. "A Jamaican, by birth. I won't have you insulting this fine lady or me."

"Oh, a LADY, is she?" said Crooked Jaw. His companions laughed. "Well, now, darkie. Let's see if she shags like one."

Crooked Jaw looked at his shipmates. "What do you say? Shall we have a go with this piece of ginger?"

A crushing blow from Balthazar's clenched right fist flattened Crooked Jaw's nose and sent him flying onto his back.

The other two sailors rushed forward. Balthazar grabbed the closest one by the shoulders and hurled him to one side against a brick wall. The third sailor, and the last still on his feet, drew a knife and was about to plant it into Balthazar's back when Katarina stepped between the knife-wielding sailor and her beloved. The blade entered Katarina's chest and pierced her heart. When she crumpled onto the cobblestones, she was already dead. The three sailors took off running down the alley, headed, no doubt, for the safety of their ship.

Balthazar knelt beside Katarina; he held her lifeless body in his arms and wept hot tears mixed with rage that stung his cheeks as they glided down his face.

Balthazar scooped Katarina into his arms and carried her into the jungle. He took her to a secluded place where they often went to feast, dance, and imbibe the camaraderie other Weirdwolves provided.

† † †

Balthazar and six close friends, all Weirdwolves, waited until after midnight before they reentered Kingston and proceeded past the City Watch unchallenged.

After crushing the Night Watch's skull, they boarded the *Minotaur* and made their way below deck to the crew's quarters.

Balthazar and his friends wasted no time looking for the three sailors responsible for Katarina's death; they killed everyone aboard. However, when Balthazar did find Crooked Jaw asleep in his hammock, Headstone awakened the sailor by cutting out his tongue and eating it. When they had had their revenge, Balthazar and his friends quietly departed and returned to the jungle.

In Jamaica's Heart of Darkness, Balthazar buried Katarina Bukowski, along with the dreams he made.

There is an ancient adage: *If you want to hear God laugh, tell Her your plans.* [68]

---

[68] Author unknown.

24.

In Due Course

Had someone of good breeding with above-average intelligence told Szah Zhah Kopeč, *"patience is a virtue*[69]*,"* Szah Zhah would have gutted such a *hüsenpilfer*[70] with a dull, butter-knife. Why? Because, at its very root, to have "patience" means "to willfully suffer," and willfully suffering was something Szah Zhah successfully eluded for two hundred years.

True. Two centuries had passed since Szah Zhah's last *menses*, but what did occur, ever so faithfully every twenty-eight days, give or take a day when the moon waxed full, Szah Zhah became hungry for blood—Homo Sapiens' blood, rich in iron and free of disease. A-Positive, when she could get it from girls with fluff for brains.

It was just such a craving that guided her over the waves and through the fog to the lighthouse on Bette's Chin and the dwelling where the O'Haras once happily resided.

It would be three weeks, at minimum, before the craving returned. For now, Szah Zhah was content with the meals Headstone prepared. How she managed for herself without him close at hand is a question for the Ages; however, the thought of someday not having him around made her shudder, so she made a point not to

---

[69] Obviously spoken by a *hüsenpilfer* who never suffered a wit, also known as a *Bliss Ninny,* first cousin to a *Backwoods Bruce*!

[70] A *"Backwoods Bruce"* is another damn near insufferable sort—a bloviating dolt, known, more simply, as a *Know-it-all*!

contemplate it. Mostly when he was off on a dangerous errand, as he was then; some people are good at shutting out uncomfortable thoughts—what others pay psychologists and psychiatrists a pretty penny to sort through and recycle. Szah Shah, however, was of the former and nary the latter.

† † †

The sound of the dory bumping against the side of the *Horror* made Szah Zhah giddy; it always did because it was the sound of Balthazar returning. It was no different for Balthazar. Each time he returned, the look on Szah Zhah's face was worth the many dangers he faced when out in the world at her behest.

Balthazar and Szah Zhah were not merely man and woman in the conventional sense, meaning two sides of the same coin; they were otherworldly beings, creatures whose fates interlocked and had remained that way while the years passed like grains of sand through an hourglass.

† † †

After securing the dory to the stern of the *Horror*, Headstone scarcely had time to catch his breath when Szah Zhah stepped into his muscular arms and kissed him hard on the mouth. She reached down between his legs and squeezed his love app(s).

"I've missed you, my Nubian prince," she said.

Her husky voice was full to the gunnels with desire; still, first things first. She released her grip on her paramour and stepped back.

"What of the girl, my love? The little mouse? Did you find her?"

"Rejoice, Mistress, I did indeed find your 'little mouse.' The New England Association of Weirdwolves is maintaining constant vigilance over her every move."

"Truly, Balthazar? They can do this?"

"Yes, but it won't be easy long term, my pet. Weirdwolves have lives of their own, and all but a few work full time. But, yes. We can do what you have asked. There is nowhere the *fasz* can take the girl without the Gray Brethren knowing."

"WONDERFUL, Balthazar. The news you bring is wonderful. I haven't been able to eat a thing since you went off on business."

"Anything you want from Room Service?" said Headstone.

Szah Zhah laughed a naughty lusty laugh that marinated in her belly before she yelled, "Loin chops, my beautiful *Tonton Macoute*! RARE!"

25.

Corned Beef on Rye

Miles Standish hadn't taken long to contact the U.S Marshal's District Office in Albuquerque, New Mexico. Mesa had discovered a promising lead, and Standish wanted the New Mexico office to reach out to the District Office in Central Illinois to determine if one of the traceable items stolen from the National Guard armory in Peoria, Illinois was a motorcycle with a side-car attached.

When the answer came back in the affirmative, Standish and Mesa celebrated by having lunch in O'Doole's Irish Pub, much to the chagrin of O'Doole, who, although mightily tempted, kept from spitting on the corned beef on rye before it left his kitchen.

After the waitress delivered two schooners of cold beer and their lunch, Mesa turned to Standish: "You don't think the old man spit on these, do you?"

Standish was keenly aware of the tricks Irishmen played on those they disliked and was about to bite into his corn beef on rye, heavy with mustard and sour pickles, then hesitated. That was enough for Mesa. He also knew such ill-natured pranks happened to law enforcement officers the world over.

Sitting as they were at the bar, Albert Mesa took his sandwich apart, bit by bit, with a knife and fork. After a thorough examination, Mesa concluded his lunch was safe to eat. Verily, it turned out to be a damn good corn beef on rye. The key is to use the right mustard.

Standish turned the Zippo lighter Mesa found side to side, examining it. "Which direction do you think Fiáin is going?"

Mesa swallowed a mouthful of corn beef and dill pickle, washed it down with a gulp of cold beer, then dabbed the mustard away from the corners of his mouth.

"This close to the border?" said Mesa. "I'd say he's headed north to Canada."

"I agree," said Standish. "Which is why we're going to pay our respects to our colleagues at the District Office in Portland."

"You want to drive to Portland, Oregon?" said Mesa.

Standish groaned. "No! Portland, MAINE!"

"I thought the District Office was in Augusta?" said Mesa. "Augusta, Georgia?" said Standish.

"No. Augusta, MAINE."

"Are you saying that's where the capital is? Augusta, MAINE?!"

"Yes," said Mesa.

Standish grinned. "Jeez, Louise. I must've forgotten that! Damn! Let this be a lesson to you, Mesa— you're never too old to remember something new."

"Won't argue with that, partner," said Mesa, using a smidgen of his capacity for patience.

"Fiáin has a head start, but we're going to get that bastard," said Standish. "Let's tell the Chief in New Dublin what you found."

† † †

"You're certain?" said the Chief, looking at the two marshals standing shoulder to shoulder in front of him. Chief McKuen returned the Zippo to Marshal Mesa.

"Yes," said Mesa, pocketing the lighter. "One-hundred percent."

"It's true, Chief," said Standish. "Have your people check what's out there drying in the mud. And the lighter? That HAS to be Jonny Fiáin's."

"So, what you deputies are suggesting is that Jonny Fiáin set fire to the house and left those tracks?"

"Yes," said Standish.

A mixture of weariness and worry took over McKuen's voice. "The O'Haras. They have a nine-year-old daughter. Angel. We recovered no trace of her among the ruins. After what Deputy Marshal Mesa discovered, I can't exclude the possibility that Angel O'Hara might still be alive."

"Holy Mary, Mother of God," said Standish, a man not at all religious. "Fiáin probably murdered the parents, set the house on fire, and kidnapped the daughter!"

"Hold on right there, Marshal Standish. You don't know that. I don't know that. The truth is, we don't know squat, except two folks are dead, and the fire was allegedly an act of arson, allegedly perpetrated by Jonny Fiáin." It helped remind Chief McKuen he was a lawman, using words like allegedly, and perpetrated.

"Yes," said Mesa. "The tracks are from a 1943 Harley- Davidson WLA, mass-produced during the war with a sidecar attached, the same as was taken—"

"Deputy Marshal Mesa means 'stolen,'" said Standish, interrupting.

"All right," said Mesa. "STOLEN, from the National Guard armory in Peoria, Illinois by Jonny Fiáin and his gang."

Chief McKuen leaned back in the large oak swivel chair he preferred over the modern metal office chairs being mass-produced, now that the war was over. The chair was a present from the New Dublin Lions' Club for the chief's fiftieth birthday. It was also in recognition of McKuen's continued success in minimizing crime throughout the county. It was only right the community should give him something more than the niggardly amount the City Council was paying him.

"We'll go out there again and check for ourselves," said the Chief. "But if you're right, this damn well changes everything."

"Oh, we're not wrong, Chief," said Standish. "But why does it change everything? I don't follow."

"The family that died that night—" "The O'Haras?" said Mesa.

"Jonny Fiáin wouldn't murder Paddy and Sarah," said Chief McKuen. "Christ! They were best friends. Jonny and Paddy served together in the Marine Corps. Jonny Fiáin may be a killer, but he's no murderer."

"Fair enough," said Standish, "but I trust my gut, and right now, it's telling me Jonny Fiáin set the fire and has the girl."

"If that's true," said McKuen, "Then I'm obliged to contact the FBI. They have jurisdiction when it comes to kidnapping. If Fiáin takes Angel out of state, Angel being under-age, and all, that opens another can of worms."

Chief McKuen watched the two marshals leave his office before grabbing his wastebasket and upchucking what remained of his breakfast.

† † †

In their vehicle, driving toward Portland (Maine), Mesa used Jonny's Zippo to light a rum-soaked Crook, Crooks being the kind of cigarillo he was fond of smoking. Plus, Mesa enjoyed the collateral notion of 'smoking crooks'; not that he particularly enjoyed killing 'bad guys," Mesa did what he needed to do, and he did it exceedingly well.

Mesa also didn't object to doing the driving while Standish stared out the window, deep in thought, like he always seemed to be when they were going somewhere. It was as if Standish was playing a game of chess with Fiáin, planning his moves. *Then, again*, Mesa told himself, *maybe Standish isn't thinking at all. Perhaps Standish is a 'Checkers' man and hates Chess?* Mesa didn't have any way of knowing. In any case, he enjoyed these moments of silence. It gave him time to ponder the evidence. Mesa didn't agree with most of what came out of Standish's mouth, but so far, it hadn't mattered. The former Texas Ranger would continue to give Standish the benefit of the doubt until it did matter, which is to say when their lives were on the line.

As they entered Portland's City Limits, Standish looked at Mesa and grinned. "I just figured out how we're going to get the bastard. We're going to use the girl as bait. When we do, Fiáin's going to bite. That's when we'll hook him. Just you wait and see, Albert."

"What about the FBI?" said Mesa.

"What about them? They have their jurisdiction. We have ours. As the saying goes: 'May the best team win!' Hell! That's going to be us! You feel me, Partner?"

"Can't say as I do," said Mesa.

"Well, forget the F-B-I! Angel O'Hara is going to be our *Trojan Horse*, and Fiáin's *Achilles Heel* all in one."

Albert Mesa took driving seriously. He kept both hands on the wheel in the "10 and 2 o'clock" position to wit. He preferred that over the "9 and 3 o'clock" position favored by bus drivers, truckers, and the California Highway Patrol.

Standish sensed a look of skepticism straddling Mesa's face.

"For crying out loud, Mesa! Have you never read the *Iliad* by an old Greek, by the name of Homer?"

"Nope," said the former Texas Ranger, "I'm more of a Zane Grey guy. You know, 'Riders of the Purple Sage'?"

26.

Hope

Chief McKuen thought it best if everyone was together when he gave them the news. Lawrence McLaughlin and Seamus O'Hara elected to stand, as did Father Timothy, an androgynous sort. The good father was there because he Baptized Angel and thought his job demanded he be present. Rose McLaughlin and Alyssa O'Hara seated themselves across from the Chief.

McKuen could see the dread in the faces of the O'Haras and McLaughlins. The Chief had tasked Annie Liebowitz, his stalwart receptionist, with notifying both sets of parents, telling them only that the Chief wanted to see them immediately in his office.

"I'm so sorry," said Annie. "I don't know what it's about."

That was true. Annie didn't know why A.J. McKuen wanted both sets of parents there. But after twenty years with the Chief and the New Dublin Police Department, Annie's instincts told her *the news* wasn't that good.

Father Timothy had the same grave expression as he always wore. No matter what, his emotions seldom varied when reciting Mass, performing a Baptism, or eulogizing parishioners when it came time to shovel sod over them. After fifty years of sermonizing and hearing Confessions, if Father Timothy believed in anything any longer, he kept it hidden. Some of his devoted flock thought the old priest stashed his faith away with the bottles of Irish Whiskey and Single Malt Scotch he kept hidden in his Study.

"Let's have it, Chief," said Lawrence McLaughlin. McLaughlin's voice was the same authoritative voice he used when questioning his accountants and lawyers regarding his finances or the details of his cannery operation. "You got us down here for a damn good reason. Didn't you?"

McLaughlin was undeniably tense, but with good reason. Something the Chief made allowances for, regardless of who it was addressing him.

"Yes," said the Chief. His voice sounded flat, void of emotion, even to him. He looked up at the clock on the wall.

"Are you expecting someone else, A.J.?" said Seamus O'Hara. He and the Chief occasionally went fishing together in the fall and had always been on the best of terms.

"Yes, Seamus, I am. And they're late."

"Please don't keep us waiting, Chief Standish," said Rose McLaughlin, close to tears.

"I'm sorry, folks. I won't." McKuen cleared his throat and took a deep breath. "I don't want you to get your hopes up, but there's reason to believe Angel's alive."

The reaction from the two mothers was the loudest. They lurched out of their chairs and embraced their husband; then, the women hugged, except for Annie Liebowitz. She was operating her station behind the Front Counter. Everybody hugged, apart from the Chief and the priest.

The Chief was relieved but thought it prudent to maintain a businesslike demeanor, so he didn't react, which some would argue is a reaction all its own. Fair enough. Father Timothy's lips twitched a bit, but he quickly looked up at the ceiling with his eyes closed. No telling what that was all about.

"Where is she, Chief?" said Lawrence McLaughlin, pulling in the reins on the emotional eruption taking place around him.

"Yes, A.J.," said Alyssa O'Hara. "Can you tell us where our granddaughter is?"

"I can't say where Angel is, folks. But I believe she's with Jonny Fiáin."

The parents and priest exclaimed "Jonny FIÁIN!" in unison, loud enough to ripple the water in Betty's bowl, Betty being McKuen's goldfish:

27.

An Eagle Drops In

It was two p.m. the same day when a swarm of unsmiling young men in gray flannel suits from the Federal Bureau of Investigation arrived in New Dublin. They were driving 1947 Ford Station Wagons with blond wood paneling on the sides. FBI Director J. Edgar Hoover wanted the men of his youthful agency to look top-shelf and feel good about themselves and their work defending America and the Constitution against all enemies—foreign AND domestic. Fords were the answer.

It is also true that J. Edgar's Second-in-Command and lover, Clyde Anderson Tolson, procured these spiffy Ford Station Wagons (soon known as "Woodys") from a car dealer the Bureau arrested in Chicago the year before. The FBI suspected the dealer of having ties to Organized Crime—a euphemism for *La Cosa Nostra*.[71]

Americans have always been good at making deals—the car dealer was no exception; neither was J. Edgar Hoover.

---

[71] *La Cosa Nostra* (Italian meaning "Our Thing"), also known as the Mafia or simply, the Mob comprising Italian and Sicilian gangsters as portrayed theatrically in books and in films such as *The Godfather*.

✝ ✝ ✝

Special Agent Neil Pauley graduated *summa cum laude* from the *College of Hard Knocks* in 1939 and immediately enlisted in the United States Army. As an Army parachutist, he first saw action in North Africa.

In the desert in Tunisia, a Fascist Italian Carrier Pigeon dropped an incendiary device intended for General George Patton's Headquarters (H.Q.). The ensuing fire caused a panic in the adjacent Battalion Mess Hall. Soldiers trying to flee nearly trampled Pauley to death; nonetheless, putting himself at great peril, Pauley insisted on staying behind to gather what he could of the silverware and food trays. Because of the trauma and mild burns he sustained, Pauley was furloughed to England to recover from a form of shell shock triggered whenever he came close to a pigeon, stool pigeons excepted. Now, anyone who has lived in or traveled to England, especially the city of London, will tell you: England is no place to have *pigeon phobia*—they're EVERYWHERE! On a more positive note, Pauley did discover what a *bidet* was all about when he mistakenly defecated into one.

✝ ✝ ✝

On D-Day, June 6th, 1944, Pauley once more parachuted behind enemy lines. He landed in the French coastal province of Normandy; got separated from his unit; blundered into a lost, rag-tag squad of Pathfinders, and went off with them, hoping to find other members of his platoon. That didn't happen!

Together, Pauley and his new buddies killed a swarm of Nazis from a *Waffen SS* Regiment, then skedaddled for safety. After hiding in the forest through the night, the next day, they found refuge in the village of *St. Germain-de-Varreville.*

It was in *St. Germain-de-Varreville* where Pauley surrendered his virginity. He gave himself willingly to Madame Celeste Soleil, the young widow of the deceased Mayor, a man forty years older than his comely wife at the time of his mysterious demise from rat poison. One should never leave that stuff willy nilly around the house. That's how nasty accidents happen.

The unwedded bedding of Corporal Neil Pauley took place in the widow's dead husband's wine cellar. For a day and a night, the corporal learned what wine went best with what *entre*, along with other terrific stuff critical to a young man's evolution. It wasn't so much the young soldier's rosy cheeks or boyish good looks; it was his willingness to learn, along with his embryonic, fawn-colored mustache, that tickled the widow's fancy.

Bedding this young man from Hornitos, California (home to the original Ghirardelli's Chocolate factory), was the least the widow could do to show her appreciation to the United States of America. After all, Pauley was risking his life to liberate France from the tyranny of the Nazis. Soon, after that, adequately schooled by the widow and wiser for it, Neil Pauley and the other lost sheep of the Allied Expeditionary Force left St. *Germain-de-Varreville* to rejoin the war in earnest.

† † †

As the American army neared Berlin in early 1945, Pauley's commanding officer's praises brought Pauley to Wild Bill Donovan's attention. Already a legend, Donovan was a maverick in the word's best sense and commanded the Office of Strategic Operations. The OSS was a covert Special Operations unit that conducted hit-and-run missions, primarily assassinations and sabotage, behind enemy lines. None but a few in the Pentagon and the Under Secretary of War, Robert Patterson, knew the OSS existed. To the President, Franklin Delano Roosevelt, they were his private army of "spooks."

† † †

"Chief Standish, I'm Special Agent Neil Pauley, with the FBI." Pauley proffered his official photo ID. "We have jurisdiction over the O'Hara abduction. As of right now, I'm taking charge."

"Of course," said Chief McKuen. "If there's anything I can help you with, Agent Pauley, let me know."

"Thank you, Chief. You can start by providing me directions to the homes of the grandparents: the O'Haras, and the McLaughlins."

"It's right here, Agent Pauley." He handed Pauley a slip of paper with the addresses. "There's a map of our town out front. Missus Leibowitz will show you where you need to go."

"I appreciate that," said Pauley. He turned to leave McKuen's office.

McKuen got to his feet and exclaimed, "I don't think Jonny Fiáin kidnapped Angel O'Hara!"

Pauley stopped at the door and looked back at the chief. "What makes you say that?"

"I've been wrestling with this day and night," said McKuen. I know Jonny Fiáin. He may be many things, and maybe they aren't all good, but Jonny's no kidnapper. If he has Angel O'Hara, there's a good reason for it."

Special Agent Pauley took a moment before replying. "For both their sakes, Chief, I hope you're right."

McKuen went to his office door and closed it. Returning to his desk, McKuen telephoned the O'Hara's, then the McLaughlins, and let them know who to expect within the hour.

28.

Different Than Before

Jonny was performing routine maintenance on the motorcycle when Angel stepped out of the back of the chateau accompanied by the doctor. To see Angel walking without her cast had been a jolt for Jonny, like the change in the color of her eyes and the way she seemed removed from the death of her parents as if it was merely a footnote in her life, something that took place decades, not weeks, before.

† † †

"What's in there?" said Angel. She flicked her head toward the outbuilding that was once a barn behind the doctor's chateau.

At the sight of Angel and the doctor, several full-grown Rottweilers started barking and ran to Van Helwing's side. Pained by the full-throated noise the dogs made, Angel raised her hands over her ears and winced.

"I agree," said Helwing. "They're loud, I know. But they're marvelous watchdogs. Quiet, you beasts!"

The dogs fell silent.

Angel repeated her question. "What's inside the barn, Doctor Helwing?"

"Hah! That's no barn, dear girl. It's where I do my research. But you must never enter there. Do you understand, Angel?"

Angel nodded.

"Good," said Helwing. "Let's continue our walk. There's something I want to show you. I think you'll like it."

† † †

Angel stopped: "Did you hear that?"

"What?" said Helwing.

"Look." Angel pointed.

A hundred yards distant, they saw two deer—a doe and her fawn, nibbling berries. Most certainly, the doctor hadn't heard the deer, not at all, nor had he seen them.

They hadn't gone much further when Angel stopped again. She looked up at a large evergreen tree. In the trunk of the evergreen was a hole in which a squirrel sat chewing on a nut. The squirrel's cheeks puffed out from the amount of food in its mouth, and the sight of it made Angel laugh.

"Someone should tell it to chew with its mouth closed," said Angel, as she resumed walking.

This phenomenon is most strange, thought the doctor. *The girl hears sounds and sees things impossible for an ordinary human to distinguish.*

When they reached the pond, Doctor Helwing took a cargo-pocket *baguette* inside his mackinaw and handed it to Angel. "For the ducks," he said and smiled.

Angel smiled. She pulled the *baguette* apart and cast bread as far from the shore as she could make the pieces sail. The ducks were fine with that and came at flank speed to help themselves to Angel's offerings.

However, the sound of their quacking caused Angel to back up several yards and hold her hands over her ears.

She did this with a pained expression on her face while ducks jostled and jockeyed to get at the bread.

When the ducks claimed the last piece of *baguette*, they moved away, and their quacking dropped off, going from an aquatic cacophony to intermittent single quacks.

Angel returned her hands to her sides.

"Are you all right, Angel?" said Helwing.

"All that quacking," said Angel, "it hurt my ears."

"Mine, too," said Helwing. "Jonny told me about your mother and father, Angel."

It was a lie, but a small lie the doctor could abide. "I'm very sorry, my dear."

Angel looked at the doctor. "Why?"

"Why?" said Helwing, repeating Angel's question.

"Yes," said Angel. "Why are you 'sorry'? You didn't do anything wrong."

The doctor smiled and took a moment to reflect: *In terms of psychological development, truth be told, this girl is no ordinary twelve-year-old.*

Doctor Helwing was, of course, correct. The creature's attack had inexplicably left Angel changed, physically and mentally. She was no one's little girl— not any longer.

"Angel, your power of sight and hearing are much more acute, more so now, than before—yes?"

"I guess so, Doctor. They seem pretty normal to me, though."

"Of course, of course," said Van Helwing. "But tell me, are there other changes, things about yourself that you find different now?"

Angel took a moment to study the doctor's question. "Yes," she said. "I smell things from far away, and I can see at night."

"In the darkness," said Van Helwing.

Angel nodded.

"Does Jonny know?"

"No," said Angel. She started toward the house.

Van Helwing watched her with a sense of amazement. Angel looked back over her shoulder: "Coming, doctor?"

† † †

Early November made for a predictably chilly evening. Jonny and Angel were dressed for it and sat drinking hot chocolate on the doctor's back porch. Jonny wore his shoulder-holster and .45 beneath his leather jacket; his shotgun rested across his lap. Neither of them spoke, both preoccupied with their thoughts.

Whiskey remained inside the chateau to be near Doctor Van Helwing. Hey—the old doctor loved to cook, and he spoiled Whiskey with an abundance of table scraps.

Whiskey had been the runt of the litter, the last of six to emerge. He looked sad and forlorn in a cage at eight weeks old that sat up high and faced a busy street in downtown Buffalo, in upper state New York.

Jonny had come out of a bar fortified by several shots of Irish Whiskey and was motivated to look for a present for Angel, something her mother, Sara, might approve of that year. Passing by on the sidewalk, through the plate glass window of a pet store, Jonny came face-to-face with "Angel's present."

The owner of the puppy mill told Jonny the unnamed puppy was a "runt"; then he asked: wouldn't Jonny be "interested" in a "classier," more expensive "pedigree"?

That was when Jonny scooped Whiskey into his arms, and off they headed, for New Dublin, Maine.

Whether Jonny Fiáin paid for Whiskey before leaving the store is open to debate.

The sound of the porch door opening alerted Jonny to the doctor's presence.

"Douglas O'Doole is on the line."

29.

Through the Grapevine

A sergeant in the Irish Republican Army (IRA), and a volunteer from County Clare, Douglas O'Doole, slipped into Canada unnoticed in 1916 with the help of a young veterinarian and sympathizer with the Irish cause calling for Home Rule, Luther Van Helwing. Soon after that, and again with Van Helwing's assistance, primarily, Van Helwing's connections, O'Doole secretly crossed the border from Canada into the United States.

The burly Irishman had fled Dublin in a fishing trawler with a sizable bounty on his head—payable in Sterling silver by the Right Honorable Chancellor of the Exchequer of England. With O'Doole was his future wife—lovely young Molly Hatchet.

O'Doole knew where he would most likely find Jonny Fiáin, no "ifs" about it.

† † †

"I'm here, Mister O'Doole."

"Good to hear your voice, Jonny. Now listen, lad—there are men from the government here, lots of them. It's about Angel O'Hara. They believe you have her."

"I do," said Jonny.

"Well, the FBI thinks you kidnapped her."

There was a long pause at the other end of the line.

"Jonny? You there?"

"I'm here."

"Watch yourself, lad. They're a humorless bunch of nancies and well-armed. The Word is, the Agent-in-Charge was a Commando during the last dust-up in Europe."

There was a long pause at the other end of the line.

"I wouldn't have it any other way," said Jonny.

"Of course, you wouldn't, lad. I figured as much."

"Humor me a moment, Mister O'Doole, if you will. What are the *Mary Nelsons*[72] in town saying?"

"The worst, as you can imagine. Lad. They're hiding their daughters and want to see your head on a pike in the town square.

Jonny chuckled. "I guess some things never change, ay, Mister O'Doole?"

"Aye, lad. Right you are. Now take care of yourself and Angel. The lads and I are here for you when you need us."

"I know."

"Well, then, Jonny Boy, hug Angel for the lads and me."

"I will. I'll do that. Thank you, Mister O'Doole." Jonny hung up the telephone and returned to the back porch, this time with Whiskey. Angel lifted Whiskey onto her lap.

"How is Mister O'Doole?" said Angel.

"You could hear me talking when you were clear out here?"

"Uh, huh," said Angel. "Is everything okay?"

---

[72] A *Mary Nelson* is an IRA name for a gossip monger, generally, a bitter, old woman, who thinks nothing of trashing someone's reputation for the brief amount of attention she derives from same.

"No, Angel, darlin'; everything's not okay. The Federal Bureau of Investigation—the FBI—think I kidnapped you. They are in New Dublin right now, probably interviewing your grandparents, the O'Haras, AND the McLaughlins."

"What are we going to do, Jonny?"

"I'm not sure. One thing's for certain: we have to let your grandparents know you're okay."

† † †

Jonny knew the FBI would probably tap the phone lines of the O'Haras and the McLaughlins and attempt to trace any calls to them. It didn't matter. He would deal with it.

† † †

"No one's answering, Jonny," said Angel.

"Let it ring a few more times."

Finally, someone did answer. It was Seamus O'Hara.

"O'Hara residence."

"Hi, Bumpa. It's me. Angel."

"Praises be, Angel sweetheart. Where are you? Are you okay? Your Nana and I have been sick with worry."

"I'm fine. I'm in Canada with Jonny."

"Oh, my goodness," said Seamus. "Where in Canada, Angel darling?"

Michael and Rose McLaughlin, Sarah's parents, listened from the kitchen. Lawrence McLaughlin was quietly furious the FBI had set up operations in the O'Hara's house, not his own.

Rose McLaughlin was at peace being in the O'Hara's modest dwelling. The thought of having so many strangers roaming around in her five-bedroom, three-bathroom mansion with her Oriental rugs and costly art collection greatly disturbed her.

"Let me speak to Jonny, please," said Seamus. "Okay, sweetheart?"

"Okay. Jonny's right here. Tell Nana I love her."

The line went dead. Seamus looked at the FBI lead investigator, Special Agent Pauley, and shrugged. Pauley looked at the agent monitoring the call in an attempt to trace its origin. The agent moved his head in the negative.

"Not enough time to get a trace, sir."

"Cheeseburger!" said Pauley, under his breath. *Cheeseburger* had become Pauley's swear word of choice since the end of WW II.

Pauley felt a tightening in his gut and surmised that Jonny Fiáin was on to them. Why else would he abbreviate the girl's call? Somehow, Jonny Fiáin had found out that the heat was on, so to speak, Pauley would bet on it. He looked around the O'Hara's Living Room at the eight agents assigned to him, who J. Edgar Hoover likewise tasked to find Jonny Fiáin.

"Heads-up, people!" said Pauley. "Fiáin knows we're here; he knows what we're doing. We will have to be quicker than him if we want to get the girl back and Fiáin with her. Got it?"

Pauley scanned the faces of the men in the room. They nodded. The telephone rang. Pauley nodded to Seamus O'Hara.

From her kitchen, Alyssa O'Hara watched with the McLaughlins, unaware that she was clinching the kitchen counter so tightly her knuckles were white from lack of blood.

"I wonder if these FBI men will be staying for supper?" she asked herself softly.

The telephone rang again. Seamus grabbed it and lifted it to his face. "Hello? Jonny?"

"Yes, Uncle Seamus. It's me. Listen. Sorry about the disconnect. Angel was in danger, and she was injured. I had to get her somewhere safe where she can get better, and she is getting better. I'll bring Angel to you; I'm just not sure when that'll be. She needs time to heal. Do you and Aunt Alyssa trust me?"

"Yes! We believe you, Jonny, and we trust you. Now take good care of Angel, and bring her back safe." Seamus sobbed into the phone: "Tell her we love her, Jonny!"

The line went dead.

Special Agent Pauley looked at the technician. The Technician gave Pauley a thumb up.

"Got him, Mister Pauley! They're in Fredericton, New Brunswick, Canada. He's calling from a public telephone inside a Duckworth Department Store."

"YES!" said Pauley, allowing a sudden burst of enthusiasm to escape, same as if he just hooked a twelve-pound Rainbow trout.

"Hot damn—we got him!" *Maybe Jonny Fiáin isn't on to us after all,* Pauley thought (more like hoped).

† † †

Meanwhile, one-hundred-and-twenty miles north of New Dublin.

"Did you get that?" said Standish, speaking to the technician from the Marshals Service in charge of monitoring and recording calls to the O'Hara residence.

The Marshals assigned to Standish were doing this inside the Control Room of the Atlantic Bell Building in Portland, Maine. In this room, telephone personnel processed thousands of calls every hour. The room was an office for fifty lady telephone operators, receiving and routing calls, along with female Supervisors who moved swiftly from station to station on roller skates.

"Yes, sir," said the technician. "Every word."

"Good work, gentlemen," said Standish. "Come on, Albert. The District Marshal wants to hear that, whatever-it-is, you've been formulating for getting this bastard."

"It's just an idea, Miles—a theory," Said Mesa. "That's all." Albert Mesa wasn't one for counting chickens, *et cetera, et cetera*. Still, Mesa believed in his gut he was correct thinking through Fiáin's next move.

"Outlaws and water," he told himself aloud, "always seek the path of least resistance."

30.

Az Álmok Fogadója

[The Inn of Dreams]

Off the coast of New Brunswick, Canada, in a fog bank, the *Horror* rested at-anchor. Sailing north from Maine, they had passed through a fishing fleet where Szah Zhah was once again able to satiate her blood lust, vital to maintaining a healthy head of hair, clear complexion, and sharp claws. It should go without saying, Iron-rich blood, preferably A-Positive, was the key to Szah Zhah's longevity and youthful visage when she wasn't airborne doing bad bat stuff.

† † †

While the *Horror* bobbed ever so gently in eerily placid waters for that part of the world in November, Headstone decided to whip up some *Halászle* (Hungarian for, *Fisherman's Soup*); which, the ocean below provided plenty. With it, he would make *Töltött Káposzta* (stuffed cabbage leaves). The cabbage for the *Töltött Káposzta* came from an Icelandic fishing trawler that Szah Zhah visited while stretching her wings one dark, cold night a week before over the north Atlantic. Szah Zhah did this while Headstone had gone to check with the New England Chapter of the Gray Brethren, whom Szah Zhah charged with maintaining eyes on the "little mouse."

So! While Headstone orchestrated supper in the galley, the not-so-subtle aroma of *Halászle* and *Töltött Káposzta* simmering in the pot reached Szah Zhah's especially sensitive nostrils and lulled her to sleep. And while she slept, she dreamed of days gone by, when she was a young girl, and of her time at *Az Álmok Fogadója*—The Inn of Dreams, in Kopeĉ.

† † †

"My, oh my! Underneath that dirt, you truly are a pretty girl," said Madame Alucard. The Madame said this while two scullery maids scrubbed the shivering, undernourished thirteen-year-old seated with her knees to her chest in a large, oakwood tub filled with hot water.

Not knowing what to say, Szah Zhah said nothing. Meanwhile, the two women, being of the simple sort one expects to find in rural towns such as Kopeĉ, giggled as they scrubbed Szah Zhah as though they were trying to rid a frightened fish of its scales.

"Watch what you're doing, you clumsy sows," said Madame Alucard.

The women averted their eyes from the scowling face of their employer and nodded contritely; they resumed bathing Szah Zhah as they would a newborn lamb.

Madame Alucard took Szah Zhah to a dressing room, a scaled-down version of what one might expect in Vienna's venerable *Hofburgtheatre*[73]. As matters would have it, Madame Alucard was once a thespian and an accomplished actor by all accounts. But that was many years before her beauty began to fade. When her looks went south, her career as an actor followed. As they say, fame is fleeting, but Alexandria Alucard was prescient and prepared early for her later years and a future apart from the theatre.

Szah Zhah looked upon the many gowns hanging on the racks; wide-eyed, she gasped as a child might on Christmas morning when beholding colorfully wrapped presents arrayed beneath the fragrant, candle-bedecked boughs of a sweet-smelling fir tree.

Madame Alucard was no dummy. She knew Szah Zhah's worth, which is to say, monetary value. Szah Zhah's tender age and the fact she was unsullied determined her value. That Szah Zhah was a virgin was a condition precedent to the sale. Something Madame Alucard's trusted doctor, Doctor Roger Vadim, ascertained before the transfer of ownership.

But there was another *force majeure* at work: the law of physical attraction if you will. Madame Alucard felt herself inexplicably, irrevocably, and irreversibly drawn to Szah Zhah. It happened when the madame's carriage passed by the Romany Fingos' camp. The wizened,

---

[73] *Hofsburgtheatre*. Opened in 1741, it is the national theatre of Austria, in Vienna. It was there, in 1960, at the Hofburgtheatre that bricklayer turned bodybuilder, turned actor, turned governor of California, Arnold Schwarzenegger, first tried on a pair of tights and found them to his liking [Almanac of Unapologetic Facts. Misty Bay Books. Volume 1. 1st Edition. 1948].

world-weary Madam and purveyor of prurient pleasures to beasts in the guise of men was captivated the first time she saw the lithesome, black-haired girl with fiery, violet eyes.

The madam's headstrong attraction to the dark-haired girl was not surprising, considering Alexandria Alucard was a true daughter of *Lesbos*[74] and devotee of *Sappho*.[75]

What to say? The heart is fickle and wants what it wants. That's about all one can say about that blood-pumping muscle; that is, without bloviating or waxing poetic.

"The dark, green one," said Madame Alucard. "See it?"

"It's beautiful."

Madame Alucard took a gown off the rack and held it up to Szah Zhah.

"It comes from Japan," said the Madam, "it's called a *kimono*. The fabric is silk, derived from caterpillars in an ancient land, far away, that Chinamen call *Cathay*[76]. Feel the material, Szah Zhah."

Szah Zhah ran her fingers lightly over the fabric. "It's smooth, like the inside of my thigh."

Madame Alucard felt the breath sucked out of her and almost swooned. It happens.

---

[74] Lesbos (also called Lesvos or Mitilini), is a Greek island in the northern Aegean Sea off the coast of Turkey. It's famous as the birthplace of the ancient Greek poet Sappho. Lesbos is also known for its ouzo (an anise-flavored liqueur) every bit as potent as Captain Jonny Stint's brand of 151-Rum!

[75] Sappho (Aeolic Greek, for "Sapphire"). A lesbian poet admired by Plato, Sappho was born on the Isle of Lesbos in the northern Aegean Sea and is revered today by lesbians worldwide as their patron goddess.

[76] Today, in 2020, China is simply a land mass that in 1949 that, after many years of war and revolution, became home to the scourge of the earth: despots, thugs and international gangsters known as the CCP, the Chinese Communist Party, the sponsors and proliferators of the Novel Corona Virus manufactured by lab rats in Wuhan Province, China, People's Republic of.

For a moment, the madam felt feint before this beautiful, violet-eyed girl. "I wore it when I was in the theatre."

"I don't know what that is," said Szah Zhah.

"Oh, *ma petit chou-chou,*"[77] said Madame Alucard. "I can see there is much I need to teach you."

That was the very moment the Madam of *Az Álmok Fogadója*—The Inn of Dreams decided she would keep Szah Zhah for herself; that the only bed the dark-haired beauty would share would be the Madame Alucard's, and no other.

However, that didn't stop Madame Alucard from using another pair of hands around the Inn. So, Szah Zhah worked a full day, six days a week—as a chambermaid.

Nights, of course, were a much different matter.

---

[77] French, for "My little cabbage."

31.

Necessary Trifles

At Jonny's suggestion, Angel and the doctor took Helwing's 1939 Plymouth 4-door sedan to the village when they returned from their walk.

When Angel showed no interest in dresses and closed-toe, low-heeled dress shoes in the adolescent girls' section of the local department store, Doctor Helwing relented.

"Very well, *ma Cheri*. Let's look elsewhere."

Angel saw what she wanted in a window display down the street and around the corner from the department store. In Baudelaire's Emporium, Angel found bib-overalls from the Levi factory in Bowie's Creek, North Carolina; a pair of black Keds sneakers; cotton athletic socks; Long Johns, and a woman's, long-sleeve, Pendleton wool shirt, made in Portland, Oregon. Angel wanted the Pendleton because her mother had worn one just like it. It was Sarah's favorite cold-weather shirt.

Meanwhile, Jonny Fiáin also had matters to attend to, with a master calligrapher and lithographer named Claude Debussy. Debussy was also a master forger. A Frenchman by birth, Debussy remained in Paris during the second great war. There, he forged documents for persons attempting to escape from France and the Nazi occupation. After the war in Europe ended and the Third

Reich lay in ashes, Debussy, his wife, and infant son immigrated to Canada

Calligraphers and lithographers were not in high demand in New Brunswick, Canada, so Debussy went to work in a candle factory. That was 'by day.' At night, he pursued his old career, forging documents. But not for those fleeing lethal persecution from the oppressive might of rogue nations; instead, he did it for the members of the Underworld, men and women who could pay top dollar for his services. And who were these denizens? In a word—criminals. It didn't matter to Debussy. Acute poverty has a way of refining the principles men and women live by, making moral principles manageable, if not wholly forfeit.

"What will it be this time, Jonny?" said Debussy. "Passport? Driver's license? Birth certificate? Something new, perhaps?"

"Let's start with a passport."

Debussy took paper and pen in hand. "For you, Yes?"

"Yes. And one more—for a nine-year-old girl named Angel."

† † †

After dinner, Angel sat with Whiskey in the doctor's Study, near the fireplace, wearing her new garments and listening to the Roy Rogers Radio Show on the NBC network, sponsored by Goodyear Tire and Quaker Oats cereal.

The show that night featured Roy Rogers telling the story of Tom Barnes, Texas Ranger, and had a few Western tunes sprinkled in, songs like *"You are my Sunshine"* and the *"Yellow Rose of Texas."*

Jonny poked his head inside the door. "What are you listening to, Angel?"

"Roy Rogers and Dale Evans."

"I can barely hear them," said Jonny.

It was true. Angel had turned the volume down so low that Jonny could barely hear. Angel looked at Jonny and shrugged.

"I can hear them just fine, Jonny."

"Okay. I'll leave you and Whiskey to your program." Jonny returned to the dining room and resumed sitting opposite the doctor.

"It's just like you said, Doc. But why? Why should Angel be hearing and seeing things so differently than before that thing attacked her? And why isn't she crying her eyes out over the deaths of—" Jonny had to stop; his eyes grew moist; his voice wavered. "Paddy and Sarah?"

† † †

"After breakfast, Jonny, will you teach me how to shoot?"

Jonny calmly spread butter and jelly on a piece of toast and nodded thoughtfully.

"Will you, Jonny?"

"Can you tell me why?"

"So, I can kill Szah Zhah," said Angel.

It was all the doctor could do not to cough up a mouthful of tea. Jonny paused from what he was doing.

"Who?" said the doctor.

"The creature that murdered my mother and father. Her name is Szah Zhah."

"How do you know this?" said Helwing. His eyes had widened as if to let in more light.

"Because it's what she told me while I was hiding in the closet. She said my blood tasted like Marzipan."

The doctor looked at Jonny. "Impossible," he said.

"No," said Angel. "It's what she said, just before Jonny came into the room and shot her butt full of buckshot."

"I believe you," said Van Helwing. "But you need to focus on getting better, Angel."

"My thoughts, exactly," said Jonny.

"After what you have endured," said the doctor, "you need time to heal, Angel—completely. Mind and body. Do you understand?"

"My body has healed, Doctor Helwing. And there's nothing wrong with my mind."

"You're only twelve years old, dear girl," said Helwing.

"What's that mean?" said Angel.

Jonny grinned. "I think what the doctor means is that now isn't the time to be thinking about revenge. If Sarah and Paddy were here, they'd tell you the same thing."

Angel stood. "If my dad were here, Jonny, he'd ask you why you aren't hunting the thing that murdered him and mom."

"Angel," said Helwing, "that's not fair. Not to your parents, and not to Jonny. Please. Sit. It's good you're talking about your feelings. However difficult, expressing what you're feeling is normal and healthy in the aftermath of such a traumatic event."

Angel just stared at the doctor with her head tilted quizzically to one side.

"Do you understand that word, Angel Traumatic?"

"No," she said. "And I don't think I want to."

"Well," said Helwing. "A trauma is an injury to living tissue caused by an extrinsic agent. Talking about it will help you."

Jonny remained silent. He wanted the doctor to have his say, no matter how Angel might regard it.

"You say talking about my feelings will help me," said Angel.

"Yes. Absolutely. I know it will," said Helwing.

Angel took a deep, controlled breath; she glanced at Jonny. He was staring at his coffee cup, frowning. Angel looked back at the doctor.

"Will talking about my feelings help to catch this—Szah Zhah thing, whatever she is, and kill her?"

"Excuse me?" said Helwing

"You heard her, doctor," said Jonny.

It was at that precise moment, sitting at the table in Doctor Luther Helwing's dining room, that Jonny Fiáin realized the little girl he once knew, the precocious Tomboy he loved, whose birthday he always strived to attend, was gone. FOREVER!

In her place was someone older, far older than nine years on earth would suggest. Jonny wouldn't need to remind himself of that again; Angel's violet eyes would suffice.

The doctor flinched. His upper lips quivered. "Well, no, Angel. I don't think it would help, not in that regard."

"I like you, Doctor Helwing," said Angel. "You've been very kind, taking care of me and letting me stay here. But I AM in touch with my feelings."

She looked at Jonny. "Jonny? I want you to teach me everything you know. Will you?"

Jonny took a deep breath, waited a moment, then exhaled.

"Yeah, Angel darlin'. I'll teach you what I know."

In 1949, at thirty years of age, Jonny Fiáin knew lots of things and was ignorant about a whole lot more. But he had a particular skill-set that set him apart from the herd, and now he was eager to put that skill-set to work again.

Sitting quietly at the kitchen table, Jonny took a sip of coffee. Apart from Paddy and Sarah, he never promised anyone anything, but this much he promised himself: *If it takes killing this thing to make Angel right in her head, I'll do it myself.*

32.

Best Laid Plans

"T*he best-laid plans of mice and men often go awry*" That was what Jonny kept thinking, sitting by himself in the doctor's study. Except, his version of the expression cited above was more succinct—**FUBAR**[78]!

Jonny was drinking his third cup of coffee laced with Bourbon while mapping out a plan to get Angel home to New Dublin and the relative safety of her grandparents, which is to say, the O'Hara side of the family.

It was no secret. Sarah's parents, Michael and Rose McLaughlin, despised Jonny for being "a bad influence" on their daughter and Paddy O'Hara. True, they thought Sarah had married beneath her station, taking Paddy O'Hara as her husband. They blamed Jonny for Paddy enlisting in the Marines rather than staying home, exempt from being drafted as a sole surviving son. That way, Paddy could have worked for Lawrence McLaughlin at his cannery and been a full-time husband to McLaughlin's daughter—war or no war.

† † †

Coast Guard Patrol Boat 476 pulled alongside the schooner, a scarce thirty yards separating them from the

---

[78] An acronym popular with American soldiers and sailors since Valley Forge and the War of Independence.

dark-haired woman standing at the railing, smiling and waving and wearing funny clothes. Chief Petty Officer Cotton raised a megaphone to his mouth, took a deep breath, and shouted:

"Ahoy, there! "Identify yourself!"

"Of course, Captain. "

† † †

That beautiful but strange young woman twirling a pink parasol over her head had suddenly elevated Chief Petty Officer Cotton to the rank of captain, caused the crew of the 476 to laugh like men in dire need of shore leave. A sharp glance from Lieutenant JG (Junior Grade), Andrew Blythe, silenced them. Being at sea on a Coast Guard vessel is a serious business; sissies and smart-asses best not apply.

Lieutenant Blythe took charge of the situation by taking control of the megaphone.

"Ahoy, *Horror*. I am Lieutenant Andrew Blythe in command of this vessel. Please identify yourself."

"Of course, darling. My name is Szah Zhah Kopeĉ."

"We see no crew aboard. Where is your crew?"

"In the galley, making *Apple Strudel*."

Lieutenant Blythe turned to CPO Cotton and said, "Something strange is going on over there, Chief."

"I agree, Lieutenant," said Cotton. "I feel it in my bones."

Lieutenant Blythe returned the megaphone to his mouth and shouted, "Prepare to receive a boarding party."

"Are you going to rape me?" said Szah Zhah.

"No!" said Lieutenant Blythe (more like, yelped). "That's a disgusting thought. Most certainly not." He was yelling so loudly now, his nose bled.

"Then what does that mean, darling?" said Szah Zhah.

"It means we are coming aboard to inspect your vessel."

"Wonderful," said Szah Zhah. "It will save me the trouble of flying to yours."

Bewildered, Blythe, and Cotton looked at each other.

"Break out the sidearms, Chief. No telling what's over there."

"Aye, aye, Lieutenant Blythe."

† † †

Young, rosy-cheeked lieutenant JG Andrew Blythe was correct, more than he could have possibly imagined. The officers and crew of Coast Guard vessel 476, Boston Sector, were never seen again.

† † †

"What makes you think Jonny Fiáin is going to use that abandoned bootleggers' road?" said Peter DaVinci, District Chief Marshal for the North-Eastern Corridor, the United States, based in Portland, Maine.

"It makes sense, sir," said Mesa. "If Jonny Fiáin thinks the FBI is hunting him and the O'Hara girl, he won't risk driving across the border from New Brunswick, or even Quebec, using logical, established crossing points."

Mesa moved to a wall map and pointed: "Maine has twenty-four land ports of entry along the six-hundred and eleven miles it shares with Quebec and New Brunswick. FBI and Customs Agents are going to have every one of those points of entry nailed down. Make no mistake, Chief Marshal. Jonny Fiáin will be expecting that."

"All right, Marshal Mesa, what do you propose?"

"I suggest you allow Marshal Standish and me, and two, maybe three sharpshooters, to set up camp on our side of the border, right there!" Mesa thumped the map hard with his knuckles. "Where the old bootleggers' road crosses into the States."

"What makes you think Fiáin won't simply put the girl on a bus in Canada and send her back; that is if he didn't kidnap her? And why, sharpshooters? I want Fiáin apprehended and returned to New Mexico to stand trial on the original warrant, not assassinated!"

"I'd like to answer that, sir," said Standish.

DaVinci nodded. "Go ahead, Miles."

"Fiáin," said Standish, "is as dangerous as dangerous gets, but he's not particularly vicious. But, yes, I repeat: he IS extremely dangerous. It's hard to guess what he'll do. But I don't believe he'll allow himself to surrender."

"Why is that?" said DaVinci.

"He's Irish," said Standish. "They're a stubborn, prideful race."

"And a decorated ex-Marine," said Mesa. "No way in Hell Fiáin will surrender."

"One more thing," said Standish. "And I think it's important."

"Keep talking," said DaVinci.

"Everything I've been able to learn about Jonny Fiáin tells me Fiáin didn't kidnap the O'Hara's daughter. I believe he had a damn good reason taking her from the lighthouse keeper's house on Bette's Chin that night. He's protecting her. I don't know from what, and we won't know unless and until we get the girl back."

"Good work, gentlemen. I'm going to sign off on your plan, except for any damn sharpshooters. I want Fiáin alive. Got it?"

† † †

When Special Agent Pauley made it clear to the Mucky-Muck Higher-Ups just who he was after, he had no difficulty obtaining a team and the resources he needed to apprehend someone with Jonny Fiáin's abilities.

To the FBI, Jonny Fiáin was a thief and a gun-runner, pure and simple. No matter the wounds he suffered or the medals he garnered serving his country in the Pacific, he had, in their eyes, turned his back on all that is good and wholesome to become a renegade, an outlaw, and an extremely dangerous one, at that. It bothered Pauley that the man he was after was a decorated combat veteran like himself. Sure, they had fought on opposite sides of the world, but it had been the same damn fight.

What? Pauley wondered, *would make Jonny Fiáin turn his back on everything he ostensibly fought and risked his life for?*

† † †

Deputy Marshal Mesa watched his partner finish a second helping of Apple pie, *a la mode*.

Standish grinned. "I'm telling you, Albert. You really should try this pie. It's sensational."

Mesa was quiet, deep in thought. Standish took a drink of coffee and swished it around his teeth.

"You were with the Texas Rangers for twenty years before you applied with the US Marshals' Service."

"That's right," said Mesa.

"I bet you fellas killed quite a few Mexicans."

"That's right," said Mesa. "We did."

"Did that bother you at all? I mean, you being--" Standish hesitated.

"What?" said Mesa. "Ethnically, Mexican?"

"Well, yeah," said Standish.

"Not a bit," said Mesa. "Truth is, I've killed more gringos and half-breed Indians than I have Mexicans. How about you, Standish? You kill any white-skinned, blue-eyed bad guys since you've been a US marshal?"

Standish grinned. "Well, now, Albert, you know I have. Most of the fellas I killed didn't want to get taken in. Not counting Nazis, I mean."

"You, too?" said Mesa.

"Yeah," said Standish. "Armored Corps. Third Division. You?"

"Airborne," said Mesa. "101st."

Standish reached his hand across the table. "Damn proud to meet you, Marshal Mesa."

They shook hands.

"I believe I'll have some of that pie, after all," said Mesa.

33.

Adieu, Ma Terrible Beauté

When Madame Alucard learned from a maid that Szah Zhah enjoyed sexual congress in the wine cellar with Brutus, the local Cobbler's son, the Madam, collapsed from a stroke and died the next morning. Eyes closed, the only words that escaped her lips were in French: "*Adieu, ma terrible Beauté.*"

The Madam's creditors heard the news within hours and descended on the village Magistrate to press their claims against Madame Alucard's estate.

Because the Magistrate was thoroughly corrupt and sold his integrity for peanuts, the creditor who got to him first, a detestable human being by the name of Farkas, told the Magistrate, whose name was Balogh, that he would accept an 'Accord & Satisfaction,[79]' for Madame Alucard's debts.

What did that mean? This particular matter meant that Farkas would accept payment other than gold or silver for what Madame Alucard owed and would not proceed to court to prosecute the case.

"Tell me, Farkas," said Balogh, "if not money, what will you accept to settle Madame's debt?"

---

[79] An **accord and satisfaction** is a **legal contract** whereby two parties agree to discharge a tort claim, **contract**, or other liability for an amount based on terms that differ from the original amount of the **contract** or claim. **Accord and satisfaction** is also used to settle **legal** claims prior to bringing them to court [Wikipedia].

Bingo!

"I will accept the indentured servant woman called Szah Zhah and one or two others, Honorable Magistrate," said Farkas.

"Ah! A Fair bargain can no robbery, be," said the Magistrate. "Done!"

† † †

Farkas gave the Magistrate his due; then, he put Szah Zhah inside his carriage with two other young women and headed south. Bound for the seaport of Rijeka, on the west coast of Croatia.

† † †

To amuse themselves the first hour of their eleven-day journey, the three women sang songs they all enjoyed like *Charlotte the Harlot, Poke, Poke, Poke the Goat,* and a universal favorite of travelers, *Ninety-Nine Bottles of Schnapps on the Wall.*

When Farkas could stand no more of their singing, he spiked the girls' hot chocolate with *Laudanum* and settled back to read a German translation of *The Wealth of Nations* by the Scottish Economist & Philosopher Adam Smith. Yes, Farkas was a *shmok*, but he was a businessman, first and foremost, and he wasn't stupid, just wickedly insensitive.

Amazing what people did with their lives before Smart Phones.

† † †

After an otherwise uneventful journey, the carriage reached the seaport of Rijeka on the Balkan Peninsula. Farkas obtained lodging for the women and then promptly locked them in their room while meeting someone. He met a Turk, a purveyor of beautiful, young females, selling them to not devout Muslims in the Levant; men who could afford to buy such chattels, sex slaves precisely, with gold, silver, or fox furs. It was nothing personal, Farkas told himself, just business.

Fortunately, there was a window in the room that looked out over the harbor. Szah Zhah sat there while Farkas was away, enthralled by the sights, sounds, and smells that greeted her. Verily, she had never been near the ocean or, in this case, the Adriatic Sea. Nor had she seen boats and ships and seagulls before.

This experience, another "first" for Szah Zhah, seared itself into her brain and took her breath away; until she could look out the window no more and joined the girls on the bed for a game of dice.

The Turk whom Farkas met in the tavern nearby the Inn was a swine named Ali Ben Babba. Once the gold was in Farkas's hand, Farkas gave the Turk the key to the room where the girls were waiting.

The ship Ali Ben Babba owned was a two-mast affair built by a rug merchant in Lebanon. The Turk proudly named his vessel, *Dürüst Ali*, which, in Turkish, means "Honest Ali." Built to Ali Ben Babba's specifications, he meant to carry cargoes: slaves, wines, and olive oil, mainly, but the *Honest Ali* was not exceptionally fast, not even with the wind behind it. A fatal design flaw.

Alas, the Turk's vessel sailed south into the Ionian Sea, past the Italian peninsula's boot-heel, where the absolute worst kind of pirates, the scourge of the Mediterranean Sea, overtook the *Honest Ali*! Who were these sea rats? In a word—they were Sicilians.

† † †

"Pity me, kind sirs," said Ali Ben Babba, speaking halting Italian to his Sicilian captors.

The Sicilians laughed. Too bad for the Italian-speaking Turk, Ali Ben Babba, and his Muslim crew. True, the Sicilians were many despicable things. Still, they were also Catholics, so they cheerfully cut the throats of everyone aboard the "Honest Ali," except for the three women they found rolling dice in the cargo hold.

As luck would have it or not, the brutally handsome Sicilian who led this merry band of cutthroats spoke French and English and Swahili, as did Szah Zhah, except for Swahili. She had learned to speak Romany, the language of the gypsies, along with German and Hungarian (Magyar). She learned to speak French and English from her lover and former employer, Madame

Alucard, during the eight years Szah Zhah shared the Madam's bed.

Verily. Every dark cloud has a silver lining. Or so Szah Zhah believed.

† † †

The captain of the pirate vessel, Salvatore Luciano Gambino, a Seventh Generation Sicilian, born into a sardine fishing family in Palermo, took an immediate fancy to Szah Zhah, as did his foul-mouthed parrot, Lola, who, like her owner, could swear in three languages, including Swahili, and had an affinity for Corsican wines, female parrots, and tincture-of-poppy from Afghanistan.

Lola began life as an egg that nearly got poached off Africa's Ivory Coast, where Gambino's ship had dropped anchor. Whatever distraction it was, it must have been serious for Salvatore Luciano Gambino to put aside thoughts of breakfast that morning and then to hurry ashore with malice aforethought and foul intent.

When Captain Gambino returned to his ship that night, the egg was gone, but, in its place, was a tiny hatchling—a gray parrot, known as an *African Gray*, and a resident of central Africa's rainforests, from the Côte d'Ivoire to western Kenya. No doubt about it—for a bird, Lola was hot—I mean, steaming! The African Gray, the largest parrot in Africa, grew silver feathers as it aged and sported a white mask and a bright, reddish tail.

Not having any children of his own, Salvatore Luciano Gambino assumed the care and feeding of the African Gray, much the same as he would if she was the product of his loins—a daughter if you will, who he named in his *Ultime Volontà e Testament.*[80] Her name? Lola.

To suggest Lola was a remarkable creature understates the truth. This particular parrot was an undeniable, irrepressible force of nature, not unlike the *Novel Corona Doctor Fauci Wuhan Lab Virus* of 2019.

† † †

To satisfy the demands of his crew, Captain Salvatore Luciano Gambino let them have their way with the women, but only two of them. Szah Zhah was off the menu.

This swarthy Sicilian had no way of knowing, not in 1750, but after a day and a night in Szah Zhah's arms, he came down with an acute case of *Pheromone Poisoning* (PP). Lola tried to warn him, but he cast her warning and caution to the wind. It wasn't the first time a father failed to heed the warnings of his daughter—take, for instance, King Priam of Troy, whose daughter Kassandra, a seer, no less, tried to warn him, saying: *Hediye Veren Yunanlılara dikkat edin.*[81]

Exactly! A lesson too late for the learning, whatever the hell that means.

This timeless malady occurred while Captain Gambino's ship, *Il Bello Ratto,*[82] remained on Cruise Control while the crew stayed drunk and occupied with the other two women 24/7; which is a polite way of saying Gambino's crew would one day roast in Hell, and

---

[80] Italian, meaning: Last Will & Testament.

[81] Trojan (Turkish), meaning: *"Beware Greeks Bearing Gifts."*

[82] Italian, meaning *"The Handsome Rat"*

deservedly so for their dastardly lack of good manners and political correctness when it came to gender equality.

Fottuti Sicilianos! They are the absolute worst when it comes to pirates!

As any qualified expert in Pheromone Poisoning's field will explain, men with acute cases of the same become irrational, more so than usual, and cannot focus on what needs doing. Simply put, men with acute Pheromone Poisoning become possessed inexplicably attached to the object of their desire, pretty much to the exclusion of everything else, even food. For Captain Salvatore Luciano Gambino, the source of his twisted manifestation of desire was Szah Zhah Kopeĉ—In the buff.

Parenthetically, Captain Gambino's parrot, Lola, became so unhinged by the uninhibited display of carnal abandon taking place in the immediacy of their shared space, Szah Zhah had to feed Lola *hashish*; that and throw a comforter over the large gold cage that housed the parrot.

FYI, the cage was custom made in Florence, Italy, by Giuseppe Zanetti & Sons.

God's Truth! You can't make this stuff up!

34.

Corsican Brothers

Just as day broke, somewhere in the Mediterranean, they lay in bed sharing a cigarette.

"You were magnificent, my love," said Salvatore. "S*tupendioso*—Yes?"

"It was okay," said Szah Zhah.

Salvatore pushed himself up onto his elbows. "Huh? Just, okay? What was wrong?"

"It was *okay*, Sal," said Szah Zhah. "It can't be *magnifico*, or *mandato dal Cielo*, all the time."

"It can't?" said Salvatore.

"No, Sal. Not for a woman, it can't."

Salvatore Luciano Gambino was dumbfounded. Never before had a woman talked to him that way, mercilessly wielding Truth to Power, not ever, certainly not in Sicily. Maybe Sal's mom spoke to him that way, but that would have been when Sal was a little boy. Besides, mothers are allowed certain liberties.

† † †

With all the fornication taking place aboard *Il Bel Topo*, no one was the wiser when at dawn, two pirates known as the *Corsican Brothers* brought their ship, a Corsair that bore the name, *Les Frères Corses, Ltd.*, alongside *Il Bel Topo*.

Without firing a shot, the twins and their virile crew boarded Gambino's boat wearing only their speedos and quickly dispatched Salvatore's crewmen, who couldn't fight; they were delirious, spent. As for the two women upon whom the crew satiated their unspeakable lust, they were cold to the touch—dead. It is impossible to know whether the Sicilians were aware of that salient fact, but the Corsican marauders caught two of Sal's crew *en flagrante* with the corpses.

The Corsican Brothers, whose names were Francois and Jean, knew Salvatore Luciano Gambino well. Gambino was a ruthless competitor, who liked to stick it to the French, generally, and the Corsican Brothers, specifically, whenever an opportunity presented itself. Worst of all, Gambino was Sicilian.

Francois and Jean wasted no time. They circumcised Sal Gambino; then, they cut his throat and tossed him and his crew overboard for the sharks.

The Corsican Brothers looked at Szah Zhah. She huddled in the far corner of the cabin, holding a sheet to conceal her toned, curvy, twenty-something milk-white body.

"Do you speak French?" said Francois. He was the oldest, accustomed to speaking first.

Szah Zhah nodded.

Jean pointed to the drying blood on the floor of the cabin.

"What is that pig, Gambino to you, Mademoiselle?"

"Dead?" said Szah Zhah.

That was the funniest thing the Corsican Brothers had heard for a very long time; they laughed uproariously for about thirty seconds.

"Would you like to come with us?" said Francois.

"Very much," said Szah Zhah.

"We are homosexuals," said Jean. "So is our crew."

"So, you need not fear us raping you," said Francois. "Not on our ship."

"How very kind of you," said Szah Zhah. "May I bring Lola?"

† † †

The Corsican Brothers were twins, and, yes, they were gay; they were also cross-dressers who graciously made their wardrobe available to Szah Zhah, who loved to play dress-up more than anything in the world. There! Do you see the truth of it? Another silver lining!

† † †

The Corsican Brothers had a Gay Pride Conference to attend on the island of Ibiza, 150 kilometers south, as the Magpie flies, from the city of Valencia where *El Cid* [83] defeated the Moors on the east coast of Spain in the 11th century; so, naturally, that's the course the Twins set.

As predetermined, Szah Zhah and the parrot went with them. Day and night, Lola's potty mouth and ribald wit delighted the twins for hours on end. When they could take no more, someone would throw in the towel and cloak her cage. For Szah Zhah, it was terrific having another girl on board.

Leaving her life on land for the first time, Szah Zhah learned an invaluable truth in her not-so-sweet, altogether brief existence; to wit, there are precious few dull moments aboard a pirate ship.

---

[83] Charlton Heston (1923-2008).

† † †

After six more days sailing in the nude, *Les Frères Corses'* crew dropped anchor in a sheltered cove in Ibiza.

Happy to see land again, Szah Zhah was dazzled by the clear, deep, sapphire, and turquoise-colored waters surrounding the island. She had no way of knowing that the Mediterranean Sea would become a cesspool of contamination where pregnant women dare not swim, two hundred and seventy years later.

While the crew skinny-dipped in the tranquil waters of the cove, Szah Zhah went with the Corsican Brothers in the lifeboat to shore.

"We won't be more than an hour," said Francois.

"Swim. Explore. Do whatever you want, Szah Zhah.," said Jean. "We'll find you."

And that's what Szah Zhah did; she had a quick dip in the water; then set off down the beach holding a pink parasol from *La Trovatore* in Rome, courtesy of the twins.

True to their word, the twins returned on time to where they and Szah Zhah parted company. It wasn't until a second hour passed that Szah Zhah appeared.

† † †

Francois and Jean sensed it immediately; something was amiss. Szah Zhah staggered along the beach toward them. The twins called to her, but she appeared stunned; her lips moved but issued no words. When they hastened toward her, Szah Zhah collapsed at their feet, face down in the sand.

"Sunstroke?" said Francois.

"No, brother," said Jean. "I fear this is something more."

It was "…something more." Something MUCH more!

35.

That Dog Don't Hunt

"That dog don't hunt," said the tall man standing closest. He had dark, beady eyes, what some call "pig's eyes," and appeared to be a woodsman, possibly a hunter with a fuzzy head of wiry black and silver-streaked hair.

South of the Canadian border, in upper-state New York, Vermont, New Hampshire, and Maine, it was deer season. Maybe it was deer season in New Brunswick, Canada, or so Jonny wondered. It didn't matter. The two men were where they had no business being and had been since Jonny and Angel arrived at the doctor's in *Sans Souci*; of that, Jonny was certain.

Like his red-haired companion but taller, the man had two to three weeks' worth of whiskers. Their Mackinaw coats and forest-green, wide-pleated corduroy pants reeked of grime, sweat, and campfire smoke, the kind of spicy cocoon that hunters ease into after a week without bathing. Both men carried Remington 783, Bolt Action, .30-06 Springfield, 22" rifles. They held their long guns cradled in their arms, where they could be brought into action quickly should a target present itself.

Jonny smiled. His hands were in the pockets of his Mackinaw, out of sight. He looked down at Whiskey sitting on the gold and brown leaves that blanketed the forest floor and smelled of seasons past and decay. Whiskey stared at the two men, and his tail wasn't wagging. That, alone, told Jonny just about everything else he needed to know.

"You're right, buddy," said Jonny. "That dog don't hunt. Not a lick. But you know what he can do? I bet you can't guess?" Jonny smiled at the pinched faces of the two men. They didn't look the least bit interested in the dog, just Jonny.

Jonny watched the color drain from their faces, a telltale sign they were about to do something dangerous. When a white man gets angry, he gets red in the face, but when he's ready to fight, his color will drain; his face turns pale, like wax; adrenalin starts to flow, and he might lick his lips. Parts of his body, often his fingers or eyelids, will begin to twitch just before he strikes.

"Well, fellas, if you're not going to guess, I'll just come out and tell you. Whiskey here, that's his name; Whiskey—he can smell a rat a mile away. That's how I found you out here, trespassing on Doc Helwing's land."

The smile never left Jonny's face. He learned that in Juvenile Hall, to control his body and not tip his hand. The number of visits he made to the Dean of Discipline after pulverizing bullies testified to that.

Just as the hunters brought their rifles to bear on Jonny's chest, Jonny's .45 came out of his pocket. The first bullet hit the redhead square in the chest, knocking him onto his back, killing him instantly. Jonny's second bullet struck the tall man up high, making a hole the size of a silver dollar in his upper chest as it spun the tall man to the ground.

Writhing in pain, the tall man began to elongate into something other than human.

"No, no, no, whatever you're doing, don't!" said Jonny.

The tall man's arms and legs bulged and lengthened, ripping apart the fabric of his garments.

"Stop, dammit!" said Jonny. He pistol-whipped the fellow unconscious; then, and only then, did the strange transformation end. The tall man slowly took on his former appearance, but not before Whiskey bit off one of the man's ears. The ear was still encrusted with silver-black fur when Whiskey swallowed it.

† † †

Angel and the doctor heard the gunshots from the back porch. Whiskey returned first, barking excitedly.

Doctor Helwing went into the house. Angel had already gone outside and was standing beside Whiskey when the doctor returned, with his shotgun in hand.

It wasn't but a minute later that Jonny appeared. He was dragging the wounded, unconscious hunter that wasn't altogether human by the coat collar.

"I know this man," said Van Helwing.

"Yeah?" said Jonny. "Well, he and another fellow have been hanging around your property since Angel and I got here. Any idea why that would be, Doc?"

"None, Jonny. That other man, did he have a full head of unkempt red hair?"

"That would be him. Who are they, Doc?"

"The Clinton brothers—immigrants from Arkansas. They own a diesel engine repair service in *San Souci*. Leastwise, until today, they did. How did you discover their presence?"

"I had help, Doc. My gut, and him." Jonny looked at Whiskey. "I didn't say anything at first, thinking maybe you knew they were around."

"No, Jonny. Not at all. And I would just as soon the authorities didn't hear a word of this."

"Me neither, Doc. I'll go back later and bury the brother."

"Yes. Of course. A good idea. What about this one?"

"I'd appreciate it if you could keep him alive for a while, Doc. I want to know what the two of them were doing out here."

Doctor Van Helwing sighed. "Very well," he said. "Help me get him to the barn."

The doctor handed his shotgun to Angel to hold; then, he and Jonny dragged the bleeding, unconscious hunter to the barn.

"You better wait inside the house, Angel," said Jonny.

"No. If that man has anything to say, I want to hear it."

36.

Digging for Truth

W ith all the changes he witnessed taking place with Angel and the totality of the circumstances being what they seemed, Jonny knew better than to argue or belabor the matter.

"All right, Angel. Grab a leg."

† † †

As they entered, the doctor triggered a switch that flooded the barn's interior with bright white light from overhead lamps, not unlike an operating room.

The inside of the barn was not what Angel expected. Instead of dirt, the floor was ivory-colored linoleum. Shelves lined three of the four walls almost to the ceiling. On the shelves were five-gallon glass jars, each containing a formaldehyde and water solution known as formalin.

A positive outcome to any surgery is, of course, a somewhat subjective matter dependent in the main on whether the patient survives. Fair enough.

While Angel looked on, Jonny and the doctor lifted the wounded man onto the table. It wasn't the first time the doctor had used wide leather straps to hold down the recipient of his tender mercies and scalpel. There were straps to secure the upper arms, forearms, abdomen, thighs, knees, and ankles.

"Holy cow, Doc!" said Jonny. "What have you been operating on that requires straps like these?"

Van Helwing finished tightening the last bolt across the man's ankles; then, he looked at Jonny.

"*The Undead*," said Van Helwing.

It wasn't the doctor's reply that got to Jonny so much as it was the matter-of-fact way Van Helwing said it.

The tall man opened his eyes. "I've said all I'm going to say. You can tell that to the Little Mouse standing there."

Angel almost leaped onto his chest: "What did you call me?" she said.

"Forget it, Angel darlin'. He's talking garbage."

"No," said Angel, "THAT'S what Szah Zhah called me. Remember, Jonny? I told you that."

Jonny lowered his head to where he could talk into the tall man's ear. "I believe the good doctor closed that hole a little too soon, buddy."

That said, Jonny placed the forefinger of his right hand on the angry red flesh seared over the tall man's wound. He poked until the flesh gave way, and his finger sank to the first knuckle. The tall man winced but remained silent.

"Feel like maybe you want to talk now, pal?" said Jonny; he forced his finger deeper, to the second knuckle.

That was all it took; the tall man began to growl and strain against the straps that held him prisoner. Angel, the doctor, even Jonny stepped back as the man's body started to shape-shift, just as it had in the forest after Jonny shot him and killed his brother.

When the tall man's head began to change into an immense wolf's head, the creature's expanding chest snapped the strap. Jonny wasn't going to wait. He yanked out his .45 and emptied the clip into the creature's head. Blood and brain matter spattered on the floor and nearest wall as if Jackson Pollock[84] had visited the barn.

Each time Jonny fired a round, the explosion sent Angel to her knees, hands tightly over her ears. When the shooting stopped, Angel ran from the barn, Whiskey on her heels. Whiskey would live out his days, deaf in one ear.

Jonny caught up with them outside.

"I'm sorry about that, Angel, but I had to kill that thing before it broke free. Your ears are bleeding. Can you hear me okay?"

Angel waited for the ringing in her ears to subside. "What!?" she said.

The color drained from Jonny's face.

"I'm kidding, Jonny. I hear fine."

"Gawd dammit, Angel! Don't ever do me like that again. We're leaving here. NOW!"

"What about the doctor?"

"Don't worry about Van Helwing, Angel. He'll be fine. Besides, I have a feeling the good doctor knows more about that thing than he's willing to admit. Get packed. We're leaving."

"For where?"

"I don't know. I'll figure that out later."

---

[84] A disturbed individual who made a ton of dough hurling paint onto canvas in New York City in the 1950s and 60s, maybe even the 70s and 80s.

† † †

"Tell the Brethren that they just left," said Van Helwing. "Yes! Just now. No. I don't know. My guess is, he'll go back the way they came."

The doctor hung the telephone up and poured himself a Brandy, a stiff one. "I'm sorry, Jonny," he said, talking to the Brandy glass. "A life for a life. That is what you owe ."

37.

Turn, Turn Again

Six weeks passed without Balthazar uttering a word.

Six weeks after Katarina Bukowski's death, all Balthazar did was sit in darkness inside the *Cave of Contemplation* on the leeward [85] side of the island.

The cave was well-hidden in Jamaica's undeveloped interior. There, Initiates into the Gray Brethren could go when confused or in pain, to meditate on their new reality as Weirdwolves. Food and water were left each morning outside the entrance, and silence was the rule. Those who could not resolve their dilemma, or their grief, or the magnitude of the transformed selves they became, died in that cave, their bones intentionally left inside for the next *Initiate* to ponder. Tough love!

On the seventh day of the seventh week at the seventh hour, Katarina Bukowski appeared to Balthazar, bathed in a bluish-white light—as a ghost, perhaps, perhaps as a *Spirit*. Who knows? She showed up unexpectedly.

"Why are you still here, my love?" she said. "Why are you not hunting with the Brethren?"

---

[85] The leeward side is the sheltered, protected, or shielded side.

Balthazar was beside himself. "Is that you, Katarina?" He forced himself to his feet. He reached out to embrace her, but she was no more substantial than mist, and he stumbled through her.

"I have crossed over, Balthazar. I am no longer as I once was. You should know that. There are great things ahead for you. Be brave, my love. Claim them! It is not your fate to die in the Cave of Contemplation. You are stronger than that. Go! Bring honor to the Brethren. Do it, Balthazar. Do it now!"

Balthazar watched Katarina's non-corporal form evaporate into the darkness. Once more, he was alone, but the great sadness that weighed on him lifted.

Without lingering another moment in the prison that his mind made of the cave and confident his vision of Katarina was real, Balthazar sought the light beyond the entrance. Something inside told him he was indeed something more than he could have ever dared hope for before Katarina.

After a night celebrating Balthazar's return to the pack, complete and whole, in body and mind, at dawn, the Brethren returned to the commonplace lives they lived inconspicuously, many of them on Jamaica: as shopkeepers, merchants, rum makers, weavers, nannies, dyers of cloth, and fishers. All necessary to the island's economy. All respectable.

All but the Spanish and French were welcome in Kingston, Jamaica. Except for maybe the Dutch, they, too, had managed to warrant a citation on Governor Trelawney's shite list; that was as of breakfast, New Year's Day, 1751. The reason was simple. The Dutch West Indies Company undermined Great Britain's monopoly on the slave trade with its colonies in America, the Caribbean, and Brazil.

For Balthazar, it meant returning to Kingston's waterfront and reopening Katarina's Boutique, where tourists could purchase such novelties as arrived weekly in the cargo holds of merchant ships and pirate ships.

"I'm fit to kill all those damnable Dutch," said the Hanoverian[86] born and inbred King of England, George II, the last British monarch actually to lead an army in battle.[87] He said this in a letter to his royal puppet-in-charge, Governor Trelawney. "Blast it all, Trelawney; I give you ships, men, a nice place to live. Now do something about those Dutch devils!"

† † †

That morning, Balthazar Headstone had nothing on his mind in any way similar to what Governor Trelawney and King George II had on theirs. It stands to reason; Headstone was free to follow his bliss, not so for Trelawney and George II. Each was locked-in to what Fate had decreed: gilded lives of servitude for both, with madness and gout thrown in for good measure. The reason subjects bow low to dignitaries, like kings and queens, governors and the like, is so the so-called *crème de la crème* won't see the unwashed masses, the rabble, ordinary folks, if you will, laughing as these great, pusillanimous personages go past in their carriages and finery.

---

[86](German: Haus Hannover), whose members are known as Hanoverians, is a German royal house that ruled Hanover, Great Britain, and Ireland at various times during the 17th through 20th centuries.

[87] In 1743, at the Battle of Dettingen, during the War of the Austrian Succession.

Headstone opened the boutique, just as he had so many times before with Katarina at his side. It didn't make any difference to Headstone that he couldn't see Katarina. In his heart of hearts, in his soul, he could feel her presence, and she wouldn't leave. It happens!

Just inside the door, golden dust hung in the air like mist, illuminated by the early morning sunlight streaming through the windows. As Headstone stepped inside, he inhaled Katarina's scent; it was pervasive on everything she touched, and it comforted him as he dusted the shelves and the trinkets that cluttered the boutique and storeroom.

Several of the Brethren, male and female, came by the boutique to check on Balthazar and welcome him back to Kingston throughout the morning. Friendship can be a healing balm, all its own, and Balthazar was grateful for it. He knew his Aunt Lily loved him, but to have the genuine affection of so many brothers and sisters with whom he shared such an extraordinary bond, well, for Balthazar, it was his version of Paradise on earth.

At Six Bells, Captain Bartholomew Hawkings of the HMS Defiance seated the mysterious, dark-haired beauty for supper in his Quarters for the last time. They found her lashed naked to a raft, sunburned, delirious, and dehydrated, not far from the island of Madeira. She had no memory of who she was or how she got there. These Englishmen aboard the Defiance knew nothing about the woman, although her accent suggested she was from the Balkans, possibly Macedonia. While stewards placed food on the table, Captain Hawkings leaned close to her. With no dress aboard the Man-O-War to give her, she was clothed the same as an ordinary seaman in the Royal Navy and wore white, button-up trousers rolled six-inches above her ankles; leather sandals, compliments of the Ship's Carpenter; she also wore a white linen, long-sleeve shirt from Captain Hawkings, and wore a blue woolen waist-coat, with gold buttons, given to her by a thirteen-year-old Midshipman named Horatio Hornblower.

"Tomorrow, dear lady," said Captain Hawkings, "we will arrive at Kingston, Jamaica. I sent advance word of our coming to Governor Trelawney by way of a dispatch I entrusted to the captain of the *Lady Thames*. Being faster and smaller than the *Defiance*, she should dock a full three days before we get there."

The dark-haired beauty scanned the faces of Captain Hawkings and the officers present. Tears began to form in the corners of her violet eyes, eyes that could mesmerize and enchant the pants off a powder monkey.

"Thank you, Captain Hawkings. And to all your fine officers and sailors, I say, thank you. I shall never forget your many kindnesses, beginning with fishing me from the clutches of the cold ocean."

Captain Hawkings and his officers laughed. Despite her ordeal at sea, the woman's self-effacing wit and cheerful spirit had endeared her to the entire ship's company.

"Our pleasure, dear lady," said Hawkings. Most assuredly, our pleasure."

"Hear! Hear!" echoed the officers

† † †

It was around mid-day when Balthazar's attention drifted toward the alley outside Katarina's Boutique. A mob of perhaps fifty men, women, and children were hurrying toward the docks the way they would witness a hanging, which, in Kingston, is free to watch and always draws a festive crowd. Besides being curious, Balthazar decided to lock the door to the shop and join them.

Balthazar Headstone found himself standing among several hundred other curious onlookers crowding the waterfront, where the HMS *Defiance* docked and was unloading cargo onto the pier.

He suddenly felt someone tug his arm. Headstone looked down to see a street urchin no more than five or six years old, pulling his sleeve.

"Please, sir," said the urchin, "may I sit on your shoulders? I want to see the lady, but I can't see over the crowd."

"What lady?" said Balthazar.

"Put me on your shoulders, and I'll tell you."

Headstone smiled at the cheeky little bastard. "Very well, little man. Fair is fair."

Headstone hoisted the urchin onto his broad shoulders.

"There!" said the urchin, and he pointed toward the *Defiance*. Balthazar looked toward the Man-O-War as he moved through the crowd; then, he saw her coming down the Gangplank, escorted by the ship's Captain and several Royal Marines, two in front, two behind.

Headstone tilted his head and sniffed the air. Her scent was strong, like Katarina's. *What has she done?*

Headstone wondered. *Why is she under guard like that?* Then he noticed her left arm draped through the Captain's right arm, the way he'd seen married women on the island do when escorted through town by their husbands. *She's no prisoner at all,* he exclaimed to himself. *But who is she? And why is she dressed like an ordinary sailor?*

Balthazar continued to watch as the ship's captain escorted the young woman to a waiting carriage with the Governor's emblem decorating both sides of its gloss black doors.

Headstone was standing close enough to see that, even in men's clothing, and without the stuff white women use to paint their faces, the woman getting into the carriage was beautiful, by any measure, with black hair that hung past her waist. A woman with a face that could haunt a man into an early grave. A face that could launch a thousand ships of greedy Greeks to rape and plunder the lands across the Hellespont; a face that could drive a man ten kinds of crazy should his love be unrequited; the type of face with a nose and ears just so; a face that at all hours of the night could compel a man to abandon his sleep and run to the market to get her a pint of pineapple *sorbet*. Pineapple! Pineapple! Pineapple! In short, the kind of face with just the right lips—lips that could make a man forget his sweet, infirm old mother and where he may have stashed her if *the Face* had willed it so.

It happens.

38.
Who's in Charge Here?

By the time Special   Agent   Pauley and his eight-member team reached the abandoned Lookout Tower used by the Forest Service, it was still early morning. Ample time, thought Pauley, to set up an ambush site before settling in to wait for Jonny Fiáin and his gang.

The "Boss of bosses" in Washington, D.C., J. Edgar Hoover himself, was adamant: "*Bring in Jonny Fiáin, dead or alive, but under no circumstances allow an incident that complicates our relations with the [expletive deleted] Canadians.*"

Hoover made no mention of the little girl Fiáin allegedly kidnapped. Probably just an oversight by the FBI's Director.

Named "Twisted Timber Road" by a Canadian-American logging consortium in the early 1900s, this narrow, one-lane dirt road later became known as "Blood   Alley." That was after bootleggers and various competing mobs, Italian and Irish, discovered it.   It was the proverbial *Silk Road*[88] for moving liquor and other contraband from Canada into the U.S and guns and untaxed cigarettes from the U.S into Canada, all *via* the border with Maine.

When the States repealed Prohibition in 1934 with the 18th Amendment to the U.S. Constitution, and booze

---

[88] The path overland from the Occident to the Orient taken by the famed Italian adventurer and explorer, Marco Polo.

was again legal to make and consume, commerce through "Blood Alley" came to a full stop. The road was dirt, and over time became rife with obstacles—potholes and fallen trees.

Using a motorcycle, even with a sidecar, Jonny Fiáin could navigate the terrain without much ado; not so for other vehicles, apart from what the military used overseas during the war: jeeps, tanks, off-road transport trucks, self-propelled howitzers, reconnaissance blimps, those kinds of things.

Riding with Special Agent Pauley in a drab, olive green, 1944 Willys jeep were two FBI agents: Marquez and Gibson. Behind them were two additional jeeps, each with three agents. These young men were an integral part of J. Edgar Hoover's vision for the future of federal law enforcement. Hoover scorned the caricature of the poorly educated, pot-bellied southern sheriff who, in Hoover's mind, represented law and order at its worst, and in many cases, he was correct.

The jeeps were "on loan" to the FBI from the Department of War; it was reconstituted in 1947 to become the Department of the Army and ultimately became the U.S. Department of Defense. Whew! Just in time for the five undeclared wars and numerous, sundry global "interventions" that would soon follow.

Commensurate with his *war against organized crime,*" J. Edgar Hoover created a small army of these "G-Men"! Crimefighters, *par excellence*, dedicated to the proposition that the world was "up for grabs," and almost a "lost cause"; that America was now the last best hope for humankind and worth defending. It made sense to Hoover to hire as many combat veterans as he could recruit, provided they had what J. Edgar called "the right stuff." He would use them to bolster the ranks of his domestic crime-fighting force.

Pauley tapped the driver, his good friend, Marquez, on the arm and pointed. "After we get around that curve up ahead, Gabe, pull over, and let's see what's what."

"You got it, L-T," said Marquez, shouting over the noise of the engine and the sound of the wheels churning dirt and loose rocks.

† † †

Born in Shawnee Mission, Kansas in 1920, Gabriel Marquez had been a Staff Sergeant in the 34th Infantry Division, 133rd Infantry Regiment, and had won a Bronze Star in Italy "for demonstrating conspicuous valor in combat."

There are no two ways about it: Gabe Marquez was Special Agent Pauley's good friend and second-in-command, a position Marquez took seriously. Pauley hand-picked every one of the men on his team; their motto: "We get it done."

† † †

When they finally reached the Fire Lookout Tower, Pauley signaled to his team to pull over and stop. They had arrived at the old road where it started through dense forest north, to Canada. As they rested, Pauley addressed his men.

"I know it's not going to happen, men, but if things go south for whatever reason, the Fire Lookout tower will be our primary fallback position."

"Well, now, that ain't going to happen, L-T," said Marquez. "Isn't that right, gentlemen!"

Pauley's team answered enthusiastically and in unison: "Hell, yes!"

After stretching their legs and draining their bladders, Pauley and his team got back into their jeeps and started away.

As they rounded the next bend, Pauley couldn't believe his eyes. Blocking the road was a "Deuce and a Half" or "Jimmy," as G.I.s fondly referred to them.[89]

Marquez slammed on the brakes; the jeep skidded to a stop. The two vehicles behind did likewise. Pauley got out and signaled to his men to gather around.

Pauley looked at the ground and kicked a softball-sized rock with the toe of his boot. "Cheeseburger!" he said, loud enough to set a murder of crows to flight.

"Cheeseburger" was Special Agent Pauley's curse word of choice, now that he was no longer being shot at most every day as he was during the war. Gabe Marquez and the others knew better than to snicker or laugh. The ironic thing is, Pauley's wife, Judy, could make a sailor blush with her choice of expletives if and when Pauley forgot to put the trash out on Sunday night.

C'est el vie entre les draps.[90]

---

[89] "Off-road," vehicles, these 2 1/2-ton, 6 x 6, troop transport-cargo trucks G.I.s fondly called a "deuce-and-a-half," or not so fondly, a "Jimmy," depending on the mood and morale of the soldiers who rode in back, space permitting, the original "Deuce and a Half," thousands of them, formed the backbone of the famed Red Ball Express that kept British and American armies supplied, as they pushed eastward after the Normandy Invasion, June 6th, 1944.

[90] French, meaning "That's life between the sheets."

† † †

"Smoke 'em if you got 'em," said Marquez to the agents as they got out of the jeeps.

Pauley took Marquez aside. " There's something not right here, Gabe."

"I got that same feeling, Boss," said Marquez.

"Weapons at the ready, gentlemen," said Pauley.

Pauley's team unslung their firearms: Thompson .45 caliber submachine guns and Winchester, 1907 .351 caliber self-loading rifles. Their sidearms were a mix of models popular with law enforcement agencies across the country: Smith & Wesson .357s, Colt .38s, Browning .45 caliber semi-automatics.

"All right, men," said Pauley, "Let's shove the 'Jimmy' off to the side."

As Pauley and his team approached the truck, five words boomed through the air, spit-out by a man concealed in the dense tree line.

"Hold it right there, fellas!"

"Identify yourself!" said Pauley, taken unawares and knowing somebody had caught him dead-to-rights in the open with his pants around his ankles.

"Oh, no. You, first!" said the Voice, calm but authoritative.

"We're with the Federal Bureau of Investigation."

Pauley and his team brought their weapons to bear, pointing them toward the forest.

"No need for that, fellas." said the Voice. "We're all on the same side here. Right?"

"Really?" said Pauley. "Okay. Just WHO would WE be?"

"I'm U.S. Deputy Marshal, Miles Standish! With the United States Marshals Service, and a direct descendant of THE, Miles Standish."

There was a pause.

"No doubt, you've heard of us?" said Standish.

Pauley looked at Marquez. Marquez shook his head and grinned.

"Can't say any of us have heard of you," said Pauley. "Or your ancestor."

There was dead silence for several seconds.

"Are you DENSE," said Standish. "Not, ME! The United States MARSHALS Service! You've heard of THEM, haven't you!?"

"Oh!" said Pauley. He winked at Marquez. "Let me ask my team if anyone's heard of your organization."

"You're a real Wisenheimer, G-Man!" said Standish. "Now, let's see some identification. Otherwise, my boys are apt to think you might be part of Jonny Fiáin's gang and hose you down with lead."

"Oh!" said Pauley. "Well, how do we know YOU aren't part of Fiáin's gang?"

"Look!" said Standish. "If we were his gang, you'd all be dead."

"Maybe yes, maybe no. I don't know about that. But it looks like we have ourselves a Mexican Standoff."

"Hey!" said another voice from a place of concealment. "No need to bring RACE into this!" It was Deputy Marshal Mesa.

"Now you've done it, G-Man," said Standish. "That was my partner, Marshal Mesa. I believe you just insulted him."

Marquez leaned close to Pauley and whispered: "Do you believe these yahoos? Let me try to goose this along, Boss."

Pauley   glanced   at   his   wristwatch; then   nodded.

"This is Special Agent Gabriel Mar--QUEZ. We need to sort this out," And I mean, fast." Marquez played up his Mexican accent. "And we need to do it BEFORE Fiáin shows up! With or without his gang. *Comprende,* Marshal *ME--SA*? *Comprende,* ya 'all?"

Pauley licked his lips. They were chapped, close to cracking. Deputy Marshal Mesa?" said Pauley in a purposeful but polite voice. "I apologize if I offended you or anyone else. It was a thoughtless metaphor, and I shouldn't have used it. So, what do you say, Marshal Mesa? Let's sort this out. How about you, Marshal Standish? Sound good?"

"Just peachy," said Standish. "How about you and I meet in front of the deuce-and-a-half where everyone can see us. Then I take mine out, and you take yours out, and we see who has the biggest?"

"Excuse me?" said Pauley.

"Badge, " said Standish. "Biggest, BADGE!"

Pauley chuckled. "You got yourself a deal, Marshal."

39.

The Gown

Alone on the bed in the stone dwelling he once shared with Katarina Bukowski, Headstone tossed and turned, unable to sleep. *Who IS she,* he wondered. *She looks no older than me. And what brings her to Jamaica?* Headstone parted the mosquito netting over the bed and got up.

Stepping outside, he felt a Trade Wind blowing past. Above him, the indigo-colored sky hosted countless stars shining bright with blue-white light, the same light as Katarina was awash with when she appeared to Balthazar inside the Cave of Contemplation.

† † †

Headstone held his arms to his sides and breathed. It was the kind of night he and Katarina so very much delighted. Changing into their other selves, they would run through the jungle, exhilarated by the savage strength their bodies possessed. And later, at the hidden waterfall, merging their bodies into one Energic Being. And when spent, they lay exhausted in each other's arms, overwhelmed and speechless by the sheer ecstasy of possessing two selves to choose from and yet be identical.

Headstone made his hands into fists, beat upon his chest, and cried loud and long unto heaven. "Have you not punished me enough!? If you do not deliver me from my torment—destroy me!"

††††

Anyone's guess why Headstone chose to change form and steal through the night to the Governor's Mansion. But that's what he did.

Easily avoiding the Night Watch patrolling Kingston and evading the prying torches of the Hessian Grenadiers who served as the Governor's private security force, Headstone crept through the darkness, scaled the brick wall, and dropped into the landscaped botanical gardens behind the mansion.

Out of the shadows, three Doberman Pincers rushed him; Headstone, as Weirdwolf, rose onto his back legs and growled. His reaction caused the Dobermans to flee in terror, back to the relative safety of their kennel in need of prolonged therapy.

††††

With her notorious coterie of female friends, gossip mongers really, Margaret Trelawney insisted on dressing the mysterious "girl" from abroad for the party. It was their way of welcoming *"her"* to Jamaica, and let's be honest, appraising her *"wares."*

The young woman's arrival was the most exciting thing that anyone (who was anyone) could recollect on Jamaica. Those fortunate enough to be invited that night wanted to meet not only "the girl," but the gallant sea Captain whose daring and heroism saved her from a certain and horrible death.

† † †

Eschewing *Robes à la Française* for more sensible, infinitely practical, British designs, designs patently warranted by the inhospitable Caribbean climate, Margaret Trelawney picked out a gown she had not yet worn—or bought.

She hadn't worn the dress for (1) fear of having to answer to her husband for its cost and (2) for having put on a good deal of weight during the last Hurricane Season, which had made the gown an impossible fit.

"Ma Saison en Enfer," she called it: "My season in Hell."

In any event, the gown was beautiful, guaranteed by its designer, Sir George Herringbone, to make the Creole women on Martinique green with envy; that is, provided they knew of the dress's existence; which they did, courtesy of a spy who was none other than Margaret Trelawney's black maid, Fifi.

There are no secrets close to the Equator.

"You look beautiful, my child," said Missus Trelawney to the black-haired beauty whose extraordinary eyes sparkled like amethyst gems. "Doesn't she, ladies?"

"Yes, yes," came a chorus of affirmative replies.

"She is beautiful, indeed!" said one.

"The gown is to die for!" said another.

"Truly, Margaret, she makes the dress come alive."

That last comment from her supposed "best friend," Libby Rice, was one the Governor's wife didn't need to hear.

Men should not fault women for how they speak when men are not around.

† † †

When a downstairs maid told the women that Captain and officers from the warship, *Defiance*, had arrived, the island's female social elite cleared out. They did so like Bulldogs after a meat cart, leaving the young woman standing alone in front of a free-standing, full-size looking-glass. That's how life went in Jamaica then.

True, she told herself. *The gown is breathtaking, but who am I to wear it?*

It was precisely that moment when she heard a "tap-tap-tap" tapping sound on the glass of the French Doors behind her. The doors opened onto a balcony overlooking one of many torch-lit fountains on the Governor's estate.

Then, this black Adonis, this son of Vulcan, opened the door and stepped inside. When she turned, she saw him standing there, his naked, seven-foot frame glistening with sweat; he was like an impossibly perfect statue sculpted from black marble. As he drew close, her breath leaped from her body; she swooned into his arms.

† † †

When the nameless woman awoke, she found herself on a carpet of sweet-smelling rose petals that gave off an aroma of freshly cut peaches. There was an abundance of Honey Suckle and Night Blooming Jasmine that also filled the air.

Near where the young woman lay was a natural pool fed by a waterfall. On the grass, and the smooth flat rocks around her, burned no fewer than a hundred, non-denominational Cathedral candles.

For the Weirdwolves on Jamaica, this was one of their most sacred sites, where marriages were performed and consummated. And, no, to this day, it is not mentioned in Travel brochures.

She pushed herself up into a sitting position and saw him sitting across from her.

"Are you going to rape me?" she said.

"No," he said. "Why would you even ask me that?" There was something in his voice that sounded hurt by the question, offended even.

"It seems to be on the minds of most men I meet," she said.

"I am NOT *most men*."

She noticed he was still naked. "I can see that."

Several awkward moments passed.

"Nice dress," he said.

"Thanks," said the woman. "It's not mine."

He laughed. A deep, full-throated laugh originated inside his belly, where, ideally, laughter should originate.

"It is now," he said.

She looked down at the dress.

"I suppose your right," she said softly and smiled. "I suppose it is."

† † †

Governor Trelawney's Redcoats scoured the island for the "missing" young woman allegedly from the Balkans, along with Margaret Trelawney's one-of-a-kind gown made of Chinese export black & silver silk-brocaded satin with a matching stomacher of silk and silk chenille, looped fringe.

It might be worth noting (again): *"That damnable dress!"* as the Governor referred to it, was designed by none other than Sir George Herringbone, with a shop in London, on Seville Row, and another under construction on Portobello Road, near Ladbroke Gardens, that was in walking distance from *Julie's Wine Bar.*

The search went on for three days to no avail. If the job as Governor of Jamaica had taught Trelawney anything, it was this: *"Sometimes you're the dog; sometimes you're the tree."*[91]

Headstone and the woman took refuge with Aunt Lily because none but simple folk and Weirdwolves ever stopped at her grass-shack condo.

† † †

With Aunt Lily's help—help that comprised an herbal potion warmed between the breasts, accompanied by chanting *A-cappella*, the violet-eyed woman's lost memory returned—intact.

"I know who I am," she said.

They were seated outside, enjoying Aunt Lily's version of *cafe latte* and *croissants.* There was no jubilation in her voice, no celebration; far from it, she sounded saddened by this drug-induced revelation that restored her Memory's orbit.

Aunt Lily stood. "You two need to talk. I'm going to Trader Joe's. Anything we need? Anything you want?"

"We're almost out of coffee, Auntie," said Headstone.

"You want more organic French roast?"

---

[91] A home-spun truism attributed to an 18th Century Buccaneer named *Handsome Jonny Stint*, Captain of a Jamaica sloop named *La Bruja Del Mar* (aka, the *Sea Witch*).

"Yes," said Headstone. "Medium grind, please."

"How about you, sweetheart?" said Lily. "Anything I can bring you from Kingston?"

"Skin lotion?"

"I'll make something special for you when I return, my dear. No need to buy that imported hog crap from Paris, don'tcha know."

"Thank you, Aunt Lily," said the woman.

"*Oui, Cheri*," said Lily. "But, of course."

"I remember my name now. It's Szah Zhah."

"How very nice," said Aunt Lily. "You must tell me more when I return."

Aunt Lily grabbed her *Giorgio Armani iguana-skin* fanny-pack and departed.

"I've done bad things, Balthazar."

"I don't care," said Headstone. "What's in the past is past, and now is now."

"You don't understand, Balthazar. I am something different than I was, and I will go on doing bad things. Whenever the moon waxes full."

He laughed and took her into his arms. "Then we will do bad things together, my love, for I, too, have been changed." He saw confusion in her eyes. "I will show you," said Balthazar as he kissed the tip of her nose. "Tonight."

"The moon will be full tonight, yes?"

He nodded.

Szah Zhah began to tremble. As an indescribable fear crowded her face, Balthazar drew her close and licked her ears until she cried "uncle," and her fears departed.

For the first time in her sweet, brief, unhappy life, Szah Zhah Kopeĉ felt safe, protected, and loved—truly loved.

As Handsome Jonny Stint would say: *there is always, always, always a silver lining; sometimes, one merely needs a dark cloud to see it.*

40.

The Long Way Home

As they started away from Doctor Luther Van Helwing's estate, Angel could feel the cold kisses of snowflakes on her face. But once the motorcycle gained speed, all Angel felt was cold wind stinging her cheeks.

Just outside the San Souci City Limits, Jonny stopped at the first roadside diner they came to. Called *Bonnie Lou's Country Kitchen,* it was renowned for its breaded veal, marinated chicken gizzards, coffee, and rhubarb pie.

In 1949, there were no fewer than seventy-eight thousand, three-hundred and twenty-one roadside diners in Canada and the Continental United States combined. And in all these roadside eateries, customers could expect at least one frumpy, middle-aged woman with blue hair and mandarin-red lips, named Ruby, to be on duty, waitressing. God's truth. And *Bonnie Lou's Country Kitchen* was no exception.

Ruby came by twice to refill Jonny's coffee cup while Angel ate a late breakfast of scrambled eggs, ham, and bacon, and a short stack of blueberry pancakes, smeared with butter and drenched with Syrpul.[92]

"That's a pretty daughter you got there, mister," said Ruby. "Oh, my, but you have beautiful eyes, sweetie."

"Thank you," said Angel, then she smiled: "All the better to see you with."

---

[92] Syrpul is a Canadian variant of maple syrup.

A perplexed look came over Ruby, Jonny, also.

"All right, sweetie," said Ruby. "If you say so," Ruby winked at Jonny and went off.

"What the hell was THAT about, Angel?"

"There's something about her. Something I don't trust. She's not who you think she is. I can sense it."

"She's a waitress in a diner, for Pete's sake, Angel. She doesn't have any say about who comes here, and we don't have any say as to who our waitress is. That's just the way things are. There are all kinds of people you'll be meeting in life. Try to relax and get along."

"Like that man who turned into that thing in the doctor's barn?"

"Judas Priest, Angel! That's not what I meant. Anyway, I wish to God you hadn't seen that. I'm sorry you did."

"Don't be. I'm glad I saw it."

"Okay, kiddo," said Jonny. "you're starting to worry me again."

Angel belched a mini-belch, then neatly stacked her plates, utensils, and used a paper napkin on top to make it easier for the busboy to handle.

From somewhere in the kitchen came the sound of dishes crashing on the floor. It was loud enough to make Jonny flinch and look. A minute, maybe two, passed in silence; Jonny took a sip of coffee.

"Are you feeling okay?" said Jonny.

Angel gave him a puzzled look. "Yeah, Jonny. I feel great."

"So, sounds don't bother you now?"

Angel laughed. "No, Jonny. I just turn the volume down in my head, like I would a radio."

"For real?"

"Yes. I just concentrate and do it. I don't know how, but it works."

Jonny nodded thoughtfully. "Nothing else bothering you?"

"Like?" said Angel.

"It's been less than a month since—" Jonny stopped.

"Since Szah Zhah murdered my mom and dad?"

"Yeah," said Jonny. "Since that THING murdered the people I love most in this world, apart from their daughter, and it makes me angry to hear you talk about that monster like you know her."

Angel used her spoon for fishing a marshmallow out of her cup and sighed. "Sarah and Paddy are gone, Jonny. Nothing can bring them back. If I could feel sad, I would, but I don't; so, I won't. It can't change anything. As for, 'that thing'? I'm sorry it bothers you that I call her 'Szah Zhah,' but that's her NAME!"

"Okay, okay," said Jonny. "Calm down."

"I AM calm, Jonny. YOU'RE the one that's not!"

The diner wasn't full by any means, but heads were beginning to turn and look in Angel and Jonny's direction.

From behind the cash register, Ruby gave Jonny a sympathetic look as if to say: "Boy, oh boy, mister, you have your hands full with that one, don't you?!"

A couple of minutes passed before Angel spoke. This time her voice was impassive, calm, almost detached.

"Something else, Jonny; I think Szah Zhah and I are, well, somehow connected."

Jonny almost choked on the coffee he was about to swallow. He took a deep breath. "Connected? How the hell do you figure?"

The heads of a few patrons turned to look and give Jonny the skunk-eye before going back to minding their own business if ever they were.

"Sometimes I sense her presence as if she's thinking about me, wondering where I am."

"Well, that's—" Jonny checked, hesitated. "That's just great." He took out his wallet and placed a few dollars on the table. "Let's go."

Angel felt a tightness suddenly grip her belly, which made it difficult to breathe. Then, just as suddenly, the intense biting sensation she felt in her gut vanished; her breathing returned to normal.

"Are you okay?" said Jonny.

Angel nodded. She took a deep breath before answering. "Yes."

† † †

Ruby watched Jonny and Angel leave on the three-wheeler before she tossed a clean-up cloth onto the seat of an unoccupied booth. She hurried down the hall to a public telephone on the wall. She lifted the receiver off the hook, dropped several Canadian nickels in the coin slot, and dialed a number she knew by heart.

After a single ring, someone answered.

"It's Ruby. From Bonnie Lou's. They just left. Pass it on."

Ruby hung the phone on the hook and went to the Ladies Room to powder her nose.

† † †

They hadn't gone far when Jonny pulled into a Filling Station to top off the Harley's gasoline tank before crossing the border. There was no sign of the sun, just a thick November mist that left a delicate blanket of moisture on everything it touched.

While Jonny was inside, paying for the gasoline, Angel ran a brush over Whiskey's fur, something Whiskey needed and enjoyed.

When Jonny returned, he held two paper cups, one with coffee and another with hot chocolate topped with marshmallows.

Jonny flicked his head in the direction of a picnic table sheltered on three sides by a sheet metal roof, not warm, given the time of year, but it would be dry underneath.

"We need to talk, Angel, darlin'. Come on, Whiskey. You, too."

When they were seated at the table, Jonny gave Angel the hot chocolate; steam overflowed the top of the cup and vanished in the air.

"Sorry," said Jonny. "They didn't have any big marshmallows, just the little ones."

Angel shook her head. "That's okay. It'll be fine. What is it you want to talk about? Is it about taking me back?" Jonny nodded.

"I was hoping I could stay with you, Jonny. Me and Whiskey both."

Jonny took a sip of coffee. He put the cup on the table and turned it clockwise; he repeated the motion counterclockwise. He did this several times while Angel waited to hear him say something—ANYthing!

"You don't want us with you," said Angel. "Is that it?"

He looked at her, disbelieving what he heard. "No, Angel, that's NOT it."

"Then tell me, Jonny."

Jonny took a minute, getting the words right in his head before he spoke. Jonny took another sip of coffee. Angel watched the steam leave his mouth and evaporate in the air.

"I've done some bad things, Angel. And the law isn't going to forget. They won't stop looking for me. I'm on the run, little darlin'. I can't do what I need to do to survive, not if I'm worried about the two of you, you and Whiskey. I promised Paddy I'd protect you, and I will, Angel. Even if that means I have to leave you behind. Besides, the O'Haras are worried sick about you."

"I know that. And I love Bumpa and Nana." Angel blew on the surface of her hot chocolate to cool it, then nonchalantly said, "I don't know about grandfather and grandmother, McLaughlin. I don't see them much. Except when I have to. I don't think they liked my dad much."

"It's complicated, Angel. Some folks have a hard time showing their feelings. But that doesn't mean they don't love you. Anyway, your grandparents will sort all that out. But first, I have to get you back, safe and sound, one way or another. I figure we'll go to Bangor. Once we're there, I can put you and Whiskey on a train to New Dublin. That's the way it's got to be, for now, anyway."

Does that mean you're *not* leaving me forever, Jonny?"

"Put THAT out of your head. We'll see each other again. Bet your boots; we will. I'm a lot of things, little darlin', but I'm no quitter, and I'm not going to quit on you, so don't you quit on me."

A minute passed in silence; they just looked at each other.

"Jonny?"

"Yeah?"

"I can see in the dark."

"Judas Priest, Angel. For real?"

"Yes."

"You keep piling them on, young lady, one wonderment after another."

"Jonny?"

"What, Angel darlin'?"

"What about Szah Zhah?"

41.

A New York Minute

Szah Zhah and Headstone sailed down the coast to New York Harbor, checked into their private suite at the Waldorf-Astoria in Manhattan, then went crazy on each other.

Later, while having Martinis in their room, Headstone noticed Szah Zhah suddenly double-over in excruciating pain.

"Are you all right, my love?" he said.

Szah Zhah straightened. "I'm fine. Really."

"What was it?" he said. "Too many olives?"

Szah Zhah's jaw relaxed; she tried to smile. "I believe the little mouse and I are somehow connecting. Communicating, you might say."

"So! You DID turn the girl?!"

"No, Balthazar. I told you. The *fasz* shot me before I got to her. But something wonderful must have happened when I clawed her. What else would explain it!?"

"Will wonders never cease!" said Headstone, and he kissed her playfully on top of her head. The telephone on the nightstand near the bed rang. It was the Front Desk. Headstone answered.

"Thank you." That was all Headstone said. He put the phone on the receiver and turned to Szah Zhah. "I'll be right back, my love."

This man-wolf turned heads everywhere. He was seven feet tall, wearing ivory-white linen slacks that morning, a long-sleeve, white muslin shirt, alligator shoes, and an alligator belt. No wonder Balthazar

Headstone turned every white head he encountered down the long hallway to the elevators.

When the nearest elevator door opened, an elderly white couple from Buffalo froze in place at the sight of the black giant about to enter.

The uniformed black elevator operator, Ernie, grinned and bid the couple, "Have a wonderful day, folks."

The elderly couple averted their eyes and hurried past Headstone for their room. Headstone had seen and heard it all as a black man who traveled extensively for two hundred and some odd years. He knew that real power rested in the hands of the social and political elites, which is to say, white people; hence, it behooved him and Szah Zhah to cultivate white friends in high places and a good many more in low-lying areas.

It is also true that, in the course of two hundred and some odd years, Szah Zhah and Headstone amassed a considerable fortune; indeed, they represented *Old Money*, or so one could rightly say but in a hugely tong-in-cheek kind of way.

A photograph of Headstone and Szah Zhah appeared in the High Society Section of the New York Times one year before; when they were having lunch at the Waldorf-Astoria with the not so Honorable Mayor of New York City, William O'Dwyer. Also present was Headstone's good friend, acclaimed Baritone, actor, and political activist Paul Robeson. Walter Winchell, Sheila Graham, Virginia Wolfe, Graham Greene, and Tennessee Williams were also present. In such company, Szah Zhah and Headstone quickly received New York's stamp of approval. In bars, theaters, hotels, and restaurants, they were made welcome, but then, that's New York, where wealth and social status announce one's identity in advance of their arrival.

Life often dances on a ball of subtle distinctions; this was especially true for Balthazar and Szah Zhah: Weirdwolf and Vampire Bat. In post-war Europe, France, particularly, a black man with a white woman would cause little or no stir, but that was Europe, not the United States, not in 1949.

Black men still lived under a covert threat of lynching in the Old South, and blatant discrimination in all forty-eight of the United States limited the work blacks could find to achieve a quality-of-life worth living. America had always been "the land of promise," but a Promise that proved elusive, just beyond reach, for all but a few people of color.

In the hotel's Main Lobby, Headstone went to one of several private booths where there was a public payphone. Inside a phone booth, Headstone dialed a number and waited. The phone rang once; then, someone answered.

"Very well," said Headstone. "Do it. But, remember, the girl is not to be harmed. Once you have her, send word to me!"

After Headstone ended the call, he stopped by the Front Desk. He ordered room service: *Beluga Caviar* from the Caspian Sea, and a bottle of *Dom Perignon*, 1936, the same year Szah Zhah won the title of "*Miss Budapest*" in the nation-state of Hungary, later occupied in 1945, by Josef Stalin and the Red Army.

As Headstone started toward the elevator, he thought of Szah Zhah waiting for news of the "Little Mouse."

They had been together for two centuries, and it bothered him not at all when she took young women as lovers. But why she fixated on a twelve-year-old child was beyond his ken. *Does she yearn for a child of her own? A daughter, perhaps? But she knows that cannot be!* Those were his thoughts on his way back to their room. Still, Headstone loved Szah Zhah more than life itself; simply put, there was nothing he would refuse her. So! He would tell her to be patient, plant kisses up and down her elongated Modigliani neck to her fat lips, and the caviar and champagne would fortuitously arrive by then.

Outside, rain lashed the streets, cars, and pedestrians, adding drama to Manhattan, with lightning and thunder crashing. Storms pleased Balthazar and had since he was a boy named Sunday, so very, very long ago.

Exciting and grand is life, Headstone told himself as he stepped inside the elevator. He knew better than to switch the words around, life being too vast, too expansive to define, with one or two adjectives.

Headstone noticed a look of weariness and resignation in Ernie's wrinkled, cordovan-brown face. He wondered how long the man had been at his appointed task taking wealthy hotel guests to rooms he couldn't sleep in himself. Ernie had probably never even seen the inside of one of those rooms, not ever. Leaving the elevator, Headstone handed the old man a crisp, clean, one-thousand-dollar bill and walked off.

The elevator operator looked at the bill; his hand trembled. Ernie held the paper closer to make sure he was seeing what he thought he was seeing. He was! The 22nd and 24th president of the United States and the only president in American history to serve two non-consecutive terms in office[93], Grover Cleveland.

Forgetting how bad his knees were, Ernie chuckled and jumped up and down.

"Oh, man-o-man! The ol' lady gunna be happy to see Ernie tonight. Hah! Oh, yeah! Oh, yeah! Gunna git some lovin' tonight."

---

[93] 1885–1889 and 1893–1897

42.

Bullets are Forever
(But Not Little Boys)

Jonny saw Angel frantically motion to stop. He coasted to a halt where the ground was somewhat flat.

"We're almost there, Angel. The border's just ahead."

"Something bad is out there, Jonny. Waiting for us. I can feel it."

"Dammit! I've been thinking the same thing."

"Ever since we left the doctor's, I've sensed eyes on us, Jonny. I felt it again at the filling station when you gassed up. And I feel it now. We should turn around and find some other way."

"Angel, darlin'. There isn't another way. The authorities will be watching the border crossings. They'll have my picture at every checkpoint. This way is our best bet. I gotta try, little darlin'."

Angel nodded. There was no disguising the grim look etched on her face.

"Okay," she said. She wrapped her arms around Whiskey.

"Hold on tight," said Jonny. "I ain't stopping for no one, NO how!"

† † †

Deputy Marshal Standish, along with Special Agent Pauley, finalized the details of what would transpire once they had Jonny Fiáin in custody. It came neatly down to this: If Fiáin were captured alive, the U.S. Marshal's Service would assert jurisdiction on the ground that they have the higher equities. In the alternative, should Fiáin choose to fight and be killed, they agreed on what should happen next. They based their claim on the date of the original warrant issued by a federal judge in New Mexico for Fiáin's arrest.

If, however, Fiáin was killed while resisting arrest, the FBI would be entitled to Fiáin's corpse and the distinction of announcing Angel's return to her grandparents in New Dublin.

The crackle of static through a trans-receiver, a U.S. military SCR-536, "handie-talkie" slung over Standish's shoulder got everyone's attention.

"Mesa to Standish, over."

"Go ahead, Albert. Over"

"They're coming! Fiáin. The girl. And a dog. Over."

"Okay, Albert," said Standish. "Good luck, amigo. Over."

Standish hung the handie talkie on the branch of a tree beside him. He looked at Pauley and grinned as he removed his sidearm from its holster.

"Okay, Agent Pauley. Let's get this bastard and go home, heroes."

† † †

Albert Mesa didn't care a whit for Standish's plan. He thought it entirely too risky for the girl and argued vociferously for another approach. Standish had seniority, however, and it was his call, not Albert Mesas.

Special Agent Pauley bit his tongue and remained neutral while the two marshals argued. He had already conceded that the Marshal's Service had jurisdiction; besides, if Standish's plan went south, the fault would be the Marshal's Service, not the FBI's.

"For the girl's sake," said Marquez, "I hope this works."

"Me, too," said Mesa. "Me, too."

In the time he and Gabriel Marquez had been around each other, they found themselves, in a word, bonding. It went unspoken, but each was more than a little grateful for the other's presence there that day.

† † †

No one knew where the shot came from that hit Standish on his left ear, taking the top half of his head off.

More shots rang out; bullets hissed through the air. Agent Gibson looked down at half-a-head, one eye and brain matter sliding off his boots onto the ground.

"Who's shooting!?" said Pauley.

The agents crouching for cover, those Pauley could see, had dumb, blank looks mirroring their bewilderment.

"Well, shoot back!" said Pauley with all the force his lungs could muster.

"At what, sir!?" said Gibson. "We don't see anyone shoot?"

"Cheeseburger!" said Pauley, for the last time in his life. "Then shoot the [expletive deleted] trees!"

Pauley's men began spraying the forest with bullets from their Thompson submachine guns and Winchester rifles for a full minute.

"Hold your fire, men!" said Pauley. His mouth and throat were parched, and the acrid smell of cordite filled his nose and hung in the air over the heads of the agents.

The forest was again silent; then came the eerie, high-pitched sound of wolves howling. There was no way of knowing how many throats the howls issued from, but they seemed to be many and were everywhere.

† † †

"What do you think?" said Agent Marquez, staring at the end of the rope they held in their hands.

The rope was "High-Grade Triple-Braided" hemp fiber made in South Carolina, approximately one inch in diameter. Mesa and Marquez held the free end while the rest of the rope lay across the road, somewhat camouflaged with twigs and leaves. The other end was tied securely around the trunk of a Blue Spruce directly across from the two lawmen.

"I think it's either going to yank our arms from their sockets, or it'll sweep Fiáin off the bike. In either case, our arms are going to be damn sore tomorrow."

"Well, that's just great," said Marquez, thick with sarcasm. "I was planning on doing some fly fishing. Soon as this is over."

Mesa and Marquez looked at each other. In the near distance, they heard the sound of a motorcycle coming their way. They also heard something else, something completely unexpected: the loud report of gunshots, accompanied by wolves howling, lots of them, from all parts of the forest.

They heard gunshots from just ahead and the sound of wolves howling. Angel realized she was holding her breath when she saw what appeared to be a long snake stretched across both sides of the road. Clearly, her eyesight was more acute than before the bat wounded her.

"Jonny!" she said (more like shouted) over the sound of the engine and pointed.

Too late. The "snake" leaped straight into the air and caught Jonny square in the chest across his heart. Angel heard Jonny grunt, and he flew fly backward off the bike.

Riderless, the three-wheeler swayed to one side and was headed straight for the dried, decaying husk of a fallen tree. In a fraction of a second, Angel tossed Whiskey into a patch of bracken, covered her head, and braced for the impact she knew was coming.

"If you can get the girl," said Marquez. "I'll cuff Fiáin."

"That works," said Mesa.

As Mesa started to find the sidecar, he instinctively chambered a round in his Remington 12-gauge pump shotgun, loaded with .45 caliber slugs. Forget deer; Armorers in the Marshals Service crafted these bullets to bring down a Grizzly bear; that, or an *Abominable Snowman*[94].

---

[94] The name given to the race of bi-peds guarding the gates to Shangri-La in the Himalayan Mountains of Tibet and distant cousins of the Sasquatches inhabiting the Pacific Northwest.

Mesa saw two FBI agents and the State Police officers abandoning their cover places, backing up while shooting continuously. Still, Mesa couldn't see the attackers.

† † †

Jonny was on his back, barely conscious. A small pool of blood formed around his head where it had made contact with the hard clay. Marquez was about to pull the .45 caliber from Jonny's shoulder holster and toss it when a creature—a giant wolf-like thing, or so he hastily surmised, lunged from the bushes.

Marquez couldn't believe his eyes; he reached for his service revolver and fired. The bullet grazed one of the creature's arms. The agent didn't have time to get off a second shot; the beast tore into his chest and neck with teeth and claws.

† † †

Jonny's vision returned, although his head felt caught in a vice. He saw a man on his back on the road being torn apart by something that resembled a wolf but with a more massive head and body. Jonny's ears rang from the impact of the fall, but now, added to the cacophony inside his head, was the mind-numbing screaming he heard as the creature tore the man's entrails from his body.

While the creature busied itself with its kill, Jonny rolled onto his stomach and crawled toward thick patches of emerald green bracken lining both sides of the road. Jonny had done a lot of crawling on his belly in the

Marine Corps, mostly when his life was on the line, just as it was then. He knew how to slither quietly and quickly, and that's what he did. There was nothing he could do for the man in the road. No. It was every man for himself time, kill or be killed, time.

† † †

Mesa could see the motorcycle where it crashed into a fallen tree. The impact had thrown Angel out of the sidecar. She was stunned but sitting up when Mesa got to her. Before he could ask if she was okay, Mesa heard Marquez screaming as a beast ripped the FBI agent's entrails from his body.

Mesa gently touched Angel's arm; she looked at him, and her violet eyes flashed. "You're one of the men chasing Jonny Fiáin."

"Yes. I'm Deputy Marshal Albert Mesa. And right now, I gotta get you out of here, young lady."

"You don't know what you're facing, do you, Marshal Mesa?"

"No," said Mesa. "Do you?"

"Yes. I think so."

"What do they want?" said Mesa, momentarily taken aback by Angel's violet eyes that lit up when she spoke.

"Me," she said. Her voice was perfectly calm. "They want me."

"THAT'S not going to happen," said Mesa. "Let's go. "Where?"

"There's a Fire Watch Tower I saw on the way in, not far from here. It's as good a place as any to hide."

Angel looked around. "Whiskey?"

"Who?" said Mesa.

"My dog. I've got to find Whiskey."

Mesa helped Angel to her feet. "We got to go now, Angel. He's a dog. They're smart. They know how to take care of themselves. You're coming with me, young lady. Even if I have to carry you!"

Before Angel could answer, a Weirdwolf jumped onto the fallen tree and growled. Mesa raised the shotgun and fired. The slug entered the creature at an upward angle at the base of the throat and exited through the back of its head. Mesa fired two more rounds in quick succession, creating a hole large enough to accommodate a Tom Brady regulation-size football in the creature's chest.

"That's no wolf!" said Mesa.

"You're right, Marshal Mesa," said Angel. "It's a man. Or it was."

At that moment, the creature began changing into a human form.

"Holy Mary, Mother of God," said Mesa. "You're right!"

No. Angel was wrong. It wasn't a man at all. It was Ruby in the buff; Ruby, the frumpy waitress with blue hair and mandarin-red lips from Bonnie Lou's on the Canadian side of the border.

"Can you run, Angel?"

"What about Jonny?"

"Right now, I don't give a rat's whisker about Jonny Fiáin. Come on!"

They started away from the din of gunfire, and the screaming and the terrible sounds the Weirdwolves made each time they made a kill.

43.

Up, Up, & Away

Agents Pauley and Gibson were the only men of their team to make it as far as the Jeeps; the others were dead. The Jeeps were where the FBI agents had parked them, directly behind the deuce-and-a-half, near the Command Center and ambush site. That intense good feeling that accompanied seeing their best means of escape turned to bitter ash in their mouths; the Distributor caps were missing and the spark-plug wiring torn apart, rendering the jeeps useless. It was the same when Gibson checked under the hood of the deuce-and-a-half. If they were going to escape with their lives, it would have to be on foot.

"What do we do now, Mister Pauley?"

Pauley inserted a fresh magazine into the BAR, the Browning Automatic Rifle he grabbed when the ammo for his Thompson ran out. A quarter of a mile away came creatures in a pack, some running on all fours, some on their back legs, upright, straight out of the tree line.

"We RUN!" said Pauley.

The agents ran until their lungs felt on fire, but the creatures, ten or more, steadily closed on them. Then they saw it, just ahead. The abandoned fire watchtower the Forest Service manned in the summer months.

Pauley was a short distance ahead of Gibson and about ten yards short of reaching the first of three zig-zagging flights of stairs when a gunshot rang out from the direction of the forest. Pauley heard the agent cry out; he turned and saw Gibson on his knees, a gaping hole in his abdomen from a 30.6 firing hollow-points. Gibson had a look of disbelief frozen on his face when a second shot blew the top of his head away. Pauley fired a burst from his BAR toward the area where he saw a muzzle flash from the sniper's second shot. He didn't wait for the sniper to target him next.

Pauley ran! As fast as his nearly spent legs would allow.

Three flights of metal stairs zig-zagged to the top of the lookout station. Pauley ascended the first flight of stairs and stood on a small landing where he hesitated long enough to look back. The creatures were a scarce ten yards away from reaching the stairs. He leveled the BAR at those closest and fired. Large chunks of fur and flesh flew off their bodies in bloody clumps—three creatures fell in a twisted heap.

The sniper must have been changing to another position, perhaps one closer to the tower, because no bullets sought him as Pauley hurried the rest of the way up the second and third flights of stairs, heart pounding in his chest.

He kicked open the padlocked plywood door and went inside a 10' x 10' room furnished with a cot, a table, a wooden swivel chair, a woodstove, and a First Aid kit, mounted on the south-facing wall. Rectangular windows faced north, south, east, and west and afforded views over the forest top. Looking north, Pauley could see to Canada. The last thing Pauley had on his mind was enjoying the view and with good reason. The sniper's next bullet smashed through the north-facing window. It missed Pauley but showered him on the left side of his face and scalp with glass fragments. Why it was at that moment, Pauley thought about the fascist Italian Carrier Pigeon that nearly caused his demise in Tunisia, almost a decade before, is anyone's guess.

Mysterious is the mind.

Jonny hadn't crawled but five yards when he came face to face with a large pile of fresh, partially digested scat[95]: bear scat. It was still warm, with a mixture of pine seeds, wild berries, grass, and small chips of animal bone and fur. Something had frightened the bear, really bad. "You ain't the only one, Br'er Bear," Jonny whispered.

Not to look a gift horse in the mouth, Jonny scooped bear scat into his hand and rubbed it over the arms of his leather jacket; it had been a Christmas present from Paddy and Sarah, way back when.

When Jonny heard the sound of twigs and dried leaves snapping a few yards ahead of him, he eased his .45 from the holster, cupped the grip with both hands, and rested on his elbows, waiting.

He saw the feathery tendrils of an emerald green fern brushed aside, revealing Whiskey's face staring back at him. Whiskey went up to Jonny, sniffed his jacket, and retreated with a whimper.

"Believe me, boy. I smell like this for a reason. Now let's find our girl."

When Angel and Mesa came to a shallow stream meandering north to south, they stopped. They had only to go fifteen feet down an incline to reach the water.

---

[95] Poop. Kaw-kaw. Shite. Excrement. Doo-doo.

"Thank you, God," said Mesa aloud. "Come on, Angel. We're going to get our feet wet."

"So, they can't track us by our scent," said Angel.

"That's right. You are one smart, little lady."

"I'm not that smart, Marshal Mesa, and I'm not little; besides that, I'm too young to be a lady."

Mesa didn't know what to say. "Okay, Angel. We're going to go with the stream, south."

"Okay."

"Great," said Mesa. "Now watch your step. It's steep, and the soil is soft."

Mesa couldn't help but wonder as they started down the bank: *Maybe it's all the red meat her generation's eating?*

They reached the water, and with each step, they carefully planted their feet on and over moss-covered rocks and the soft gravel bottom that shifted beneath their feet as they proceeded south. They could hear gunshots coming from two different locations ahead of them, neither from far away.

Whiskey stopped, his ears perked up; then Jonny heard it, the sound of many voices participating in what seemed a heated debate. The voices came from the other side of a ravine that Jonny and Whiskey were traversing.

"Stay, Whiskey."

Whiskey whimpered and stretched out on his stomach on the spongy, dark hummus that carpeted the ground throughout much of the forest. He did this while Jonny stealthily made his way through the bracken, out of the ravine, and slithered his way up the other side.

Atop the ridge, Jonny concealed himself behind the hollow trunk of a fallen tree. He looked down at a clearing where he saw no fewer than forty partially nude men and women conversing loudly, shouting while putting on clothes left on the hoods of a dozen or more parked passenger vehicles.

"Y'all can't leave," said a lean, dark-haired man with sharp features and nose like the curved beak of a hawk. "The girl is out there, somewhere, and our orders are to get her."

A stubby woman with red hair hitched up the bib-overalls she was putting on; then, she poked the dark-haired man on the chest with her forefinger. "How many brothers and sisters are we supposed to lose to find this girl, Curly!?"

There was a loud murmur of agreement from the others getting dressed.

"That ain't the point, Maggie," said Curly. "We gave Balthazar Headstone our word we would help."

"Dammit, Curly, we have! Haven't we?" said the redhead. "We lost seven of our family this morning, maybe more. We won't know until we recover the bodies. And how long before more lawmen show up? We did our best. Now it's time to go. I've got a beauty salon to run, bills to pay, and food to put on the table. We all do! But we can't very well do it if we're dead."

The others, dressed now, shouted their approval with what Maggie, the redhead, was saying. Curly was on his own.

"Well, I ain't giving up. My word is my bond. And if Balthazar Headstone says the girl is important enough to risk our lives to grab hold of, so be it."

"Then you're a damn fool, Curly. I love you, brother, but you're a damn fool." Maggie scanned the faces of the others. "Let's go home, folks, honor our dead, and forget about today."

Jonny watched as those below tied tarps over the back of two pickup trucks where at least fourteen badly shot up bodies, ten men and four women, were stacked like cordwood.

Jonny watched as everyone in the clearing below returned to their vehicles and drove off except for Curly.

Curly began lacing up his logging boots. He did this sitting on the tailgate of his 1938 Chevy half-ton pickup truck while cursing the others as cowards for leaving him alone to accomplish their mission. Curly was another gift horse[96] that Jonny wasn't going to look in the mouth.

Jonny unsheathed the K-bar[97] he kept on his belt and crept up behind Curly to the front of the pickup. From there, he moved along one side toward the back.

Crouching by the left rear fender, Jonny grabbed a rock the size of a hardball and lobbed it over the back of the truck. It worked. Curly leaped to his feet, minus one boot, and looked for the source of the sound. Enough time for Jonny to come around from behind; then, slit Curley's throat, literally from one unwashed ear to the other. Curly crumpled to the ground and was bleeding out when Jonny knelt beside him.

---

[96] The old adage: *"Never look a gift horse in the mouth,"* has been around for a long, long time. Back in the day, when a farmer (anyone, really) purchased a horse they would first check its mouth, gums, and teeth, to make certain there was no indicia of rot or disease. If the mouth was in good shape, the horse was considered worth buying; which only left the price to haggle over. Hence, if you're getting the damn horse for FREE, don't be so rude as to first look in its mouth.

[97] Marine Corp combat knife.

"I'm sorry I had to kill you, Curly. I would have liked to ask you a good many questions, but that's just how it goes, I guess. I'll be taking your truck. Okay?"

Curly was bleeding out. Only a stream of pink bubbles emerged as he tried to speak through the deep gash in his throat.

Jonny whistled. Whiskey came running, and off they went—in Curly's truck.

44.

Hell, Hath No Fury

"Why don't you come out in the open, you son of a bitch," said Pauley, shouting his lungs out. "Let's settle this like men." He knew it was a stupid thing to say, but he said it anyway.

"Too bad, lawman," came a distinctly feminine voice, loud and shrill. "Yours truly is ALL woman, and you, sitting up there like a coon up a tree. You know you're licked, so toss that machine gun out the window and come down? I promise I'll kill you fast, won't hurt a bit."

Pauley already felt like his head was splitting apart, and now, THIS!

"You may be a woman, but I'll tell you something: you're NO, lady!"

That, too, was a stupid thing to say, but he said it anyway.

Pauley stood and fired off a burst from the BAR. He heard her laughing.

"What the hell are you shooting at, lawman? I'm over here, you dumb bastard!"

She fired another round that traveled three-thousand feet per second and went through the east-facing window, just missing Pauley's head. She had relocated her position. At that point, Pauley thought it prudent to upend the desk and sit behind it. As he sat on the floor, he conceded to himself that his adversary was competent; no, better than just qualified, a marksman who knew how to anticipate the movements of his prey and to account for wind and elevation. Where, he wondered, had she learned such skills?

"Hey, Annie!" said Pauley. He knew if he kept shouting, he would be hoarse by nightfall. Or, he'd be dead, and it wouldn't matter a whit if his voice quit on him.

"How'd you know my name, lawman?" said Annie, the sniper.

"Seriously," said Pauley. Your name is ANNIE?"

"Yeah, dick-head. Did someone rat me out, or was it just a lucky guess?"

Pauley laughed, as much from battle fatigue as from the irony of his predicament.

"Neither," said Pauley. "I called you 'Annie' as a compliment! After a famous female Sharpshooter in the Old West named Annie Oakley."

Pauley could hear her laughing.

"Well, beat a turd with a stick, lawman! That's who my pop, Curly, named me after. Annie Oakley."

"Isn't that something," said Pauley.

"Lawman!"

"What?" said Pauley.

"How is it you showed up here today?"

"We came to apprehend and arrest a fleeing felon who's been hiding in Canada. Why are you here?"

"We're here for the girl."

"The girl!? What's the girl to you?"

"To me? Nothing. It's the master, the head of the Brethren who wants her."

"Who's that, if you don't mind my asking?"

"Hah! said the woman. "If I told you, Lawman, I'd have to kill you."

"Isn't that what you're going to do, anyway?" said Pauley.

There were a few seconds of silence before she replied. "You're right. Okay. The leader's name is Headstone. Balthazar Headstone. And he's the real deal! The bee's knees!"

"That's an impressive name," said Pauley.

"Isn't it, though?"

"Is he here today?"

"Oh, hell, no," said Annie. "He has other things to do. Besides, the Exalted, Great Grand Wolf has us to do his bidding."

"Lucky man," said Pauley. "Or should I say, lucky wolf?"

Another few seconds of silence passed.

"Are you mocking me, mister, and insulting the Master?"

"No, said Pauley. "I wouldn't dream of it. I'm just trying to wrap my head around everything that happened."

"Me, too," said Annie, the sniper. "But I'm still going to kill you, sooner or later, so you might as well get the waiting over and make it sooner."

"Okay," said Pauley, " Let me think about it."

† † †

Angel and Marshal Mesa had quit the stream when it meandered into the open, away from the forest. The breeze was blowing into their faces, and Mesa knew it was a blessing; still, if the direction of the wind changed, there was a good chance the sniper would catch their scent and redirect her fire onto them.

They were probably no more than twenty yards away from where she knelt, taking shots at the FBI agent in the tower.

"What do we do now, Marshal Mesa?"

"I don't know, Angel. The tower is too far away to make a run for it from here. I could try to sneak up behind the shooter, but if the wind changes and that thing picks up my scent, she'll probably give me a lead shampoo."

"I have an idea, Marshal Mesa. But you're going to have to trust me."

† † †

"Hello," said Angel. She stood behind a tree, no more than five yards from the sniper's blind.

Annie spun around and fired. The bullet thudded into the tree.

"Please! Don't shoot," said Angel. "It's me! The girl you're looking for."

"Okay, said Annie. "Come on out where I can see you. And no tricks."

"I don't know any tricks," said Angel as she stepped into the open.

"So, you're the one," said Annie.

"Yeah, I guess so," said Angel. "Do you know Szah Zhah?"

"Lady Szah Zhah," said the sniper. "To us, she's LADY Szah Zhah."

"Okay," said Angel. "Well, I'm Angel O'Hara. And the first chance I get, I'm going to kill Lady Szah Zhah. What do you think of those apples?"

"Cocky little bunghole, aren't you?" said Annie.

"I'm just honest," said Angel.

"Well, you sure got sand, Angel O'Hara. I'll give you that. Do I need to tie your hands, or are you going to come nice and quiet?"

"The second one," said Angel. "It's been a crummy day, and I want it over with."

"Yeah," said Annie. "Me, too."

"That makes three of us," said Mesa, as he stepped out from behind cover. "Drop the rifle, lady."

The color drained from Annie's face; her mouth sagged open, the pupils of her eyes dilated. When Annie looked at Angel, she saw a trace of a smile on Angel's face; she looked again at Mesa and muttered a string of cuss-words as she brought her rifle to bear. Too late! Mesa had her dead to rights.

Mesa fired three deafening rounds from the shotgun in quick succession, knocking Annie off her feet and flying several yards onto a small evergreen.

Deputy Marshal Albert Mesa made the sign of The Cross before he holstered his sidearm. Mesa drew his sidearm and went to where Annie, the sniper, was bleeding out. Her eyes were open but glazed over, and her mouth was gasping, contorting like a fish out of water. One does what one can, yes?

Annie's days as a sniper and a Weirdwolf were over.

45.

Gaelic for 'Wild'

If one spends half a lifetime believing they know where they're going, surely, the other half they spend finding out.

Jonny Fiáin thought he was going to Hell. It hit on him as far back as the Third Grade at Saint Thomas Aquinas School. There, he and Paddy O'Hara got their knuckles soundly smacked. It was a daily event. Not by Sister Evangeline, but by Brother Timothy, with his gold-plated, 12" ruler. Since that time, Jonny Fiáin seemed hell-bent on proving his childhood ability for prognosticating correct.

† † †

Jonny waited until nightfall before driving to Doctor Van Helwing's estate outside *San Souci*. He couldn't take the chance that someone, anyone, would recognize the pickup he took belonging to the man-thing formerly known as "Curly." Jonny had in mind that darkness was his only friend, his only ally, apart from Whiskey.

Jonny left Whiskey in the truck by the side of the road, then walked fifty yards, or so, down the dirt driveway to the doctor's front door. There had been no barking from the dogs chained outside the barn, so Jonny picked the lock on the doctor's front door and let himself inside.

There were lights on which suggested the doctor was elsewhere, most likely his barn.

Jonny poured himself some of the doctor's *Napoleon Brandy* and waited.

† † †

It was two in the morning when Van Helwing re-entered his house by way of the back porch. As he stepped into the kitchen, he found Jonny Fiáin waiting for him at the breakfast table with a bottle of Napoleon Brandy and two snifters, the one Jonny was drinking out of, and a second, empty snifter. Jonny's .45 was resting in his hand.

Doctor Van Helwing looked exhausted and wore a surgical gown heavily stained with blood.

"Sit down, Doc," said Jonny. His voice was cold, void of emotion.

"Jonny!? What are you doing here? Is Angel with you?"

"Lose the gown, Doc, and sit. I'm not going to tell you a third time."

"Very well."

Van Helwing reached behind him and undid the knot holding the surgical gown in place. The doctor let it fall on the floor. He sat across from Jonny.

"What's wrong, Jonny? You sound agitated. Has something terrible happened? Is Angel all right?"

Jonny came out of his chair, reached across the table with his .45, and slammed the barrel against the side of the doctor's head. Van Helwing cried out and clutched his ears. Blood began to trickle through the fingers of his left hand, just above his temple, where the blow landed.

"I want answers, Doc, and you're going to give them to me. If you don't, I'm going to kill you and leave here bitterly ignorant. Savvy?"

The doctor nodded. "May I wash the blood off my hands and get something for my head?"

"No," said Jonny. "You may not. Start talking."

"Where, Jonny? Where do you want me to start?"

"The two brothers I killed on your property. They were after Angel and me. Why?"

"They were under orders to take custody of Angel. You were in the way. It wasn't personal, Jonny."

"It was for me. What do these things want with Angel O'Hara?"

"It's complicated." "Well, uncomplicate it."

"May I first have some Brandy, Jonny? My throat feels parched."

"No. Now answer the question." Jonny cocked the hammer of his .45.

"Okay, okay!" said the doctor.

"The Gray Brethren in Canada retained me decades ago for their medical and health needs."

"Why? Cannocks have socialized medicine. What did these creatures need you for?"

"Because the authorities would ask too many questions. The Grey Brethren prefer anonymity. I could treat their medical problems, and no one, certainly not the government, would ever be the wiser. No records, no forms to fill out, no authorities. Surely you can understand their need for privacy?"

"I don't give a rat's ass about their need for privacy. Tell me what these things want with Angel."

"For reasons sufficient to herself, Jonny, the Queen of the Full Moon Night, wants Angel. That's all I know. To that end, she tasked her consort, Balthazar Headstone, to enlist the help of the Gray Brethren dwelling along the Atlantic seaboard."

"This, queen'," said Jonny. "Would her name happen to be Sup Zup, or Blah Blah, something like that?"

Van Helwing's eyes widened. "Yes. It would. Except, her devotees address her as Lady Szah Zhah."

"Good for them," said Jonny. "But this would be the same creature who sliced up Angel, almost killing her?"

"Yes."

Jonny took the bottle of brandy and poured two-fingers worth into the empty snifter in front of Van Helwing.

"Go ahead, Doc. Wet your whistle. You earned it."

Van Helwing smiled nervously and drank half the contents from the glass. He sighed heavily.

"I gotta admit, Doc, that's damn fine, Brandy. Expensive, I bet?"

Van Helwing nodded, chin to his chest, like a despairing boxer in his corner with his 'cut man,' waiting for the bell to sound the next punishing round.

"Tell me about these creatures," said Jonny. "This group, the Gray Brethren. Who are they?"

"They're an ancient society, tribe, race, species; I don't exactly know what to call them, Jonny. I can't tell you how long they've been in existence because I honestly don't know. But as you've seen, they can shape-shift from human to wolf and vice versa."

"The one with the silver dollar name?"

"Balthazar Headstone."

"Yeah. Tell me more about Balthazar Headstone."

Van Helwing's shoulders relaxed. He gulped the remainder of the Brandy in his hand.

Jonny smiled and poured the doctor two-fingers more.

"Balthazar Headstone is the Exalted, Great Grand Master of the Gray Brethren. He and Lady Szah Zhah have been together for over two centuries. They are powerful beings and, together, amassed considerable wealth. But like all creatures, they need to feed. For Lady Szah Zhah, that means every twenty-eight days when the moon waxes full. Weirdwolves, like Balthazar Headstone, eat whenever the mood strikes; they live for the pack and the thrill of the hunt. In the main, they are shy creatures and try to blend with their surroundings. To some extent, they live apart from society, as much as they can, without drawing attention to themselves. Otherwise, they hide in plain sight doing things others do. "

Van Helwing finished what was in the glass and wiped his mouth dry with the back of his hand. "That's all I can tell you, Jonny. I don't know anything more."

"How can I find these two, Doc? Headstone and Szah Zhah?"

"That's impossible, Jonny. If they are not on Lady Zhah Zhah's schooner, the *Horror*, sailing any one of the Seven Seas, they could be anywhere, anywhere in the world. No, Jonny. You won't find them. They'll find you."

Jonny drank his brandy. He returned the .45 to the holster under his left shoulder. "Got any Mink oil, Doc?"

"You're not going to kill me?"

"I'm tempted. You betrayed me, and you betrayed Angel. But you also saved her life, and that counts for one helluva lot with me. No, Doc. I'm not going to kill you. My leather jacket is rank with bear scat; I mean to clean it."

46.
Look Homeward, Angel

Pauley heard the gunfire and decided to risk getting his head shot off to have a look. He stared past the shattered glass of the east-facing window and looked in the direction of the sniper's last approximate position.

He saw them as they emerged from the tree line. U.S. Deputy Marshal Mesa and what had to be Angel O'Hara; approached the tower waving parts of a white handkerchief that Mesa had torn in half.

Pauley looked at his watch for the umpteenth time. It was just past three o'clock. Too early for backup to arrive. Unless and until Pauley's team failed to check-in, others would assume that the stakeout was proceeding apace, meaning nothing remarkable had happened.

Pauley stepped outside and used the catwalk to get to the east side of the tower. He placed the BAR over the railing to cover Mesa and the girl should they need it.

"Come on," said Pauley. "I've got you covered."

Angel and Mesa ran the rest of the way.

† † †

"Agent Pauley," said Mesa, "this is Miss Angel O'Hara. Angel, this is Special Agent Pauley."

"Call me, Neil," said Pauley. He extended his hand to shake.

Angel ignored the FBI man's hand. "You're one of the men after Jonny Fiáin, aren't you?"

"Well, yes, Angel, I am. I'm with the FBI."

"I'm not going to shake hands with you, Agent Pauley." Angel glanced at Mesa. "Neither of you. Jonny Fiáin is my best friend. He saved my life, and he's been looking after me. He was only trying to get me back safe, to New Dublin. You gentlemen may think you know all there is to know about Jonny, but you don't."

Angel went to a corner of the room with no glass shards on the floor and sat cross-legged. She leaned back against the wall and closed her eyes.

"And that's all I have to say about that."

Mesa and Pauley looked at each other. Mesa shrugged. "Maybe we should get this placed cleaned up a little since it looks like we'll be spending the night."

"Right," said Pauley. "I'll gather some firewood."

"Okay," said Mesa. "While you're doing that, I'll look for a broom."

Angel stood. "I'll go with Agent Pauley and gather firewood.

† † †

Angel was sitting by the woodstove with Marshal Mesa, warming their hands when Special Agent Pauley returned. The only thing Pauley had in his hand was the flashlight he took with him.

"Sorry, folks," said Pauley. Whatever those things are, they took everything out of the jeeps and the deuce-and-a-half, everything we didn't nail down. It looks like we go hungry tonight."

"They call themselves, Weirdwolves," said Angel.

Mesa and Pauley exchanged looks. "Say again, please?" said Pauley.

"Yes," said Mesa. "If you don't mind, Angel, Agent Pauley, and I would like to hear everything you know about these creatures... these, Weirdwolves, as you called them?"

Angel nodded. "Okay," she said. "Hold on a sec." She reached into one of the pockets of her Pendleton. "I have a Hershey bar we can share."

† † †

Pauley and Mesa listened attentively to Angel's story beginning with the night Szah Zhah Kopeč murdered Angel's parents; then the flight with Jonny to Canada, her convalescence at Doctor Van Helwing's, followed by her and Jonny's first encounter with the Gray Brethren.

Angel quietly stood and removed her Pendleton; she pulled her thermal shirt up over her shoulders, allowing the two lawmen to see where Szah Zhah's claws raked her.

For what must have been two or three minutes, neither Mesa nor Pauley spoke. If their minds weren't reeling from the events of the day, they were reeling now.

"You believe me, right?" said Angel.

"Speaking only for myself," said Mesa, "I believe everything you've told us. The scars on your back say a whole lot more, as well."

Angel looked back and forth at the two men.

"Why am I expecting one of you to toss in a big, fat, 'BUT,' right about now?"

"I can't speak for the U.S. Marshals Service, Angel," said Pauley, "BUT, the higher-ups at the FBI are going to come unglued as soon as I report it was a big, fat, hairy-legged Vampire bat who murdered your mom and dad, and a terrorist organization known as the Gray Brethren, who murdered eight FBI agents, six Marshals, and twelve State Troopers from Maine's Department of Public Safety. Oh, I almost forgot, terrorists who also just happen to be half-human and half-wolf."

"But you were HERE; you saw them!" said Angel. "Weirdwolves almost killed you! Both of you!"

Mesa and Pauley remained silent for several minutes. Mesa looked squarely at Pauley.

"The way I see it, we can wait up here for help to come. Or tomorrow, we can take our chances and hoof it back to the highway. Once there, we can flag down a motorist to take us to the nearest telephone."

"Sounds like a plan," said Pauley. He looked at Angel. "Marshal Mesa and I need to contact our superiors so we can get you to your grandparents in New Dublin soon as possible. Sound good?"

Angel nodded. What she thought she would keep to herself—for now, anyway.

Angel and the two lawmen sat quietly, listening to the snap, crackle, and pop from inside the woodstove. Around midnight, Angel moved to a corner, curled herself into a ball, and closed her eyes.

Mesa and Pauley continued their conversation, whispering to each other so Angel could get some rest and because they didn't want her to hear what they both feared: *Who on earth was going to believe them, or her? Think about it: Weirdwolves? A huge, smelly, hairy-legged Vampire bat named Szah Zhah? And how were they going to account for the violent deaths of so many good men?*

Given she could hear a pin drop ten yards away now, Angel wondered about that also: who was going to believe her?

Although neither man mentioned it, both had heard wild but unsubstantiated rumors from Roswell, New Mexico, and repeated by nationwide newspapers. Stories regarding a flying saucer, of all things that had crashed in the harsh, barren waste, of the New Mexico desert; moreover, that corpses of several extra-terrestrials had been recovered and taken to a secret base widely known as 'Area 51.'

God's truth!

The U.S. Army said it was merely a meteorological balloon that crashed near Roswell. "No need for alarm, folks."

Yeah. Right.

For the remainder of the night, Mesa and Pauley took turns stoking the fire in the stove while keeping a close watch on the stairs lest Weirdwolves return.

They didn't.

† † †

They stepped off the last stair-step to the ground just after dawn and started walking south toward the highway.

It was then when New Dublin's Chief of Police, A.J. McKuen, appeared in his police cruiser with its 'cherry top' flashing and siren blaring. Accompanying Chief McKuen was Officer Robb Royce and Seamus "Bumpa" O'Hara, who rode in the back seat clutching the 20-gauge shotgun Paddy gave him one Christmas for pheasant hunting.

Behind McKuen's police cruiser came a dozen more vehicles led by Douglas O'Doole driving his 1937, Atlantic gray Plymouth made out of battleship iron. Packed inside with him were an uncle and two brothers; together, they owned a fishing boat that sailed out of New Dublin when the weather gods allowed.

Behind them were an assortment of pickup and delivery trucks filled with doughty Irishmen from the Old Country, along with their New World progeny, all residents of New Dublin, all friends of the O'Haras, and all of them armed.

The last vehicle in this wholly unexpected convoy belonged to none other than Father Timothy. On the seat beside him was a lacquered, black cudgel, known in Ireland as a *shillelagh*. The good father had made it from a stout, blackthorn stick with a large knob at the top and could shatter a skull or a coconut with ease. No one invited the priest to come along; it's just that no one was willing to tell him he couldn't.

Seeing her "Bumpa" in the Chief's cruiser, Angel shouted and waved her arms. Albeit somewhat sheepishly, Pauley and Mesa did the same.

† † †

Chief McKuen walked to where Pauley and Mesa were standing by their lonesome. There wasn't a dry-eyed Irishman among the rescue party. Even Father Timothy was a trifle misty watching Angel, and her grandfather reunite outside the Chief's cruiser.

"It's great to see you folks, Chief McKuen," said Mesa.

"Marshal Mesa. Agent Pauley," said McKuen. "You fellows look a bit worse for the wear."

"Yesterday was a long day, Chief," said Pauley, "and night."

"And to tell you the truth, Chief," said Mesa, "we were hoping to see some backup about now from the FBI and the Marshals Service."

McKuen looked at the two lawmen a moment. "Who?" he said, then he walked off.

Pauley looked at Mesa. "What the [expletive deleted]?" Pauley had dropped "cheeseburger" from his lexicon twenty hours earlier.

McKuen stopped and looked back at the two, too stunned to reply lawmen. "I imagine you fellas are hungry. We'll leave you food and drink and let your people know where to find you."

That said, Chief McKuen whistled loudly, raised one arm, and circled his hand in the air. "Let's go, boys!"

The Irishmen returned to their vehicles. Angel and Seamus O'Hara got into the back seat and hugged.

Flabbergasted, Mesa and Pauley looked on as the New Dublin Fenian Home Guard circled them and headed south, back toward the highway with their horns and McKuen's siren blaring.

"What do you want to do, Agent Pauley?"

Pauley stared at the food and beverages the Irishmen left.

"Right," said Mesa. "Let's eat."

Szah Zhah's Complaint
New York, New York
December 1949

Headstone could hear her before the elevator stopped at the 48th floor where they had a suite at the Waldorf Astoria in Manhattan. Theirs was one floor below the Penthouse, which, at the time, was occupied by none other than the so-called *Prince of the Underworld*, the mobster Francesco Castiglia, also known as Frank Costello.

As Headstone stepped into the hallway, he saw hotel guests in varying degrees of undress looking in the direction of the suite from which the sounds emanated. Not just "sounds," but screaming, sometimes shrieking, and in decibels so loud, glass shattered every time she hit a high note.

Stay with someone in a marriage long enough, and you're liable to come away with a fair understanding of who and what you're dealing with. It doesn't have to be a "marriage," *per se*; shacking up will suffice. The point is, stay with someone long enough, and you're bound to get to know them—their biology, psychology, the whole *tamale*. It may be that you get to know them more than you wanted to—to the point you want to leave them, or worse, but that's another matter entirely.

After two hundred and twenty years together, Headstone was acutely aware of Szah Zhah's many faces and moods and *vice versa*. However, through the years, Balthazar Headstone kept his keel on an even trim and charted his life on a course as faithful and constant as *Polaris*, the North Star. Rarely did he allow himself to enter into a storm, which partly explains how he ascended over time to the position of *Exalted Grand Master of the Gray Brethren*, an honor not easily attained and harder still to maintain.

Outside the door of Szah Zhah and Headstone's suite was the General Manager of the Waldorf Astoria, Claude Pepper, his Administrative Assistant, Rene Derriere, and the Head of Hotel Security, Tommy "Three-Fingers" McGurk, on loan from the Lucky Luciano Crime Family.

"What's going on, Claude?"

"Can you not hear for yourself, Monsieur Headstone? Lady Szah Zhah is destroying your suite, upsetting our guests, upsetting me, upsetting my employees."

"And pissing me off royally," said McGurk, with an unmistakable New Jersey accent. "Let's face it, gents, that broad is one dizzy dame!"

Whatever Headstone felt that second about Szah Zhah, the Waldorf Astoria, the screaming, McGurk, all of it, his expression provided no clue. Not even his eyes, dark as the abyss and momentarily fixed on Tommy' Three Fingers' McGurk's Adam's-apple.

"Please! Mister McGurk!" said Claude Pepper. "I can't have you speaking that way about one of our treasured guests. Monsieur Headstone and I will handle this like gentlemen." He turned to Headstone. "Won't we, Monsieur?"

"Of course," said Headstone. *"Parlons en Française?"*

"Oui bien sûr," said Claude Pepper.

At that same moment, the fierce sounds inside the suite abruptly ended. The General Manager sighed with relief. Headstone, however, gave no outward sign of emotion. Instead, he spoke to the General Manager in French, leaving Three Fingers McGurk shaking his head disparagingly as he walked away.

"Plainte à ce sujet, Claude, et je vais acheter le Waldorf-Astoria, licencier tout le monde et l'ouvrir à la racaille de New York. Maintenant, en ce qui concerne les dommages à la chambre, je vais payer pour un remodelage complet. Quant à l'inconfort causé à vos invités, dites-leur que leur chambre et pension pour la semaine prochaine seront payées, compliments de Lady Szah Zhah. Faites-en part aux journaux et vous feriez mieux de prendre le prochain bateau pour la France. Comprends-tu, Claude?"

The following is a rough translation of what Headstone told the General Manager:

"Complain about this, Claude, and I will buy the Waldorf-Astoria, fire everyone, and open it up to the sewer rats of New York. Now, as to the damage to the room, I will pay for a complete remodeling. As for the discomfort caused to your guests, tell them their room and board for the next week will be paid for, compliments of Lady Szah Zhah. Leak any of this to the newspapers, and you had better catch the next boat to France. Do you understand, Claude?"

Claude Pepper understood perfectly. Every impeccably spoken word.

† † †

Once they were alone, Headstone sat Szah Zhah beside him on a long couch opposite the wet bar.

"Who told you that, my love? That was for me to do."

Resting her head on Headstone's shoulder, Szah Zhah's eyes remained shut. Her cheeks were still crimson, her eyes swollen from crying.

"It was that horrid little man in Canada, Doctor Van Something."

"Van Helwing?"

"Whatever!"

"What else did the doctor say, my love? It is imperative, I know."

"He said he had a message for me. A message from the American *fasz* who shot me in the butt."

"Jupiter's cock! That DICK! Tell me the message, Szah Zhah!"

"Don't shout at me, Balthazar. I'm right here beside you."

"Forgive me, my little cabbage, but what was the message?"

Szah Zhah began to sob.

"Tell me, little dove; I am here; the American *fasz* cannot harm you. What was the message?"

"He's going to kill me, Balthazar. Slowly."

"What!?" said Headstone.

"Yes," said Szah Zhah. "First, he's going to saw off my claws, my wings, my legs; then my milk bags; then my ears. He said the last thing I feel would be his long *schlong* around my throat as he chokes me with it."

"The American said THAT!?"

"I think so."

The American fasz[98] Szah Zhah refers to is a former Marine named Jonny Fiáin. An outlaw and fugitive from justice, Fiáin, told the doctor to tell Szah Zhah he was

---

[98] A Hungarian slur, meaning dick!

going to "cut her head off." That's it! That's all! For reasons sufficient to himself, Doctor Van Helwing took obvious liberties with Jonny's message.

Now, back to the story.

"The American is just saying these things to frighten you, my little pussy cat."

"Well," said Szah Zhah, between sobs, "He [expletive deleted] succeeded! I don't understand, Balthazar? I never did ANYthing to him. I don't even know what he [expletive deleted] looks like!"

Balthazar smoothed Szah Zhah's hair back out of her eyes."

"Balthazar?"

"Yes, my Turtle Dove?"

"There's something else. Something you need to see."

"What?"

"I'll get it."

Szah Zhah got up and trotted off to the Master Bedroom. She returned a moment later with *Les Prophéties Perdue de Nostradamus.*[99] She placed it carefully on the coffee table in front of the couch and opened it to a place she had marked with a raven's feather.

"Read it, my love. Out loud, please," said Szah Zhah. Her voice trembled, and her hands shook.

"Very well, my Love," said Balthazar. He looked at the passage written in French and began to read it out loud, in a clear, impassive voice: "*Du vieux monde elle viendra, Une fille de l'horreur ailée. Elle, dont le nom*

---

[99] The Lost Prophecies of Nostradamos, circa 1555.

inspire la peur, dans les cœurs et l'esprit des hommes. Elle régnera deux cents soleils; cette reine de la nuit de pleine lune, quand, du Nouveau Monde, une enfant déchirée et née de son toucher, sortira pour la détrôner."

"Well?" said Szah Zhah. "Do you not see it, Balthazar?"

Balthazar pocketed his reading glasses and looked at Szah Zhah.

"You think this girl-child is the one, *born by your touch, come forth to dethrone you?*"

"She is!" said Szah Zhah. "I wasn't able to turn her, but I tore her flesh. Somehow, someway, it was enough to transform her into something different than she was."

"Something more like you?" said Headstone.

"Perhaps. More or less, yes," said Szah Zhah. "Something more like me."

Balthazar and Szah Zhah left the Waldorf-Astoria that afternoon in a white, 1948 Stretch-Limousine, just as two police cars and an ambulance pulled over in front of the hotel and parked. Someone had discovered the Head of Security, Three-Fingers McGurk, at the bottom of an elevator shaft. McGurk was flat-out, forty-eight floors of DEAD! Every bone in his body was either fractured or broken.

As the limousine continued toward Pier 17, where Headstone moored their schooner, the *Horror*, Balthazar couldn't get the American out of his mind.

"I need to meet this man," Headstone said aloud. "He interests me.

"Can't you simply kill him and bring me his heart?"

"In good time, my love. All things in good time. First, I need to think through the prophecy you chanced upon."

"It wasn't by CHANCE, Balthazar. Fate MEANT me to find it! And Fate chose YOU as the messenger. It cannot be otherwise."

Szah Zhah's face turned deathly pale. "I think I'm going to be sick."

Balthazar pulled the sash that rang a bell in the driver's compartment. The driver pulled over in front of *Number One Broadway*. Headstone lowered the window beside him. Szah Zhah leaned across his lap with her head out the window and barfed on the sidewalk, spattering passersby. When she could vomit no more, Szah Zhah wiped her mouth with the back of her hand.

"I need some 7-Up, Balthazar. It will help settle my tummy."

"Of course, my little bat. Of course."

48.

Pick Up Sticks

Mesa and Pauley took the provisions the Irishmen left into the tower; smart move since neither could be certain the creatures wouldn't return. "*Weirdwolves*," Angel called them.

Two days later, around one pm, an official vehicle from the Maine Department of Public Safety, a flat-black Buick escorted by four State Troopers on motorcycles, appeared on the scene.

Mesa and Pauley came down from the tower to greet them. A young man with a pasty white face and rose-colored cheeks got out of the passenger side of the Buick. He wore a two-piece, dark wool suit, black, lace-up shoes, and a class-tie that marked him as a "Yale Man," His hair was cut short in a flat-top and held in place with Butch Wax.

When he saw Pauley and Mesa, he smiled broadly. It was cold that morning, and steam escaped his mouth when he spoke;

"Marshal Mesa! Special Agent Pauley. Am I ever glad to see you." He extended his hand. "I'm Gavin Needleman, Special Assistant to Governor Payne, and liaison to the Federal Bureau of Investigation and the U.S. Marshals Service. I'm here to take you, gentlemen, to Augusta, straightaway."

"What about the men out there?" said Mesa. "The ones who didn't make it?"

"Someone will take care of them directly," said Needleman.

"What's that mean?" said Pauley.

"It means National Guard Search and Recovery teams are on the way, and a temporary morgue is being set up in the High School Gymnasium in Mount Pleasanton, just down the road."

"Why aren't our people here, Mister Needleman?" said Mesa. "FBI and Marshals Service?"

"There weren't enough FBI or Marshals left in Maine to respond. They're up north, watching bus terminals, railroad stations, and checkpoints on the Canadian border. Look. The Governor has it on good authority that yesterday was an 'unmitigated disaster.' Is he wrong?"

"No, Mister Needleman," said Pauley, "he's not wrong. Yesterday was fubar! Maybe the worst day of my life, and I've had some terrible ones."

"Ditto that," said Mesa. "But who IS, this 'competent authority? If you don't mind me asking? "

"I don't mind at all, Marshal Mesa. The caller said his name was Jonny Fiáin. I believe he's the 'fugitive from justice' you gentlemen came to Maine to apprehend. Am I correct?"

Pauley had to restrain Mesa from dropping Needleman with a right cross to the chin.

"You sonuvabitch," said Mesa.

"We need to be going now, gentlemen," Said Needleman; he smiled and gestured toward the Buick with an effeminate sweep of his hand. "If you don't mind

† † †

Jonny drove Curly's truck toward Quebec. He planned to ditch the pickup at a truck stop near the border at *Saint Pamphile*, then hitch a ride, him and Whiskey, on a truck headed south. But it had to be just the right track, with just the right driver.

† † †

Creedy White Owl worked for *'Pamplona Paper Products,'* a Maine-based U.S. corporation that processed fir trees from Canada, trees that once reached two-hundred feet and more into the vast expanse of a leaden-gray, Canadian sky. Fate designated the wood to become rolls of toilet paper and paper cups for water dispensers. Creedy's daughter tied her father's snow-white hair into a single long braid that rested on his shoulder like a sleeping snake.

Creedy stuck his head out the window at the checkpoint on the American side of the border and greeted the Customs Official.

"Hey, Henry!" said Creedy.

"Hey, Creedy," said fifty-four-year-old U.S. Customs Official Henry Zanzinger. He had a clipboard tucked under his left armpit and held a coffee mug in his right hand, steam trailing off the top. As he stood, he picked his feet up and down on the cold cement.

"Where you fixing to march off to, Henry?" said Creedy, a broad grin on his face.

"Hah!" said Henry Zanzinger. "That's a good one, Creedy. It's my damn circulation, and this [expletive deleted] frozen ground doesn't help."

"So, when you gonna retire, Henry?" said Creedy.

"Hah!" said Henry Zanzinger. "Soon as you, you old fart. Never! Who you got with you?"

Jonny turned so the official could see him. Whiskey was sitting in the middle, head up and alert, between the two men.

"I got my nephew, Jonny, with me, Henry. I'm trying to get him a job with Pamplona as a stick driver. That's Jonny's pup, Whiskey, drooling on my knee. Jonny, this is my pal, Henry Zanzinger. He was in the Corps, just like you, 'cept Henry fought in the Great War. Didn't you, Henry?"

"Damn straight. I almost got buried in Belleau Wood, along with a whole lot of friends. Good boys, every one of them."

"You were with the 4th Brigade?" said Jonny. " The Germans called your battalion Devil Dogs."

"Hell, yes, they did! Sure as I'm standing here freezing my butt off. Who were you with, son? It's Jonny, right?"

"Yes, sir. I was with the 1st Marines, right up to V-J Day."

"Well, God Bless you, Jonny, and 'good luck! I hope you get that job. If you do, I'm sure to see you coming and going like I do your uncle Creedy."

"Thank you, sir," said Jonny.

"Oh, hell, don't call me 'sir,' son; I work for a living. Call me, Henry."

"Okay," said Jonny. "Glad to meet you, Henry."

"Great meeting you, Jonny. Damn, it's cold out here."

"*Semper Fi*[101]," said Jonny.

On the driver's side, outside-mirror, Jonny could see Henry Zanzinger saluting him while Creedy White Owl went through the gears, and the truck gained speed.

---

[101] *Semper Fi* [Latin] meaning: Always Faithful. The slogan of the United States Marine Corps.

"I owe you more than I can repay, Creedy," said Jonny.

"You don't owe me nothing, young man. Just watch your top-knot, and stay safe, you and your pup."

"I sure mean to try."

For most of the ride back to New Dublin, Angel slept soundly with her head resting on Seamus's shoulder. Sheriff A.J. McKuen and Officer Robb Royce didn't say but a few words during the ride back. The three men knew there would be no end of questions coming at Angel from umpteen directions all at once, not to mention what the newspapers would do once they sank their teeth into Angel's mysterious disappearance, the deaths of Angel's parents, and Angel's harrowing experience at the border. The three men were in full agreement: let Angel enjoy what peace she can.

† † †

When the convoy reached downtown New Dublin, Seamus gently awakened his granddaughter.

"Hey, Angel girl, you'll want to see this."

Ahead, strung across Main Street, was a banner that read:

Welcome home, Angel!

Sheriff McKuen and Deputy Royce turned their heads toward the back seat and said in unison, "Welcome home, Angel."

The Sheriff turned on his siren and flashing red light. Sounds of honking from the convoy of vehicles led by O'Doole followed Angel into town.

It was December 1949, a Saturday, December 10th, to be exact. New Dublin was in a festive mood and alive with Christmas decorations, and a holiday spirit flourished on the faces of the men, women, and children. There were large wreaths made of holly on lampposts, a forty-foot Douglas Fir in Central Park that at night would light up the snow-covered ground with a thousand strings of cherry red, frosted white, deep amber, emerald green, and sapphire blue bulbs. Throughout the downtown, loudspeakers on lampposts played Bing Crosby, Doris Day, and Perry Como Christmas carols from noon to eight pm. And O'Doole's pub hosted a dance every Saturday night at the Veterans Memorial Hall.

Angel rubbed sleepy seeds from her eyes as the vehicles drove in a slow procession down Main Street, garnering stares, smiles, waves, and thumbs-up from folks on the sidewalk, curious as to what the fuss was about.

By now, news of Angel's ordeal had reached just about every one of the two-thousand, two-hundred-and-one registered voters of New Dublin, Maine.

What with newspaper coverage of Angel's "kidnapping" and her "miraculous" rescue from one of the FBI's "10 Most Wanted" outlaws in America, like as not, Angel was an overnight celebrity.

† † †

Aboard the *Horror*, Szah Zhah hurled the stack of newspapers carrying word of the debacle at the border off the bed. Parenthetically, the bed was massive, a four-post, canopied pallet once owned by none other than Marie Antoinette.

On the deck above, Headstone was attaching new, all-weather sails to the two masts. Headstone, or for that matter, Szah Zhah, could now raise or lower the new sails electronically by merely triggering a switch.

The previous month, Headstone installed two Rolls Royce marine engines that could propel the *Horror* without the benefit of sails, at speeds up to fifty knots[102] on a calm sea. This time of year, the Atlantic Ocean would be rough and tumble and, as a rule, unforgiving.

Maybe not the best time to sail south for peace-of-mind, thought Headstone; *still, perhaps Szah Zhah would welcome a trip somewhere warm before the guano hits the fan.*

Headstone knew that, realistically, a vacation wasn't going to happen, not just yet anyway, as long as Nostradamus's prophecy about the girl hung over them, overshadowing their lives with foreboding. The girl was all Szah Zhah could think about; she even dreamed about the "little mouse." The point being: the more Szah Zhah's attention was on Angel, the less energy she had for Balthazar. Not exactly rocket science. Weeks before, Balthazar was merely jealous of Angel O'Hara and wished her a life of unspeakable difficulty. Now, with the advent of the prophecy, he found himself wishing something worse for Angel O'Hara.

Headstone lamented the fact Sigmund Freud was dead, having died a paltry ten years before. That was in

---

[102] A "knot" is a nautical measurement of speed. One knot equals 1 and 1/8 miles, per hour.

1939, just as another war was breaking out in Europe[103]. Freud liked Szah Zhah, and Szah Zhah liked Freud, or "Siggy," as she called him. They had a connection; Freud was someone apart from Headstone, in whom she could confide.

Once, in Vienna, Austria, Headstone invited Freud to tea at *Das Crazy Sausage*, on *Trostlose Straße,* in the heart of the old city. Headstone hoped the excellent doctor would impart what Szah Zhah disclosed about Headstone's sexual proclivities, given that Headstone possessed a forked penis, and his bedroom inclinations were legion.

Freud laughed. "Not for ten-thousand Swiss Marks, my friend. The code of doctor-patient confidentiality binds me. I simply cannot tell you what your paramour discloses in the course of her therapy."

"I understand, Doctor," said Headstone. "Forgive me for diving into forbidden waters."

"Hah! No worries, dear man. I can tell you this Balthazar, Szah Zhah loves you beyond measure. She trusts you the way ancient mariners trusted the North Star, the one constant in the heavens they could use to chart a course. I can also say without reservation, Szah Zhah is nuts. One-hundred percent, bonkers! She tells the most delightful stories, though, stories spanning centuries. My God, just last week, she told me about having spent a romantic night with Marie Antoinette in 1788: THE Marie Antoinette. Her stories are so rich with details, such vividity! Alas, I must say, Szah Zhah is, in so many respects, a little girl trapped in a woman's body.

---

[103] Nazi Germany invaded Poland on September 1st, 1939, triggering the Second World War; which, at the beginning, pitted France and England against Hitler's Germany, Mussolini's Italy and Emperor Hirohito's Japan.

Enchanting as the day is long, with an imagination to rival H.G. Wells and Jules Verne both. I recommend that you entrust Szah Zhah to an insane asylum for enhanced treatment, but I realize you would never agree to that."

"No, Doctor, Freud. I would not."

That was in 1929, the last time Headstone saw or spoke to Sigmund Freud.

The right ear, meaning one that hears, TRULY listens, is not easy to access, especially on short notice. Just ask Vincent Van Gogh!

What to do? Headstone asked himself as he left *Das Crazy Sausage* on *Trostlose Straße*. And, now, twenty years later, aboard the *Horror*, Balthazar was still asking himself: *What to do?*

49.

Blazing Saddles

J. Edgar Hoover set his reading glasses aside and looked at Special Agent Pauley sitting across the table from him. Clyde Tolson, the FBI Administrator primarily responsible for personnel and discipline, was also present.

After lighting a match to it, Hoover tossed Agent Pauley's handwritten statement of facts concerning the events leading up to, during, and immediately following the debacle in the forest into a wastepaper basket and watched it burn.

"That's pretty imaginative stuff, Special Agent Pauley," said Hoover. "The kind of crap I'd expect from a hysterical nine-year-old girl, NOT one of my best field agents!"

"Sir?" said Pauley.

"I believe what Director Hoover is suggesting," said Assistant Director Clyde Tolson, "is that, when he and I appear before the House Committee on Un-American Activities tomorrow to explain how eight of our finest agents lost their lives in the line of duty, murdered by something that tore them limb from limb, it would be best if you could simplify your account of the events of December 9th. With that in mind, Special Agent, we prepared a statement for you to read when it is your turn to testify before the committee."

Tolson handed a single piece of paper to Pauley to read. As Pauley began reading, his eyes grew large, his mouth sagged open, and his upper lip trembled. He placed the paper on Hoover's desk.

"Apart from the date," said Pauley," not one word is accurate. Not one, gentlemen."

"Are you saying we can't count on you," said Hoover, to make that statement before the committee?" His puffy red cheeks swelled with anger. "Are you forgetting it was ME who hired you, Special Agent Pauley!?"

"No, sir, I'm not. But I'm not going to lie to Congress, either."

J. Edgar Hoover brought the flats of both hands down hard on his desk. "I told you, Clyde. I told you we had a water-walker on our hands. Goddammit, Pauley. You'll do as I order, or you'll never work in this town again. What'll it be, young man?"

Pauley felt his back straightening, the way it did when he was in the army on a forced march and let his seventy-pound rucksack slide off his shoulders after a twenty-mile hike. Pauley placed his badge, ID, and service revolver on Hoover's desk.

"That suits me just fine, sir."

'Special Agent' Pauley would be plain old Neil Pauley, husband to his wife, Judy, and dad to his four daughters, Collette, Estelle, Lucy, and Angie. *I don't need a badge for that,* Pauley told himself.

When he finished dotting the Is and crossing the Ts on his separation papers, Pauley bought a bag of hot, roasted peanuts and walked to the deserted Lincoln Memorial. He stood in the shadows of that marbled hall and looked into the world-weary face of the American President he most admired.

Neil Pauley left Washington, D.C., that same day. Forever.

Mesa drove the same company car he and Marshal Standish drove to Maine. He reckoned he was two days shy of Albuquerque when he stopped for the night in Lincoln, Nebraska.

Mesa didn't mind making the drive back to New Mexico alone, not at all; it gave him time to think about everything that had taken place recently east of the Mississippi. But it did feel odd, even somewhat eerie, not to have Standish around. Mesa thought if he turned quickly, he might see Standish's ghost staring out the passenger window.

When Standish wasn't singing, he was forever telling jokes *Amos & Andy*[104] made famous. Now Standish was dead. Poof! Gone! Unless the GREAT THAT gets fed up having Standish around and sends him back to earth as an angel or something.

Mesa banged the desk bell and waited for the Night Manager at the Moon Glow Motel to show up. As he waited, his eyes caught sight of the headline on the front page of a newspaper left on the counter. It read as follows:

"Massacre in Maine!"
Only three left alive! Authorities Hush-Hush!

Mesa felt his meeting with the Director of the Marshals Service went reasonably well. They would give Mesa a full year's Severance Pay and a favorable letter of recommendation. That, in exchange for keeping

---

[104] A popular radio comedy show that featured two white men in the roles of two black men, Amos & Andy, and a third white man, in the role of Kingfisher, also a supposed black man.

his mouth shut about what he saw that day near the border.

"Look out, Rainbow trout," Mesa said aloud as he left the Marshals Service Headquarters in Arlington, Virginia. "Albert's coming!"

After checking into a single room with a queen-size bed, green wallpaper, and yellow cornstalks painted on the walls; Mesa went to the bar. Far from crowded, he was the only one there, apart from the bartender.

Mesa stared at what he ordered (a shot of Tequila, with a Schlitz beer chaser) and recalled what Director Robert Wise said in the Hall of Heroes in Arlington:

"Miles Standish died in the company of his friends, performing the duties he enjoyed most in the job he loved. His bravery will set a standard by which every Deputy United States Marshal will hereafter follow."

"Amen to that!" said Mesa. He raised the shot glass and looked at his reflection in the mirror behind the bar.

"Here's to you, partner. Rest in peace."

No sooner had that liquid fire burned its way down Mesa's gullet; he hurled his empty shot glass at the mirror with every bit of force he could muster. Mesa struck his reflection dead-center, right between the eyes, creating a spider web of fractured glass.

As it turned out, the mirror in the bar of the Moon Glow Motel in Lincoln, Nebraska, was custom made by the Libby-Owens glass factory in Toledo, Ohio.

After the US Marshals Service agreed to pay $13,000.00 (a hefty sum in 1949) for a new mirror, sixty days later, ordinary citizen-civilian Albert Mesa was released from Lincoln County Jail and invited never to return.

As Mesa got on a Greyhound bus headed west, he looked back over his shoulder and shouted, "Adios, mother [expletive deleted]!"

To whom he was directing that epithet remains unclear.

50.

Heartache Builds Muscle

"I want to see mom and dad," said Angel to Seamus and Alyssa O'Hara. "Where are they buried?"

Angel's paternal grandparents looked at each other before Alyssa abruptly left the room.

"We had Paddy and Sarah cremated, Angel," said Seamus.

Alyssa returned with a brass funeral urn. "We have their ashes, Angel. We were only waiting to find out what you wanted to do."

"Do?" said Angel.

"Yes, Angel," said Seamus. "With the ashes."

"The house on Bette's Chin is the only home we had. I think that's where they'd like to be."

"Then that's what we'll do, sweetheart," said Alyssa.

"I'll grab my coat and warm up the car," said Seamus.

"I'll make some sandwiches and hot chocolate to take along. Does that sound good, Angel?"

"It sounds wonderful, Nana."

Angel lassoed Seamus and Alyssa with her arms and hugged them until all three had tears running down their cheeks.

Outside, the sun managed to burn through the marine layer allowing patches of blue sky to emerge. It looked like a beautiful day after all.

Another silver lining!

† † †

There wasn't much wind that afternoon, and what wind there was came from offshore. Angel was mindful of how the wind blew as she removed the lid from the urn, stood to one side, and poured the ashes out. She did this thinking that the breeze coming from the ocean would disperse Paddy and Sarah's ashes over the property yet be far enough away from the terrible, charred foundation where they once lived, laughed, and loved.

"No more tears," said Angel as she emptied the urn, "Dust to dust, ashes to ashes."

Seamus and Alyssa O'Hara looked on from some twenty yards away, standing outside the car where Seamus parked. They didn't know it, but despite the sound of waves crashing below the cliffs, Angel could hear Seamus and Alyssa softly converse, speaking as they were, just above a whisper:

"This was good for her," said Seamus. "Bringing the ashes and all."

"Not for me," said Alyssa. "Bette's Chin gives me the creeps. It always has."

"Aye," said Seamus. "Maybe it wasn't a bat; maybe it was a banshee[105] that did the evil here, Alyssa?"

Alyssa crossed herself. "Don't be speaking of bats and banshees, Seamus O'Hara. Are you daft!?" Alyssa leaned her body against Seamus and sighed.

"I don't think she's well, Seamus."

---

[105] **Banshee** [Irish] "woman of the fairy mound" or "fairy woman") is a female spirit in Irish folklore who heralds the death of a family member, usually by wailing, shrieking, or keening [Wikipedia].

"How could she be? After everything she's been through!" said Seamus O'Hara.

"Yes, of course, but, look at her—walking as if she never broke her little leg in three places! And her eyes? So violet; so cold, they are, like she sees through things! She's not the same granddaughter we had before."

"Yes, she is," said Seamus. "She's just a wee bit different now."

† † †

Lawrence McLaughlin's attorney, Charles Arthur Keller, waited until the Downstairs Maid finished pouring coffee before he spoke.

"Larry. Rose," said Attorney Keller, "a custody proceeding is an unpleasant experience. You need to know that from the get-go."

"It can't be any more unpleasant than seeing Angel raised by the O'Hara's. Hellfire, Charles! They have nothing to offer Angel. Rose and I have everything she needs or ever will need. As matters presently stand, Angel is the sole beneficiary of our trust. Isn't that right, Rose?"

"Yes, darling."

"I realize that, Larry," said Attorney Keller. I was the architect of your Living Trust—remember?"

"Of course, of course. So, what do we do to get the ball started with this *custody* business?"

"It doesn't please me to say this, but it may come down to getting *mean*. I mean, plumb, mad-dog mean!"

"We can do *mean* if we have to."

McLaughlin turned and looked at his wife. "Can't we, Sugar Rose?"

Rose McLaughlin reached across the table; she covered her husband's hand with her own. "Whatever you say, dear."

"Fine, I'll get started on the paperwork," said Keller.

51.

Fact-Finding

"The week before Christmas, Chief of Police, A.J. McKuen knocked softly on the O'Hara's front door. He removed his hat when Alyssa O'Hara appeared.

"Good morning, A.J.," said Alyssa. "Come in. Have a cup of coffee with us. Seamus and Angel are finishing breakfast, and I just baked a fresh batch of *Apple Piffles*."

"Alyssa, I need you, Seamus, and Angel to follow me down to the station. It's urgent."

† † †

"Thank you all for agreeing to meet with us today. My name is Luke Marmot, Assistant Director of Internal Investigations for the Federal Bureau of Investigation. To my left is Marie McElroy, of Counsel, for the US Marshals Service. To my right is Roger Cleaver, Director of Internal Affairs for the Maine Department of Public Safety. After everything you've been through, Miss O'Hara--"

"ANGEL!" said, Angel. "My name is Angel. I don't know any, 'Miss O'Hara.'"

The Court stenographer, who could have been Lucille Ball's freckle-faced twin, grinned.

"Oh! I see," said Luke Marmot. "Then, Angel, it is." Marmot smiled a smile that wasn't a smile; instead, it was something closer to a grimace.

In the corner, a psychiatrist on loan to the FBI, Phil Dokes, seemed to think Angel's response was significant and made a notation to that effect on a yellow pad resting on his lap.

"Okay. Angel," said Marmot, "We want to be as brief as we can, but we do have some questions for you."

"Then," said the father of Angel's dead mother, Lawrence McLaughlin, "I suggest you get on with it, so we can all get the hell out of here."

McLaughlin was visibly troubled. His attorney, Charles Arthur Keller, tapped McLaughlin lightly on the wrist, cautioning him to remain quiet. Not such an easy thing to do for a self-made millionaire who owned most of New Dublin, Maine.

"Fiddlesticks," said McLaughlin, under his breath.

"Miss O—" Marmot hesitated. "Angel?"

"Yes?"

"In your own words, please tell us what happened from the time you were abducted by Jonny Fiáin, up to your return to New Dublin with Chief of Police, McKuen. Can you do that for us, please?"

"I already told Chief McKuen all there was to tell."

"Yes," said Marmot. "But this time, we're going to record your statement."

Marmot looked over at the Court Stenographer. Her name was Grace Goodnite. She raised her hand, 'hello.' Angel replied in kind. Marmot gestured at the three microphones in front of Angel, one for each governmental agency present.

"If you wouldn't mind?" said Marmot, with the same awkward smile as before.

Angel looked at Seamus O'Hara. He smiled reassuringly.

"Okay," said Angel. "First, and this is the last time I'll say it: Jonny Fiáin did NOT kidnap me. After I came home from trick-or-treating with my friends, Megan and Andrew, I went inside my house and found my parents on the floor. I believe my dad was already dead, but my mother was still alive. On top of her was the most frightening thing I've ever seen—a monster."

"What kind of monster, Angel," said Luke Marmot.

"Can you describe it?"

"Yes," said Angel. "It was a huge, fat, hairy-legged bat, with wings that looked like stretched, dried-up leather. And it had claws, and its eyes were purple like mine are now, and it smelled like seaweed and dead crabs all mixed together."

Angel glanced at the corner. The psychiatrist was taking notes as fast as he could scribble on his yellow pad.

"It was drinking my mother's blood. When it saw me, I ran, sort of, for the stairs. It swung one of its wings at me and clawed my back. I got out of the kitchen, past my dad's body, up the stairs to my room. I pushed a dresser in front of the door and then hid with my dog, Whiskey, in the closet. I could hear the monster come up the stairs and force its way inside my room. That's when it spoke. It was a woman's voice I heard. She said her name was Szah Zhah and that my blood tasted like marzipan. She was about to open the closet door when I heard a gunshot. She screamed and smashed through the window and part of the wall. I guess she flew away. The closet door opened, and there was Jonny Fiáin. He saved my life. He said we couldn't be sure the monster wouldn't come back, so he would take me somewhere safe. I was bleeding pretty badly, and I felt like my back was on fire.

Jonny put Whiskey and me into the sidecar of Jonny's motorcycle, and we rode away from New Dublin, all the way to Canada, to a little town called *Sans Souci*, not far from the city of Fredericton."

"I don't remember the ride there, but Jonny took me to a doctor friend of his named Luther Van Helwing. It was the doctor who gave me Rabies shots and sewed me up. I was unconscious for a week. When I woke up, I was different."

"Different how Angel?" said the Marshals Service representative, Marie McElroy.

"The leg I broke mended before it was supposed to. And my eyes changed color to what they are now. I could hear, smell, and see things better than ever. Jonny didn't want to worry me, but he sensed something followed us to Canada and watched us at Doctor Van Helwing's. The things that we're watching are part human and part wolf. They're called Weirdwolves. They're shape-shifters. Jonny killed two of them after they tried to kill him and capture me. One of them said they obeyed orders from the bat who wanted to kill me and called herself Szah Zhah. Jonny knew I wouldn't be safe any longer at the doctor's, so he decided we should come back to New Dublin, the same way we got into Canada. On the way back, we knew something was still out there, following us, and Jonny figured it was the Weirdwolves. What Jonny didn't know was that you folks were waiting for us in the forest also. Jonny flew backward off his bike. Before it crashed, I tossed Whiskey into a clump of bracken. I rolled out of the sidecar. A good man named Marshal Mesa found me and helped me escape. One of the Weirdwolves he killed was a waitress on the

Canadian side of the border called Ruby. I recognized her after she changed back into human form.

"Oh, boy," said the exasperated, disbelieving representative from the Maine Department of Public Safety, Roger Cleaver. "Are you saying it was these wolf things that killed those State Troopers and the others? The men from the FBI and the Marshals Service."

"Please, Roger," said Luke Marmot, "Let her finish her statement."

Angel's eyes flashed angrily. "Marshal Mesa and I made our way toward a fire watch station. He killed a sniper trying to kill an FBI agent who was firing back from the tower. It was Agent Pauley. We spent the night there. In the morning, Chief McKuen and grandpa O'Hara came and got me."

"Thank you for your time Angel," said Marmot. "We're glad you're home, safe and sound."

"Merry Christmas, Angel," said Marie McElroy from the Marshals Service."

"Humbug," said Roger Cleaver, the representative from the Maine Department of Public Safety. "There's something fishy about you, young lady."

"Don't you dare talk to my granddaughter that way!" said Lawrence McLaughlin.

"It's okay, Grandfather McLaughlin," said Angel. "I think he lost some of his friends that day."

"You're damn right; I did!" said Cleaver.

Lawrence McLaughlin tried to reach across the table and sock Cleaver in the jaw. His attorney pulled him back as Chief McKuen stood and shouted. "Enough!"

"You should have told me, Seamus," said Lawrence McLaughlin.

Seamus O'Hara shrugged. "I had no say in the matter.

I'm sorry, Michael."

"There wasn't time, Mister McLaughlin," said Chief McKuen. "It was Douglas O'Doole who Jonny called, and Jonny specifically told O'Doole to bring Seamus and no other family. He knew there might be more trouble out there."

"Fiddlesticks!" said McLaughlin as he pushed himself away from his attorney's embrace. "Fiddlesticks! I'm Angel's grandfather, the same as Seamus, here, and I had a right to be there when you brought her home, dammit."

"I'm sorry, Mister McLaughlin," said Chief McKuen. "But that's the way Jonny wanted it."

"Jonny!? Jonny Fiáin!? Since when do you take orders from a common criminal, Chief McKuen?"

McKuen shrugged. He wasn't going to argue the matter.

"I don't know why you hate Jonny, Grandfather McLaughlin," said Angel, "but he was my dad's best friend, and he saved my life. TWICE!" Angel's eyes flashed; hot tears gathered on her cheeks.

"The meeting is over, folks," said Chief McKuen.

The federal and state representatives exchanged uncomfortable looks, gathered their microphones and tape recorders, and departed.

"Come on, Michael," said Keller, the attorney. "Time to leave."

The psychiatrist, Phil Dokes, put his notes into his briefcase and hastily departed. He had an urgent telephone call to make to someone at Black Briar, in upper state Maine.

The Court Stenographer, Grace Goodnite, came over to Angel. "You're a fearless young lady. May I hug you?"

"Sure," said Angel. "I'd like that." They hugged.

"Merry Christmas, Angel," said Grace Goodnite.

Angel nodded. She knew what people said to each other that time of year, but right then, she found those words empty, void of meaning, removed from her present reality, fluid as that reality was.

Angel watched the stenographer exit with the others, then softly sighed, "I miss you so much, Jonny.

52.

Amongst Friends

"Are you sure you feel up to it, Angel," said Alyssa O'Hara. She and Angel were alone in the bedroom that Jonny once shared with Paddy until Jonny went to the Bangor Reformatory for Boys.

Several years later, Paddy fled the nest when he married Sarah McLaughlin, on condition he accepts a job as a mechanic at the cannery Sarah's father owned. The O'Hara's had left Jonny and Paddy's room just as it was, an expanded moment, two boys, frozen in time.

Angel sat on Paddy's bunkbed and ran her hand over the bedspread and pillow. She had seen Jonny and her dad's old bedroom a hundred, maybe a thousand times, but that day it felt different, as though Paddy and Sarah might suddenly walk into the room smiling as they swept Angel into their arms and hugged her.

"Angel?" said Alyssa O'Hara.

Angel blinked. "Yes, Nana, I feel up to it."

† † †

The Veterans' Memorial Hall in New Dublin could comfortably sit four-hundred and fifty people. That is how many bodies appeared to be in attendance that afternoon, a week after Angel's return to New Dublin.

Angel was the Guest of Honor, seated at a cafeteria table placed on the stage. Sitting with her were both sets of grandparents—O'Haras and McLaughlins, along with Douglas O'Doole, Chief McKuen, Father Timothy, and New Dublin's Mayor, Tobey Maguire.

Headley Lamarre, a reporter with the *New Dublin Clarion*, was also there. The *Clarion* boasted a bi-weekly circulation of three thousand copies, but most folks read it for the Comics each Sunday due to a chronic scarcity of local news. In 1949, one could enjoy such gripping serials as *Terry and the Pirates, Lil' Abner, Cap Stubbs & Tippie, Little Orphan Annie, The Katzenjammer Twins,* and Angel's favorite, *Popeye*. *Popeye* was Angel's favorite because Popeye reminded her of Jonny Fiáin.

"I'll make this short and sweet," said the Master of Ceremonies, Douglas O'Doole. "Our very own Angel O'Hara is back, safe, and sound. And tonight, we're here to let Angel know how much we love her, just as we dearly loved her parents, Paddy and Sarah O'Hara, Keepers of the Light on Bette's Chin. God rest their souls.

Throughout the Hall came tears and some crying, quelled when O'Doole raised his ham-sized hands to end it.

"Well," said O'Doole, "enough said. Let's eat! And a merry, merry Christmas to every one of you."

Standing behind O'Doole, Father Timothy stood on his tip-toes and cleared his throat loudly into one of O'Doole's cauliflower-shaped ears. O'Doole wasn't born with that ear; it took a good deal of beating on it to achieve such a profound shape.

"The devil take me for a fool!" said O'Doole. "Pardon me, Father. Folks, we'll start serving soon as Father Timothy gives us a right and proper blessing."

† † †

Father Timothy started with First Corinthians and ended with Ecclesiastes, "…there is a time to everything, under Heaven….".

What solace the priest's invocation provided to Angel's friends and the O'Hara's that afternoon is debatable.

Michael and Rose McLaughlin felt like they were sitting on the dark side of the moon, despite daylight entering through windows and the Hall festively lit. True, the McLaughlins didn't have many friends, apart from Lawrence McLaughlin's business cronies, none of whom were present in the Veterans Memorial Hall that day.

The people who were present were simple, dignified, working-class folks. They wanted to hear words that would comfort and abide with them awhile, along with the baked ham, roast turkey, potatoes and gravy, hot rolls, pumpkin, and Mince pie they would soon consume.

Suffice to say, the mob greeting Angel that day was predominantly Catholic (most days of the week), along with a spattering of Protestants and as many, or more, closet atheists. Angel's pals from Grade School were there, including Megan and Andrew Crabtree, but as Angel scanned the faces of those present, young and old, alike, she suddenly wished she was invisible. If only she had a magic ring like Bilbo Baggins, she would put it on, disappear and leave the Shire in a heartbeat! No differently, Angel wanted to leave New Dublin to find Jonny Fiáin and Whiskey, no matter what. She had made her mind up about that, and nothing else mattered— nothing!

There was a whole lot more that Angel wanted to learn, what she needed to learn, and Jonny Fiáin was the key that would unlock the terrible knowledge she sought.

During the banquet that followed Father Timothy's invocation, Seamus O'Hara went to the microphone and thanked everyone who had participated in Angel's recovery in a voice weighed down with emotion. In his remarks, Seamus made no mention of the FBI or the U.S. Marshals' Service. Was that fair to the FBI and the Marshals' Service? The equities remain somewhat split as to that, six of one, half-dozen of the other; so, who cares? Certainly not Angel. She liked Marshal Mesa and Special Agent Pauley, but they were two of the men who wanted to bring down Jonny Fiáin, and THAT was not to be forgotten or forgiven.

When Larry McLaughlin got up to speak, the intentional talking of the crowd and clatter of plates and utensils were so loud he simply gave up after thirty seconds and sat. The only persons in the Hall who felt bad about McLaughlin's reception were his wife, Rose, and Angel herself. She had wanted to hear if her grandfather McLaughlin had anything to say worth hearing. He didn't.

When O'Doole introduced the Mayor, Tobey McGuire, the good-natured laughter and booing were so loud that, like Lawrence "Larry" McLaughlin, he gave up and returned to his seat between Rose McLaughlin and Father Timothy.

When Douglas O'Doole raised his hands, calling for quiet, the audience responded. To the chagrin of Lawrence McLaughlin and the Mayor, a silence fell upon the Hall. Those in attendance knew it was Angel's time to speak. Everyone was hungry to hear in Angel's own words what occurred that fateful night, October 31st, 1949.

"Ladies 'n gents," said O'Doole, "we're going to hear now from the pride of New Dublin, herself—our very own Angel, Miss Angel O'Hara."

The applause was prolonged and heartfelt, and as Angel walked from her place at the table without wearing her cast and without limping, there was many a gasp from the audience. Angel's previous condition necessitating a cast on one of her legs was a well-known factoid, at least in New Dublin. The Hall became silent.

When Angel reached the stand-alone microphone, O'Doole adjusted its height to accommodate her.

"Hold your mouth about three inches away from the silly thing, darling," said O'Doole, in a whisper, "then go ahead and talk as if we were having a conversation, just like we used to do in my pub, waiting for your mom."

Angel nodded.

"It's nice," she said, "seeing all of you. Thank you for coming."

Enthusiastic applause interrupted Angel, then quickly died, allowing her to resume.

"But you all need to know something," said Angel. "I'm not happy to be here. Too many terrible things happened—to my family, and the families of FBI, U.S. Marshals, and Maine State Troopers that monsters killed

near the Canadian border when they tried to arrest Jonny
Fiáin."

There was a great deal of murmuring that rippled
through the audience as folks tried to assimilate what
they were hearing out of Angel's mouth.

"But I didn't need to be rescued. It was only the night
my parents a big, fat, hairy-legged Vampire bat named
Szah Zhah murdered my parents——that I needed
rescuing."

It was at this point audible gasps of shock and
disbelief issued from many inside the Hall. People began
whispering, not maliciously, but simply not
comprehending what they were hearing—no fault in that.

"My mom and dad always said there was no such
thing as monsters. They were wrong. There are. Believe
me. Monsters are real. I know. A monster killed my
parents and came close to killing me."

Lawrence McLaughlin, keenly aware of the
audience's reaction, turned beet red, the arteries in his
neck trebled in size, and appeared about to explode.
McLaughlin stood and shouted: "Angel! Stop! Stop
talking like that! For the love of your mother and
father—stop!"

Things Children Say

Seamus O'Hara and Douglas O'Doole joined Angel at the microphone, shielding her from Lawrence McLaughlin and a chorus of nay-sayers that were now shouting epithets at her.

"Let Angel speak," said Douglas O'Doole. "I, for one, believe every word, and I'll not suffer anyone silencing her!"

"Aye!" said several other voices in the Hall. "Let Angel speak!"

Father Timothy couldn't take it; after what he heard, he needed a drink, a strong one. He just shook his head, got up from the table, and walked offstage.

"Go ahead, sweetie," said Seamus O'Hara. "Let them hear what you have to say."

"Absolutely!" Said Headley Lamarre, the reporter from the *Clarion,* sitting at a table closest to the stage. She was using shorthand to get Angel's every word. Several others also wanted to hear what Angel had to say. They were standing at the back of the Hall. Two were there together, and none of them were residents of New Dublin. One was from the Governor's office—the same man who relieved Pauley and Mesa from the Fire Lookout Station near the Canadian border, Gavin Needleman, Special Assistant to Governor Payne of Maine. The other two were dressed identically, in black. They wore black Fedoras and sunglasses and stood stiffly with their arms folded across their chests. No one from New Dublin recognized them; most just wrote them off as city slickers come to gawk.

"If it weren't for my dad's best friend, Jonny Fiáin, I wouldn't be here today," said Angel. "I'd be dead. And now the FBI and the Marshals' Service are chasing after Jonny when they should be hunting for the monsters responsible for killing over thirty people—THEIR people! That's all I'm going to say about that. Anyway, thank you for being here for me."

The Hall remained silent until Angel's friends, Megan and Andrew Crabtree, shouted, "We love you, Angel!"

Angel took Douglas O'Doole and Seamus O'Hara each by the hand and looked into their faces.

"I want to leave."

O'Doole looked at Seamus O'Hara and said: "The lads and I will clear the way."

† † †

They had just reached the O'Hara's faded green, 1947 2-door Chevrolet when they were intercepted by Lawrence McLaughlin, with his wife, Rose, in tow. With McLaughlin was his attorney, Charles Arthur Keller.

"Angel, dear," said Lawrence McLaughlin. "Your Grandmother Rose and I were hoping you would come and stay with us, at least until things settle down. We've kept your mother's old bedroom just the way it was before she got married."

Before Angel could reply, Seamus O'Hara came around the front of his car and stood beside Angel.

"You mean you kept Sarah's room the same as before she married my boy, PADDY?"

"I'm talking to Angel, Seamus. It doesn't concern you."

"Anything that has to do with Angel concerns me, Michael."

Lawrence McLaughlin's attorney, Charles Arthur Keller, stepped between the two men.

"Gentlemen," said Keller, "what you're doing in the middle of this public parking lot is unseemly and can't be good for Angel. Now is not the time to argue the matter of *custody*."

"I've already decided that," said Angel. "I want to stay with the O'Haras."

"What?" said Lawrence McLaughlin, baffled.

"With Grandfather and Grandmother O'Hara," said Angel.

"Angel," said McLaughlin, "You're not well. Rose and I can see you get the best of care. The best of everything. The O'Haras can't do that for you. I can."

"Come, Michael," said Keller, the attorney. "Now is not the time, nor is this the place, to litigate."

"Litigate?" said Seamus O'Hara, as if something foul had just entered his ear.

"Damn straight," said Lawrence McLaughlin. "We'll settle this in court, Seamus!"

With that, Charles Keller urged his client away to McLaughlin's 1939 Rolls-Royce Phantom III Four-Door Cabriolet. The Chauffeur had the engine running, and Rose was sitting in the back with the heater and defroster running full blast.

"I don't understand," said Angel, "why is he so angry? Grandfather McLaughlin never showed any interest in having me around. He was always too busy."

Seamus O'Hara opened the passenger side door for Alyssa and helped her inside. Angel got in the back.

"That was before they lost their only daughter, Angel," said Alyssa O'Hara. Now that Sarah's gone, you're all that's left to remind them of your mother."

Angel thought a moment, then nodded. She and Alyssa waited for Seamus to scrape the snow off the windshield.

Lawrence McLaughlin roared past in his Phantom III, shaking his fist out the window at Seamus, and shouting, "Don't bother coming to work on Monday, Seamus. You're fired!" The steam spewing from his mouth could easily have been Luciferian Smoke[106].

Riding in the front with the Chauffeur, Lawrence McLaughlin's attorney lowered his eyes and sadly shook his head. The one aspect of his work that bothered him, in fact, the ONLY part that bothered him, was assisting his clients, persons of prominence, generally, accomplish or obtain what they had no business achieving or obtaining.

"Lady Justice isn't blind," Supreme Court Justice Felix Frankfurter once said, "She's gagging."

Before Angel could get inside the back of the O'Hara's car, the reporter, Headley Lamarre, rushed up.

"Angel!" said Lamarre. "The monsters who killed all those lawmen, what were they? What did they look like?"

"They were scary. Like wolves, only worse, and much larger."

Seamus O'Hara appeared. "Come on, sweetie. Let's go."

Headley Lamarre brought her camera up to bear. There was the flash of a lightbulb, and that, was that; she had taken Angel's photograph without so much as, *"By your leave?"*.

"Thanks, Angel. You were great! Welcome home!"

---

[106] Hot, nasty, worse than Skunk-Weed! The worst kind of smoke imaginable [Almanac of Unapologetic Fatcts. Misty Bay Books. Volume 7. 1st Edition. 1948].

† † †

The *New Dublin Clarion* ran a special edition of the paper that week. The front-page headline read:

"Monsters Are Real!"
Claims 9-years-old New Dublin girl

Lawrence McLaughlin went so far as to hire a private security firm to keep non-residents off Elm Street where the O'Hara's, and now Angel, resided. Likewise, Chief McKuen posted his best officer, Robb Royce, once a good friend of Paddy and Sarah O'Hara, directly outside the house in a patrol car. Angel enjoyed having Officer Royce around. At lunchtime, Alyssa O'Hara would send Angel with soup and sandwiches to give to Royce, and Angel would sit in his prowl car and listen to Royce recount the good times he spent with Angel's parents. Angel enjoyed hearing Robb Royce's stories from the past, and Royce loved telling them.

As for going to school, Angel didn't. The school was out for Christmas vacation.

54.
Implausible Deniability

Angel and the O'Haras sat on one side of a long, scarred, walnut table inside the old courthouse's conference room built in the summer of 1865, after the War of Succession between the North and South[107].

On one side of the table were Angel and her paternal grandparents, Seamus and Alyssa O'Hara. Chief A.J. McKuen sat just inside the door to guarantee privacy for the proceeding about to take place. At one end of the table sat the Court stenographer, Grace Goodnite; at the other end, sat Judge Love. The judge was known to be tough but fair-minded; he was there to see that the rules were at all times adhered to following principles of due process.[108]

Across from Angel sat Lawrence and Rose McLaughlin, accompanied by the McLaughlin's attorney, Charles Arthur Keller. Alongside them at the table were three mental health experts.

It was snowing outside, but inside the room, an electric heater hummed steadily, making the place tolerable, notwithstanding the grim reason the conference room was in use on a Sunday morning.

There was one other person present. Sitting in the corner of the room, observing, was the Chief Administrator for the State of Maine's *Black-Briar*

---

[107] The United States' Civil War [1861-1865].
[108] Due Process is a legal term which essentially means fundamental fairness, from which certain legal rights stem and must be recognized in any legal proceeding, when someone's life, liberty, or property is at stake.

Asylum for the Criminally Insane. The Administrator's name? Felicia Bear Claw.

Bear Claw often appeared as an expert witness for the Prosecution in criminal trials when the Defense raised the Affirmative Defense of Insanity to mitigate a defendant's guilt for the crime or crimes alleged.

Judge Love, a teetotaler, had already mandated no smoking of pipes, cigars, or cigarettes; nor the chewing of gum, spitting, cursing, or using the Lord's name in vain. Moreover, any "untoward" displays of emotion would not be "countenanced."

† † †

Angel wore long underwear under a pair of pleated, forest green corduroy trousers, along with the Pendleton she got in *Sans Souci* the day she went shopping with Doctor Van Helwing. On her feet, she wore sheepskin trappers' boots lined with fleece, an early Christmas present from "Bumpa" O'Hara.

Angel smiled as she eyed the strangers arrayed opposite her. Angel sensed that whatever they would ask, and however she answered was somehow of great importance. She was, of course, correct.

† † †

Seventy-seven-year-old Judge Richard Love was not dressed in black judicial robes but wore a three-piece, dark blue suit, a white button-down shirt, and a black-tie. What Angel found strange, however, was that the Judge was wearing wool socks without any shoes. Angel tapped Seamus's arm. As he looked at her, she flicked her head in the direction of the judge's feet.

Without looking, Seamus O'Hara whispered into Angel's ear: "I know."

Judge Love cleared his throat. "First, in case anyone is wondering why I have no shoes on, it's because I walked here from Church wearing a leaky pair of rubbers. Said boots are drying out in my private chamber as I speak. Now. Angel O'Hara. Do you know why you're here today?"

"No," said Angel.

"What?" said the Judge.

"That's my fault, your Honor," said Seamus O'Hara. "I couldn't bring myself to tell her—not exactly."

"Which is why you're unfit to have custody of Angel," said Lawrence McLaughlin. "You don't have the stomach for it!"

Judge Love brought the flat of hand down hard on the table. "I will not tolerate a second such outburst from you, Larry McLaughlin!"

"Our apologies, your Honor," said Charles Keller, McLaughlin's attorney. "It won't happen again."

"Well, it damn well better not," said the judge. This hearing may not be taking place in my courtroom, but my word is the law." Judge Love looked at Seamus O'Hara. "Well, Mister O'Hara, what exactly DID you tell your granddaughter?"

Angel cut her grandfather off before he could answer.

"He told me that Grandfather and Grandmother McLaughlin wanted custody of me so they could get me the help I need."

"Hmm. And did Seamus O'Hara explain what that help might be?"

"Yes, Judge," said Angel. "He said it was a truckload of poppycock."

The Judge chuckled but just as quickly cleared his throat a second time.

Angel removed a piece of hard candy from her Pendleton pocket and held it toward the Judge. "Would you like a piece of horehound candy, Judge? It's good for a parched throat."

"Yes, I believe I will. If you would be so kind as to pass it down."

"Sure," said Angel. And that's what she did; she passed a piece of horehound candy toward the judge.

After Judge Love had unwrapped the lozenge and popped it into his mouth, he said, "Young Lady. You're here because—" The Judge hesitated.

"Well," he said, but again he stopped. He looked up at the clock on the wall, then turned back to Angel.

"Because some people think you're not right in your head. Do you understand what I'm saying?"

"No," said Angel. "Because my head doesn't feel wrong, not even a smidgin."

When Seamus O'Hara laughed, Judge Love gave him the skunk-eye.

The Chief Administrator of Maine's Asylum for the Criminally Insane, Felicia Bear Claw, then spoke. "Your Honor? At this juncture, may I offer the court my assistance?"

"Gladly, Miss Bear Claw," said the judge. "It's no secret; I'm no fan of custody OR mental competency proceedings."

55.

The Die is Cast

"Angel?" said Miss Bear Claw.

"Yes?"

"Do you know the difference between truth and fiction?"

"I think so."

"Good. Will you please tell everyone here what you think the difference is?"

"Okay," said Angel. "Truth is real. Fiction isn't. It's something made-up."

"Very good, Angel," said Miss Bear Claw. "You're here today because the story you told about what happened to you and your parents the night of your birthday sounds like fiction—not truth."

"Not to the missus and I, it doesn't," said Seamus O'Hara.

"Your Honor?" said Felicia Bear Claw.

"Interrupt again, Mister O'Hara, and out of the room, you go. Am I understood?"

"He understands, your Honor," said Alyssa O'Hara. "Don't you, Seamus?"

Seamus scowled and nodded.

"Well, good," said the judge. "Now, where were we?"

"Clarifying Angel's understanding of truth and fiction, your Honor," said Felicia Bear Claw.

"Yes, that's right. We were. Thank you, Miss Bear Claw. Please proceed."

"Thank you, your Honor. Now, Angel, are you also asking us to believe the story you told about what happened to you near the Canadian border when you were with Jonny Fiáin is also true and not fiction?"

"You keep saying my 'story,' as if I got it out of a comic book. I didn't. Everything I told Chief McKuen and the men from the FBI and the Marshals Service and the State Troopers was the truth. I DIDN'T lie! Not about ANY of it!"

Angel's eyes flashed angrily. She pushed her chair back and stood. "May I leave now, Judge?"

"I realize," said the judge, "that being here isn't easy for you, young lady. But you are a material witness to some very terrible crimes—crimes committed in your presence, and you're the only one who knows what happened. Now, please, Miss O'Hara, sit down."

When Angel looked at Seamus O'Hara, he nodded in the direction of her chair. Angel sat.

"Just a few more questions, Angel?" said Bear Claw.

"What?" said Angel, not disguising her sudden loathing for the woman.

"Do you truly believe, in your heart of hearts, that your parents were murdered by, and I'm going to quote you now: 'A huge, fat, hairy-legged vampire bat, who could speak English, named Szah Zhah'?"

"I don't have to believe it," said Angel. "I was there! I KNOW it!"

Nothing Like Truth

(To Settle the Stomach)

"And is it your *truth*," said Bear Claw, "that wolves murdered the brave men who lost their lives near the Canadian border? Wolves who could change into human form? I believe you may have even used the expressions, Weirdwolves and shape-shifters?"

"It's not, MY truth," said Angel. "It's THE truth. Every word I've said, whether you believe me or not."

"Your Honor?" said Bear Claw.

"Yes, Miss Bear Claw?"

"I believe my colleagues and I have heard enough to be able to render a determination."

Judge Love looked at the psychiatrist, the psychologist, and the Medical Doctor individually. "Is that correct?"

The three nodded in the affirmative.

"Very well," said the Judge. You four ladies and gentlemen will adjourn to the Law Library across the hall. When you're ready, I will hear what you say and entertain recommendations in my private chamber. Until then, the rest of you are free to stretch your legs inside the courthouse. But nobody leaves." He looked at Angel. "And I mean, NOBODY! Listen up! Miss Goodnite was sweet enough to bring homemade cake and cookies. Enjoy yourselves. But do it quietly!"

† † †

After Felicia Bear Claw and the medical experts aired their "findings" before Judge Love privately, his hands became fairly well tied. Not bound with ropes, mind you, but by the laws and statutes on the books in the state of Maine in the year Nineteen-Hundred and Forty-Nine.

Angel O'Hara would be confined for an indeterminate period in the *Black-Briar Asylum for the Criminally Insane*, commencing immediately. Here's how it went down:

[10:10 am.]

Doctors Felicia Bear Claw, Hilda Rasmussen, Cecil Wonton, and Louis Lipchitz, II, adjourned to the law library to confer before rendering a determination to Angel O'Hara's state of mind; specifically, is she nuts? Or is she nuts?

[10:12 am.]

"Esteemed colleagues," said Doctor Bear Claw, "this child is a veritable cornucopia of pathologies. Clearly, after trick-or-treating with her friends on Halloween, I believe Angel O'Hara murdered her parents while in a sugar-induced rage. Later, unable to cope with the horror of her actions, Angel created a monster to take the blame. Same as the bloody aftermath near the border, when Jonny Fiáin and his gang brutally murdered those law enforcement people.

"I, for one, said Doctor Hilda Rasmussen, find myself intrigued by Angel's relationship with the criminal friend of her deceased father, Jonny Fiáin."

"It has all the makings of an Electra complex," said Doctor Cecil Wonton.

"Jonny Fiáin is no doubt a surrogate father figure," said Doctor Louis Lipchitz, II. "Moreover, the anger she harbors is considerable—I believe she poses a threat to herself and others."

"Yes," said Doctor Wonton, "Angel O'Hara is a time bomb waiting to go off."

"I concur with that assessment, Doctor Wonton."

"Thank you, Doctor Lipchitz."

"I was most intrigued," said Doctor Rasmussen, by her self-absorption. The way she emphasized the "changes" that occurred to her, following the death of her parents."

"I noticed that too, Doctor Rasmussen," said Doctor Felicia Bear Claw. "I believe this girl is a paranoid schizophrenic with an Electra Complex who poses an extreme threat to herself and the public-at-large. What say you?"

"Harrumph, harrumph!" said Bear Claw's esteemed colleagues.

And, well, that was that.

[10:20 am]

Doctors Bear Claw, Rasmussen, Wonton, and Lipchitz deliver their "findings" to Judge Love in Chambers in the presence of two Federal Marshals. The latter was there to take custody of Angel O'Hara, and they had the "papers" to prove it.

"The Department of Justice regards Angel O'Hara as a Material Witness to multiple murders," said U.S. Deputy Marshal Timothy Olyphant. "Murders perpetrated by Jonny Fiáin and his gang on members of two federal and one state agency near the Canadian Border, last November. As of now, we are taking custody of her."

"Your Honor," said Doctor Bear Claw, "my colleagues and I understand the significance of the government's position, but it is OUR professional position that Angel O'Hara is criminally insane. We believe she murdered her parents and should be committed to Black-Briar for an indeterminant time, where we can treat her afflictions."

"She has more than one?" said Judge Love.

"Uh, huh," said the four doctors in unison.

"Boy, oh boy," said the Judge.

"Judge," said Marshal Olyphant, "Marshal Grabazz and I aren't leaving here without the girl. That's just the way it is, your Honor. You have the necessary papers in front of you, authorizing you to release Angel O'Hara into our custody."

"Hold your horses, sonny-boy, this all coming at me like a runaway train."

"Your Honor?" said Bear Claw.

"Quiet!" said the judge. "Everybody! Just be quiet! I need time to think."

Tick-tock! Tick-tock! Tick-tock!

[10:25 am]

Court Stenographer, Miss Grace Goodnite, stops at the drinking fountain in the hallway outside the Conference

*Room.   Already there is U.S. Deputy Marshal Timothy
Olyphant, wetting his whistle.*

"How's it going in there?" said Grace Goodnite.

"With the eggheads, you mean?" said Olyphant.

*Grace thought that was funny, referring to the
medical people as "eggheads," so she laughed.*

*"That's funny," said Grace. "So, what's going to
happen now, Marshal Olyphant?"*

*"Looks like the kid's going to the loony-bin."
Olyphant raised his finger to the side of his head and
spun it in circles. "She's mixed-up. I mean, whacko! My
partner and I are taking her to Black-Briar. That's my
guess."*

"Oh, my," said Grace Goodnite. "Oh, my, my!"

*"How's it going in the Conference Room?" said
Marshal Olyphant.*

"The cake and cookies are wonderful."

So! The upshot of Judge Love's thought process was
to Judicially mandate the United States Marshal's
Service to deliver Angel O'Hara to Black-Briar, the State
Asylum for the Criminally Insane, and into custody of
Black-Briar's Chief Administrator, Felicia Bear Claw.
The Marshals Service would maintain a presence at
Black-Briar, should they think the risk to Angel
warranted their continued presence there. Angel would
be, after all, in protective custody," ironic as it sounds.

Her confinement would last until the government
obtained testimony from Angel O'Hara sufficient to send
Jonny Fiáin to the electric chair at Leavenworth Federal
Penitentiary in Kansas.

† † †

[10:32 am]

Grace Goodnite returned to the Conference Room, looked at Angel, and broke into tears. Sobbing, this sweet court stenographer who never hurt much more than a fly in her entire life spills the beans as to what she learned from blabbermouth, U.S. Deputy Marshal Timothy Olyphant.

57.

For Every Action

"Loose lips, sink ships."

"For every action, there is an equal, opposite reaction."

Angel didn't make that up; Judge Love didn't make that up; neither did Marshal Timothy Olyphant or Doctor Bear Claw make that up. It's what one of the *Laws of Physics* dictates. Isaac Newton and Stephen Hawking kind of stuff.

Thus, when the two U.S. Marshals entered the Conference Room with Bear Claw and the judge, the tiny delicate hairs on the back of Angel's neck stood. Thanks to Grace Goodnite's warning, Angel knew what was about to happen.

"I'm not going!" Angel said (more like, screamed). "I'm not going!"

She grabbed a fistful of cake off the paper plate in front of her and hurled it. The Marshals ducked; the cake sailed past them, striking the judge on the chin.

"Enough of that, young lady," said the judge (more like, shouted). "Stop that, right now!"

That remark prompted Angel's grandparents to stand and hurl their uneaten cake and cookies at the judge, the Marshals, and Bear Claw, forcing the four to retreat to the hallway.

† † †

On his way back from the lavatory, Chief McKuen intersected them.

"What's all the racket about?" Then, McKuen noticed the gob of cake and frosting clinging for dear life on Judge Love's chin.

"Don't say a word, Chief," said the Judge (more like, growled). "Don't say a word." With that, the judge wiped the cake from his chin. Perhaps it was his "Inner Boy," the *Tom Sawyer*[109] that resides in every grown man that couldn't resist tasting the residue of cake on his fingers.

"Not bad. Devil's Food," said the judge. "Not bad at all."

"What do you want to do, Judge?" said Marshal Olyphant (more like, demanded).

"Do?" said the Judge, suddenly quite cheerful. "I'm going home. That's what I'm going to do. The rest of you are welcome to muddle on, by all means. Merry Christmas!"

And that's what he did! He put his worn-out, old rubber boots on and trudged home where Connie, his wife of fifty years, would have something tasty prepared for lunch. You see, Judge Richard Love was a simple man with simple needs, unlike the [expletive deleted] bankers who would turn the financial world on its ear fifty-nine years later.

---

[109] Tom Sawyer, the best friend of Huckleberry Finn, is the creation of Samuel Langhorne Clemens, [1835-1910] who wrote: *The Adventures of Tom Sawyer.* Known by his pen name, Mark Twain, Clemens was an American writer, humorist, entrepreneur, publisher, and lecturer, and lauded as the "greatest humorist [the United States] has produced." William Faulkner called him "the father of American literature." [Wikipedia]

✝ ✝ ✝

Angel and her grandparents, working together in concert for the first time, shoved the large conference table in front of the door, barricading themselves inside. Done, they looked at one another.

"What do we do now?" said Lawrence McLaughlin.

His attorney, Charles Arthur Keller, had the good sense to occupy a corner of the room when the cake and cookies started flying in the face of legal compliance.

"Well," said Keller, "you can pray the federal government, along with the State of Maine, go easy on you all for obstructing justice and interfering with an ongoing criminal investigation."

McLaughlin looked at his lawyer. "Charles, you're fired!"

Charles Arthur Keller placed the legal documents pertinent to Angel's custody hearing into his briefcase and snapped it shut. He looked at McLaughlin and smiled how a chess player does after eluding a checkmate by his opponent.

"No, Larry. I quit! Now, how about someone opens the damn door so I can leave."

Before anyone inside the Conference Room could say, "no," someone outside pounded on the door. The voice that followed was a familiar one.

✝ ✝ ✝

"Come on, folks. Open up," said Chief McKuen. "Judge Love's gone home. And there are some very distressed people out here who want to see this end peacefully."

"Then, they should leave, too," said Seamus O'Hara from the other side of the door.

"That's right!" said Lawrence McLaughlin. "They should just LEAVE!"

"That isn't going to happen," said U.S. Deputy Marshal, Timothy Olyphant, shouting at the top of his lungs. "Marshal Grabazz and I want the girl, and we want her NOW!"

Marshals Olyphant and Grabazz leaned their shoulders on the door and shoved. Nothing! The door didn't budge.

"Enough!" said Chief McKuen.

† † †

Angel and the others, sitting on the table, continued to listen as Chief McKuen tried to dissuade the Marshals from, quote, "inflaming the situation."

A rock suddenly crashed through one of the windows of the Conference Room. The only one not sitting on the conference table shoved against the door, Charles Arthur Keller retrieved the rock from the floor. Tied around the rock was a piece of paper torn from a grocery bag with a message written on it.

Keller removed the note and dropped the rock to one side.

"What's it say, Counselor?" said Seamus O'Hara.

"Yes—read the damn thing, Charles," said Lawrence McLaughlin.

Keller held the note out in front of him. "It's for Angel."

Angel hopped off the table and took the note from Keller's hand. The message was brief—It only read:

"Hang tough, Angel!"

† † †

Outside the door, Officer Robb Royce joined Chief McKuen. On Bobb's heels came Douglas O'Doole and a half-dozen Fenian vigilantes from O'Doole's *Breakfast Club*, all of them carrying truncheons and nightsticks.

"Now hold on!" said the Chief (more like, shouted). "Everybody, just hold your horses! This place is the Courthouse, for Christ's sake! NOT the O-K Corral!"

† † †

Hearing what was happening beyond the door, Angel looked at the others as she pocketed the note. "This is wrong," she said. "I don't want anyone else to get hurt or killed because of me. I love all of you and what you're trying to do, but we need to open the door— now."

58.

Love's Labor's Lost

Balthazar Headstone was working at his desk in the forecastle of the *Horror*. He'd long ago converted it from crew's quarters to an office, an office where he could ostensibly attend to financial matters, the same that governed his and Szah Zhah's lifestyle. It was, in truth, a place he could retire to on deck, forward of the foremast, to think things over without Szah Zhah assuming he was sulking over something having to do with her. However, that is what Balthazar Headstone was doing—brooding over Szah Zhah's obsession with Angel O'Hara and writing Sympathy Cards to the families of the Gray Brethren, who died near the border trying to capture Angel O'Hara.

So distracted was he that he didn't notice a tugboat called the *New Jersey Dame* coast past close enough for the deckhand to toss the latest issue of the *New Dublin Clarion* onto the deck of the *Horror*. That was no mean feat, speeding issues of the bi-weekly paper from New Dublin, Maine, all the way to Pier 17, with its views of the iconic New York Skyline and the Brooklyn Bridge.

Light snow was falling when Szah Zhah entered the forecastle, unannounced and naked but for platform pumps of silver/black leather from *Jildor Shoes* and an ankle-length Mink coat. The coat was a gift from Angela Lansbury when Szah Zhah stayed the night following the premiere of *Samson and Delilah*[110] three days before, on December 21st, in New York City. That took place while Headstone was conferring with representatives of the Gray Brethren in the Hamptons, having rented the summer compound of Joseph P. Kennedy,[111] senior.

In Szah Zhah's hands was the latest issue of the *New Dublin Clarion* and a frosted pitcher of Martinis, chock-full of fat green olives from the island of Crete.

"You're sulking again, darling," said Szah Zhah, "and I want you to stop."

Szah Zhah dropped the paper down on the desk in front of Headstone. "Look, my beloved." Her voice was awash with glee like a girl whose peers just voted her Prom Queen.

On the cover was a photograph of Angel taken by the *Clarion's* lone reporter, Headley Lamarre, as U.S. Marshals Olyphant and Grabazz escorted Angel to a waiting government vehicle for eventual transport to *Black-Briar Asylum for the Criminally Insane.*

"What the Gray Brethren failed to do at the border," said Szah Zhah, "the little mouse has done for us—just by telling the truth. Look, Balthazar. She will be in a box with no way out. She will be trapped!"

Headstone looked at the photograph of Angel and the headline above it, that read:

Court Orders Girl Committed
Experts say, "Angel is Bonkers"!

---

[110] Sampson and Delilah (1949) from Paramount Pictures, starring Victor Mature, Hedy Lamarr, George Sanders and Angela Lansbury.
[111] Joseph P. Kennedy, senior (1888- 1969). Wealthy American bootlegger, businessman and politician.

Headstone removed his reading glasses, placed them on the desk, and pointed to the stack of thirteen cards in envelopes ready for mailing to Canada.

"What are those, my love?" said Szah Zhah.

"Sympathy cards for the families who lost loved ones last month near the border."

"Oh!" said Szah Zhah; she put the pitcher of Martinis on the desk, along with two Martini glasses. "You're still bothered by that, aren't you?"

Headstone frowned, then slipped a file folder under the pitcher that was now sweating moisture to protect his cherry wood desk—a desk once owned by *Napoleon Bonaparte*—from watermarks.[112]

"Of course, it still bothers me, Szah Zhah. They were decent, hard-working Weirdwolves, all of them. My greatest fear is more will die because of that girl. And why? Because you believe she's the one from the prophecy."

"She IS the one from the prophecy!" said Szah Zhah (more like, screeched).

"We don't know that with absolute certainty, my love."

"What will convince you, Balthazar? When that *fasz* cuts my head, OFF!? Will THAT convince you!?"

Tears poured from Szah Zhah's eyes, ruining her mascara, sending rivulets of color down her cheeks. She clutched the pitcher of Martinis to her chest and started to exit the forecastle. She stopped and turned around.

"I'm going back to the Waldorf. As soon as you decide to cheer up, you know where to find me. Oh, and

---

[112] A Man-Cave is a sacred place, inviolate, to be respected and protected, and that includes the furniture.

if you decide you want to play hide-the weenie tonight, forget it! Plan on me having a headache."

† † †

Later that afternoon, Headstone posted those same sympathy cards in a mailbox on 49th Street, a stone's throw from his hotel. Soon night would fall, and the dazzling lights of New York City would mask its ugliness.

Walking along the sidewalk toward the Waldorf, Headstone stopped and did a double-take, for there, across the street, through the plate glass window of *La Trattoria Siciliano,* he espied his beloved. She was sitting at a table in the company of their neighbor, Frank Costello, who lived in the Penthouse above them.

Headstone had no difficulty recognizing the so-called *Prime Minister of the Underworld.* Still, it was the presence of a half-dozen well-dressed gangsters, Costello's bodyguards, standing outside the restaurant in front of the entrance that confirmed what Headstone suspected. *What are you doing, Szah Zhah?* Headstone wondered. Simultaneously, with the crystal-clear vision he possessed, Headstone saw Szah Zhah hold the worn, leather-bound *Les Prophecies Perdue de Nostradamus* in front of the mobster.

Costello took the book carefully from her hand and appeared to be reading a page that Szah Zhah marked for his attention.

After several minutes, Costello nodded thoughtfully, then put the book down. Szah Zhah extended her hand; Costello took it in his own and brought that proffered appendage to his lips and kissed it like he was Rudolph [expletive deleted] Valentino.

"No, no, no, Szah Zhah," Headstone said aloud, standing in the middle of the sidewalk, inadvertently becoming an immovable wedge for passersby in both directions. It was clear to Headstone that Szah Zhah no longer trusted him to purge her of what she believed was true, without equivocation—that Angel O'Hara was the child from the prophecy and had to die that Szah Zhah might live a VIP, to wit, the *Queen of the Full Moon Night.*

"What are you doing, my love!?" Headstone asked aloud as pedestrians hurried past. "What have you done?"

Balthazar hailed a taxi. Remarkable as it was, a taxi stopped. Not so remarkable, after all—the driver was a black man, a Haitian *émigré*.

"Where to, sir?" asked the taxi driver.

"Penn Station, please. I have a train to catch."

† † †

The train ride north from Penn Station to Fredericton, New Brunswick, Canada, took nine hours and forty-six minutes, including an unplanned stop while a steel gang cleared snow and debris off the tracks.

Headstone spent most of the trip in the deserted Bar Car, looking out the window at the frozen landscape while thinking through his next move.

† † †

It was just after midnight when a taxi owned and driven by a Weirdwolf named Ben Periwinkle pulled up and coasted to a stop in front of Doctor Luther Van Helwing's house in *Sans Souci*.

"I won't be long, Benjamin," said Headstone.

"I'll be right here, Exalted Grand Master."

The doctor's dogs chained near the barn ceased barking once they heard their master's shrill whistle out the upstairs bedroom window. That was followed by the sound of the front door opening and shutting.

† † †

"Exalted Grand Master," exclaimed Van Helwing.

"Hello, Luther," said Headstone.

The doctor stepped back as Headstone lowered his head to accommodate his height and entered. He followed Van Helwing into the doctor's library.

"It wasn't your place, Doctor, to relay a message from our enemies to the Queen of the Full Moon Night. That was for me to do."

"Exalted Grand Master," said Van Helwing; "the American held a gun to my head; he forced me to call our Queen and say all those terrible things."

"Including strangling her with his *schlong*?"

"What—!?"

"Did you NOT hear me?" said Headstone (more like, bellowed).

Before the doctor could reply, Headstone tore the doctor's left ear completely off and dropped it at Van Helwing's slippered feet. Hopping around in a tight circle, the doctor howled with pain. Headstone removed a handkerchief from his camel-hair overcoat and gave it to Van Helwing to stem the flow of blood running down his neck and over his night-shirt.

"Exalted Grand Master," said Van Helwing, "when I insisted to our Queen that Fiáin's message was for you, and you, alone, she said she'd tear me limb from limb if I didn't '*cough it up, fast*'!"

"I see," said Headstone. "That does sound like something she'd say. Now, how might I get in touch with Jonny Fiáin?"

59.

Yellow Brick Detour

"Please don't cry," said Angel. "I'll be okay, Nana. I promise."

It was the day after Christmas. A tearful Alyssa O'Hara remained on the front porch; her husband Seamus accompanied Angel to the vehicle that would transport her to the *Asylum for the Criminally Insane* in upper-state Maine.

Seamus held a single piece of luggage with the few belongings Angel was allowed to take. In addition to what she was wearing for the trip, her wardrobe comprised slippers, pajamas, and a bathrobe. Everything else, Black-Briar would furnish, a bed, meals, toothbrush, toiletries, medical and psychiatric care—and as to the latter, lots.

The two marshals, Olyphant and Grabazz, stood outside their vehicle, holding twelve-gauge, pump shotguns, watching both ends of Elm Street where the O'Hara's lived. It was early, the street was quiet, and snow covered the road and the front yards of the houses.

"Your Nana and I will come to see you every Sunday, sweetheart. We promise."

Wearing a too-tight chauffeur's uniform., the Driver, a muscular man with an unsmiling face and a flattop, took the suitcase from Angel's Grandfather's hand and placed it in the trunk. Seamus O'Hara held the rear door open for Angel and winked. "You can do this, Angel," he said. "We'll have you back here before you know it."

Angel hugged her grandfather close. "Take care of Nana."

Angel got into the back seat. Waiting for her with a quilted shawl covering her legs, Doctor Felicia Bear Claw greeted Angel with a smile, the likes of which would embarrass Captain Hook[113] and the damn crocodile, both.

† † †

"There are other girls your age at Black-Briar, Angel. Did you know that?"

Angel made no reply; instead, she continued to stare out the window as they drove through New Dublin.

"You may not believe it now, but, trust me, Angel, you'll make friends. I promise you."

There were some pedestrians out and about, not many, but with most stores closed for the holiday, those who were out seemed to be simply stretching their legs on a beautiful Christmas afternoon.

As Doctor Bear Claw's limousine turned onto Main Street, there, standing on the street, waiting to greet Angel, was O'Doole and New Dublin's Fenian Home militia. They were intent on following behind to guarantee that Angel arrives safely at Black-Briar.

Angel waved to O'Doole, and he and his associates piled into their cars and trucks and followed the doctor's limousine.

Doctor Bear Claw turned and looked back through the rear window at the convoy of Irishmen following.

"Have those men no better thing to do on Christmas?"

---

[113] Peter Pan's nemesis, much maligned, and misunderstood.

"You mean, like take someone away from the people who love and believe her when she tells the truth?"

"Angel, you're not well. But you will be. Become my partner as we commence your therapy, and together we'll make you better. You'll see."

"I'm sorry, Doctor, but I won't be staying that long."

"Oh!" said Doctor Bear Claw. "You won't be?"

"No, Doctor. I won't."

"Well, Angel, dear, the sooner you accept the fact that you're ill and need my help, the sooner I can make you well. And on *that* day, you can leave Black-Briar."

"So," said Angel, "we're NOT going to be *partners*?"

"That was a figure of speech, Angel. I think you're old enough to realize that. But, now, I'm curious, young lady. Why did you say you won't be staying 'that long'?"

"Because Jonny's going to come for me."

"What!?" said Doctor Bear Claw. "The criminal every law enforcement agency in the country is looking for—coming for you?"

"Yes," said Angel.

"Oh, you poor child. You are delusional." The doctor laughed as she adjusted the shawl across her lap, leaned back, and shut her eyes. "We have a long drive ahead of us, Angel. I suggest you rest those beautiful eyes of yours a while."

Angel turned and looked out the rear window at the convoy following her and waved.

† † †

Seeing Angel looking back at them, O'Doole turned his headlights on and off and waved.

"Don't you worry, Angel. Don't you worry about a thing."

60.

No Lark in the Park

In July 1853, New York's State Legislature set aside more than 750 acres of land centrally located on Manhattan Island, thus creating America's first major public park.[114] What Manhattanites first referred to as "the Central Park" eventually became known as "Central Park." Socially conscious reformers understood creating a genuinely magnificent, landscaped public park would improve public health and contribute significantly to the formation of civil society. What they could not have foreseen, not in a million years, was Central Park becoming a feeding ground for a two-hundred-and-twenty-year-old Hungarian Vampire Bat who answered to the name *Szah Zhah*.

✝ ✝ ✝

January 3rd, 1950, was the first night of the first Full moon of the New Year. It was also the first time Szah Zhah and Balthazar Headstone had been apart on New Year's Eve in two hundred years.

Love stinks!.

---

[114] New York's Central Park Conservancy.

† † †

The recently completed *Kate Wollman Ice Skating Rink* in the east end of Central Park was a huge success, touting over three-hundred-thousand skaters in its first year of operation.

Thirty minutes after the rink closed for the night and Central Park emptied of visitors, Arnold Birnbaum and his son, Willy, began the necessary work emptying over two hundred trash cans placed around the rink to transfer said trash to a much larger bin for collection the next morning. They had a system whereby they set off in opposite directions and would meet at the entrance—a clear division of labor twixt father and son. Done with their work, they would sit on their favorite bench, drink hot chocolate, eat their sandwiches, and look at the stars. And that's what they did that night—Arnold Birnbaum and son. They were interrupted, however, halfway through their hot chocolate when an immense winged creature swooped out of the darkness and, with clawed feet, took Arnold and Willy by the neck and flew off— with them screaming helplessly at the benignly indifferent stars above them.

Father and son, what remained of them, were discovered the following day in a densely wooded park section. The police searched and searched but found no clues upon which to base their investigation.

One theory put forward attributed the deaths of the two fully-grown men to alligators sneaking out of the City's sewers in the dead of night in search of a good meal. Hey! They ARE down there! Generation after generation, ever since the first moron from Brooklyn returned after wintering in Florida, with baby alligators in a shoebox.

61.

De Hombre a, Hombre

O'Doole led the way through the pub to his office in the back. He shut the door and gestured toward one of several chairs in front of his desk.

"I'll stand, thank you."

O'Doole was impressed. He was standing opposite a man taller than himself, which was quite a rarity, let alone a black man wearing expensive, custom-tailored clothes, and well-educated by the way he spoke, with a manicured, British accent; a man whose physicality, just to look of him, seemed poured from molten iron.

"Are you here alone?" said O'Doole.

"I am."

"You're a brave man, waltzing in here by your lonesome, Mister—?"

"Headstone. Balthazar Headstone."

"What can I do for you, Mister Headstone?" O'Doole's tone of voice was a hair short of hostile.

"I want a meeting with your friend, Jonny Fiáin," said Headstone. "Doctor Luther Van Helwing said you could arrange it."

"Oh, he did, did he? The doctor has a big mouth," said O'Doole.

"As to that, you'll get no argument from me," said Headstone.

"By the looks and sound of you, Mister Headstone, you strike me as an important man. Am I right? Are you an important man?"

"I didn't come from New York to verbally spar with you, Mister O'Doole. Your ties to the Irish Republican Army are of no interest to me, no more than the fact that the British government is still offering a bounty for your capture. My business is with Jonny Fiáin."

O'Doole looked at Headstone, then seated himself behind his desk, took a bottle of Irish Whiskey from a drawer along with two shot glasses.

"Are you a drinking man, Mister Headstone?"

† † †

Headstone looked around before stepping onto the deck of the lobster boat owned by Douglas O'Doole, his uncle, and two brothers. As they cast off from the dock, visibility was low due to the fog blanketing the coast; the bell buoy ringing offshore was a constant reminder of the danger venturing out at night presented.

† † †

Headstone stood with Douglas O'Doole on the bridge. Steering the boat was O'Doole's uncle, who would sound the foghorn every sixty seconds to alert other vessels of its presence. One of O'Doole's two brothers was below deck in the engine room; the other brother stood at the bow holding a flare, the red flames it spewed cast an eerie light against the backdrop of the fog.

"You seem quite comfortable on the ocean," said O'Doole.

"I am, Mister O'Doole."

A flare exploded in the air, two points off the starboard bow. The flare became an orange ball of flame descending slowly through the fog, alerting the men aboard the trawler to the presence of a fishing trawler, its engine idling, approximately thirty yards away.

O'Doole's uncle cut the engine, allowing the trawler's momentum to put her alongside the lobster boat. As O'Doole and Headstone climbed aboard, a voice called out:

"You'll find him in the galley."

The voice belonged to the captain of the fishing trawler, Zeke Larson. Larson stepped from the wheelhouse with a lantern emitting light sufficient to reveal several thick, wax-colored scars that ran the length of his face, something the blades of a thrashing machine, or a man highly skilled with a *stiletto* might sculpt during a Pier-6 brawl.

Jonny sat at one end of the table used to serve meals on. In front of him was the Devil's portion[115] of a bottle of *l'Coq Noir*, 151 Rum from the Caribbean island of *Saint Croix*. His shotgun rested on the table, along with two glasses. One glass was empty. Fiáin's glass, however, was half-full.

"Good to see you alive, lad," said O'Doole.

Jonny smiled at the grizzled Irishman, then gestured for his passenger, Balthazar Headstone, to sit.

"What can I do for you, Mister Headstone?"

---

[115] The *Devil's Portion* is a bottle (usually of rum) half full. What inspired Robert Louis Stevenson to write, *"The Bottle Imp."* [Almanac of Unapologetic Facts. Misty Bay Books. 1st Edition. Volume 1. 1948].

"I am very well aware of the steps you've taken to protect the girl, Angel O'Hara. From the time you set fire to her parent's house and fled on the three-wheeler."

"Ah!" Jonny took a long sip of rum. "So it was you, watching from the tree-line."

"Indeed, it was. And had I been there at the border the day you returned from Canada, we would not be having this conversation now."

"Maybe not," said Jonny. "Who's to say?"

"Yes, well, in any event, I want to make a deal with you, Mister Fiáin."

"I'm all ears."

"You want the girl free of that horrible place. I believe its name is Black-Briar. And I want Szah Zhah Kopeč free of the girl, Angel O'Hara. Simultaneously, Mister Fiáin, I realize you're a wanted man, a situation not likely to change anytime soon."

Headstone lifted his right hand. "May I reach into my pocket?"

Jonny placed one hand on the stock of his shotgun and nodded. From inside his coat, Headstone produced a manilla envelope and slid it across the table to Fiáin.

"What's this?" said Jonny, taking the envelope into his hand.

"A letter of introduction to the Branch Manager of Lloyds of London in Bermuda, where I have opened an account in your name. In that account, waiting for you, is five-hundred-thousand dollars, Mister Fiáin. Enough money for you and the girl to disappear and start a new life where you need not look over your shoulder every waking moment. Or live aboard a trawler—delightful as it must be."

Jonny ignored the sarcasm. "What do you want in exchange, Mister Headstone?"

Headstone finished what rum remained in his glass.

"From you, Mister Fiáin? I want your word that you will not attempt to avenge the deaths of the girl's parents. We've both lost people important to us. I say *enough is enough*. Let us part in peace, committing never to see one another again."

A full minute passed, each man studying the face of the other for a telltale sign of betrayal in the offering.

"What is she, Headstone?"

"Excuse me?"

"This thing you care so much about; the thing that killed my best friends and savaged their daughter. What is she? From behind, she looked human, but what punched through the wall and flew off wasn't—it had wings! So, what is she, or it, or whatever the hell you call her?"

"It's complicated," said Headstone.

Jonny glanced around the galley and shrugged. "I'm not about to rush off. Uncomplicate it. If you don't mind."

"Very well," said Headstone. "Szah Zhah is all-woman, Mister Fiáin. She wasn't always the Queen of the Full Moon Night, but—THAT is whom you wounded. In truth, in mind and body, Szah Zhah is no more than twenty years of age, more or less, but, two-hundred years ago, she became the thing you shot."

"Became, *how*?"

"Are you a religious man, Mister Fiáin?"

"No."

Headstone smiled. "It doesn't matter."

Jonny poured them each more rum.

"Szah Zhah was cursed, Mister Fiáin. By *Asmodeus,* a prince of the *Seraphim,* cast out of Heaven, along with the Prince of Darkness and his minions."

"Lucifer."

"Yes, Mister Fiáin—Lucifer."

Jonny whistled through his teeth and grinned. "This gets better and better by the minute."

Headstone nodded. "I understand how this must sound, Mister Fiáin, especially to a non-believer. Should I continue?"

"By all means."

"Very well." Headstone tossed back the rum in his glass with one gulp. "You see, Szah Zhah is no different than you and me in that she, too, requires sustenance. Szah Zhah must feed; she requires blood—preferably human, from young girls with iron-rich blood and fluff for brains. But that isn't always available, so she makes do with what she can find. She had no malice in her heart when she killed your friends, Mister Fiáin; it wasn't personal—she simply had to feed."

"Because of this... curse?"

"Yes. Precisely. When Szah Zhah wandered innocently into a cave on an island near Africa over two hundred years ago, *Asmodeus* was there, disguised as a great bat. He would have drained Szah Zhah of her blood, ending her life, but she begged him to spare her. And he did. But at great cost. Her soul! Szah Zhah is forever damned, Mister Fiáin, condemned for all eternity to be the thing you shot."

They sat in silence for the better part of a minute before either spoke.

"What about you, Headstone?" said Jonny. "What's your story?"

"Not nearly as colorful as Szah Zhah's, Mister Fiáin, However, I, too, am damned. Condemned for all eternity to dwell in this outer ring of hell that we call, earth."

Headstone undid several buttons on his shirt and pulled his collar to one side. He leaned into the lantern light. There, on Headstone's neck, were two scars, once deep, puncture marks.

"You see," said Headstone. "I, too, was changed. Like those you killed at the Canadian border, from a mortal creature to one destined to live on. It was Szah Zhah's gift to me."

"That's some gift," said Jonny.

"Yes," said Headstone, buttoning and straightening his shirt. " Believe me, Mister Fiáin, when I say there are days I tire of living, but… I never have tired of loving her. I daresay, I never will. My primary responsibility is, as it's always been—to protect Szah Zhah. Most of the time, that means protecting her from herself."

Jonny extended an open hand. "You have yourself a deal, Mister Headstone."

As they shook hands, Jonny could feel a fraction of the black man's strength in Headstone's grip.

Headstone stood. "One more thing, Mister Fiáin. I'm afraid Szah Zhah has hired some very bad men to kill the girl."

"Who?"

"Have you heard of a mobster named Frank Costello, boss of the Lucky Luciano crime family?"

Jonny nodded. "Yeah. I've heard of him."

"If I could have," said Headstone, "I would have stopped her, but—"

"When?" said Jonny, interrupting. "When will they make their move on, Angel?"

Headstone shrugged. "Sooner than later, I fear."

† † †

The following evening, Jonny Fiáin left the trawler's relative safety and rowed a dory ashore.

A few minutes before midnight, Douglas O'Doole received a telephone call. The only sound he heard was "*dot-dot-dot*," followed by "*dash-dash-dash*," followed by "*dot-dot-dot*"; Morse Code for S-O-S.

It was enough to cause O'Doole to leave his pub early and return home where he found Jonny Fiáin, immersed in shadow, sitting in the parlor, shotgun across his lap. The curtains were closed; only a single dim light was on.

"That best be you, Jonny, in my favorite chair."

Jonny stood. "Was I right?"

"Aye, lad," said O'Doole. "The Feds are still out there, looking for you. There are two across the street in a Station Wagon. They followed me here from the pub. Cheeky bastards. They don't even try to disguise what they're doing."

"And that's why they'll always be a step or two behind," said Jonny. "Listen, Douglas, that black fella you brought to see me."

"Jesus! Joseph! And, Mary!" said O'Doole. "Have you ever met such a one as that one? Dress me in bloomers if he doesn't have a killer's grip, the likes of which I've never felt before."

"Headstone and I made a deal," said Jonny, "one that will benefit Angel, and me, once I get her out of Black-Briar."

"What kind of deal, Jonny?"

" Live, and let live. THAT kind of deal."

"Oh! THAT, kind of deal. Jesus, Jonny! Do you trust him?"

"Yes, Douglas. I do. But there's a downside. The one thing Headstone cares about is the thing that murdered Paddy and Sarah and almost killed Angel. This same creature has hired the Luciano Mob to kill Angel."

"Seriously!?" O'Doole plumped himself down on the couch. "Saints preserve us, lad!"

"Aye, Douglas, it's bad, and we haven't much time to organize."

"The boys and I are ready, Jonny."

"Thank you, old friend."

† † †

Jonny slipped out a rear window, climbed O'Doole's backyard fence, and dropped to the other side. He made straight for where he left the dory on the rocky beach, dragged it into the water, and rowed like a man possessed, back to Zeke Larson's trawler, offshore, where it was waiting.

"Where, to?" said Larson, once Jonny was back aboard.

"Long Island," said Jonny. "Sooner, the better."

"Consider it done," said Larson. "But this squares us, right, Jonny?"

"Yeah, Zeke," said Jonny. "It'll square us. Now, let's go!

End

of

Book One

Follow the author at Amazon.com

Book Two of the Angel O'Hara Demon-Slayer Saga

Revenge of the Vampire Bat

is scheduled for release in the fall of 2021.

Also by Jon Christopher

Beowulf the Bear's Son, 2nd Edition. (700 pages. Paperback. Perfect binding).

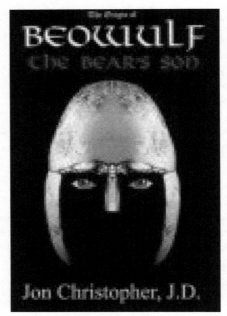

Based on the oldest existing poem in the English Language, "*Beowulf The Bear's Son*" is an Origin Story and epic saga that recounts the legendary adventures of a Sixth Century Norse warrior who, favored by the gods as a child, is raised by a she-bear and shaman until Fate returns him to the world of men to become the greatest warrior of all time.

Lockup (Paperback. Perfect Binding. 139 pages. Screenplay format).

Falsely accused and arrested for brandishing a dangerous weapon, an aged homeless man finds himself down the "rabbit hole," among a cornucopia of colorful characters while incarcerated at the County Jail.

Robin, Stevie Nicks & Me, 2nd Edition (Paperback. Perfect Binding. 183 pages). A rock & roll Memoir, 1966-1977.

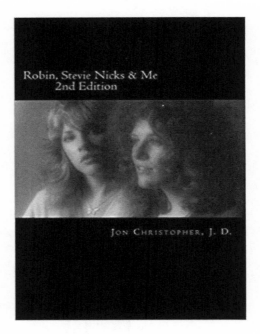

Photograph by Herbert Worthingtoon, III

Revised and expanded, the second edition of "*Robin, Stevie Nicks & Me*" is an intimate, backward glance at 1966-1977, a tumultuous time in America's history that defined a generation and forever changed the music and culture.

"*Robin, Stevie Nicks & Me*" is brutally honest, at times raw, and offers a rare look at one of rock & roll's most celebrated icons, Ms. Stevie Nicks

The Gypsy (Paperback. Perfect Binding. 131 pages).
Mystical realism, in screenplay format.

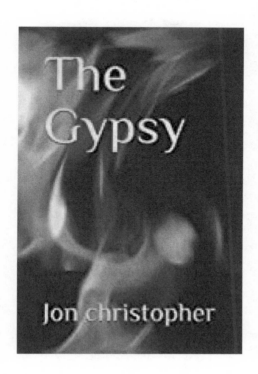

1876. An idealistic young priest and the lovelorn wife of
a brutal rancher confront the supernatural when a
mysterious horseman rides into a drought-stricken valley
in Old Mexico.

It's FaVre, Not FaRv, You Bobbleheads: How Brett Favre, the NFL, and the media let America go to hell in a jockstrap. (Paperback. Perfect Binding. 200 pages).

A celebration of language encompassing wit, humor, and satire, *It's FaVre Not FaRv You Bobbleheads* takes to task issues of celebrity, race, and politics in America while providing whimsical and lyrical insights into the art of tilting at windmills.

It's FaVre Not FaRv is a hilarious parody centered on the three-times former football great Brett Favre. Warning: contains colorful language, rife with clichés, truths, half-truths, untruths, violence, and partial nudity. In other words, everything football fans expect on Sunday.

Acknowledgments

For all my faults, flaws, and failings, I do not count ingratitude among them. Time waits for no man, but while it lasts, I will acknowledge some very fine folks whose presence in my life leaves me smiling.

They are Lachelle & Michael Pettit and their daughters, Alouette, Evangeline, Eowyn & Ireland, Jim & Bette Truitt (RIP), Toni & Terry, and son & Tom. Silvia & Ray Faulstich, and their daughters, Brittany & Sarah. Barry & Veronica Davis, and their children, Teresa, Gregory, and Beri. Neil E. Pauley, (Robin Snider (1948-1983), Laura Thorne, Lisa (Keeper of "the lights") Jessica White, Cathy Carter, Erik Bjornstedt (1948-2020), Don Williams, Alan "Al" Vail, Mike Bobb, Jim & Susan Kasser, Elena & Alex Lobado. Stephanie Doherty, Ingrid Boulting, Kris Kassel, Mary Floyd & the Pineapple Power Stars, Alexandra Vincent, Lydia & Robin, here at the Best Western motel, and all the wonderful folks at the Ventura County Humane Society, along with the hard-working folks in the Public Defender's Office.

Truly, I am the luckiest man alive.

Jon Christopher

June 30, 2021   Bakersfield by the Se

About the Author

The sole progeny of a young Irish dancer from County Clare and an American naval Commander, Jon Christopher, was delivered atop a pool table in the Officers' Club in Coco Solito, Panama, by an 'Ear, Nose, and Throat' specialist shanghaied from the bar.

Christopher weighed in at seven pounds, eight ounces, and, apart from having gills between his ribs, and webbed feet, was free of abnormalities.

An old man in a dry month, Christopher lives on the road with the last of his fur-children, Misty Moos brother, Bayou Bay

Fini

Made in the USA
Columbia, SC
12 August 2021

43085076R00231